DEATH'S DISCIPLE: BOOK ONE

DEATH'S DISCIPLE

EMMA L. ADAMS

DEATH'S DISCIPLE

DEATH'S DISCIPLE: BOOK ONE

EMMA L. ADAMS

This book was written, produced and edited in the UK, where some spelling, grammar and word usage will vary from US English.

Copyright © 2023 Emma L. Adams
All rights reserved.

To be notified when Emma L. Adams's next novel is released, sign up to her mailing list.

Edited by Sarah Chorn.
Proofread by Patricia Long.
Cover art by Deranged Doctor Design.

PROLOGUE

Yala watched the King's funeral pyre burn, the light of the dancing flames reflecting in her fellow soldiers' eyes. A cascade of grey smoke billowed from the courtyard, disappearing into the sky.

Four robed Disciples stood at the corners of the pyre, orange flames streaming from their outstretched hands, while mourners gathered in rows according to their status. The soldiers occupied the western side of the courtyard, with each commander forming an orderly line before their respective unit with the captains standing behind. Despite Commander Sranak's broad frame shielding her from the heat of the flames, the wooden cane Yala held had grown uncomfortably hot, and her proximity to the pyre made it obvious to her sharp eyes that no bodies lay upon it.

Even with the best efforts of the king's scouts, His Majesty's body had never been recovered from the depths of the ocean that lay between Laria and Rafragoria, and neither had those of his closest guards. Crept upon and slaughtered by Rafragorian assassins, according to the sole survivor of the attack who'd later died of his wounds. Yala's grip tightened on the cane, which she'd borrowed to ease the pressure on her injured leg while she stood through the hours of eulogies and funerary rites. Despite the heat searing its surface, the wooden stick was a solid foundation amid the unreality that had cloaked the past few days like a drug-induced haze.

One would think attending the king's funeral would have lessened her impression of being the recipient of an elaborate joke, but the lack of any bodies to burn made some inappropriate corner of her mind wonder if the king himself would walk in at any moment and declare his miraculous survival. It would hardly be the most improbable occurrence she'd witnessed in the past week.

Get a fucking grip on yourself, Yala. He's dead.

His son, Prince Daliel, addressed the crowd from a raised platform on the northern side of the pyre, calling the ceremony to an end. As one, the four Disciples lowered their hands, and the flames died. No doubt they'd have to burn a cornucopia of offerings to their deity upon the altar for supplying them with a funeral's worth of holy fire, unless they'd already done so. She wasn't familiar with the particulars of the contract between the Disciples of the Flame and their revered god, but they would be the last to leave the courtyard.

While the attendees began to depart, the remaining embers on the pyre dimmed, leaving little more than a flurry of ashes that drifted on the wind. Ordinarily, the ashes would signify the departure of the occupant's soul to the afterlife, but without a body ... well, the new king wouldn't thank her for implying that His Majesty's soul had been seized by the god of Corruption, Mekan, and dragged down into some ghastly hell, so she kept those thoughts to herself.

A shiver danced up her spine despite the lingering heat, and it took her a moment to notice Commander Sranak had begun dismissing each squad one by one. Yala loosened her grip on her cane and stretched her cramping leg, hearing the other members of her squad stirring behind her. Saren caught her attention first; he stood on her left, stood stiff-backed and grim, his usually unruly long hair pulled back behind his ears and his eyes puffy from lack of sleep. Every day since their return she'd been woken in the night—if not by her own nightmares than someone else's, disturbing the barracks with tortured screams.

Next to Saren stood Vanat, whose eyes flickered towards Yala with concern when he thought she wasn't paying attention. Machit was further to the left, nervously fiddling with the sleeves of his jacket, while Viam's arm was bound in a sling, her forehead gleaming with sweat from the heat. Next to her was an empty space where Dalem would have been, and the last team member, Temik, stood as far from Yala as custom would allow. She felt the heat of his glare as acutely as the flames as she waited for dismissal. Her wounded right leg ached for rest, and the flickering ashes from the pyre stung her eyes.

Commander Sranak's even pace halted in front of Yala. "Captain Yala, the prince—ah, king, would speak with you."

Her heartbeat skipped. "Now?"

"Yes." He gestured to the area north of the pyre where the soon-to-be king waited amid his newly promoted retinue of guards—including Superior Datriem, leader of the Disciples of the Flame. The Superior's white-robed presence lingered in the corner of her vision as she followed the commander around the pyre, past the white-cloaked Disciples at each corner.

Yala's cane tapped against stone with each step, the spasms of pain in her right leg were as acute as the day after she'd landed. Likely she'd walk with a limp long after the gaping wound healed to a scar. The injury wasn't her first, by far, but if the future king intended to strike back at

Rafragoria for the death of his father, she'd have to spend the battle in the capital recovering rather than on the back of a war drake. Not that anyone knew his intentions outside of his advisors, but that hadn't stopped an endless slew of rumours from flooding the barracks over the past few days.

Yala rarely joined those debates. King Tharen's death had left her with a churning mass of questions that went far beyond the petty concerns of who would be promoted to join the new king's personal guard. Even the matter of retribution ran second in her priorities to her desire to know *why* they now found themselves clustered around a pyre instead of beneath a display of fireworks above Ceremonial Square to celebrate their victory over Rafragoria.

The future king watched her approach, dressed in funerary white with a simple golden headdress intended to suffice until his proper crown was constructed. No doubt each twist and whorl held a specific meaning—Viam might know them—but all she could think was that he must be baking in the heat. Then again, she thought the same of the white-robed man nearby, whose pious stance showed nothing of the fire he could summon to his fingertips at will. Or to be more accurate, at the will of the god of the flames, Dalathik.

We all obey someone, she thought wryly. *Whether it be man or god.*

Yala halted in front of the future king, hoping he wouldn't take offence by her inability to kneel. *Except him, maybe,* she amended her thoughts, lowering herself into a bow that caused her injured leg to give an aggrieved spasm of pain. "Your Majesty."

"Captain Yala," he said. "I'm told you led the last mission my father ordered."

Her back straightened, tension rising from her core as the mass of questions inside her threatened to come spilling out.

She'd expected the mission to be of little concern to a man who'd lost his father in frankly bizarre circumstances, and who found himself abruptly in charge of a nation he hadn't expected to lead for decades to come. Why would one minor, unfinished mission be of any concern to him?

Unless ... unless he knows why King Tharen sent us there.

"I did," she answered. "King Tharen ordered my team to scout ahead of the army and secure the island before Rafragoria did. Regrettably, the island was destroyed, and— one member of my squad met a tragic death alongside the Rafragorian contingent. The rest of us barely escaped with our lives."

Her words drew a look—subtle but sharp—from Superior Datriem. The briefest flicker of anger cut through his serene expression, and her nerve faltered for a similar instant. If she spoke the full truth to the future monarch, would the next body to lie on a pyre be her own?

"My father would grieve with you, too, if he lived," Prince Daliel said gravely. "Neither of us ever expected that I would take the throne this soon, but I will do my best to live up to his legacy."

Yala frowned, unsure how he expected her to respond. With confidence? Reassurance? He was awfully young, she thought—barely older than she'd been when she'd first joined the army at sixteen. "I'm sure you will, Your Majesty."

"I intend to make some changes," he added. "The wars with Rafragoria have wrought a terrible toll on the nation in recent years, particularly on our economy."

"Undoubtedly, but..." *But they killed your father,* she thought. According to whispers that had travelled from the palace into the barracks, Prince Daliel didn't share his father's desire to demonstrate Laria's military might at every opportunity, but she'd thought he would at least consider putting Rafragoria in their place for sending assassins to

EMMA L. ADAMS

slaughter their king instead of facing him on the battlefield. "I'm sorry, Your Majesty, but what do you mean by 'changes'?"

Was she being reassigned to a different squad? If so, wouldn't the commander have told her himself? An uneasy feeling stirred in the pit of her stomach when the future king did not respond right away. After a short pause, he said, "I intend to disband the flight division."

"Disband?" Repeating his words back at him made her sound dense, but what else was she supposed to do? Thank him? Her injured leg would make it impossible for her to perform effectively as a foot-soldier.

"It was not an easy decision to make," he said, "and I had no desire to dismiss someone of your abilities without any compensation. Due to the sacrifices your team made to fulfil my father's last orders, I'll ensure that you receive sufficient compensation to enjoy a comfortable retirement."

Retirement? Yala had long thought she'd be *dead* before she retired and being offered money to walk away from the only life she'd known left her with no response but blank-faced disbelief.

The suitable reply dredged itself up from the depths of her mind. "Thank you, Your Majesty."

No doubt he thought he was doing her a favour, and hells, maybe he was. Anyone would be happy to walk away from the threat of imminent death to a life of cosy indolence, and she'd been a fool to believe for an instant that he might have any answers to offer her. There was no sense in dwelling on what might have followed if King Tharen had survived to greet them upon their return, rather than leaving his well-meaning but clueless son to pick up the pieces after his death.

"You will have a home in the barracks until everything is settled," he added. "Ask Commander Sranak for the

6

details. Thank you for your service to the nation, Captain Yala."

Custom told her to bow and leave, but instead, she found her mouth moving of its own accord. "Your Majesty, did your father ask you to do this?"

She heard a sharp intake of breath from the commander behind her, but she could hardly believe he'd stripped away the livelihoods of a hundred loyal fliers when his father's pyre had scarcely burned to embers. Even if he thought the flight division was too costly to manage—and she had to admit, she'd often wondered where the money to feed and raise the menagerie of war drakes came from—Rafragoria's remote islands were reachable only by sea or sky, and Laria's military had no naval faction. Prince Daliel had effectively ended three decades of war in an instant ... assuming Rafragoria didn't decide to continue to wage a one-sided conflict. *What in the gods' names is he thinking?*

"My father never expected me to take over from him so young, so he gave me no such requests," Prince Daliel answered. "That said, there will be no more war."

"What if Rafragoria threatens us again? They've already proven they can't be trusted to adhere to any reasonable demands." *Such as not assassinating our monarch while our backs are turned.*

Commander Sranak cleared his throat. Loudly.

The king's brow wrinkled, but his youthful face showed more sadness than anger at her outburst. "The Rafragorian assassins' actions were reprehensible, but my father was a combatant, and he knew the risks of actively participating in the war. In the past, the Rafragorian rulers have always adhered to the accords set out between our nations."

Yala's mouth hung open as her common sense sought to wrangle her tongue under control. Rafragoria *hadn't* adhered to the accords, not if they'd been intending to double-cross them on the island as well as murdering King Tharen, but it was hard to prove anything when the only witnesses aside from herself were dead.

"I … suppose they have, Your Majesty." She'd likely sundered any chances she might have had of winning the monarch's favour in future, but this might be their first and last encounter, and in a few short days, she'd be nothing more than a civilian. A well-off one, but not someone with the ear of the king. "Thank you, and my condolences on your loss."

She could say no more, not in front of an audience, so she gave an awkward half bow and turned to rejoin her squad.

Commander Sranak snagged her arm on her way past. "What in the name of the hells was that, Captain Yala? Have you no sense of decorum?"

"Did *you* know he intended to remove my entire squad from their positions?" She cast a glance at the lingering soldiers, who comprised most of the flight division. Had the King expected *her* to tell them all that they were no longer employed by Laria's military? "The entire flight division, in fact?"

His mouth sagged open. "As of a few hours ago, yes. I'm sorry for that, but it's not our place to question His Majesty's decisions."

"It's done now." The sound of her cane on the cobbles echoed like a door closing on her heels. Regrets for her own actions were hard to come by when so many others would be affected by the monarch's choice.

"What're you complaining about?" said the commander. "You get to retire early rather than dying in the saddle."

Yala supposed he was right, but living was far more complicated than dying. She almost envied Dalem for not having to witness the aftermath. "Do *you* think Rafragoria is likely to threaten us again?"

The commander blinked, his moustache twitching. "How in hells should I know?"

"You know more than I do." Frustration burned beneath her skin like an itch. "They killed King Tharen. Is there nobody else who wants, I don't know, justice?"

"Justice is reserved for the gods alone."

She flinched, gripping her cane to cover up her reaction. She had no argument to the notion that justice was the domain of the gods, and nobody ever said the gods were *fair*.

Dalem was dead, King Tharen was dead, and the rest of her squad had money enough to retire for the rest of their lives. If that was the will of the gods, the messages were decidedly mixed. Yet it wasn't they whose eyes watched her back, but the white-robed figure who'd watched her from the king's side. Calculating, silent, but taking note of every word she said. As if to ensure she didn't overstep the mark.

His last words to her rang in the back of her mind. *Leave at once, before Dalathik's righteous flames claim your lying tongue.*

She'd spoken no lies, but even Prince Daliel would have no reason to believe her.

Maybe she shouldn't be concerned. The future king seemed decent enough, and while his kindness might simply be a mask, she'd never get close enough to see beneath it. He didn't want soldiers at his side, but scholars and priests. Maybe that was recipe enough for a changed nation, but Yala wasn't optimistic enough to believe Laria's militaristic history would be so easily buried.

"Yala?" Vanat called to her, drawing her eyes back to her squad. "What is it?"

She drew in a breath and spoke. "I have good news and bad news. For all of us."

1

Blood sprayed across the wall of the cabin. Yala yanked her dagger out of the insect she'd impaled, rubbing the welt on her shoulder with her free hand. She'd heard the bloodfly's strident whine in the background but hadn't expected the bulbous insect would have the audacity to slip through the nets covering the windows and take a bite out of her while she'd been dozing in her hammock.

"Rather you than me," she said, tossing the dagger back into its corner. At one time she would have reprimanded any member of her squad who treated their weaponry with such callousness, but those days were long gone.

Look at the state of me, talking to fucking wildlife. She'd been on her own for too long, that was the problem. Limping back to the hammock, she settled into the fraying fabric and let its gentle rocking carry her into a doze.

Not for long. A scraping noise sounded against the side of her wooden cabin, and she lifted her head. Her home was deeply enmeshed in the trees, an intentional choice on her part, but every so often a well-meaning local dropped by to offer her a basket of freshly picked sunfruit or baked bread. The scraping noise didn't sound as if it belonged to a human, though, and it was too loud to be one of the mischievous kekins that occasionally snuck into her cabin and wreaked havoc when her back was turned.

When a low growl followed, Yala swung her legs over the edge of the hammock, her heart racing. *That's no kekin. Nor a bird, either.*

Her bare feet touched the wooden floor, prompting a familiar ache in her leg. The old wound liked to remind her of its presence every so often, though nothing remained but a curved scar a shade lighter than her brown skin. Wishing she hadn't tossed her dagger aside, she reached for the whittled cane she kept beside her hammock.

Keeping one eye on the window—or hole, as Vanat would have called it, though she'd argue that the lack of glass was an aesthetic choice—she edged towards the corner where she'd thrown her dagger and retrieved the weapon. Then, Yala yanked back the misshapen piece of fabric masquerading as a curtain and found a giant eye staring back at her.

With an oath, she recoiled. *A war drake? What in the hells is it doing this deep in the jungle?*

At one time, the sight of a large reptilian beast had been as familiar as her own squad, as had the mixture of anticipation and nerves that preceded a flight. Her mind brimmed with memories of sitting on a similar beast's back and soaring above the waves, the wind in her hair and a squad to protect with her life.

Now, her squad had scattered, and the war drakes returned to the wild from which they came. This was no trained steed but a mere animal, and from the way its nostrils contracted below its pitch-dark eyes, it smelled prey.

In one swipe of a curved claw, the wild drake ripped the curtain aside, exposing the inside of her cabin. Yala backed out of range of its curved claws and sharp teeth and tongue, gripping a dagger that seemed laughably inadequate, but she hadn't brought any larger weapons with her when she'd left the capital. The walk had been arduous enough without the added weight of spears or swords, and she'd never been much of an archer.

The war drake pawed at the inside of the room, snagging her hammock, and yanking it to the ground. The blade-like claws missed her retreating form by a finger span, and she held her breath, weighing the odds of dealing a killing blow before its claws ripped out her throat. Not high, she had to admit. The beast could smell that she was just out of reach, judging by the guttural noises that escaped its throat, but sooner or later its claws would snag on her bad leg and reel her to her death.

Yala backed into the furthest corner of the cabin, uttering a silent reprimand towards her past self for her indifference towards security. Nobody ever came out here, and the room was the perfect size for one person who didn't want to limp too far to reach anything—but now, her only means of escape was through the jungle. Despite the thick trees impeding the beast's motions, the chances of evading its sharp claws were stacked against her.

Wood cracked and splintered as the war drake's clawed foot delved further into the room. Yala threw herself flat to avoid being impaled, a motion that drew a protesting ache from her leg. Gripping the dagger, she drove the point of the blade upward and into the joint between two of the beast's clawed toes.

A snarl escaped the war drake, but to a beast of that size, such a wound was little more than the prick of a needle. Yanking the dagger out, she bit back a gasp when the heel of the war drake's foot struck her chin. Stars winked before her eyes like a fireworks display, and hot blood trickled down her chin. Staggering to her feet, she gripped the wall with one hand as she made her way around the beast's flailing foot.

The scraping noises around the window grew louder as the beast shoved more of its huge body inside the cabin. The wood was sturdy enough, but it would eventually give under the creature's weight; she'd once seen a rampaging war drake tear its way through a wooden fence when it had escaped its paddock. Such incidents were rare, but it wasn't unheard of for one to escape into the countryside, indiscriminately slaughtering livestock and humans alike.

On the other hand, they didn't generally wander into the jungle, and she'd moved as far as possible from the paddocks in which the military's war drakes had once been kept. The beast couldn't possibly know a former rider lived inside the cabin, but Yala had to admire the irony in meeting her end at the sharp claws of one of the beasts that had once been at the centre of her world.

Holding herself flat against the wall, Yala edged towards the wooden door and leaned against the handle until it gave way, enabling her to step out into the humid heat of the jungle. Hoping the constant sounds of insects buzzing and birds' cries in the treetops obscured her clumsy feet, she backed out of the cabin's shadow.

Yala could imagine how her squad members would react to her standing within reach of an enraged war drake without any means of defending herself, but despite it all, a curious part of her wanted to see if it had ever worn a heavy iron chain around its neck. War drakes weren't loyal to a single rider—or anyone for that matter—but years of training left a mark that was not so easily forgotten.

She couldn't tell if this one was old enough to have flown in the war; its wings were bunched behind its back, its rear claws digging into the undergrowth while its front claws ripped their way into the cabin like a child opening a gift. The reptile might never have been one of hers, yet she didn't want to slay the beast if she could help it. It was only obeying its instincts, and after the king had dismantled the flight division, the war drakes might have found themselves as confused as she and her squad had been. They'd originally been from the vast plains and mountains of the northern continent, some five hundred years or more back, and the modern world contained few habitats suitable for beasts bred in captivity for war.

Even the wilder jungle in Laria's south could little accommodate their large wingspans and huge feet. Low-hanging branches scraped against the drake's sloping, horned head as a growl slipped between its sharp teeth. Its pitted eyes were fixed on the cabin, but she knew that if she fled, its sharp ears would hear her uneven steps wading through the thick undergrowth. The ground in front of her cabin was flatter, softer, and enabled her to tread silently until she stood in the beast's immediate shadow.

Given its hunched position, she didn't need a stirrup to mount the beast, and if she sat on its back, it would be less likely to take off one of her limbs. Her leg would be an impediment, but the motions were drilled into her bones. She moved carefully, the cool mud sucking at her feet and a thin sheen of sweat gathering beneath the curls on the back of her neck.

As the beast shifted, one of its wings opened a little and forced her to come to a sudden halt. The war drake's sharp ears picked up on the sound, and its head swung to the side, pinning her to the spot.

Heart in her throat, she met its eyes as a rider would have. "I'm not your prey. This is my home, and I'd appreciate it if you left me in peace."

The drake couldn't understand her, of course, but the

sight of the deep scars on either side of its neck—the marks of the chain it had once worn—sent a thrill through her. It *had* been trained by a handler, and despite the years that had elapsed, it would still recognise certain commands.

"Stay," she warned, suffusing her voice with the steely calm she'd employed as a rider. "*Stay.*"

Yanking its claws free from the cabin, the beast roared. *Or maybe not.* Yala threw herself to the ground and rolled under its scaled body, then crawled into the thicker undergrowth on the cabin's other side. She'd dropped her cane, but when she groped around in the bushes, she found a loose stone instead, which she palmed. When the beast began sniffing at the undergrowth in search of its escaped prey, she took aim and tossed the stone at a nearby tree.

The war drake's head spun towards the noise, allowing her the chance to crawl into a more dignified position. Her leg protested the abuse, but no sooner had she reached for a low-hanging branch to pull herself to her feet than the beast swung its tail around, shaking the undergrowth and causing her to lose her footing.

As she landed on her back, a wild impulse drove Yala to reach up and wrap both arms around the beast's scaly tail, using the momentum to swing both of her legs off the ground.

Clinging to the war drake's tail like a sloth to a branch was the sort of reckless manoeuvre that would have earned her a week cleaning out the paddocks as punishment when she'd been a novice, but there was nobody here to shout recriminations or yank the war drake's chain to stop it from biting off her face. Instead, a sideways clamber brought her into a sitting position upon the beast's tail.

The war drake snarled at its unwanted passenger and lashed its tail again, but she held fast, using the swaying motion to claw her way up the ridges lining its spine. In less time than she'd expected, she reached a sitting position with her knees on either side of its thick neck.

"This familiar to you?" she hissed into its ear. "You've had a human on your back before, haven't you? Many times."

Scales scraped against her legs through the thin fabric of her trousers, reminding her that if the beast decided to take her for a flight, she'd suffer a lot of pain. Her old drakeskin trousers were somewhere in the mess the beast had left of her cabin, along with the gloves she'd worn to protect herself from its sharp teeth. A growl rippled through her mount's heavy body, and it beat its wings as if to dislodge her.

Perhaps she'd put too much stock in its instincts submitting to the memory of its former handlers, but she had one last trick up her sleeve. Leaning forward, Yala pressed the point of the dagger to the vulnerable skin of the underside of its neck.

"Feel that?" she whispered in its ear. "It's not easy to kill one of you on the battlefield, but everyone who's ever fought in the flight division knows your weak spots."

Unlike a war drake equipped for battle, this one wore no armoured plates. If she stabbed it in the neck, it would bleed out … eventually. Whether it'd perish before it ripped out her throat was debatable, but while the beast didn't understand human speech, the sharp point of the dagger against its neck spoke for itself.

"Keep still," she crooned in its ear, affecting the tone she'd used when breaking in a new mount. "Hold."

The beast shifted, its wings bunching behind its back as it sat to attention. A rush of triumph seized her, vanishing an instant later. She might sit on the back of a war drake as if nothing had changed, but she was older and achier, and the beast had ruined her fucking *house*.

"We're the same, really," she said to the war drake. "Sorry to say that I don't have any of that fancy spiced meat

Commander Sranak used to feed you. I won't let you feed on the nice humans who live near me, so you'll have to go and find prey somewhere else."

The war drake's body vibrated with a growl, but it didn't move. *Someone trained it well.* She tentatively squeezed her legs around its neck but didn't give the command to fly. As much as she'd missed the sensation of soaring over the open sea, it wasn't worth risking a grim fall to her death for the sake of a cheap thrill.

The beast growled, wings bunching as if to take off despite her unvoiced command. Inspiration struck, and she hastily swung her good leg over its side before giving the order. "Fly."

As Yala slid to the ground, she tried to angle herself so that her good leg took her weight. The impact jarred her wound regardless, but the war drake ignored her muffled oath and launched into flight.

Branches tangled in its wings as the war drake crashed through the canopy, leaving a trail of broken trees in its wake. The air currents stirred up by its flight broke through the humid heat of the jungle like sun through clouds, bringing the bittersweet memory of Yala's first time watching a war drake in flight. She'd been unpacking her meagre belongings in the barracks on the day of her arrival when she'd heard the cry and stuck her head out of the window in time to catch the gust of wind rippling from the practise field. She'd laughed in delighted surprise as the cool air whipped her hair back, the majestic sight of the winged beast carrying its rider captivating her attention.

Even subsequent less-than-pleasant experiences of watching riders lose limbs to sharp claws or fall to their deaths hadn't erased the simple thrill of the moment, which in hindsight, ought to have been a sign of her fate. Those who gladly walked in the jaws of death had no place in the current state of Laria.

Yala returned to her cabin and swore at the mess the drake had left behind. The simple task of finishing her nap would be impossible until she disentangled what was left of her hammock from beneath her upended belongings.

Retirement, she reflected, was not as sublime as she'd been led to believe.

2

Kelan followed the mercenaries downriver, heading deep into the heart of Laria's southern jungle. Their dug-out canoe served its purpose, but their progress was slow enough that he could have gone back and forth from their destination several times in the time it took them to round a single curve of the river. Then again, since he had the ability to fly, that was hardly a fair comparison to make, and he had little doubt that they'd appreciate his help with the journey.

One of the mercenaries jerked upright when he spotted Kelan, his eyes widening at the sight of the strange, cloaked intruder hovering a foot above the riverbank. Kelan flashed their group a reassuring smile before taking a gliding step towards their canoe, his feet hovering slightly above its wooden edge to avoid tipping it sideways. Three men occupied the cramped space, clothed in dirt-stained gear and laden with battered oars.

"Greetings," he said. "Are you by any chance on the tail of a certain bounty?"

"Who are you?" A large man with a straggly beard halfheartedly drew a knife from his belt, though he must know he hadn't a hope of skewering someone out of reach without upending the canoe. "You're one of those ... Disciples."

"Whatever gave me away?" Kelan took another step across the air so that he stood directly above the helm of their canoe. "I'm Kelan of Skytower, and I'm following a rumour of a large reward on offer for the life of a particular individual."

In truth, he'd eavesdropped on them for the past ten minutes, so he already knew their purpose in heading south. What he didn't know was precisely *why* this woman was worth so much money, or how they expected to find someone who didn't seem to have a fixed address.

"Looking for a share, are you?" growled the man. "I thought your people had enough money."

"Not at all," he answered. "We need to make a living the same as the rest of you, though we have certain advantages at our disposal. Take this, for instance."

The mercenaries gripped the sides of the canoe as he conjured a faint breeze that steered their vessel around the riverbend without anyone having to lift an oar.

"What d'you want, then?" asked the bearded man. "You help us steer, we give you a cut of the bounty?"

"Good, we understand one another," said Kelan. "You'll have an easier time finding your target with the aid of a navigator. I can scout ahead, though ideally, I need to know some landmarks."

"There aren't any," grunted the man at the back. "This woman—soldier, they said—lives in isolation in the jungle."

"Interesting." He'd heard the same rumour, but he'd found it a little hard to believe she was alone. "There must be a settlement within reach of her home. Even the Disciples of Life live in enclaves."

Not that a group of mercenaries would know much of the

4444

44

Disciples of Life, and in truth, neither did his own people. Each branch of Disciple was mostly estranged from the others, with the result that he'd needed to get a little more creative than he'd initially anticipated to find a lead that might help him with the task Superior Sietra had given to him.

"If there's a settlement, I can find it," Kelan added, when the mercenaries made no reply. "I have a question to ask of you, though, before we leave."

"Yes?" asked the man at the back, whose dark brows twitched with distrust. A fair reaction, not unwarranted; Kelan intended to betray them, after all. "What question?"

"What kind of abilities does this woman have?"

He spoke in casual tones to hide his curiosity. He might not have been able to make any headway in the capital, but a rumour of a person with magical abilities who didn't belong to a Temple of one of the five gods—Flame, Sky, Earth, Life, and Sea—was worth a second look. At this point, such rumours were all he had to go on.

The mercenary hunched at the back answered in a low voice. "They say she rips out the hearts of men and devours them."

Kelan stared for a moment, fighting the urge to burst into laughter. "Ah—I assume you've taken precautions?"

"It's not funny," growled the mercenary.

"Absolutely not." He hid another laugh with a cough behind his hand. "Interesting. I'm intrigued to meet her."

"Not just you," said the bearded man. "We're sharing the prize."

"We certainly are." He lifted a hand, conjuring up a breeze to steer their canoe around another bend. "I think we need to get a move on, don't you?"

———

It took Yala the rest of the day to clear the debris from outside her cabin. There was nothing to be done for the claw marks, but she decided that the deep gouges in the wooden exterior added character and might deter any locals from bothering her in future. The annoyance of trekking an hour back and forth for supplies was a small price to pay for privacy, and until now, the only predators she'd encountered had been the insects that so desired the taste of her blood. It wasn't unheard of for raptors or wyverns to wander the forest in search of prey, but not war drakes.

Given the flight division's demise, the beast couldn't possibly be an escapee from a military operation. Even in her remote location, word would have reached her if the king had reversed the decision he'd made in his youth, and he hadn't reneged on any of his other promises thus far. There had been no more wars between Laria and her neighbours in the half decade or more that had elapsed since her encounter with the king at his father's funeral.

Yala picked up the frayed fabric that had once been a hammock and set about fixing it back into place. The one thing that could be said for her accommodations was that returning the cabin to its previous state was a relatively straightforward job; it contained no other furniture, and most of her belongings were stored in cloth sacks. After spending her entire adult life sleeping in dormitories with scarcely a handspan between each sleeping mat and sharing a single bathhouse, having an entire room to herself seemed an extravagance. The need to walk out into the forest to take a piss and occasionally waking to wild kekins rifling through her bags were minor inconveniences.

If the war drake came back, though, she ought to take some precautions. Leaving the hammock, Yala tracked down the sack that contained her old army gear and pulled out the finely made drakeskin trousers she'd once worn as a rider. Matching gloves would shield her hands from its teeth, but the rest of her body would remain vulnerable. She might be experienced at handling war drakes that had already been subdued, but that one had worn no chain, and her gear would be of little use if it marked her as prey again.

She tossed the gloves aside, irritated with herself for entertaining the idea that picking up her uniform would do anything to improve her situation, and the faint sound of movement drew her attention to the gaping hole that had once been a window. *Is the war drake back?* No, it would have made more noise, but the sense of being watched stole upon her like the subtle scent of decay.

Grabbing her discarded dagger, Yala moved to the window—and for the second time that day, she found a pair of eyes staring back at her. Human, this time, but her instincts had already kicked in. As she drove the dagger towards the intruder, the short young woman sprang backwards with a cry of alarm, the point missing its target by a finger span as she raised her hands palm-up to indicate she was unarmed.

Yala, who'd barely stilled the dagger before it reached its mark, caught her balance against the side of the window with her free hand. "Who are you?"

"My name is Niema." To Yala's utter astonishment, the woman bowed at the waist, as if she were a noble or a high-ranking officer. "You're Captain Yala, right? I'm sorry I startled you."

Yala let out a disbelieving huff. "Haven't been called 'captain' in a while, but yes, I am. Why are you here?"

The woman was dressed oddly, wearing nothing but a misshapen tunic that hung off her small frame, but her brown skin and curly dark hair were unmistakeably Larian. "I met a friend of yours," she answered. "On the road."

"Vanat sent you." Yala lowered the dagger. *That's how she knows my name.*

Of all her former team members, it couldn't have been anyone else. The last she'd seen, Vanat had been living in Setemar—a few days' walk from her location but considerably closer than the capital. Niema, however, didn't look as if she came from the city. Her odd tunic-like garment was not made from fabric but from countless stems woven together. Her shoes, too, looked to be made of threaded reeds—practical enough for the jungle, but five minutes on the rough cobbles of the capital, and they would fall apart.

Niema inclined her head. "He said you lived somewhere out in the jungle, and I questioned some locals until I found your cabin."

"If he wanted to convince me to return to the city, why didn't he come in person?"

Given the war drake, it might be for the best that he hadn't, but sending a stranger on his behalf didn't sound like Vanat.

"It'll be easier if you talk to him yourself," said Niema. "He's staying in Setemar, he told me."

"That's not where you came from." A nagging sense of familiarity surrounded the woman despite Yala's certainty that she'd never seen her before, and it didn't escape her attention that Niema was surveying her with equal curiosity. Her scars often attracted attention; while her leg was covered, a thinner scar bisected her right cheek, and no doubt she still had dried blood on her chin from the war drake's attack earlier. Niema's face was blemish-free … save for a faint birthmark on her neck, forming the outline of a leaf. Not a birthmark, in fact, but a tattoo. Recognition hit her. "You're a Disciple of Life."

"I am," she confirmed. "And you're Yala Palathar."

A Disciple? Didn't the Disciples of Life live in enclaves

deep within the forest, without any contact with the outside world? Why had Vanat sent one of *them* to find her? "I'm sorry, *why* are you here?"

"I've come to warn you, Yala." She drew in a breath. "It's my belief that you are in danger."

"Danger." The woman's matter-of-fact sincerity left Yala utterly nonplussed. "If you're here to warn me that a wild drake is going to disturb my nap, you're several hours too late. Otherwise, please enlighten me."

She'd never heard of the Disciples of Life delivering warnings, though she'd be the first to admit her knowledge was as patchy as a worn coat. Dalem, the only member of their squad who'd received a formal temple education, had said the Disciples of Life were surpassed in elusiveness only by the Disciples of the Sea; they lived in small enclaves scattered throughout Laria's southern jungles and rarely took in outsiders. No doubt their inhospitable location was partially responsible.

Niema chewed on her lower lip as though considering how to respond. "It's difficult to explain. I don't know how much you know of the Disciples of Life—"

"A little." Frankly, she'd have preferred to keep it that way. "I wasn't aware you could see into the future."

"We can't," she said. "However, we occasionally receive insight from the god of life Herself, and this time, Yalet saw fit to bless our enclave with a shared vision warning of grave danger. When we spoke to the other enclaves, they had received the same message."

"A vision warning of … what danger, precisely?" What in the gods' names did this have to do with *her*? Yala had never had anything to do with the Disciples before the mission that had ended her career, let alone after. Unless… "Another war? Is Rafragoria planning to take advantage of our weakness?"

"I cannot share the details," Niema said. "The words of

Yalet are for Her Disciples alone. However, I will say that you have a part to play in this."

"Me?" Were all the Disciples of Life so damned cryptic? No wonder the other Disciples avoided having anything to do with them. Ominous warnings of danger did not make for pleasant dinner conversation. "Why me? I'm not part of your, ah, enclave. Also, I'm retired."

If this hypothetical danger did involve Rafragoria, it made sense for His Majesty to put out a plea for former soldiers to return to the city, but Niema might have recommended any other flight squad leaders who didn't have an injured leg or a comfortable home to retire to. Recent incursion aside, her life in the jungle had been perfectly adequate. Unless the king didn't know the war was going to take place yet, of course, but why would Niema warn her first and not the monarch?

"My enclave leader, Superior Kralia, sent me to deliver the message," Niema said. "If you wish to reunite with your friend, I'll gladly accompany you on the road."

"You ... no." Yala needed to slam the door on the young woman's assumptions before she found herself bound to a promise she'd never made. "I'm not leaving my home. Sorry to disappoint you—and Vanat, too, wherever he is—but I have no intention of going anywhere."

Hurt flickered in Niema's eyes. How old was she? Everyone under twenty-five looked like a child to Yala, which left her with no frame of reference, but if Niema had little experience with the outside world, no wonder Yala's scars and hostility hadn't drawn any curious questions.

"I see." Niema took in a steadying breath. "I will be waiting in the village if you change your mind."

"I won't." If Niema wanted to waste her time, though, she was welcome to. "Please don't disturb me again. I gave my answer."

Yala turned her back and returned to picking up the

pieces of her life that the war drake had callously tossed in all directions. Despite her professions to the contrary, she'd intended to prepare for the possibility of the war drake's return, so she picked up the drakeskin gloves and trousers and added them to a pile of essentials to take with her should she need to flee.

Inside this single room was everything she owned, or everything she'd taken with her when she'd left the capital. She'd handed her uniform and weapons back to the commander, aside from her drakeskin clothing—with the demise of the flight division, it wasn't as if the army would need them—and had deposited most of her money at a bank in Dalathar. She was frugal enough to know she wouldn't need most of it to maintain a simple existence, but she'd kept a bag of coins underneath a loose plank of wood in the corner.

She lifted the plank, revealing the small hollow beneath the floorboard to reveal both the coins and a curved claw that most people would believe had belonged to a wild drake —a long dead one. Her own blood encrusted its sharp edge, which matched the scar on her leg where it had pierced her skin. She didn't know why she'd kept it. The same reason she'd kept the drakeskin gloves, perhaps. An unwillingness to let go. When she fingered the claw's edge, a faint chill touched her shoulder, and the merest scent of decay tingled her nostrils. Shuddering, she returned the claw to the bag and raised her head to the window, hoping Niema hadn't seen. Thankfully, the other woman appeared to have taken Yala's words to heart and left.

Good. Vanat needed to accept that she'd sooner cut off her other leg than leave the jungle, and that it had nothing to do with regrets over their brief span as lovers. Yes, that had been a mistake on her part; she remembered those days with bittersweet fondness but had no desire to rekindle their relationship. It had been easier when they'd been squad leader and subordinate, but upon shedding those roles, she'd had a moment of weakness and pushed him to acknowledge the feelings he'd nurtured for years without acting upon.

The army didn't have rules against romantic entanglements between soldiers, but she'd made a point of staying out of her squad members' romantic lives. When she'd become aware of Vanat's admiration for her, she'd encouraged him to pursue other lovers instead, though she'd rarely done the same. She'd never been jealous, exactly, though she'd sometimes wished she had the same ability to easily slip into a new relationship as if trying out a new pair of gloves. For Yala, the trust had to already be there for her for her to feel comfortable, and while that had been the case with Vanat, the rift between past and present had been too vast.

How morose I am, she thought as she fixed the hammock back into place. How long had it been since the war? She'd stopped counting at five years, but it might be six or seven by now. What had she made of her life, really? Would following a vague warning from a stranger be worse than staying put and waiting for the next predator to visit her cabin to eat her?

She tried to imagine what the others would say instead. The last she'd seen of Saren, he'd been on a determined drunken expedition through every pleasure house in the capital, emerging at dawn each morning with someone new on his arm, be it a handsome dockworker or a lithe-bodied dancer. Machit, meanwhile, had married a noblewoman, of all people. Yala doubted their marriage would last, but he at least had had a sense of purpose. So did Viam; in fact, she'd put her funds from the army into her education at the University. Last she'd heard, Temik had been considering doing the same. She couldn't imagine him in a dusty study room, poring over old texts, but she'd never have imagined herself spending her days in a cabin in the rainforest and not in the sky. Life had a way of surprising you.

With her job done, Yala fell into the hammock, and dreamed of flight.

Sunlight jabbed Yala's eyes, prompting them to open. She lifted her head and groaned when she saw that the curtain that she'd hung had fallen into the room during the night, leaving a gaping hole open to the jungle. The hammock swung as she sat upright, her head fuzzy with sleep, and she watched the curtain flutter with a vague sense that something wasn't right. Silence clothed the forest; the usual howls of kekins and shrieks of birds had been absent since the war drake's incursion, but the beast wasn't outside her home. Was Niema? She certainly felt as if unseen eyes stared at her.

Yala's tiredness fled when a breeze caressed her sweat-dampened skin. The cool rush of air was as alien to the jungle's suffocating heat as a snowstorm; generally, the only reprieve from the humid dampness was to jump into a river. What was the source, another winged predator?

Yala climbed out of the hammock and snatched her dagger before heading for the window, peering out into the mass of crumpled undergrowth the beast had left in its wake. The breeze had ceased, but her instincts told her she wasn't alone.

"Who's there?" she called. "Show yourself."

A gust of air hit her arm, knocking the dagger spinning from her hand. Yala took a startled step back, scanning the thick greenery in search of her attacker, but the forest remained untouched.

What in the hells was that?

Dropping to a half crouch to retrieve her dagger without

jarring her injured leg, Yala kept her attention on the window.

"I'm getting really tired of people disturbing me," she said. "This is your last warning. Show your face, or I'll carve it up."

A tall man dressed in pale blue robes stepped out from between the trees. "You were hard to track down."

His words made little sense to Yala. "Do I know you?"

Was he a friend of Niema's? He had the medium-brown skin and curly brown hair of any Larian, but it was the blue robes that prompted a memory. Encountering two Disciples in a single day made it improbable that they didn't know one another, but the Disciples of the Sky lived in the mountains to the southwest. What was one doing in the jungle?

"Not yet." The arrogant tilt to his chin and the knowing glint in his brown eyes indicated he would not so easily be dissuaded as Niema, and Yala's shoulders tensed when he reached for a thin blade sheathed at his waist. "It would be wise of you to come with me, soldier."

"Come with you?" He couldn't possibly be serious. "Not a chance."

The man lifted a hand and sent another current of air to whip at her hair and clothes. She dove to the ground in a lunge that made her leg twinge in annoyance, and her newly repaired hammock was once again torn down. With an oath, she raised the dagger and leapt for the open window, intending to tackle her adversary.

Instead, she landed clumsily in the mud, the man having effortlessly glided out of her range. She'd known his people could call upon the god of the sky to aid them, but she'd never seen that power for herself. The man moved swiftly, his feet skimming the undergrowth and his sword slicing through vines and branches as she pursued him.

"What is your problem?" she bit out, her leg giving a

painful jolt as she was forced to twist on her heel to keep him within her sight. "I don't even know who you are."

"My name is Kelan." He gestured with his free hand and a current of air wrapped around her ankle like an invisible hand, tripping her. In another blink, he was in front of her, and she caught the edge of his blade against her dagger. Metal rang against metal, and her leg throbbed a warning. Gods, she was out of practise. She hadn't had a sparring partner in years. "If you don't want to meet my companions, I'd suggest you put your weapon away and follow me."

Yala's hand didn't so much as twitch. "I'll put my weapon away when you're dead."

"Fair enough." His next swipe aimed at her good leg, skimming the fabric of her trousers, and she felt the first stirrings of panic. He'd taken note of her limp. That wasn't good. If he took out her uninjured leg, she'd be dead before she could draw another breath.

She had to finish him off first.

When the air buffeted her face again, she intentionally fell backwards and let the undergrowth break her fall. Lifting her blade, she stabbed upward, and the point sank into his upper thigh. As he stumbled, she grabbed Kelan around the ankles and brought him crashing into the undergrowth on his back.

"Ouch." He touched a hand to the bloody gouge in his thigh. "That stings."

"Good." She aimed for his neck next, but he lifted his bloodstained hand and sent a torrent of air towards her. The attack hit her in the chest, knocking the breath from her.

Yala flew backwards, tossed like a child's toy, and landed on her back in a mat of greenery. Numbly, she lifted her head and saw a lithe female figure hurrying uphill. Niema. *Good. They're welcome to finish one another off.*

Yala pushed upright, the undergrowth tangling around

her legs. It took several breathless minutes for her to free herself, and when she next looked up, Niema was peering down at her. "Good, you're all right."

"Where's that man? Dead?"

"He ran," she said. "He was bleeding. You stabbed him?"

"Yes..." Yala trailed off. "Was he following *you?* Was he the 'danger' you warned me about?"

"I have never seen him in my life." Niema sounded a little insulted. "He didn't follow me."

Yala frowned. "Why would a Disciple of the Sky come here?"

"That ... I don't know." Niema's voice faltered. "I've never met one either."

"Wonderful." She might have spoken harsher words, but she swallowed them; despite her misguidedness, Niema had helped to drive the stranger away. Pity they hadn't learned anything except his name. Kelan.

Didn't most Disciples look unfavourably on anyone who used their gods-given gifts to hurt others? Yes, the Disciples of the Flame held no such rules, and for all she knew, those of the Sky were the same, but he couldn't possibly be a Rafragorian out for revenge on her for the number of his kinsmen she'd killed during the wars. A treaty signed some centuries prior had forbidden Disciples from getting involved in warfare, and that was *before* Laria had had a new monarch who'd sworn off warfare of any kind. Granted, Rafragoria had proven they held a flexible approach to peace treaties, but why would they hunt down her and not one of the people who'd given the orders?

No, the truth most likely lay with the Disciples themselves. Yala cast a glare at Niema, wondering what level of pressure would coax her to spill the details of whatever vision had led her here. Knowing her luck, Niema's promise of secrecy would bind her tongue even at knifepoint, and killing a Disciple of the god of life struck her as a spectacular way to meet a painful end. Yala refused to die at the hands of a god, and she gained no pleasure from unnecessary murder either.

Niema flinched. "Captain Yala—"

"Please don't call me that." Her rage abated, leaving only weary scorn, mostly towards herself for being fool enough to think true retirement had ever been an option. "That man said he wasn't alone. You should go."

Yala trudged uphill towards her cabin again without another glance behind her. Niema might mean well, but she was as much a source of trouble as every Disciple she'd met.

The Disciples of the Sky, though … now Yala thought back to her conversations with Dalem, he'd mentioned that the Disciples of the Sky often took on freelance work. Had someone hired the man to kill her? Speculating on her own would do no good, she knew, but she had years of practise ruminating on unanswered questions and had never quite dropped the habit. Like running her tongue over a loose tooth, she couldn't seem to help herself.

As she approached the cabin, the sound of rustling footsteps made her ears prick. Cursing herself for not retrieving her weapon on the way back, she spun on her heel and saw several figures among the trees.

"Yes?" she said. "Are *you* going to tell me what you want with me?"

In answer, a tornado hit her house.

3

F or the third time in less than a day, Yala flew backwards, pushed by the force of the torrent of air. Around her, trees creaked and swayed, branches tearing free, and she tumbled head over heels until her back slammed into the undergrowth. Above, branches revealed jagged shards of blue sky with scarce a cloud to be seen. There were worse places to die, but Yala had far too many questions to resign herself to her fate.

Yala lifted her head a fraction, gauging where she'd landed. The blast had sent her flying away from her cabin, which had the presumably unintentional effect of knocking her out of the other assassins' line of sight. She counted three, none of whom wore the robes of a Disciple like their companion did. Evidently, Niema had picked up a few more followers on the road, and while Yala saw no signs of her nor the Disciple of the Sky who'd so rudely flung her aside, she knew the jungle better than the average person. Unlike those three men, whose rough clothing suggested they were mercenary swords-for-hire who'd have no way of distinguishing between the regular noises of the wildlife and the sound of a human sneaking up on them.

Crouched low, Yala began to ascend the hill. She'd dropped her weapon at some point, but the would-be assassins were oblivious to her, and the nearest had a nicely sharp-looking knife sheathed at his ankle.

Yala crept through the undergrowth, using the carnage the rampaging war drake had left in its wake to conceal her approach. When she came within reach of the man's ankle, she gripped the knife hilt and gave a firm tug, freeing the weapon and causing the man to stumble.

"He—!" He cut off in a gurgle as she drove the blade into his spine. He collapsed with a muffled noise that drew the attention of another assassin.

Yala yanked the knife free and kicked the man's body aside, moving towards the second assailant. This one held a longer weapon, but these men were slow and clumsy compared to the Disciple's effortless control over the elements. He swiped at her, missed, and she tackled him around the ankles, bringing him down into the mud with her. When he tried to rise, her feet tangled in his, and she brought the knife up between them.

"Tell me," she growled in his ear. "Who sent you here?"

He didn't answer. She'd moved her knife too fast, and it impaled his chest, blood bubbling from his lips. Yala pushed herself off him and yanked the blade out, counting the bodies. Two ... there'd been at least one more, she was sure. Not to mention that Disciple of the Sky. Her leg twinged its displeasure at her rough treatment, but she had no time to assess her own injuries when her most dangerous assailant was still alive.

He'd also made a spectacular mess of her house. Yala approached her cabin, cursing under her breath. A torrent of air had ripped the roof clean off. How in hells was she supposed to fix the damage?

As she approached a tangle of beams, she tripped over a body. Not one of the people she'd killed, since he was in the wrong place—and was that his own blade sticking out of his chest?

Stiffening, Yala caught sight of the blue-robed Disciple from before, hovering a short distance from the body. Had *he* killed the man? He'd tied a bandage around the leg she'd stabbed, but it didn't seem to have slowed him down.

Kelan saw her watching and tilted his head, as if inviting her to come closer. Did he think her foolish enough to walk into range of his blade after the last time?

"What is it?" she called to him. "Aren't you going to bother to walk over to me and finish me off?"

"I hoped you'd come to me yourself."

He's playing games with me again. "No thanks. Either tell me why you want me dead or get it over with."

"I'm not going to kill you." The man moved closer, holding his hands palm-up to indicate that the thin blade he carried was sheathed at his waist. His robe and trousers were too warm for the climate but didn't impede him in any way; in fact, he seemed to hover above the ground as if the under-growth wasn't present at all.

"You tried to stab me earlier."

"You *did* stab me." He indicated his leg, where the blood had already dried against the bandage. She hadn't hit a major artery. *More's the pity.* "I wasn't aiming to kill. Unlike those mercenaries. Personally, I think four against one is hardly a fair match."

"Weren't you *with* them?"

"No, I followed them." He moved a little closer, and Yala raised her borrowed weapon. "I was under the impression you were worth more alive than dead, but they didn't appear to be the sharpest of knives."

"Who exactly put a price on my head?" It must be a hefty one for mercenaries to have come all the way out here, but how it related to Niema's warning was less clear.

"Haven't a clue," he said. "Personally, I prefer to know who I'm going to kill before I commit the act."

"An assassin with morals. How quaint." Why was he talking to her at all? "Wait, you *don't* know who wants me dead? Aren't they your employers?"

"I don't have an employer," he said. "I'm merely a curious bystander."

"A curious bystander who arrived at the same time as a group of mercenary killers?" She lifted a brow. "And who tore off my *roof*?"

"Wait, you live there?" His gaze slid from her to the pile of beams that had once been a roof. "I assumed that was some kind of penal shack for rural prisoners."

He thought he was funny, did he? "Curious bystander or not, if you don't get away from my house, there'll be one more body for the grubs and bloodflies to feast on."

With a shrug, Kelan glided several steps eastward from the sorry ruin of her cabin. "If you don't want to get eaten by a wild raptor in the night, I suggest you find new accommodations."

"If you don't want a hole in your other leg, I suggest you fuck off."

One brow rose to match her own. "There's no need to be rude."

"Trust me, I'm exercising extreme restraint right now."

She ought to kill him, but she was far too tired for another fight, especially against someone who could make the wind turn against her. If she had to die, she'd prefer it to be with a little more dignity than at the hands of an assassin who didn't even go about his job in the right way.

"Is that so?" A smile tugged at the corner of his mouth. "I think you owe me your name at least, before I leave. I gave you mine."

He didn't know her *name?* "Standards among swords-for-hire must be lower than I thought."

"You'd be surprised." He shifted his feet, and Yala tensed when she spotted the gleam of a blade hidden in his free hand. "I heard some intriguing rumours on the road. Do you devour men's hearts?"

What? Who in the hells had told him that? "No, but if you want to be the first, I'll happily oblige."

"Interesting," he said. "You must be worth a lot of money if that many people want a piece of you."

"It seems to me that if you want to get the hypothetical bounty on my head, you should probably find out if you've got the right person," she said. "If it turns out to be a false lead, it's a long way back to the capital from here."

"That won't be a problem."

The merest gust of wind drew her gaze downward to his booted feet, which hovered a finger span above the ground. She hadn't been imagining things when they'd fought—he stood *on* the air, as if the forces of nature didn't apply to him and his kind. No wonder his leg injury hadn't impacted his speed. No doubt carrying her out of the jungle wouldn't be an issue for him either.

She caught his eye, and he lifted his blade, the air stirring at his fingertips. *All right. What's one more body, really?*

Before either of them could move, however, a mighty roar shook the forest, followed by the sound of wingbeats. The assassin looked up, startled, as did Yala. The war drake was back?

Branches crunched and were swept aside in the war

drake's descent through the canopy. Yala watched in astonishment as the beast ignored her and lunged at Kelan, who scooted backwards, his feet gliding on the air as though it were solid. When the beast's claw swiped, missing him by a finger span, the assassin gave her one last disbelieving glance before he vanished amid the trees.

Yala expected the drake to give chase, but instead it landed in the mess of undergrowth near her cabin. She held her breath, every muscle in her body tensed, but despite being undeniably conscious of her presence, it did not attack her. Was that normal behaviour for a wild animal? Likely not, but it had been born and raised in captivity, and the war drakes that escaped the paddocks were usually furious enough to attack any human unfortunate enough to cross their paths. This one had only targeted her out of hunger.

Her breath caught again when its front claws ripped into the undergrowth, snatching one of the bodies of her attackers.

"You're welcome to him," she told the beast. "Thanks for the help."

Clutching its meal, the war drake took flight with a beat of its wings that once again shook the forest. Yala's teeth rattled in her skull, her instincts urging her to get out of the jungle before it changed its mind. At least she had two more bodies to offer as bait, but the locals would not be best pleased if she got into the habit of feeding the wildlife.

If she had a scrap of sense left, she'd be out of here by dusk ... after she dug her belongings out of the ruin of her house.

"Fucking *Disciples*," she spat at nobody in particular, limping back to her cabin. As little as she wanted to leave, sleeping in a room without a roof was a foolish idea ... and if more of those assassins were out there looking for her, she wouldn't last long.

No, she had to come up with another plan, preferably before nightfall. As she was digging through the ruins for her pack, Yala wasn't particularly surprised to see Niema approaching.

"Once again, you're too late." Her caustic tone was undeserved, but one would think the gift of prophecy would be a little more reliable.

"Would you have preferred me to have asked the beast to kill the man instead?" she asked. "If so, my apologies. My vows to the god of life prevent me from taking lives."

"Excuse me?" Yala's heart missed a beat. "*You* sent that beast?"

This woman was scarcely an adult. How could she have commanded a war drake? She wasn't even old enough to have served in the army when Yala had been there, and she'd no doubt never seen a battlefield in her life.

"I understand if you're annoyed," Niema said. "It sounded like he was threatening to kill you. In a polite way, mind, but still."

Yala's mouth hung open. "Were you the one who ordered the war drake to attack me?"

"Attack you?" she echoed. "No, I didn't. Why?"

"It came here before you did." She gestured at the cabin. "Nearly cost me another limb, too."

"Oh." Horror rounded Niema's eyes. "I apologise. I might not have been clear enough with my orders. I've never used my ability on a beast of that size before."

"All the Disciples of Life can command war drakes?" If so, why had they not fought in the wars? Well ... if they weren't allowed to take lives, it would defeat the purpose, and the treaty against Disciples fighting in wars applied to them, too.

"Any animal," Niema corrected her. "Except humans. That's not allowed."

The Disciples of Life have the ability to exert their will over

41

animals? Dalem's education in the temple definitely hadn't covered *that*. "Where did you even find a wild drake?"

"Your friend."

"Vanat." She huffed a laugh. It was typical of him to have tried to befriend a war drake. He'd missed flying as much as she did. "He didn't take it with him into the city, surely."

"No, they were travelling together on the road," she explained. "I think he brought it with him for protection. When I explained my abilities, I convinced him to let me use them to find you."

"That's how you found my house." *Why* he hadn't come in person—though a former rider wouldn't have been able to exert total dominance over a wild drake, even one that had been tamed by humans in the past. Everyone in the flight division had known that war drakes had to be handled extremely carefully to avoid fatalities, and the rate of riders who retired early with missing limbs was significantly higher than in the other segments of the army.

"That's right," Niema said. "He's waiting for you in Setemar, but it's more than a day's journey away."

"I'm aware. I've been there before." She ought to be more polite to someone who'd saved her life, but Yala could scarcely wrap her head around the notion of this tiny woman giving orders to a giant winged predator. "I'm going to pack."

She limped to the cabin door, glanced behind, and saw that Niema was following her. "You don't have to come with me. Two of us will draw more attention."

Niema's expression shifted from hurt to puzzlement. "I thought you knew."

"Knew what?" Yala halted, hand on the door frame. "I thought you said you'd never seen that man before. Do you know why those assassins were after me? Are they with Rafragoria?"

"It's to do with the war, yes, but they aren't with Rafragoria." Niema drew in a deep breath. "According to your friend, someone put out a bounty on the last flight squad to take part in the Rafragorian conflict."

Her words catapulted Yala's thoughts several years into the past. "The ... last flight squad? You mean..."

My squad. We're the targets.

4

Kelan waited for the soldier to leave, careful to conceal himself behind a large-leafed tree. The beast that had unexpectedly attacked him appeared to have left, but he'd waited for an hour before daring to approach the wooden cabin again.

The wound in his leg had stopped bleeding, though a dull ache persisted. The injury ought to have been a sign that he should leave the woman alone. While the mercenaries' absurd notions of her heart-devouring tendencies had unsurprisingly proven incorrect, he had not come here to leave with more questions than he'd started with. Instead, he waited, trying not to imagine how Superior Sietra would react when she found out that he'd gone on such an elaborate detour he'd ended up being hunted by a wild drake in the jungle.

The wild drake had claimed one of the assassins' bodies but the other two lay where they'd fallen, as if the woman cared nothing for cleaning up her traces. Kelan glimpsed her moving around the room through a hole in the wall that might have passed for a window and wondered what would drive someone to live in such a remote location. He already had a hard time believing she was comfortable in that shack, though he supposed its small size was adequate for a lone person who didn't care for luxuries. Her limp would make it hard to climb stairs—an old injury from a past war, he assumed.

When he next looked up, she'd stripped off her torn, bloodied shirt. Her body was compact, muscled and scarred, as he'd expected. Kelan had no doubt she'd been a soldier, but otherwise, she didn't look particularly remarkable. Curly brown hair, a scar across one cheek, lips compressed as if disappointed with the world in general. Kelan didn't have enough of a conscience to look away, so he watched her tug on a clean shirt and pick up a handwoven bag, which she slung over her shoulder. She then lifted a wooden cane and nudged open the shack's door.

Hastily, he glided back amid the trees to avoid being seen, his feet skimming the undergrowth. Even from his current position, the thick greenery was an impediment to stealth. He was used to sparse rocky paths and cool air rather than humid dampness, and he understood why everyone down here wore thinner clothes and not the robes that kept out the chill at a higher altitude. He could easily conjure up a breeze to fan himself, though Superior Sietra would have reprimanded him for using his gods-given gift for frivolous purposes. Personally, Kelan thought the god of the sky would have understood that he would have difficulty supplying Him with prayers if he lacked the ability to breathe.

Despite the breeze he'd conjured, the soldier remained unconscious of his presence as he followed her down a dirt track. Or perhaps she didn't care. She seemed remarkably unconcerned for her own safety, though she also had a pronounced knack for narrowly avoiding catastrophe. Why had that wild animal attacked him and not her? It couldn't possibly be a relation of one of the wild drakes he'd driven out of Skytower, and besides, he felt he'd been justified in his annoyance towards the beasts for their persistent attempts to raid the food supply.

At one time, they'd been steeds in the king's army, bred for war and ridden by warriors who didn't mind the risk of losing a limb or worse if their mount unexpectedly decided it no longer cared for cooperating with humans. While it made sense for the newly freed beasts to seek a new home in the mountains, he was at a loss to explain how one of them had ended up in the jungle.

Then again, I'm not entirely sure why I'm *here either.*

He hadn't lied to the mercenaries when he'd said he needed the money, but this bounty had had the most tenuous of possible connections to his mission in the capital. The trouble was, most regular folk had little knowledge of magic, much less the sort that didn't lie under the authority of one of the five branches of Disciples. When he'd heard the words 'magical abilities' in connection to a large bounty, he'd let his desire for coin overtake his common sense. The woman didn't have any abilities, and her house, if one could call it that, had contained no altars or prayer mats or even furniture. She'd uttered no prayers to the gods when her life had been under threat. Aside from the odd way that war drake had reacted to her, she'd shown no signs that she was a threat to his fellow Disciples.

Or that she rips out men's hearts. Then again, why had he expected any sense from mercenaries?

The woman walked with dogged persistence until she reached a small settlement formed of wooden huts and approached a cluster of market stalls. Sensible of her to buy supplies for the road. The villagers didn't appear to be afraid of her, but Kelan kept his distance; his robes would draw attention, and there were few travellers in the region. With her supplies packed away, the woman paused to pick out a few herbs—bitterleaf, used for medicinal purposes as well as a potent painkiller—and when she lifted her head, her eyes locked with his.

The woman's jaw twitched. "You again? Looking to make a public scene, are you?"

"Certainly not." He hadn't intended to draw her attention, though given his conspicuous attire, it had only been a matter of time. "I'm here to peruse the markets."

"I find that hard to believe."

"How much are those leaves, exactly?" He indicated the bandage on his leg, evidence of her handiwork. "Or can you spare one?"

"Now you want to steal from me as well as capturing me for a bounty?" She shoved one of the leaves into her mouth and began to chew. "If you have money, the locals will appreciate your business. If not, then leave. You've done enough damage already."

"I might remind you that the next person to stop by your cabin will find the dead bodies of your last visitors."

She worked her back teeth over the leaf, grinding it into paste. "I killed them in defence of my own life, as well you know. Nobody's going to arrest me."

Most likely true. Communities like this one policed themselves, and while the locals might turn on her after they learned of the dangers she'd drawn to their home, she seemed to have already resigned herself to leaving.

The soldier limped past, and Kelan fell into step with her, his feet skimming the dirt track. "That beast of yours was quite the surprise. I didn't know wild drakes made a habit of befriending humans."

She halted, one hand resting on her cane. "I've had quite enough of you trying to wheedle information out of me. If you aren't going to kill or capture me, why are you here?"

"A valid question, but you've overlooked the most important thing."

"And that is?"

"My insatiable sense of curiosity." He spoke half in jest, half in truth. He shouldn't have been following her, not when it was clear she had no connection to his mission, but why did everyone seem to be fixated on this woman? Yes, her bounty was worth a lot of money, but any thoughts he'd entertained of turning her in had melted. She was simply too *interesting* to hand over to a group of low-life mercenaries.

Her cane tapped against the hardened mud as she began limping again. "You're going to get bored with following me on foot when you can walk on the air."

"I like a challenge." He had to admit that the slower pace made the thick humidity more noticeable, but the walk would be far more unpleasant for her than it was for him. "Besides, I believe we're heading in the same direction."

"I doubt it." She marched on, as if she had no concern that he might ambush her from behind. Had she dismissed him as a threat so easily?

No. Her gaze flicked to the sky, and he realised the danger an instant before a gust of air buffeted him from above. He lifted his head to see the wild drake heading directly for him.

———

Yala watched the war drake's descent, this time with a little more understanding. The man beside her gave a startled curse as the drake's claws snagged the hem of his robe. He glided backwards to avoid being further entangled. Someone screamed from the direction of the market, and Yala gripped her cane tightly as she limped away from the settlement as fast as her leg would allow.

The war drake took flight again with a beat of its wings, and Niema emerged from the trees at the path's side. "Sorry. I didn't mean to scare the people at the market, but I thought he was threatening you."

"Niema." She'd wondered where the other woman had disappeared to. "He wasn't threatening me. Annoying me, yes, but not threatening my life."

"What in the hells is going on?" Kelan looked at the pair of them with confusion, as if he hadn't yet realised that it had been Niema who'd sent the war drake to attack him. Yala saw the moment his attention landed on the leaf-shaped tattoo on her neck, as his eyes widened. "You're a Disciple of Life."

"Yes, and you need to leave Yala alone."

Yala groaned. He might not have known her name before, but he did now.

"Yala," he repeated. "Captain Yala, right?"

"Not a captain." Gods, but he was persistent. "Niema, can you ask the war drake to bite his head off? Or perhaps a limb. Make it nice and slow."

The colour drained from his face. "*You* sent that beast after me?"

"Yes," said Niema. "I did. Also, I told you to leave Yala alone."

"I was just *talking* to her," Kelan protested. "You're going to the capital, aren't you?"

"As a matter of fact, no," said Yala. "I'm not."

"Setemar, then?" he pressed. "There are more mercenaries looking for you there."

"And how would you know that?"

"Because the ones currently lying dead outside your cabin overtook them on their way into the jungle," he told them. "I might have had a hand in sending their group astray, I admit."

"You're lying," Niema said.

EMMA L. ADAMS

"Of course he is," Yala said. "I don't think even *he* knows what he's doing here, except irritating me."

"Believe it or not, I'm here on the instructions of my Superior." He turned to Niema. "I gather that you are, too, since your people never leave your enclaves without cause."

"Your Superior sent you to kill me?" Yala asked, disbelieving.

"No." His jaw locked, his attention remaining on Niema. "No, and I'd prefer not to share the details in front of the likes of you."

"You're one to talk." Niema's biting tone was a contrast to her earlier politeness. Yala had known the different branches of Disciple did not typically get along—their members tended to mirror the rivalries between their respective gods —but she had no patience for more delays.

"You two can fight it out," she told them. "Niema, feel free to find me later, after he's dead."

"Dead?" Kelan gave a laugh. "Don't your people take vows against harming other living creatures?"

"Our vows can be flexible in certain circumstances."

Yala ground her back teeth over the bitterleaf in her mouth and walked on, leaving the two bickering Disciples behind. If not for Kelan's interruption, she'd almost resigned herself to Niema's company, and she did have an extensive list of questions she'd intended to ask. Whether Yala would be able to bypass Niema's vows of secrecy was another matter, but if someone had put a bounty on her entire squad, she needed to know why. Also, having someone at her side who could tell a dangerous wild beast to obey her commands would be a distinct advantage.

The war drake changed course and swooped downward again. Yala glanced behind her to see Niema gesture towards Kelan. "Leave, or I *will* order the beast to bite you."

Kelan gave the pair of them one last disbelieving look

50

before vanishing into the surrounding forest. The war drake gave a rattling growl and flew onward with a beat of its leathery wings while Niema jogged over to Yala. "I didn't realise he was still here."

"I hope he took the hint this time." How had Yala managed to go for more than half a decade without meeting any Disciples and then run into two within the course of a day? Granted, Niema had proven surprisingly fierce when she'd driven off her fellow Disciple, and Yala made a mental note not to underestimate her. "Let's not disturb the locals any longer."

No doubt they'd be less than friendly if she ventured near their settlement in the future, and it wouldn't be undeserved. Anyone unlucky enough to draw the attention of mercenaries *and* a wild drake was not a person one would want as a neighbour. Life in the untamed jungles of southern Laria was challenging enough already.

Niema easily overtook Yala's limping pace, but then she doubled back to let her catch up. "Did you walk here when you first came to live in the jungle?"

"Yes." They'd already left the trappings of habitation behind, and the overgrown dirt track barely qualified as a road. "It was a long journey. Unlike Vanat, I didn't tame a wild war drake to carry me here."

"Oh, I don't think he's using it as transport," she said. "The one time he tried to mount the beast, it nearly bit his fingers off."

"The fool." He'd had no saddle or chain, and he'd presumably lost his drakeskin gloves at this point, too. That was characteristic of Vanat, though. He insisted upon doing everything the way that *he* thought was easiest, even if it caused no end of trouble for everyone else. Including her, but what had she expected? She was the one who'd persevered long past the point where she ought to have given up on them making a relationship work. There'd been too much grief, in the end, but the same could be said for the rest of her squad.

What if people are hunting them, too? Niema's warning worked its way under her skin like an itch.

"He said that he wished there'd been another way to find you," Niema added. "It was quicker for me to send the war drake than for him to comb the area himself."

"I expect it was." The drake remained visible as a winged outline etched against the egg-blue sky. "Flying would be faster."

More conspicuous, though, especially if Kelan wasn't the only Disciple of the Sky in the region. Their ability to fly without reliance on a deadly steed had been envied throughout the flight division. She'd never heard of them using those abilities to perform assassinations, but why wouldn't they? Their god didn't seem to object.

Flying would be less painful, too. The leaf she chewed helped with some of the pain, but it wasn't a substitute for rest, and a collection of new aches and bruises made themselves known as they walked. Yala spat out the remains of the leaf and pulled another out of the pouch at her waist, prompting Niema to glance at her injured leg. "I can help with that."

"What do you mean?"

To Yala's bemusement, Niema crouched beside her and extended a hand towards her right leg. As the Disciple's palm brushed the fabric, a sensation rushed over Yala's skin as if she'd plunged her leg into cool water. The pain didn't go away entirely, but when she tested her weight on her right foot, the new aches from her recent fall had vanished, leaving only the familiar dull twinge she'd grown used to managing. She blinked, startled to find salt stinging her eyes.

"There." Niema removed her hand. "Better?"

"That's a useful ability." She hadn't known the Disciples of

Life had the power to ease pain, but once again, she had to wonder why they'd never been drafted in to help the army. Yes, their vows forbade violence and the treaties prevented them from taking part in warfare, but one would have thought a past monarch would have tried to find a way around it. If not King Tharen, then one of his predecessors.

"Yes ... but it has a cost."

Yala followed the other woman's gaze and saw that a nearby patch of greenery had begun to wither, each leaf decaying on its stem. *Ah. That's the cost.* The Disciples of Life's power over nature might be remarkable, but like the other Disciples, they had to offer something to the god of life in trade. Interesting that the god of life drained the life from other living beings despite Her followers' vows against harming others, but Yala had to admit a few leaves was a small price to pay for a less painful journey.

She inclined her head. "Thank you."

Maybe the Disciples are good for something after all, she thought. *Or some of them are.*

5

K elan's day did not improve after he left Yala and the strange Disciple of Life behind. He knew better than to continue to tail them when they had a war drake at their command—or at least one of them did—but he was left at a loose end when it came to his mission.

He wouldn't find more mercenaries to question at this remote a location, but Setemar was Yala's eventual destination, he was sure. Admittedly, he'd met another group of mercenaries when his erstwhile companions had stopped there for supplies, and he'd given them misleading directions in order to avoid being overtaken. *Maybe I don't want to see* them *again.*

If the bounty were as large as rumoured, though, there'd be others on their heels. With the aid of the god of the sky, Kelan reached Setemar's boundaries without needing to put a foot on the muddy road. Houses sprawled outward from the walls that encased its central region, forged by the Disciples of the Earth who'd founded the city several centuries prior.

When he approached the rusty iron gate to the inner city, he found his way blocked by a guard. "What's your business here?"

"Nothing in particular."

"You're armed." The muscular man eyed the blade sheathed at Kelan's waist and then the bandage wrapped around his injured leg.

"Should I not be?" Since when did Setemar need hefty security? The city was hardly the cesspit of decay and crime the capital had become in recent years. Unless things had changed since his last visit to the Inner City, which had admittedly been several years ago. "I'm here on business from my Superior."

The guard's suspicion vanished at the word, as he'd hoped, and he moved aside to let Kelan enter. He didn't typically like to draw attention to his Disciple status—it tended to impede one's efforts to blend in—but the robes would already draw attention, and he wouldn't have been surprised if he was the only one of his kind in the city.

His leg wound had begun to ache, so he made for a nearby drinking house. It was a little early, but several people were drinking already, and nobody gave him a second glance when he entered the dimly lit room. Smoke billowed from a corner where a group of miners sat smoking, and while the surly bartender gave monosyllabic answers to his enquiries about travellers in town, Kelan's mood improved considerably. A drink or three and an evening at a pleasure house would wash away the sting of the injury he'd been dealt, and who knew—maybe someone here would talk. Kelan had guessed that this would be Yala and her companion's next destination, but they wouldn't arrive until tomorrow morning at the earliest. He'd be able to ask a few questions of the locals without any concern that her irritating companion might send a war drake to bite his head off.

Her vows are flexible, are they? He sipped his drink. *Well, so are mine.*

He kept an eye on the door and felt a rush of vindication when a group of rough-looking men with muscles and scars walked in. Former soldiers, no doubt, turned mercenaries, each of whom claimed a seat at the table across from his. He angled himself towards their group and ordered a second drink. Snippets of conversation reached him, making his ears prick.

"She's supposed to be some kind of hermit," growled a masculine voice. "Lives in the jungle."

"Someone said she killed the last mercs who went looking for her," a lower-pitched whisper returned. "Nobody came back alive."

"All the more for us."

Kelan gave up pretending not to be eavesdropping. "Are you talking about the captain?"

"Who wants to know?" said the brutish-looking man who'd spoken first. "You're one of them Disciples, aren't you?"

"Yes, and I've seen her," he said. "If you're talking about who I think you are. Are you after the bounty?"

"Seen her, have you?" The man snorted. "A likely story."

"She's the one who did this to me." Kelan indicated the bandage on his leg, wondering if they'd heard the same rumours as the last band of mercenaries. "They say she devours men's hearts."

The brute leaned forward in his seat. "Nah. Their pricks, maybe. I heard she won her captain title by fucking the commander."

His companion—female, by the pitch of her voice— elbowed him in the spine. "Don't be crude. If it was that easy to advance in the ranks, you'd have made it higher than cadet."

As the others laughed at him, the man scowled. "Not my fault they ended the war before it started."

"This is all interesting," said Kelan, who rather thought that anyone who believed Yala incapable hadn't been on the receiving end of her army-issued knife, "but I have to wonder why you took a bounty to bring in one of your former comrades. Money that tight, is it?"

"Like you'd know?" The man put down his glass, hard, causing froth to spill over the sides. "Sounds to me as if you're looking for a fight."

"No, just information." Kelan reached into the pocket of his robe and pulled out one of his admittedly dwindling coins. "I can pay you for it."

"Why'd you need the bounty, then?"

"I don't." He pushed air at the coin so that it tilted onto its side and balanced on his fingertip. "Hence why I'm offering you this."

"That's a nice party trick, that is." The man watched with greedy eyes as the coin spun on its edge. "What do you want to know?"

"Who put out the bounty on her?" Kelan asked. "For that matter, do you even know the captain's name?"

"No, but there aren't too many ex-captains here," he said. "Gimme the coin."

"You didn't answer my first question."

"Who arranged the bounty?" As the man spoke, his female companion rose to her feet and walked away from their table as if bored with their conversation. "Shit, I don't know. I heard from another group of mercenaries we passed on the road."

"You came all this way for a rumour?" Then again, hadn't he done the same himself? The soft sound of the door closing indicated that the woman who'd been sitting with their group had left.

"Give me the fucking coin."

"Right, right." He flicked the coin at the men and was rewarded with the mildly entertaining sight of them scrambling on the filthy floor to pick it up.

This was ridiculous. It shouldn't be that hard to find out who wanted to pay a large sum for a retired soldier who'd committed no crime that he knew of. Unless she'd caused some grievous offence on the battlefield, but hadn't the last war ended more than six years ago?

More to the point, how could anyone possibly be sure the bounty was legitimate? He'd heard of rising desperation in the capital, but he'd thought nobody would risk their neck on the road for a rumour of coin and not the real thing. He hadn't considered that unemployed soldiers might do exactly that.

The surly bartender shot him a glare as if daring him to start something, so he returned to finish his drink before his mouth got him into trouble. Mercenaries were notoriously tight-lipped, but maybe he'd have more luck at a pleasure house. He'd heard people make confessions in the throes of passion or the luxuriating aftermath that they never would have said under other circumstances.

Tossing another coin to the bartender, he left the tavern and followed the cobbled road for a short while before he realised he was being followed. He tilted his head, allowing his pursuer to catch up.

"You're the one who was asking all the questions." The woman from the tavern stepped into view, the hood of her cloak falling back to expose a head shaved to the scalp. "You know where the captain is."

She wants to have this discussion away from her companions, does she? Interesting, though it wasn't unheard of for mercenaries to betray one another as easily as they would anyone else. Her fellow soldiers had plainly handed their morals in as well as their uniforms, but had this woman, too?

"No, I don't know where she is," he said. "I lied."

"I don't think you did." The woman moved closer, cloak shifting in such a way that exposed the blades sheathed at her waist. "There are people who'd kill for that information."

"Why?" His hand touched his sword hilt, though in truth, he had little desire for another fight. "Do *you* know who put the bounty on her?"

Her lips compressed. "They're known as the Successors, in the capital, but nobody knows who their leader is."

"Who are the Successors?"

"If I were you, I wouldn't repeat the name."

"Ah, but if I'm not going after the captain, it doesn't matter, does it?" He hitched on a smile. "That part wasn't a lie. Is there any reason she's such a valuable target? Hidden skills, or…?"

With a swish of her cloak, her daggers were hidden again. "Nice try, but I already gave you the name. If you want more, you'll have to offer me something in return."

"That's fair." His smile widened. "It might interest you to know that the captain is currently on her way to Setemar, and she's likely to arrive by morning. Are you staying here?"

She tilted her head, assessing him. "You'd better not be lying this time."

"Wouldn't dream of it." He caught her eye, pleased to see the hint of greed there. *I've got her.* "I'll buy you a drink. What do you say we finish our conversation somewhere more private?"

———

Niema walked alongside Yala, following a winding route through patches of trees. Few people visited such a remote region, but Yala didn't seem to mind the lack of decent roads. If anything, Niema had the impression she'd come here on purpose. Whenever Niema tried to strike up conversation with the other woman, Yala was taciturn with her responses, and didn't ask many questions despite her obvious curiosity about Niema's mission. She also didn't want Niema to know the details of her relationship with Vanat, though Niema inferred a little from the way she spoke of him, a wistful note to her tone that she was likely unconscious of. They'd been lovers for a time and squad mates for longer, and Yala had been responsible for his life as well as those of their fellow fliers.

That bond hadn't been erased by time or separation, a bond Niema understood. She had little doubt that she would have made similar sacrifices for her fellow enclave members, and leaving them behind had been the most challenging part of her mission. While she could sense the life thrumming in every living creature within range of her—and further afield, if she concentrated hard enough—she was bound to her enclave in a more intimate manner. The sense that five hearts beat in her chest alongside her own hadn't dimmed yet, but she'd been warned that it would fade when she was far enough away.

Some tasks must be completed alone, she told herself, echoing the words of Superior Kralia. It was an honour to be chosen, and Niema tried to focus on her gratitude rather than the unsteady impression of being unravelled like a spool of thread.

When the sun began to set, Yala slowed her pace. "We need to find somewhere sheltered to stop for the night. Did you stay in a village or inn on the way to my cabin?"

"No, I prefer to sleep out in the open." The slightest twitch in Yala's mouth indicated she thought that odd, which was a fair reaction, given the number of predators roaming the southern jungles. As of yet, Laria's government had not burned the trees to the ground to make room for farmland or grazing space for livestock. "I can find a safe place where we won't be disturbed."

Yala inclined her head with a grunt of acceptance. No doubt she'd slept in worse conditions as a soldier, and her cabin had been as basic as the few buildings in Niema's enclave. "Are you a long way from home? I'm not familiar with which part of the forest you live in."

"You won't find it on a map," said Niema. "Like your cabin, it's secluded."

Yala didn't respond. Too late, Niema remembered her home had been destroyed and she might not have appreciated the reminder. Typical, when she'd finally managed to coax her companion into making conversation.

"You don't travel much," Yala said after a short pause. Perhaps she hadn't taken offence after all, or her curiosity won out. Niema had never met someone quite so hard to read, though admittedly, she didn't have extensive experience to draw on.

"No, we're usually only sent out of the jungle to meet with the other Disciples."

Yala's mouth tightened at the last word, and once again, Niema regretted not watching her tongue. Yala's friend— Vanat—had warned her to stay away from the subject, but that would exclude almost the entirety of Niema's repertoire of conversational topics. Unless the other woman wanted to discuss the intricacies of kekin migration habits and the best days of the year on which to pick the ripest sunfruit.

"Is that why you left?" Yala asked. "I find it hard to believe that you came to find me and for no other reason."

She wasn't wrong, but when Niema opened her mouth to

reply, no words came out. She felt a tugging sensation in her chest like a rope pulled taut, forcing her into silence.

"Right, you can't tell me," Yala surmised. "Never mind."

"I can give hints," said Niema delicately. "Like I said, we're sometimes sent to meet with other groups of Disciples, though we aren't the only ones who live in isolation."

The Disciples of the Sea, for instance, had made their homes in the vast ocean to Laria's north and were equally hard to pinpoint on a map, while the Disciples of the Sky lived up in the mountains in the southwest. Only the Disciples of Earth and Flame lived in cities—the former in Setemar, the latter in Dalathar, the capital. While Niema did plan to visit both, they weren't her primary goal.

Yala inclined her head. "True, but the way my day is going, I'll find a Disciple of the Sea lurking in the river when I try to take a wash."

Niema gave her a small smile. "Possible, but unlikely. Do you want to stop here?"

Yala considered their surroundings and picked out a shady spot beneath a tree. "Did you bring food with you?"

"I know how to find plants that are safe to eat."

Yala put her pack down. "I've no doubt you can take care of yourself in the wild, but I wouldn't wander off alone in case we're being followed. Share with me instead."

"Are you sure?" Niema hadn't wanted to leave Yala unwatched in case their pursuer returned, though she could call the war drake back if necessary. She rather hoped she *wouldn't* have to ask it to tear off any limbs; while the action was within the instincts of a wild animal, the knowledge that she'd caused harm to another living creature wouldn't rest easily alongside her vows.

Yala pulled out several packages, including a sleeping mat and a few bags of dried fruit and meat, which she shared between them. Niema shook her head when offered the latter and Yala seemed unsurprised to learn that Disciples of Life did not consume the flesh of living creatures. While Niema preferred fresh fare, she had to admit that sharing a meal with Yala was a pleasant change from scavenging in the woods.

"When was the last time you visited the capital?" Niema asked as they ate. "To Dalathar?"

Yala chewed a mouthful of dried sunfruit and swallowed. "A while ago."

"I've never been." Niema hoped to coax her into telling her more of the place she intended to be their eventual destination, but Yala didn't take the bait. "Is it true that there are military parades every week?"

"I doubt the new king kept up that practise," Yala muttered. "Not if he's determined to reinvent Laria as a pacifist state."

Niema opened her mouth to ask why she thought that was a bad decision before she recalled that Yala had been a squad leader in the flight division before the current king had eliminated her job. While Niema was glad that non-Disciples no longer had to complete a compulsory term of service in the military, she wouldn't get far with earning Yala's trust if she kept reminding her of how little they had in common.

No, she needed to proceed with caution. When the time came for her to reveal her mission, Yala needed to have faith in her.

If Niema wanted to prevent the rise of Corruption, all of Laria depended upon her success at winning Yala onto her side.

———

Yala and Niema reached the outskirts of Setemar early the following morning. The clear sky made it easy for Yala to pick out the shape of the grey cliffs that arose along its northern side, from which the Disciples of the Earth had mined the stone used to create the foundations of the settlement. While dirt tracks ran between ramshackle houses on the outskirts, her cane soon tapped on cobbles as they neared the gated area that had formed the original city before the population had swelled too large to be contained within its walls.

The gate was staffed by a muscled guard who looked askance at the pair of them, taking in Yala's cane and Niema's tunic-like garment. "What's your business here?"

"Here to see a friend," Yala responded. "We're from Dalathar."

The latter was a lie in Niema's case, but the guard was already ogling at her odd clothing, and revealing her companion's Disciple status might draw unnecessary attention. If Kelan had been telling the truth and more mercenaries were staying in the city, they didn't need to turn themselves into targets.

The guard waved them in, and when they reached the other side of the gates, Yala turned to Niema. "Whereabouts will I find Vanat? Is he staying at his lodgings?"

"He didn't say." Her gaze slid over the stone apartments in which all but the well-off resided. "I can help you look."

"That won't be necessary." Yala felt a twinge of guilt when the woman's face fell, but she would prefer to be alone when she spoke to Vanat. "Thanks for your help."

The city's streets were quiet at this early hour, so if Vanat was on the lookout for her, neither would have trouble finding the other. Yala would be able to recognise him even in a festival crowd, thanks to years of having to identify her squad-mates among crowds of identically dressed soldiers, but Setemar didn't look to have seen any cause for celebration. Half the lodgings appeared unoccupied. *Moved to the capital, did they?*

The stone wall circling the Inner City towered over the rooftops, giving her a sense of being enclosed, and the tightness of the streets soon started to irritate her. At least the jungle had been sheltered; here, the buildings didn't overhang the streets like they did in Dalathar, and if a certain Disciple of the Sky was watching her from above, she wouldn't have known. *He'd better not be here.*

The Disciples had created the wall circling the central part of the city, too. It had been intended to give the impression of a stronghold but only served as an eyesore, in Yala's opinion. As if they expected to be attacked from the outside, which was laughable—nobody would waste their time trekking all the way to Laria's central province to wage war when the capital lay at its most exposed northern point and was a far more attractive target than an old mining city past its best days.

Yala's steps brought her to a familiar tavern, and she ducked inside. The room was deserted at this time of day, but she and Vanat knew the owner, Thraten. When she sidled over to the counter, his usually surly expression broke into a grin. "It's been a while, Yala."

"Yes, it has, Thraten," she said. "Where's Vanat?"

"I thought he was off looking for you."

Her brow wrinkled. "No, he sent someone else to find me, and we came here to track him down."

"You two could never have a straightforward conversation, could you?"

"That's not the point." Had Vanat gone on a drunken rant about her? Possibly yes, and she'd deserved it, too, but she wished he'd kept his thoughts to himself. "Is he staying at his old lodgings?"

"Last I heard, yes," he said. "I'll keep an eye out. What's the rush?"

Yala's mouth parted. She didn't know if Thraten was aware that someone had allegedly put a bounty on her entire squad, but she needed to talk to Vanat to gauge if he knew more details before she let word spread any further. "Never mind. I'll find him."

She left the tavern and made for the residential district in which Vanat had rented an apartment that he often lent to friends when he wasn't in the city. Like her, he'd never settled anywhere; in his own words, when you'd spent the best part of your life in flight, putting down roots was all but impossible.

Yala halted in front of the narrow apartment and knocked on the wooden door. Nobody replied, nor did she see anyone through the single dusty window. Her spine prickled. Vanat was not an early riser, and she'd frequently had to drag him feet first off his sleeping mat in the barracks when they'd been called in for early-morning training drills.

Yala pushed against the door with her cane, and it swung inward. Not a suspicious sign on its own; sleeping in shared dormitories for most of his life had made him a little lax about security, and he didn't live here all the time, regardless. Careful not to make too loud a noise with her cane, Yala scanned the downstairs room. A few piecemeal bits of wooden furniture and an ancient armchair were the only occupants, as Vanat shared Yala's tendency not to get sentimentally attached to physical objects.

She walked to the bottom of the wooden staircase and peered upward. "Vanat? Are you there?"

No reply, nor any movement. Maybe he'd gone to find her and they'd somehow missed one another on the road. The war drake must be outside of the city, though surely even Vanat wouldn't be foolish enough to sleep next to a dangerous predator; the most skilled handlers were wary enough to keep the drakes chained down when they weren't flying. No, he'd been here, recently, judging by the mud in the entryway.

She studied the floor closer, and her gaze snagged on a dark spot on the pale wood near the stairs. *Blood.*

6

K elan was jerked out of sleep by the sound of someone drawing a knife. He gripped the side of the narrow bed when the mercenary sat to sheath her knife, his mind drifting back to the previous night.

Somehow, his plan to coax answers from his female companion had disappeared somewhere after the third drink, and she'd proven to be quite impenetrable. In one sense, anyway—the pleasant ache in his legs attested that she did have some sense of cooperation, but her current body language didn't demonstrate any desire for another round. Not that the way the bed shook made him desire anything more than to stick his head in a bucket.

As she finished dressing, she gave him a brisk look. "Go back to sleep if you like."

"Wait." He lifted his head, squeezed his eyes for an instant, when the world rocked to the side, and then opened them again. "What's the rush?"

"I have a bounty to collect," she said. "You haven't changed your mind, have you?"

"On what?" He pushed upwards, wincing at the sunlight

cutting through the window of the inn's upstairs room. "No, I'm not going after the bounty."

"Good." She blew him a kiss. "Pleasure spending time with you."

He had the distinct impression he'd walked out of this game on the losing side. He gathered his clothes, doing his best to ignore the sour taste on his tongue, and dressed quickly.

When he left the room, a glowering innkeeper stood at the top of the stairs, barring his path. "Well?"

"Well what?"

"She said you'd pay for the room."

"What?" He peered into the main room, but of course she was long gone by now. Had he even learned her name? He didn't remember. "How much?"

The answer prompted him to choke on vomit, which he held back by sheer force of will—and the desire to avoid adding more to his bill by ruining the carpets. He dug into his pocket and counted out coins, certain the price had trebled since his last visit here. No doubt they were suffering from a lack of recent business.

Speaking of suffering. He left the overpriced establishment, racking his mind to remember the previous night. Had the woman given anything away? He'd wanted to know who'd put up a bounty so outrageously large that it had sent at least three separate bands of mercenaries south into the jungle to find a single retired captain, but all he'd learned was a name. *The Successors.* He never did find out who they were, but he hadn't got the impression the mercenary woman had known either, except that they had money and were willing to part with it for comparatively little in return.

Or not so little, given the amount of trouble Yala had given him. The knowledge that he'd told the mercenary that Yala and the Disciple of Life were due to arrive in Setemar that day shouldn't sit as heavily on his conscience as it did. Or maybe that was the drink. *I shouldn't have told her that. What if she tells every mercenary in the city?*

The urge to warn Yala arose, but the notion of running off to find her made his head pound worse than ever. Would she be on the road this early in the morning? No, she likely wouldn't arrive in the city until later, which gave him time to ask questions. He might have had no luck finding out anything more in relation to his mission, but something had the guards on edge.

Would the local Disciples know? He could do worse than to pay them a visit and see if they did. If not, Superior Sietra had claimed the other Disciples might be willing to discuss the rumours, substantiated or not, that someone in Laria had accessed magic never seen upon the continent before.

Niema watched Yala walk away, her cane beating a rhythm against the cobblestones. The rejection stung like the bite of a bloodfly, though she ought to have expected as much. Yala had little reason to trust in a stranger, and despite Niema's attempts to find common ground between them, she'd failed to make any headway. Yala wouldn't thank Niema for following her, but anyone she ran into in the streets of Setemar might be allied with the people who'd put a bounty on her squad. Then again, the woman could handle herself. She'd proven as much already, and Niema had a second visit to pay while she was here.

Namely, to the Disciples of the Earth.

Superior Kralia had warned her that she had no guarantee of cooperation from the other Disciples, but unlike with Yala, she had more leeway to confide the severity of her enclave's shared vision. They might not know all of her talents—and the five beating hearts beside hers had grown notably quieter the further she'd travelled from the jungle— but they would understand the binding nature of a promise to her god.

They would also know what the rise of Corruption would mean to her people.

The person she asked for directions gave her a puzzled look and pointed her to the back of the stone wall circling the central part of the city, and when Niema came within sight of the temple, she understood why. The Temple of the Earth appeared to have been carved directly into the cliffs bordering the city's northern edge. The central cliff formed a square pyramid-like shape with a towering door, while the other cliffs were shaped to resemble the broad, imposing face of Setem, god of the earth. While the exterior was certainly impressive, Niema had the impression that the interior would be suffocating and confining—at least compared to her own, but she was bound to be biased in that regard.

And on top of a nearby stone sat Kelan. Niema startled at the sight of the robed Disciple of the Sky, who looked somewhat worse for wear since the last time she'd seen him.

"Niema," he croaked. "Ah—where's your captain friend?"

"None of your business," she replied. "What are you doing here?"

"Taking a rest." He winced and pushed to his feet. A bandage was wrapped around his upper thigh where Yala had stabbed him, and his brow was furrowed as if the sunlight hurt to look at. "I wouldn't advise you to go to the local tavern. There are thieves everywhere."

"Someone robbed you?"

"Yes." He did not elaborate. "You're here to talk to the Disciples of the Earth? If so, they don't seem to be home."

Frowning, she moved to the door and rapped on its wooden surface, but she received no answer.

Kelan spoke from behind her. "Didn't I tell you?"

"Why are you here?" she asked without turning around. "I thought you were pursuing Yala on a whim."

"No," he said. "Believe it or not, I'm currently acting on behalf of my Superior … or I would be, if the Disciples of the Earth weren't hiding underground instead of taking visitors."

Niema rapped on the door again. Where were the Disciples of the Earth? She didn't know enough of their ways to know if this was normal for them, but her suspicions landed on the man behind her. "Did you do something to them?"

"Me?" Kelan sounded insulted. "If I did, why would I stand outside the door and implicate myself?"

"I haven't a clue." Rattled, she turned away and took a sharp step back when she found Kelan had moved directly behind her. "If you're pursuing Yala, I won't let you."

"I told you, I'm not going to kill her." He ran a hand through his tangled dark hair, his bloodshot eyes assessing her. "I found myself on her tail because my Superior sent me on a mission, and…"

"And you thought you could earn some quick coin?" Niema attempted to sidestep him, only for him to glide smoothly into her path. "Can you please move?"

"So polite, even to someone you dislike as much as me." He tilted his head on one side. "I wonder … are we looking for the same thing?"

"Unlikely." She spoke in clipped tones, refusing to be tricked into confiding in him. "Given that every word that comes out of your mouth is a lie, I doubt you're on a mission at all."

"Every word? Not at all." An inexplicable smile tugged at his mouth. "You know, my promises of secrecy aren't as binding as yours. If I tell you my mission, you should be able to confirm if yours is the same."

"You assume I want you to know my business?"

He chuckled under his breath. "I assume you came here to talk to the Disciples of the Earth because you were looking for the nearest source of information on anything related to unsanctioned magic. I could have told you that you're far more likely to learn of such things in taverns and pleasure houses."

"I don't doubt you've spent time in both." *Unsanctioned magic?* He couldn't possibly know her mission, but his words trod close to the truth, and for all she knew he was right. Setemar was an unknown to her, especially if the Disciples of the Earth remained behind closed doors.

"I have," he said, "but in this case, most people have remained unwilling to share their insights."

She tried to walk around him, but Kelan glided into step with her, his feet hovering a handspan above the ground. Niema cast him a sideways glance. "If you're hoping I'm an exception, you're mistaken."

"I imagine unsanctioned magic would be of great concern to your people," he said. "Especially ... Corruption."

Niema's heart missed a beat. *How does he know?* She'd thought the enclave's knowledge was shared only with her fellow Disciples of Life, though it wasn't implausible that the other Disciples had received some level of warning from their respective deities as well. This man, though ... if he saw a Disciple of Corruption pass him in the street, he'd probably wave them along and continue with his day.

"That's right," he went on. "My Superior is under the impression that someone in Laria is dabbling in Corruption. I thought her paranoid, but for someone like you to be on the move, there might be truth to the rumour after all."

"Someone like me?" *A rumour, then. Not anything definite.* If he'd been anyone else, she might have risked sharing her information, but after he'd attacked Yala, it was out of the question. He couldn't be trusted.

"There's no reason to sound so insulted." He shaded his eyes from the bright sun. "I freely admit our meeting was not what I had envisioned, but I'd be more than happy to start over."

"Start over on what?" Niema continued to walk away from the temple, hoping to shake off her companion. If anyone else were around, she might have told them he was hassling her, but the area outside the temple appeared devoid of any other visitors. Did the locals know why the Disciples had closed their doors? "We already established that you're more interested in turning in my companion for coin than in your own mission."

"I did say I changed my mind, didn't I?" To her irritation, he continued to glide at her side, his booted feet skimming the cobblestones. *Useful.* Niema's own thin sandals did little to prevent the hot stones from prodding at her feet. "I never wanted the bounty—not exclusively. The mercenaries, though, spoke of your companion possessing some ability. They disagreed on its nature, but it seemed an obvious clue."

A thrill of abject rage pulsed through Niema's blood, sharp enough to blot out the heartbeats accompanying hers. *How dare he?* "Fool. Yala's not a Disciple of Death. She's the opposite, if anything."

She slammed her mouth shut, but not before a knowing expression crossed Kelan's face. "Interesting. Do you believe Yala has the ability to fight Corruption? She has no magical talent ... though I suppose a former soldier like her does have other useful skills, especially when one is inconveniently incapable of dealing so much as a minor injury."

"You think me incapable?" Her hands fisted at her sides. "I wouldn't speak too soon."

Empty threats, but she'd already said too much. Even Yala didn't know the extent of Niema's awareness of her history. The last thing she needed was for this man to destroy the fragile partnership between her and Yala before she had the chance to gain her companion's trust.

"I didn't intend to insult you," Kelan said. "It was an observation, and a valid reason for us to cooperate rather than go our separate ways."

"I'd sooner cooperate with a bloodfly. At least they have some use."

"Ouch." The mocking tilt to his mouth gave way to something a little more serious. "Listen, I happen to know there's another group of mercenaries staying in this city who are also intent on capturing Yala, and that their employer is located in the capital. Are you sure you won't accept my help?"

"How did you—?" She broke off. "You told them she was coming here, didn't you?"

His mouth parted in surprise, which confirmed her guess. In a move that surprised even herself, she reached out a hand and jabbed her fingers into the wound on his leg.

Leaving him gasping in pain, Niema turned her back on the temple and broke into a run.

———

Yala stared at the blood for a long moment. *Vanat.* When had he been attacked? If Thraten had seen him the previous day, it couldn't have been that long ago, but she didn't know this city as well as she did the capital. Nor did she know where he might have gone afterwards … or if he'd been taken.

A knock on the front door made her reach for the dagger at her waist. *Would his attackers knock, though? Be realistic, Yala.* "Who's there?"

The door pushed inward, and a breathless and dishevelled Niema entered. Her sandals hung off her feet, and she bent double to catch her breath as Yala lowered her dagger. "What is it?"

"I thought you were being attacked." Niema lifted her head. "Apologies. It's lucky I remembered the way…"

"You aren't the only one." Yala indicated the blood droplets on the floor. "Thraten said he hadn't seen Vanat since last night."

"That's his blood?" Niema's eyes rounded. "No … those mercenaries already took him?"

"Looks that way." Cane in hand, Yala trod up the narrow stairway to the equally austere upstairs room. Her chest tightened at the sight of the neatly folded clothes stacked at the foot of the sleeping mat. Vanat had cast aside some of his habits from the army—early mornings being one of them—but not all.

She forced herself to view the room with detachment. The smear of blood on the stone wall, as if a fist had struck it. Faint gouges on the wooden floor, as though someone had been dragged towards the stairs.

"There was a struggle," she said. "Someone broke in…"

Not a difficult task when Vanat often forgot to lock his door, but the question was, *why?*

"He might still be in the city." Niema peered around the corner from the stairs below. "There are mercenaries looking for you. That's why I had to run back so quickly."

"Who told you that?"

"A certain airborne friend of ours."

"Kelan." She gave a sharp tap of her cane on the wooden floor. "You ran into him again?"

"Outside the Temple of the Earth." She backed downstairs and waited for Yala, who was reminded why she'd chosen to live in a cabin with a single floor. Each stair jarred her leg, cane or no cane, and she envisioned jabbing out Kelan's eyes with every painful step. *Did he tell them where to find Vanat?*

Gods, she ought to have stuck her knife into his neck, not his leg. Upon reaching the downstairs room, she sought more clues. "Where did Vanat keep that war drake of his? Might it have followed him?"

"I can find out." Niema made for the front door. "It might be able to lead us to him."

If he lives, whispered a voice, which she ignored. Yala would not entertain the possibility of his death until she saw the proof with her own eyes. "Then we'll go."

Niema opened the door, revealing two strangers standing outside the house. Both male, and undoubtedly mercenaries. That much was obvious from their nondescript dark clothing, the weapons strapped to every limb, and the air of anticipatory greed as they took in the pair of them.

"Can I help you?" Yala reached for her dagger with her free hand, the other tensing on her cane.

The bulky man in front bared his teeth in a grin. "If you're Captain Yala, then yes, you can."

"I don't go by that title any longer." She hefted the weapon, weighing the odds of taking him down before his equally bulky companion got a killing blow in. "This isn't my house. Who told you I'd be here?"

Surely not Vanat—and not Kelan either, unless he'd followed too. In answer, the man swung his blade at her with unexpected speed.

Before Yala could block, Niema dove in front of her and his blade glanced off her arm, spraying blood onto the wooden floor. Alarmed, Yala lifted her cane and jabbed the man in the knees while he was unbalanced, then shooed Niema behind her.

"I don't suppose you can call your scaly friend from here?" she said.

Niema shook her head. *What was she thinking?* Niema didn't even carry a weapon, but she'd tried to save Yala's life.

Yala assumed her healing ability didn't work on fatal wounds, so if Niema died, she wouldn't get up—and the war drake was nowhere to be seen. "Stay behind me. That's an order."

Whatever heroic impulse had driven Niema to dive into the path of the mercenary's sword, Yala would not give her another chance to sacrifice her life.

When the first man lunged at her again, Yala blocked the strike with the side of her cane and thrust upward with her knife, her blade parting the flesh of his throat. Blood spurted, and his companion cursed at full volume and shoved the man's hefty body at Yala.

The unexpected weight caused her to stumble, her leg threatening to give way, but Niema somehow darted into the other man's path and tripped him. Yala shoved his bulky body off and tackled her second would-be killer to the ground. Her blade sank with a wet thrust into his chest, and she growled in Niema's direction, "What did I tell you?"

Niema's attention was on the door. "They're alone, I think. There aren't any others..."

"Shit!" She tried to rise, but the dying man dragged her back down with a rapidly weakening grip. "Who are you? Who offered you money for my life?"

The man spat blood. "Why should I tell you?"

"Because I might spare your friends?"

"Not my friends." He coughed, his breath rattling to silence, and Yala disentangled herself from his body with a muttered curse. His sword looked vaguely familiar. Army-issued. *Was he a soldier?* He'd used her title, albeit in a mocking way, and the two had clearly been trained in combat, the same as she had. That knowledge further fuelled her rising temper.

"I don't think they're the ones who took Vanat," Niema ventured. "What are you doing?"

"Stealing their weapons." Yala divested the soldiers of their swords and offered one to Niema, who flinched. "Right, you can't kill people."

Tripping them and flinging herself into the path of an oncoming weapon apparently didn't count, but neither of those things would make a damned bit of difference in a real fight. She was lucky there'd only been two adversaries. Her attention went to Niema's injured arm, but the wound the sword had dealt appeared to have already vanished.

Seeing the direction of her gaze, Niema lifted her arm to show her the smooth flesh. "I'm fine. The wound was shallow. What ... what are you going to do with the bodies?"

"I'm more interested in who took Vanat."

Niema cleared her throat. "Ah—our adversary. I left him at the Temple of the Earth. He might know."

Right. "I'll kill him this time."

7

As much as Yala would have liked to track down that Disciple of the Sky and skewer him on the spot, she already had two bodies to dispose of, preferably somewhere that wouldn't lead to her getting arrested. She'd be hard-pressed to explain to any passing city guard that she'd been defending herself when the only witness was Niema, who was even more of an outsider than she was. At one time, her captain status would have commanded respect even from lowly city guards, but the title meant little now that it was no longer attached to a job.

Niema made a soft noise when Yala began to drag the larger man's body across the room. "You aren't taking them outside?"

Yala paused to lean on her cane and take the weight off her injured leg for a moment. "They can't stay in here. Not for long."

Dumping them in the nearest river would be the easiest option, but that would have unfortunate effects on the city's main drinking source, and someone might see her doing it.

This wasn't the capital, where the city guard would look the other way if they saw someone tossing a body into the cesspool that called itself a river. Carrying both bodies at once was out of the question, which increased her chances of being caught.

"I'll borrow some sacks from Thraten," she decided. "Then leave them in an alley. It's not ideal, but it isn't uncommon for mercenaries to meet a sticky end."

Not in Dalathar, it wasn't, but she hadn't known they frequented Setemar. Though it might explain the presence of extra guards at the city gates. *It's their own damned fault for letting those mercenaries in to begin with.*

Niema gave no objection to her plan, so Yala left the bodies in the middle of Vanat's downstairs room and left the house. Her visit to Thraten held another purpose: if any strangers had been in the city, they might have stopped at a local tavern. She had a hard time believing Thraten would have directed those mercenaries to Vanat's house, but how else had they known his address?

"Did Vanat tell *you* where he lived?" she asked of Niema as they turned into the cobbled street where Thraten's tavern was located.

"He did, but I had to knock on a few doors before I found the right one." Niema walked slightly behind Yala; her voice pained. A glance confirmed that Niema had removed her ruined shoes and was forced to hobble barefoot. *We'll have to deal with that later.*

When Yala entered the tavern, Thraten stared at her bloodied clothes. "What happened to you?"

"I got into a scuffle with a couple of people who showed up at Vanat's place," she said. "I don't suppose you can explain how they knew his address? They were mercs ... ex-soldiers, I think. Didn't have time to ask."

Fear flickered in his eyes. "You killed them?"

"Never mind what *I* did." Her hand clenched on her cane. "Vanat's gone. I found blood on the floor and signs of a struggle, so I'm guessing someone captured him. Did you give anyone else his address?"

His shoulders slumped. "I thought they were Vanat's friends, to be quite honest. Like you said, they were soldiers..."

Damn. She'd guessed right. Part of her wanted to reject the notion that her fellow soldiers would take up petty banditry or worse, but desperation bred difficult choices.

"Don't look at me like that," Thraten said. "I couldn't have known, could I? I've been seeing more and more of their sort around lately. They've been coming back and forth from the capital for a while. It's not that unusual."

"It is if they're kidnapping civilians." She gave him a hard stare, though she took little pleasure in seeing the colour drain from his face. "Have any of the others asked after Vanat? Or me?"

"No, they haven't." His voice trembled. "Listen, I don't know where Vanat is. You're better off asking the city guard. They're supposed to vet everyone who comes in."

"They're doing a piss-poor job, then." She rapped the cane on the floor, making him jump violently. "Next time someone comes here asking after me, you'll demand that they tell you exactly who sent them. That clear?"

"I..." He dropped his gaze, swaying like a tree in a storm. "Listen, Yala, you can't go around doling out justice at will. You're not a captain anymore."

"I'm aware." Some of her anger seeped out of her when she glimpsed Niema cowering near the door. "Someone wants me dead, Thraten, and there's a fair chance it's already too late for Vanat. That's my only concern."

He sucked in a breath. "I told you everything I know. There's nothing else I can do, is there?"

"Actually yes." She flashed him a smile without any humour. "I need two large sacks."

Several minutes later, she reached Vanat's house and pushed the door inward, already dreading the pain that disposing of the men's bodies would cause to her much-abused leg. It was unavoidable, however, and the quicker she dealt with the bodies, the quicker they could find Vanat.

Yala busied herself wrangling each body into its respective sack, wishing Niema would give her a hand. Granted, Niema had probably never handled a dead body before—or even seen one—and Yala had to admit she hadn't missed the stench. As she was tying the second sack with robe, she heard the other woman retching outside the front door.

Typical. With both bodies taken care of, Yala rested her hands on her cane, willing her leg to behave itself until the task was done.

"Can you open the door?" she called to Niema, who acquiesced without a word. Her stance was downright haughty as she watched Yala drag the first body over the threshold, prompting her to lift her head. "What? If you aren't going to help, hovering over me isn't going to make this go any faster."

Niema stepped aside with a muttered apology, while Yala began the excruciating task of wrangling both body-shaped sacks out of the doorway. "If you have a problem with how I spoke to Thraten, I'd appreciate it if you came out and said so."

Niema was silent for another long moment before she replied. "He's right… We're not at war," she said. "If you keep killing people, sooner or later, you're going to end up in trouble with the law."

"They didn't exactly give me a choice." Yala gave one of

the bodies a sharp prod with her cane to push it over a bump in the cobbles. "If you have an alternative, I'm listening."

"You might have subdued them and then contacted the city guard."

"I was too busy trying to keep them from turning me into pulp." She seized the other sack and dragged it for a few handspans before switching to the other. "Or you. I won't allow you to jump in front of me again, do you understand?"

"I—" Niema's mouth parted. "You're angry with me for that?"

"You aren't a soldier." She dropped the end of the sack. "And if you've never had a weapon in your hand and known you'd be the one bleeding out if you didn't use it, you don't get to make judgments on what I do."

"That ... that wasn't my intention." Niema self-consciously touched the faint leaf-shaped tattoo on her neck. "I told you of my vows, didn't I? Harming others is a direct violation of Yalet's will. The god of life reveres all living creatures."

"I assume Yalet has no problems with you sending war drakes to attack your enemies." *Stop talking*, whispered a voice in the back of Yala's mind, knowing she was doing nothing to help the situation by turning her sole remaining ally against her.

"Attacking other humans is within the instincts of wild animals," Niema said. "It's not a violation."

"Convenient."

Hurt bled into Niema's voice. "I was trying to help you. My enclave might not have made the same choice, but —wait."

"Wait for what?" She grabbed the sack again, which slipped from her grasp when a breeze tickled the back of her neck.

"Want me to help you with those?"

Yala spun on her heel with an oath, reaching for her weapon. The Disciple of the Sky, Kelan, descended as if he'd been watching them the whole time. "Watch it. If you get any closer, I'll find myself with three bodies to dispose of instead of two."

"It's up to you if you want to add to your burden." He turned and pointed south of their position. "I wouldn't go that way. There are city guards marching around the interior of the city wall."

"What—?" Yala broke off when he descended in a swirl of robes and grabbed one of the sacks. "What are you doing, trying to get me arrested?"

"No, I'm trying to ease my conscience." He hefted the body over his shoulder, grunting at the weight, and drifted towards an alleyway further down the street.

"I didn't know you had one." Yala seized the second sack again, but she'd scarcely dragged it a few handspans before Kelan returned, divested of his burden. "If you're expecting me to thank you for this, you're out of luck."

"No more than I deserve." He took the end of the sack from her and hauled it over his shoulder—with some difficulty, given that its occupant was easily twice his size.

"No, considering you *told* the mercenaries I was here," she said. "Didn't you?"

"It was a miscalculation." He vanished into the alleyway, and Yala heard the body hit the ground with a thud.

"How can you *accidentally* send a group of murderers after me?" She hobbled down the street, but he reappeared before she reached the alley's entrance. "Give me one good reason not to throw your body into that alley, too."

"I know who put the bounty on your head."

"Don't listen to a word he says." Niema caught up to them, puffing a little, and addressed Kelan. "I'd have thought you'd have had more sense than to go near Yala after you admitted to sending those mercenaries to attack her."

"I also helped her dispose of their bodies." He indicated the alleyway behind him. "That cancels out my transgression, doesn't it? I thought your people believed in second chances."

"Second chances?" Niema spluttered. "This is your third, at least, and if you betrayed the trust of someone in my enclave, you'd be exiled into the jungle."

"Harsh." Amusement glittered in his eyes, while Yala contemplated the odds of knocking him out of the air with a well-timed dagger throw. Not high, she had to admit; he might not be trained like she was, but he moved so damned fast it didn't matter. *Fine.*

As she made to turn her back, his feet touched down on the cobbles once more. "Didn't you want to know who hired those mercenaries? I'd gladly offer you that information ... if you answer a question of mine."

"No," Niema answered for her. "Even if you *aren't* lying, it's not worth putting ourselves in debt with the likes of you."

"That." Yala jerked her head in agreement. "I'd rather eat drakeshit than make any kind of agreement with you."

"That's fair." He gave the alleyway a last contemplative look, and then vanished in a flutter of robes.

Yala swung her head towards the other woman. "What in the hells was that about?"

"I hoped you knew." Niema frowned at the spot where Kelan had been hovering. "The last I saw of him, he was trying to get into the Temple of the Earth. They weren't answering the door."

"Did he cause that, too?"

"No." Uncertainty underlaid her voice. "I wouldn't have thought a Disciple of the Sky would have been able to subdue every member of their Temple. He wasn't in the best shape earlier. He said he was robbed."

Yala forced a laugh. "It's more likely that he was the one who did the robbing."

Though robbery was a step above murder, and Yala would find herself in trouble if he'd intentionally put the bodies in a spot within view of the city's guards. She didn't *think* he had, but now he was gone, she'd have to go elsewhere to find out where Vanat had been taken.

She returned to Vanat's house to retrieve her pack, Niema hovering at her shoulder. "Where are you going now?"

"To ask some questions." She fished her waterskin out of her pack and drank, tipping some of the water onto her shirt in an attempt to wash the blood out. "You really ought to replace those shoes. Didn't you bring any spares?"

"I usually walk barefoot." Niema eyed Yala's neatly packed clothes. "That won't be sufficient in the capital?"

"The—" She broke off. "What makes you think I'm going anywhere near Dalathar?"

"That man... Kelan... He said the mercenaries' employer was located in the capital." Niema spoke quickly. "He might have lied, but that's where you used to live, isn't it?"

Suspicion flared. "Just how much did Vanat tell you?"

When Niema didn't answer, Yala sighed and reached into her pack, fishing out a few coins. "Take these and buy yourself some new shoes. Consider it payment for helping me fight off those thugs."

And a peace offering. With Vanat gone, her list of allies had shrunk somewhat, and the last thing she wanted was to draw attention to the bodies she'd left in that alley by questioning the city guards. *Though they don't know me, do they?*

After cleaning herself up the best she could, Yala left Niema to browse the markets and made her way to the nearest pair of guards patrolling the city walls. "Excuse me."

"Something I can help you with?" One of the guards—

grey-haired and broad-cheeked—eyed her cane. "Looking for a replacement for that, are you?"

"No, I'm fine," she said. "I'm looking for a friend of mine, a former soldier. He lives in the residential district ... sometimes." *It would help if he stayed in one place for longer than a season,* she thought, as the two guards exchanged sceptical glances.

"Former soldier? Is that why you look familiar?"

"I used to be," she said. "He was in my squad."

The grey-haired man raised a thick brow. "Were you now? Must have been brief. I was in for twenty years, and I don't know you."

"I spent most of my time in the flight division." If he'd been on the ground, he'd likely seen little actual combat; most of their skirmishes with Rafragoria in recent years had taken place over the open sea.

"You flew on one of those war drakes?" asked the second guard, a younger man. "Fucking hell. You're mad."

"Have you seen one recently? A war drake?"

Vanat hadn't brought the war drake into the city, but if someone had seen it, this might be her best chance of finding him. Though she'd need Niema's skill to guarantee its obedience. *Of all the luck.*

"Sure, we see them sometimes," he said. "Why?"

It was a fair question, but if Yala told him Vanat had brought the beast here, she'd end up being the one answering questions instead of the other way around. "No reason. I really do need to find my friend, though... Did you see any of those mercenaries leaving through the gates early this morning?"

"Mercenaries?" His forehead screwed up. "You're the second person to ask that question today. No, the last ones I saw left at dusk. They come and go all the time."

"Why do you let them?" She could guess; from the sparse

crowd at the market, mercenaries were among the few visitors the city had. Shame, really. "Don't they have a tendency to make trouble?"

"The ones that do don't stick around," he responded. "If you want to know who's new in town, I'd ask at Thraten's place."

Right. Yala debated arguing and then let it go. "Thanks."

If the mercenaries had taken Vanat, they wouldn't have wanted to make a public scene. It was more likely he'd been smuggled out, not unlike the two bodies she'd hidden in sacks, without the city guards being any wiser.

Yala returned to the market, where Niema had acquired a pair of boots that paired oddly with her tunic-like garment but were at least comfortable looking. Now she was less likely to get blisters on the road, should she follow through with her plan to go to Dalathar.

As for Yala herself… "Niema, how close do you need to be to the war drake to get its attention?"

"It depends how many other people are around," she said. "Here, I can't sense anything but us."

That doesn't seem like a good sign. "Your abilities don't work outside the jungle?"

The other woman's head tilted. "They do. I should be fine when we leave the central part of the city."

Yala hoped so, because the war drake was the sole clue connecting her to Vanat. If the mercenaries had no allegiance to one another, the two who'd attacked her at Vanat's house might not have even known he'd been kidnapped. Or they might have been sent as a diversion as their allies took Vanat to the capital. *That's the problem. We don't know nearly enough.*

"Then we'll go." Yala marched onward towards the gates, privately glad to leave the enclosing walls of the Inner City behind. The Disciples of the Earth had had a deficit of imagination when they'd designed Setemar because there was no reason for them to have created a less impressive copy of the capital city with more mines and fewer decent taverns. Really, it was no wonder nobody came here to visit.

Yet the idea of setting foot in Dalathar again appealed as much as stepping in drake dung. With bare feet. *Who are those kidnappers, really?* Were they based in the capital, or was it a convenient hiding place for their illicit activities? Criminals flocked there like flies to shit, and the city itself was like a bloodfly she couldn't swat away.

The guards that waved them through the gates hadn't seen Vanat either—or otherwise didn't have any satisfactory answers on the latest mercenaries to visit—so Yala gave up on the notion of getting answers from any two-footed beings and watched the skies instead. Niema muttered under her breath, reciting a prayer or litany that Yala didn't recognise.

"What was that?" she asked, when Niema had finished. "Were you calling the war drake?"

"Not exactly," she said. "No, I was praying to my deity to grant me strength enough to call the beast back to our side. I haven't used my abilities this extensively before, but I should be able to attract its attention, once we're away from these houses."

"I don't expect it would want to land near human habitation."

"No, but my abilities... They can blunt its instincts, temporarily. I don't like to do it too often, but in the case of an emergency, like this..."

"Handy." She didn't quite know why Niema was telling her this detail about her abilities, unless Yala's comments concerning her usefulness in their fight with the mercenaries had hit a nerve. "I'd prefer not to have to use that method in a crowded street. Trust me, you haven't seen what one of those beasts can do to a person."

"No." A moment passed. "Vanat told me some of it. He

said you had a knack for handling the war drakes from the start."

"I grew up on a farm." Another peace offering, then, and a chance for Yala to find out how much Vanat had told her companion. "Moved to the capital after my parents died. War drakes are unpredictable, but so are raptors, if you get unlucky."

As her parents had. An escaped raptor had been responsible for the fire that had burned down her family's farm, killing everyone except Yala, who'd smelled the smoke and bolted before she'd realised her parents were trapped inside the barn. She didn't mind Niema asking questions about those days; the hurts were old scars smoothed by time, not jagged and aching like her right shin. Her pace slowed as the houses grew sparser, and if they did find themselves on the road again, she might have to hire a wagon. Or borrow one. *Hmm.*

Niema's attention turned to the sky, and she began to whistle. The sound reminded Yala of a bird's call, a soft and almost soothing melody that wrapped around her ears like a lullaby. "Are you calling the war drake?"

The whistling stopped. "Yes, but if I'm interrupted, I have to start over."

"I wondered if you were putting it to sleep." How the beast would possibly be able to hear her was beyond Yala's comprehension. "Also, if we walk much further, we'll be back on the road. Are you sure you want to head to the capital on foot?"

"I didn't know there were other options." Niema slowed her pace, as if sensing that Yala was displeased with the constant strain on her injury. "I can heal you again…"

"It'd be easier to hitch a ride on a wagon," she said, ignoring the offer. "You won't have to sacrifice as much that way."

"We ... don't use that word."

Yala's ears pricked at the inflection in her tone. "Sacrifice?"

Niema gave a shudder. "It's so ... blunt. We think of the process more as a transference of energy from one being to another."

"Ah." Yala ought to have spoken more carefully, given that experience of Disciples so far had shown they tended to clothe unpleasant concepts in acceptable language and did not react well to crude statements. 'Offerings' was the term the Disciples of the Flame used, albeit theirs was not a magic that could be used to heal, only burn. "Did Vanat mention anywhere we can hire a wagon? A boat might be faster, but I don't know the rivers."

"He didn't. Sorry."

Typical. Vanat had been so fixated on finding Yala that he'd neglected to make arrangements for the event of his own capture. "Then we'll have to make do."

If he'd been taken as bait for her, Yala would surely have found more clues leading her onward. Those mercenaries she'd killed hadn't even mentioned his name, and the possibility of several groups competing over the same bounty meant that she couldn't trust a word any of them said. *Not my friends*, that man had said before he'd died. Some soldiers they'd turned out to be.

The question was, why would anyone target her squad to begin with? She was no closer to answers than before she'd left her cabin, nor did she have any obvious clues linking the mercenaries to the last person who'd threatened her life.

Who to blame? She had one theory, but why would the Disciples of the Flame choose now to send mercenary killers after her? Given their own talents, why would they need to?

"Should I try calling the war drake again?" asked Niema.

"Oh, go on. Why not." Yala heaved a breath. "Unless you can tell me who to blame for this mess, I'm out of ideas."

"I don't know," said Niema. "Vanat said the gods were to blame, but—"

"You can't agree with that, for obvious reasons."

Vanat had frequently told Yala she was wasting her time blaming the gods for the actions of the living, but in the absence of any living person to blame, perhaps the gods were all that remained.

8

Niema watched Yala out of the corner of her eye as they made their way through the city's outskirts, keeping her other eye on the sky in search of the war drake. She whistled as she walked, a soothing tune that calmed her nerves following the outbreak of violence earlier. It was difficult to forget the bodies they'd left behind, nor that Kelan had escaped. She could hardly believe the man had the nerve to show his face to them, let alone try to bribe Yala into accepting his trust by helping her dispose of the bodies.

The truly infuriating part was that he'd been more helpful to Yala than Niema had, and the clues he'd taunted Yala with concerning her missing friend were weighing on her mind.

Niema told herself that she could hardly blame Yala for her mistrust, given that she'd been alone for a long time since her retirement. *That and she's no stranger to killing, while I could barely poke Kelan in his wound without running up against my vows to the god of life.* Niema had never thought of her vows as an impediment, but Yala did, and the notion rankled her.

Her whistling heightened in pitch, and Yala raised her free hand to cover her ear. She did not interrupt, however, and after several moments, a familiar winged shape appeared in the sky.

Yala let out a low whistle of her own. "Impressive."

The wild drake swooped downward and landed beside the pair of them on the wide dirt track. When Niema saw the dark blood on its claws, she sucked in a breath. "Oh, no."

"Is that human blood?" Yala approached the war drake. "Please tell me you killed the scum who took Vanat."

The war drake growled between its teeth, but Niema's abilities didn't extend to understanding its snarls and hisses. It might have simply snatched some unfortunate livestock ... or human. Niema gave another whistle, a soothing rhythm that would calm its agitation. Yala moved closer to the creature as if she had no fear, but Niema stifled a wince when her companion crouched down directly beneath its sharp teeth.

Then Yala straightened, having extracted a scrap of fabric from between its claws. "Drakeskin. This ... it's part of a glove, I think."

"Do you think it's Vanat's?"

She turned it over in her hands. "Might be. Can you tell the creature to go and look for him?"

"I'll try." The war drake could only follow basic commands, and its attack on Yala's cabin had proved that it didn't distinguish between friend and foe without her watchful eye. The scrap of fabric would help, if it did belong to Vanat. "Can you give me that?"

Yala handed her the fabric while Niema suppressed a shudder at the warm blood dotting the hard material. Meeting the war drake's pitted eyes, she gave another whistle, drawing its attention.

"Find him." She held up the material, and the beast's nostrils flared, taking in the scent. "Lead us to the owner of this."

Her murmured instructions drew a growl from the war

drake, and its legs bunched. Then it leapt into the air, launching into a glide.

"Where's it going?" Yala jabbed her cane at the sky, but they had no hope of catching the creature on foot. "Not the fucking capital. How are we supposed to get there before nightfall?"

"We can't." Niema took a step back, her brief triumph at the war drake's obedience fading. "I've no doubt more mercenaries will be on the road, too."

Yala's hands curled into fists at her sides. "Then we'll have to risk it."

A breeze tickled the back of Niema's neck, and she stiffened. So did her companion, who sharply turned to the right. "Not you again."

Niema followed her line of sight, and Kelan held up his hands to indicate he was unarmed. "If you're going to leave the city, you aren't wrong that there are people waiting to ambush you on the road."

"And you're one of them?" Yala took a half step towards him, hand clenched on her cane. "I'm not here to make deals with you, Kelan. We already had that conversation."

"If you want to reach your friend without walking into a trap, you might want to rethink that choice."

———

Kelan watched the two women exchange wary glances, but he'd caught their attention. The snippets of their conversation he'd overheard—along with their perplexing interaction with the wild drake—indicated that they were looking for some unfortunate soul who'd been taken by the mercenaries and that they were in a hurry.

"How do I know you aren't the one setting the trap?" Yala queried.

"Why is it so hard to believe I don't want to kill you?" Granted, he could have used the bounty after that mercenary woman had fleeced him, but it had taken all morning for his hangover to subside, and his head felt too delicate for a duel. "I can offer you the name of the person who put the bounty on you as a gesture of goodwill."

"Do you even know the meaning of the word?" Yala said. "In case you've forgotten, *you're* the one who set up those mercenaries to ambush us by telling them we were in the city."

"I told you, that was a mistake," he said. "Few people will part with information for free, so I gave them what I had in exchange. It wasn't I who endangered your friend. I spoke to the guards, and no mercenaries have left the city since before my arrival yesterday."

Yala's jaw tensed. "Show your goodwill, then. Go on."

"The people who put the bounty on you are known as the Successors," he replied. "I'm not sure if it's a title or name."

"The Successors?" she echoed. "How do I know you didn't make that up?"

"You don't." There was little point in being dishonest. "But it cost me all my coin to get the information and a fair bit of my dignity, too."

"I find it hard to believe you have any to lose," said the other woman, who'd watched their exchange.

He grinned. "That's fair."

"Successors," Yala repeated, her forehead scrunching. "Successors to whom?"

"That I don't know." Kelan's gaze swept from the two women to the dirt road ahead of them. "Neither did the mercenaries I spoke to. They heard the word 'bounty' and the rest ceased to matter."

"Really." Yala gave him a flat stare. "If you're trying to

trick me into leaving the city so you can murder me on the road, I don't appreciate the subterfuge."

"I told you, I'm not going to kill you," he said. "Or hand you over to the Successors. I can make my own way to the capital with ease, but if you want to get there without running into trouble, I think you're going to need my help."

"What is that supposed to mean?"

"You need transport," he said. "I know where the mercenary contingent is camped, and they have a nice wagon sitting there begging to be taken."

"Why would you help us?" The question came from Yala's companion, who'd acquired a new pair of boots since the last time he'd seen her. Given the state of her flimsy sandals and the filth the capital was mired in, she'd made a wise choice.

Why indeed. "I told you, I'm curious, and you have a knack for getting yourself out of scrapes. I also think a large group of mercenaries against one person is unfair."

Yala grunted. "Despite the gods' best efforts to the contrary. Also, there are two of us, not one."

The other woman's mouth opened in surprise, suggesting this was news to her, which further muddled Kelan's impression of their relationship. It was plain that they hadn't known each other long, but then again, he could say the same for himself, and here he was offering them favours.

"Yes, I'm also curious to know what drove one of your people to leave the jungle." He'd expressed as much to her before, but he wanted to see how Yala reacted. "Have you ever been to the capital before? You might need a guide."

Annoyance flickered through the other woman's features. "We're not here to talk about me. If you're being honest, tell us where the mercenaries are."

"All right." He'd return to the question later, and the matter of their shared quest. Yala, he was sure, didn't know the details. Either she hadn't asked, or her companion didn't want her to know. "Shall we be off?"

"Fine," said Yala. "Lead the way."

———

Yala knew that trusting her would-be assassin was unwise, but stealing the mercenaries' transport would both solve the problem of getting to the capital and slow down their pursuers, too. Besides, Kelan *had* given her a name, though it wasn't much use on its own. Or maybe that was the point. He was unscrupulous and plainly had no allegiance to anyone, save perhaps his god, but she also didn't know why he'd lie to her. Admittedly, she didn't know why he'd tell the truth, either, but if they travelled to the capital on foot, it would take several days, and that might not be time Vanat could afford to spare.

Kelan led them a short distance down the dirt road. "Wait here while I check to see if they're in the same place as before."

"You'll be seen."

"It's not me they're looking for." He glided ahead of them, and Yala followed. A wagon had been parked diagonally across the road, a simple wooden contraption with four wheels and two raptors secured to the front to pull it along. A flat roof on top kept out the sun, which seemed extravagant. *They can't be hurting for coin. That or they stole the wagon themselves.*

When Kelan saw that she and Niema had ignored his warning, he halted. "If you must watch, go around the wagon from behind, and I'll steer their attention elsewhere."

"I can convince those raptors to move," Niema whispered to Yala. "Want me to try?"

"Wait until we're in the wagon." The unintelligent wingless reptiles didn't startle easily, but their large, clawed feet could do a lot of damage. While Yala wouldn't shed a tear if they trampled the mercenaries into the dirt, they didn't need to draw any more attention to their departure, not if there were others hoping to get a piece of the bounty.

Yala approached the wagon from the side, holding her cane off the ground to avoid making unnecessary noise, and spied a woman with a shaved head talking to Kelan. A man stood on either side of her, and they appeared to be arguing. Heart in her throat, Yala crept up on the wagon and indicated for Niema to climb in first.

Niema climbed into the wagon and then held out a hand to help Yala, who shoved her pack and cane ahead of her and begrudgingly accepted the other woman's help. The wagon rocked, and the mercenaries' conversation lulled, while the raptors lifted their flat, scaly heads.

"Now," Yala mouthed at Niema, gesturing towards the raptors, whose restless feet swayed the wagon from left to right.

Niema gave a series of short, sharp whistles, and the wagon ceased its rocking motion. As their transport began to move forward, the murmur of conversation ceased.

"What—hey!" The woman whom Kelan had been talking to startled as they rattled past her group. "That's ours!"

"Not so." Kelan's voice was barely audible under the rattling of loose stones under the wagon's wheels, and the pounding of the raptors' feet.

A gust of air rocked the wagon, causing Yala and Niema to grab the side, but it righted itself a moment later when Kelan climbed in. "You're welcome."

Yala peered over his shoulder and saw the three mercenaries lying dazed in the road behind them. Kelan gave the woman with the shaved head a cheery wave. "Consider that payback for the room."

"What in hells was that?" Yala demanded of him as he withdrew into the wagon and propped up his feet on the back of the seat in front. "You had a score to settle, did you?"

"Yes, I did." He grinned widely. "Rather less of a hazardous one than yours, but nevertheless, I think our plan was a resounding success."

Yala's jaw twitched. "Did you distract their attention by pretending you were giving us up?"

"It worked, didn't it?"

Gritting her teeth, she turned her attention to the road to avoid giving into the impulse to push him out of the wagon. He *had* helped them secure their transport, after all, and the wagon would get them to the capital much faster than walking. As for whether they'd arrive in time to catch Vanat's kidnappers, that remained to be seen, since their adversaries had at least a half day's head start. "Niema, can you convince the raptors to move faster?"

"I can help." Kelan leaned out of the wagon and pushed at the air as if he was steering a boat with an unseen oar. The wagon jolted and then rattled onward, picking up speed. "I can't go too fast, or the poor beasts will get confused and drag us into a river."

"Speaking from experience, are you?" Yala stretched out her injured leg and rested her cane across her lap. "Can't you fly? There's no good reason for you to sit in here when you could get there twice as fast on your own."

"Ah, but this way gives me the chance to recuperate." He indicated his bandaged leg. "It's relaxing, too."

Yala wasn't in the mood to relax. The road northward ran through less wild terrain than in the south, but there were remaining patches of jungle that might hide attackers. Yala stole the occasional glance at the sky, but she didn't see the war drake either.

"What're you looking for?" Kelan asked. "That beast of

yours? Do you have some affinity with the creature, like your companion?"

Niema's back stiffened. "Cease the interrogation. Neither of us wants to talk to you."

"You can hardly blame me for being curious," he went on. "Those beasts aren't known for being friendly with humans. They've even been raiding Skytower in the last few months."

"Skytower." The name held familiarity; Yala recalled Dalem describing a towering construction in the southwest mountains, the home of the Disciples of the Sky. "Can't you use your abilities to drive them away?"

"Yes, of course," he said. "The trouble is, they keep coming back. It does get rather tiresome. I suspect that's why so many of my fellow Disciples spend their leisure time in the capital instead."

"Yes, you seem to have a surfeit of leisure time." Yala gripped the side of the wooden seat with one hand as they rode over a bump. "If you're chasing bounties in the southern jungles on a whim. Don't they pay you enough at Skytower?"

"Your friend hasn't told you much about the Disciples, has she?"

Niema sat up straighter. "Do I need to repeat what I said? We don't want to talk to you."

"*You* might not want to talk to me, but your companion has questions," said Kelan. "I can tell."

"Don't push your luck," said Yala. "I'm still debating whether to throw you out of the wagon."

He flashed her a smirk, as if he knew full well that she did have questions—which she did, but not concerning his life as a Disciple of the Sky. Granted, now that she thought on the subject, she recalled Dalem mentioning that each branch of Disciple received no funding from the government, so the money to keep their temples running had to come from somewhere. Many were businesspeople or merchants, some took up a trade, and others ... well, some Disciples of the Flame worked *in* the government, as the King's personal guard. Or they had at one time. For all she knew, King Daliel had tossed out that practise along with most of his army.

As for the Disciples of Life, their enclaves were isolated enough that they must be mostly self-sufficient. Yala had to wonder how Niema had expected to get to the capital alone. Yes, she could find food and water easily enough, and she had no reason to fear predators, but humans were another matter. The Disciples of the Flame weren't known for charity either.

As they continued to rattle down the road, Yala's thoughts turned to what she might find when they arrived at the capital. She rather hoped they'd catch up with Vanat before that eventuality, but if they did find themselves in Dalathar ... what would she do? Find the rest of her squad? Saren and Machit would be there, but it was anyone's guess as to whether they'd be in a welcoming mood. If she told them of Vanat's capture, they surely wouldn't slam the door in her face, though it was no less than she deserved.

Yala was jolted out of her reverie when a sudden gust of wind rocked the wagon. The raptors screeched, and the wheels momentarily left the ground before slamming down hard enough to rattle her teeth in her skull. *Shit.*

Kelan lifted his head. "We have company."

"You *did* plan an ambush." Seizing her cane to prevent it from rolling away, Yala peered over the side and spotted a blue-cloaked figure hovering above the road ahead. *Another Disciple of the Sky.*

"No, I didn't." Kelan's tone held a note of alarm. "Hang on —I'll talk to him."

He jumped out of the wagon and glided ahead of them, stirring up an air current that further tilted their seats. When the wagon gave another jarring tilt, she gestured to Niema. "We'll have to jump out before it lands on top of us."

As the wagon rocked to the right, Yala jumped clear. Her leg gave a twinge when she landed on it, but at a warning breeze from in front, she and Niema threw themselves behind the wagon as the air blasted into their path, stirring up clouds of dust and soil. The raptors screeched, and the sound of splintering wood came from the wagon as the frightened beasts tried to pull themselves free.

Peering around the side, Yala saw Kelan talking to the other Disciple of the Sky, but her attention immediately landed on several other figures at the roadside, making their stealthy way towards the wagon. *Mercenaries.*

She nudged Niema and pointed, and the other woman's eyes widened. There were at least five, too many for Yala to take out singlehandedly—especially with the Disciple of the Sky preparing another attack. Kelan's body language indicated he was arguing with the man, gesturing towards the wagon, but she couldn't hear the words, and she couldn't rule out the possibility that he was putting on an act and that they'd soon find themselves facing two Disciples instead of one.

As for the mercenaries, they stayed on the side of the road as they crept towards the wagon, presumably to avoid being caught in a stray attack from one of the Disciples. Yala swore under her breath when they drew closer, one gesturing towards their hiding place. She'd dropped her cane when she'd jumped out, and she hadn't a hope of outrunning them.

A faint whistle sounded from her side, then one of the raptors broke free of the wagon and charged straight at the mercenaries. With a rush of gratitude towards Niema, she watched with satisfaction as the mercenaries scattered to avoid being trampled by the reptile's clawed feet.

The other Disciple of the Sky shouted something, and

another blast of air forced Yala and Niema to duck out of sight. As they did, the second raptor shook itself free of the wagon and ran straight at both Kelan and the newcomer. Both flew out of the way of the beast's rampage, while Niema gave another sharp whistle that sent the raptor in pursuit of the other Disciple.

Kelan returned to their side to watch the mercenaries scatter into the surrounding fields. "Nicely done."

Yala swivelled to him. "Who was he? What did he want with us?"

"That's what I was trying to find out when you drove him off," Kelan said, a touch of ruefulness in his tone. "If I'd had time, we might have come to an understanding."

"A likely story." Yala scanned the area, but the mercenaries had vanished along with the raptors and their Disciple companion.

The trouble was, with the raptors' departure, the wagon lay abandoned at the roadside without anything to pull it along. They'd have to walk the rest of the way to the capital on foot.

9

A fter retrieving her pack and cane from the wagon, Yala found her two companions glowering at each other on the roadside.

"Why are you still here?" she asked of Kelan. "This isn't going to be relaxing. It's a long walk."

Kelan didn't budge. "Since you're without transport thanks to one of my fellow Disciples, it seems the least I can do is keep an eye out for trouble."

"Is this all to ease your conscience or is your god telling you to do this?" Niema asked in acidic tones Yala had never heard from her before.

Even Kelan appeared a little taken aback from the way his brows lifted. "No. My deity is fairly undemanding, at least compared to yours."

Niema's jaw twitched, as if she wanted dearly to push her vows aside and strike him, and then she turned to Yala instead. "It's up to you."

"Oh, let him come," she said. "We hardly have time to argue."

Cane in hand, she walked ahead of the other two, though

it wasn't long before Kelan overtook her. As far as she knew, he was telling the truth, though the gods only knew at which point his curiosity might run out. In any case, she was glad that Niema was there to guarantee that he'd face a painful death in the jaws of a war drake if he decided to betray them.

The irritating part was that Kelan knew more about the current situation in the capital than Niema. He also knew she had questions, judging by the occasional knowing glance he sent in her direction, but she ignored him, and Niema retained a frosty silence, too. Yala had heard that the branches of Disciples did not typically get along, and it made sense; as the Disciples were barred from participating in traditional warfare, they fought within their own ranks instead.

In the end, Yala was the first to speak, addressing Kelan. "I don't suppose your fellow Disciple told you any more about these mysterious Successors?"

"No, he didn't," said Kelan. "At a guess, they're an organised crime group operating in the capital. It's not that uncommon, and the fact that they drew the attention of former soldiers means they're likely targeting the desperate."

Yala looked up sharply. It made sense that some of her former comrades had been forced into crime to survive, though the thought sat ill with her. Her own squad had been better off than some, thanks to the reward their last mission granted them, but there were few opportunities left to most people who'd been in the army since childhood. "Is there an army left at all?"

"Yes." Kelan slowed his gliding pace to allow her to catch him up. "The king does keep a small army, but I gather he's more interested in diplomacy and cooperation with our neighbours than waging war on them."

Yala snorted. "Cooperation."

The Rafragorians hadn't cared for cooperating with Laria

when they'd sent assassins after their former monarch, but King Daliel had stuck to his word to put the matter firmly to rest. Yala might know little of politics, but it seemed to her that assassinating the monarch of another nation ought to have resulted in *some* consequences. Otherwise, what was to stop them from doing the same again?

"The last few decades of war have wreaked havoc on the country's economy, or so I've heard," Kelan added. "My Superior told me the previous king ran up debts as deep as an ocean trench to cover three decades of constant military action."

"Why would that matter to you or your Superior?" she queried. "I thought you had no loyalty to Laria. Or anyone."

Kelan frowned. "I wouldn't go that far. What exactly do you have against Disciples?"

Had she been that obvious? "Nothing, but I do have a certain lack of respect for people who switch loyalties as easily as changing their coat."

"Have you never changed your mind on anything?" Her answer pacified him, though, and he returned to their former topic. "I have to admit that I'm curious as to where these Successors got their funding to pay out this bounty. Unless it's a scam, of course."

"Hell of an elaborate one, if so," said Yala. "Given that they didn't know my location and had no guarantee that anyone who tried to find me would make it back alive."

"That's not unusual by any means," Kelan said. "I've taken on bounties to hunt down escaped criminals before, and there's always an unpredictable element."

"That's your job, then?" Niema spoke, derision dripping from her words. "A Disciple-for-hire?"

"What's yours?" He reached into his coat and pulled out a coin. "This is called 'money'. In the real world, we exchange it for services—"

Yala jabbed her cane in his direction. "That's enough. If you're going to bicker all the way to the capital, you can make your own way there. That clear?"

Neither of the Disciples spoke for a moment, though fury coloured Niema's face, and Kelan's eyes glittered with amusement. He gave a short bow. "Absolutely, Captain."

"Don't call me that." If she'd been capable of overtaking him and leaving him in the dust, she would have, but they were stuck with him until he decided travelling with two mere mortals was too boring to endure. "Niema?"

"Yes." A strain of hurt underlaid her voice, as if she'd hoped Yala would take her side. "I'll try not to provoke him if he returns the courtesy to me."

Kelan inclined his head. "Agreed. I'm in favour of making this journey as pleasant as possible."

"If you ignore the fact that we have to walk through a hundred fields to get to the capital, assuming we don't get ambushed on the road again."

The mercenaries were long gone, but it was the second Disciple of the Sky who was more likely to catch up. Kelan kept an eye out, occasionally leaving the path to examine the fields of grain and other crops on either side, but after an hour passed, and then two, Yala concluded that he must have returned to the capital. When the sun reached its highest point, Kelan somehow talked Yala into giving him a coin or two to enable him to glide to a nearby settlement and purchase lunch for all three of them. She might have delved into her own supplies, but fresh fare was a luxury, and she'd learned to eat whenever she could. By midafternoon, Yala's bad leg started to twinge again, despite her cane, and she reached into her pack for a bitterleaf to chew.

Niema edged closer to her. "I can help. You should have asked."

"I doubt the farmers will appreciate you killing their

EMMA L. ADAMS

crops." She lowered her voice, but Kelan's ears pricked all the same.

"Killing?" he echoed. "Who's killing what?"

"We're deciding which field to bury you in," said Yala. "If you don't keep your nose out of our business."

He blinked. "If you're considering taking a shortcut through the fields, I wouldn't advise it. The grain harvest is bad enough this year without you trampling through ... unless you want me to carry you?"

"Absolutely not." Yala dropped the subject and marched on, grinding the leaf between her teeth. "Bad harvests, debt, and unemployed soldiers on the streets. It sounds like His Majesty is doing a piss-poor job of governance."

She'd wanted to gauge Kelan's opinion on the monarch, but he reacted with little more than a shrug. "That, and the protests over the tax raises, a lot of unhappy businessmen and traders, and general unrest."

"Is there anything *good* that came out of his leadership?"

Kelan considered this. "The Parvan Empire is more willing to trade with us, since we're no longer at war with Rafragoria."

"If we had anything to trade." Laria could scarcely feed its own inhabitants, and it wouldn't have surprised Yala if everyone had preferred the constant warring, including her fellow soldiers.

Why would any of them want her dead? She'd been nothing but loyal to her nation and her king up until the last, failed mission. The other soldiers hadn't known what her squad had endured on the island, since nobody had broken their mutual pact to tell nobody of that last mission, as far as she was aware—but she was rapidly running out of other possible reasons for someone to pay money for her capture.

It can't be that. Surely.

Kelan lifted his head. "We have company."

110

Yala followed his gaze, seeing that a familiar winged shape had appeared on the horizon. The war drake. Did that mean they were close to catching up with Vanat's kidnappers? Niema whistled while they walked, a similar tune to the one she'd used to call the beast to their side outside Setemar.

When the beast swooped down to land in front of them on the road, Kelan looked mildly impressed, though he schooled his expression to a scowl when he caught Niema watching him.

"Are we close to Vanat's location?" Yala asked Niema.

"Maybe." Niema eyed the dried blood on the war drake's claws. "I thought I gave clear instructions ... though the beast might have been unable to get into the city, if that's where they took him."

"Who's Vanat?" asked Kelan.

Yala worked her jaw. "A friend of mine. The Successors took him, I think. Niema, can you tell the war drake to stay within sight of us while it leads us to Vanat?"

She stood back to watch, avoiding Kelan's questioning look, as the war drake took flight again at Niema's command. She didn't want their companion to know any more than necessary, though if Kelan hadn't been present, she might have made another attempt to pry into Niema's own mission. She hadn't appeared to recognise the term 'Successors', but that didn't exclude any possible connection to the danger her enclave had foreseen.

They maintained a steady pace throughout the afternoon, following the war drake's path northward. Yala's hopes that they might be close to catching Vanat's kidnappers began to dim, and the notion of another few days on the road held little appeal. Neither did entering the capital, for that matter, especially if conditions had deteriorated as much as Kelan claimed they had.

Yet it wasn't the new king who occupied her thoughts, but his predecessor. Had King Tharen known each clash with Rafragoria mounted Laria's debt a little higher? Had he cared? When one considered Laria's unreliable harvests and a comparative lack of trade prospects relative to their neighbours, an end to the conflict might have been inevitable, though for all she knew, the same was true of the Rafragorians. Perhaps that was why they'd opted to skip the war altogether by assassinating the king.

Niema was the first to spot the war drake's descent near a patch of trees. "I think it's found something."

"Mercenaries?" Yala ignored her leg's irritated twinge and pushed to a faster pace. "Or did it get hungry and stop for a snack?"

Kelan glided in pursuit, so fast that he appeared a blur to Yala's eyes, and she shook her head after him. "Well, it's not my problem if he gets eaten."

"Nor mine." Niema kept walking, while Yala watched Kelan halt near the drake's hunched form. While he didn't get close enough for its claws to be a danger, he appeared to be staring at something on the ground.

A rush of foreboding washed over Yala. Her pace quickened despite the growing ache in her leg, driven by the need to see the truth that had already sunk into her heart like the point of a blade.

Niema got there first, and she gave a sharp whistle that caused the war drake to launch into flight. A few painful moments later and Yala had a clear view of the body of a man lying in the mud. *Vanat.*

———

Kelan had already suspected that the body belonged to Yala's companion, but her reaction confirmed his guess. Upon reaching his side, she dropped to her knees with a bitten-off curse; one hand on her injured leg, the other reaching towards the body. Blood soaked the dirt from the gaping wound in the man's throat.

From behind her, Niema made a soft noise. "I'm sorry, Yala."

The other woman didn't reply, and Kelan managed to keep his mouth shut for once. While a list of questions was rapidly assembling in his mind—such as why someone had left the body out in the open—he thought it wise to leave Yala to her grief and shock. Niema would be better suited to comforting her than he was.

Yala answered Kelan's first question without him having to voice a word. "They left him here for me. A warning, perhaps."

"Or a trap." Kelan scanned the surrounding fields, but he didn't see anyone else within range, including his fellow Disciple of the Sky.

"No." Niema lifted her head to watch the war drake fly south, having lost interest in their group. "If it was a trap, the war drake would have unearthed anyone hiding nearby. Whoever did this … they already left."

"Why?" Kelan tensed when Yala sent a glare in his direction, but his curiosity got the better of him. "What's the point in this?"

"Ask your fellow Disciple." Yala spat the last word. "If you don't get away from us, you'll join him in the dirt."

Kelan opened his mouth to protest and then thought better of it. She likely needed time to mourn her friend, and he would do nothing but earn himself a few more stab wounds if he stayed in her company. She and Niema were capable of defending themselves should they need to, so he turned away and left at a glide without another word. Clouds of dust arose in his wake as he moved north, almost hoping that he'd run into his fellow Disciple of the Sky so he could resume his attempts to find out why he'd attacked Yala. Aside from the lure of a bounty, which he'd have had to split with his mercenary companions.

Granted, he might have intended to betray them as Kelan had with the mercenaries who he'd joined downriver—the first in a series of mistakes that had nevertheless led to the most eventful few days he'd had in a long while. As much as he'd have liked to prolong the journey to the capital in order to tease more information out of his companions, he also wanted to know if other Disciples of the Sky were in the city, whether Superior Sietra had sent them or otherwise.

As it would be nightfall soon, he moved faster than usual to reach Dalathar before full darkness. A measure of guilt pursued him for leaving the others, but they hadn't wanted him to stay, and they'd never have reached his destination before the gates closed for the night if they continued to travel on foot.

As it was, Dalathar's outer wall appeared in his vision within a matter of minutes. The city sat inland from Laria's northern shore, and from a higher altitude, he glimpsed the glittering expanse of the ocean beyond. The view might be impressive, but the smell left much to be desired. As soon as he descended on the other side of the city's interior wall, the stench of waste, human or otherwise, thickened the humid air. Now he remembered why he'd been so relieved to get outside of the city. In past years, he didn't remember it being quite so ... pungent.

Kelan conjured up a breeze to make the air more breathable and made his way through the darkening streets of the outer city. Bridges crossed the murky river, which made its sluggish way from the nobles' estates in the central part of the city to the docks in the north before spilling out into the ocean. He knew the upper city inside and out, but the outskirts were less familiar to him. If his fellow Disciple was in less savoury company, Kelan was at a loss as to where to find him. It had been pure luck that he'd found those mercenaries heading downriver on the way out of the capital.

Leave it, a voice whispered in the back of his mind. *Go and wait at the Disciples' Inn. Odds are that any Disciples in the city will show up there eventually.*

True, but he'd left one route unexplored on his last visit. Namely, the Temple of the Flame. He'd be the first to admit to holding a certain disdain for their pious tendencies and their apparent inability to see the fun in anything, but he'd never met their leader. If there was indeed truth to the rumour that someone in Laria had strayed into forbidden magic, Superior Datriem surely knew.

Yet he wouldn't easily forget the look on Yala's face when she'd left him out in the field with her dead friend. The odds were high that the man who'd died had once fought at her side before their early retirement, which Kelan had deduced was due to the new monarch's unexpected gutting of the army.

Did she have other friends in the city? Likely she did, but he was unfamiliar with the places the former soldiers frequented. No, he was better off staying in the realm of the familiar. Relatively. He'd never actually been inside the Temple of the Flame, but he knew the route through the winding cobbled streets to Ceremonial Square in the city's beating heart.

The palace complex occupied the area north of the square, while the Temple of the Flame stood at its eastern flank. Large slabs paved the ground, pounded flat by countless military processions around the colossal gold statue of King Larial, the first monarch and the man believed to have led an army across the ocean from the Parvan Empire to establish a new nation. Or so the legends told. They also said that he'd tamed the first war drake in order to cross the dangerous seas between Laria and its northerly neighbour, but Kelan found it hard to believe the Disciples of the Sky hadn't got here first.

At the eastern side of the square, a set of stone stairs led up the side of a building formed of square blocks of stone of decreasing size stacked on top of one another. Wide windows filled each wall, clothed in golden latticework, with the result that light spilled out from each side as if the building itself contained the blazing sunset. He might have thought it a trick of their magic if he didn't know that they'd intentionally built their temple in such a position that the sun's light always shone directly through its windows as it moved throughout the day, igniting the golden stuccowork on its exterior in flaming strips. A touch excessive, but since Kelan lived in Skytower, he could hardly talk about unnecessary extravagance.

After climbing the stairs, he rapped on the front door and waited to be admitted.

A minute passed before a robed man dressed in the pale orange of a novice answered. "Can I help you?"

"I'd like to talk to your leader, on behalf of Superior Sietra of the Disciples of the Sky."

The novice eyed Kelan's robes. "He's a busy man, so he might not be able to talk to you until tomorrow."

"I don't mind waiting." Kelan followed the novice through the doorway and stifled a gasp at a sudden jolting pain in his right leg in the spot where Yala had stabbed him. He found his feet no longer hovered above the floor. It was as though an unseen pressure had driven him downward, and the same discomfort pushed on him from all angles. He suspected that if he attempted to call on the power of the god of the Sky, he'd meet with nothing but silence.

He'd never stepped into a building dedicated to another

god before now, but he should have anticipated something like this. The deities themselves had no love for one another, so it was to be expected that their human counterparts would have ensured no rival's power entered their places of worship. Still, it was not a pleasant sensation—not the pain of his stab wound, but the knowledge that if the other Disciples were to turn against him, he'd have no way of defending himself.

Such was his discomfort that he didn't notice the white-robed man until he stepped in front of Kelan, his robes incandescent in the blazing sunlight streaming down from the windows both on the lower floor and above the balconies overlooking them from above. The man's hair was light grey, almost white, and gold thread formed embroidered patterns on his clothing. Kelan couldn't remember what all the symbols and patterns signified, but they spoke of devotion and strength. *This is Superior Datriem, then.*

"Superior Datriem," said Kelan. "It's a pleasure to meet you. I am Kelan of the Disciples of the Sky."

"Here on behalf of Superior Sietra, I assume," he said. "Yes, I wondered if you might visit our temple."

"You did?" Kelan hadn't been prepared for that response. "Then you know why I'm here. My Superior believes that someone in Laria might be practising unsanctioned magic. Corruption." The last word, he spoke in a whisper, in case any novices were listening in. The wide hall appeared to be empty save for the towering statue of the god of light overlooking an elaborate altar, but curious novices might be lurking out of sight on the balconies. He certainly would have been, in their position.

"No." His blunt answer made Kelan's frown return. "No, I have seen no evidence that anyone in the capital is dabbling in such magic."

"Really?" Kelan had the sense that his chance was rapidly

getting away from him, but he persisted. "It might not be in the capital, but I've heard the same from other Disciples, too. There's a Disciple of Life on her way to the city, and the Disciples of the Earth have stopped accepting visitors to their temples."

"Neither has come to me," Superior Datriem said smoothly. "Rest assured that if there was any Disciple of Corruption in the capital, I would deal with them myself, and with utmost urgency. The city has a number of substantial problems, but as of yet, Corruption is not one of them."

"I have no doubt the city has a great deal of challenges." Kelan reached for his last card to play. "I've also been told there's a new gang of some sort in the city offering bounties to ex-soldiers. Have you heard the name ... Successors?"

Superior Datriem's expression shuttered. "I know nothing about any criminals. I keep my attention on the Temple of the Flame alone."

"Understandable," he said. "If the issue was confined to my own temple, I wouldn't bring it to your attention, but my Superior did insist. I'm sure any of your Disciples would do the same."

"Luckily, there is no need to be concerned," Superior Datriem replied. "You can reassure your Superior that there is no Corruption in this city. If there was, we would burn it out with all the power invested in us by Dalathik Himself."

The temperature rose as the faintest spark of fire danced in the Superior's eyes. A reminder that Kelan's own abilities remained shuttered. No Corruption could possibly take root in here, to be certain, but why would his Superior send him on a false errand?

"All right," he said. "Thank you for your time."

The novice waited to escort him out of the temple. A sense of frustration at the lack of answers mingled with relief when Kelan crossed the threshold and found the familiar cool breeze at his fingertips again. He'd never been cut off from his connection to the god of the sky beforehand, but then again, he'd never been inside another god's temple either. No doubt the same would have resulted if he'd entered the Temple of the Earth—if the Disciples had answered their door.

Strange. Superior Datriem had been nothing like he'd expected, but someone in this gods-forsaken city must have answers.

10

Yala looked down at Vanat's body as if the force of her stare would undo his death and return him to his laughing self. She knew the numbness would eventually give way to grief, but rage would come first.

And this time, unlike with Dalem, she'd have a solid target at whom to detect her wrath.

Dalem had died to save the rest of the squad, but Vanat... He'd died for Yala alone. He'd wanted to warn her, and for that reason, he'd stayed in Setemar despite knowing that his life was at risk. Yet his death had brought no answers as to the identities of the people who hunted her squad.

"Fucking fool," she whispered.

Vanat's serene expression remained etched on his face, and gradually, practical thoughts seeped into her mind. What was she supposed to do with his body? They were at least a day's walk from the capital, and even if Niema kept the war drake from preying upon him, there'd be other predators out there. Leaving him behind was out of the question, but she'd never be able to catch up to his killers if she was encumbered.

Yala lifted her head and addressed Niema's silent presence at her back. "I can't take him back to the city with me."

What other options were there? With Dalem, there'd been no body to burn, and on some level, it had been a relief not to put him into the hands of the Disciples of the Flame. With Vanat, though...

Niema spoke. "I can help you."

"In what way?" Yala's voice was hoarse, her throat tight. "I can't burn him."

Vanat hadn't been an ardent believer in the afterlife, but every Larian was taught that cremation was the only way to ensure the spirit was freed from the body and cast into the realm of Dalathik, of the god of light and flame. Truth be told, Yala had laughed at the notion that leaving a body to rot would risk the god of death rising to claim their soul, but that was before she'd seen a dead man rise, rotting flesh sloughing off his bones, a rusted blade in his hand.

"I have a way." Niema moved to her side, shaking the thoughts out of Yala's mind. "My people ... we believe that if a physical body is returned to nature itself, their spirit will be set free and will return to the gods."

The gods don't deserve him. She did not say the words aloud, but her hands clenched.

Niema glanced at her. "I know you're probably used to doing this a different way. If you want to take him to the Disciples of the Flame, I understand."

"No." The word was harsher than she'd intended. "Go ahead."

If Niema took exception to her command, she gave no sign. She crouched beside Vanat's body and pressed her palms to the soil, murmuring to herself. Or to her god, rather. It was a damned shame there was no way *not* to involve the gods, but Vanat wasn't alive to voice an objection. Yala hated that death had smoothed out his expression and he appeared at peace for the first time since their final mission. They'd all grieved Dalem in different ways, and while he'd held it together better than some, the same shadows had lurked in the corners of his eyes, and every laugh they'd shared had been tinged with sorrow that he wasn't there to share in it.

Niema's murmuring turned to a chant, and the soil around Vanat's body began to shift. Yala's shoulders tensed, instinctively, but Niema's soft chanting kept her from lunging to move the body away from whatever was stirring beneath the earth.

Countless green stems emerged, creeping upward and sprouting leaves as they curved towards Vanat's body. In seconds he was encased in greenery, stems wrapping around his arms and leaves unfolding over his chest. Nature itself moved at Niema's command, claiming Vanat for itself.

Let it take him. His spirit was gone, she was sure, and watching him succumb to nature was a marked improvement on being engulfed in a fiery inferno. Or so she told herself. Her vision swam as the leaves crept over his face, over his eyes and his smile and every part of him she'd known. She bowed her head and whispered her goodbyes to the soil. "You can rest now, Vanat."

"There," Niema said. "It is done."

"Thank you." Her voice cracked, and when she lifted her head, she felt dampness on her cheeks. "I ... Niema?"

The other woman dropped to her knees and then abruptly toppled sideways. Yala hastened to her side, catching her shoulders awkwardly before her head hit the ground.

"I'm ... all right," Niema murmured. "I ... gave some of my own life to fuel the spell. I'll be fine after I sleep."

"Your own *life?*" Yala released her, unsure why she was

surprised that even the god of life demanded a price in exchange for Her power.

"Really, I'm fine." Niema pushed herself into a sitting position with trembling arms. "I'd sooner give my own life force than take it from others."

Take it from others? Yala had thought the god of life frowned upon taking the lives of other humans, but perhaps the custom was born of Niema's enclave and not of Yalet Herself. As she watched, Niema rose to her feet unsteadily. "I can walk a little, but we might have to stop soon."

"We can stop here." Yala wasn't ready to leave Vanat's grave yet, and Niema would be no help to either of them if she passed out.

Yes, there was the risk that Vanat's killers would come back, but Yala had seen no signs of anyone, and Kelan would have warned them if he'd seen trouble on the road ahead. Or not, considering she'd driven him off, but that couldn't be helped.

She didn't dare set up camp right next to Vanat's body, so she and Niema walked a short distance to a nearby patch of trees to settle for the night. Her leg throbbed its displeasure from kneeling on it for so long, but she wouldn't ask Niema to heal her when the other woman was barely conscious. Upon reaching camp, Niema laid at the foot of a tree and closed her eyes.

When she caught Yala watching her, Niema's head lifted. "I'm fine. I forgot how draining it is to draw upon the god of life's power directly, especially when I'm so far from my enclave."

"You've done it before?" She had the impression Niema's people didn't face death on a regular basis, though they had to dispose of their deceased somehow, and it made more sense for them to give the dead back to nature rather than burning them.

"Yes, for my mother." She rested her head against the tree again. "It's possible for my people to get sick despite our bond with the god of life, but I was able to make her death less painful."

Oh. Niema's wide-eyed innocence had caused Yala to assume she knew nothing of death, but evidently, she'd miscalculated. "That must have been hard."

Niema's eyes didn't open. "She taught me everything I know. I miss her sometimes, but the enclave helped me to endure her loss. I had doubts, before I joined them, but I'm glad I did."

"The enclave." Yala had little curiosity, but she wanted to keep talking, to put up some defence against the oncoming darkness of night. "You didn't always live among them?"

"Children don't live in the enclave," she said. "They're raised in nearby villages. My mother left shortly after I was born, but she came to collect me at the age of seven to be tested, as is custom. It's easier, that way, as not every child of an enclave member is found to have an affinity with the god of life."

"Oh." Now she thought back, Dalem had talked about the other Disciples having similar practises. There was no guarantee even a child birthed by a Disciple would inherit the same gift. "Who was your father?"

"A traveller," she replied. "It's not usual for my people to marry outside of our enclave, so he never stayed. Outsiders have a hard time understanding our shared connection, as it's not something they can be a part of."

"Shared connection?" Yala echoed. "In a magical sense, you mean? Like your bond with the god of life…"

"Exactly." Niema's voice was quiet enough that Yala had to strain her ears to hear. "When I'm near the five people I'm bonded to, I can feel their emotions as if they were my own.

This is the first time I've ventured this far from them since I joined the enclave."

Yala caught the sadness in her tone and realised that she'd underestimated how hard an adjustment this must be for Niema. She resolved to watch her tongue in future, especially as she'd managed to convince Niema to spill some of the details of what had led her here.

Not the details of her mission, however.

"Why were you chosen to leave?" Niema's lack of experience of the outside world was bound to have been an impediment, but for all Yala knew, the same was true of her fellow enclave members as well.

"Superior Kralia believed that I needed a chance to experience life outside of my enclave," Niema said. "This is a test of my skills, as well as a chance to prove myself to Yalet."

Yes, she did have some useful skills, but being able to coax animals to obey her will would be of little use in the capital. Even her healing capabilities must have their limits. *I suppose I ought to ensure she gets there in one piece.*

Why? A less welcome voice pushed into the back of her mind. *Are you sure you want to start adopting people into your squad again, given your record?*

No. Being part of her squad was no guarantee of safety. Niema had seen the proof with her own eyes, but who else would help her? Catching the other woman's curious stare, Yala asked, "How did you find Vanat?"

Saying his name didn't make her choke up with grief, not yet. That would come later, when the truth of his death sank in and she stopped imagining that he might emerge from his grave at any moment.

"I saw the wild drake first," Niema answered. "Or heard it, rather."

Fool. Vanat was lucky the beast hadn't been the one to

bring about his end. "You started talking ... and my name came up. Right?"

"Yes," Niema said. "He already knew that someone was hunting for you—"

"The Successors." Yala cast her a sideways glance. "Was that the name he used?"

"No," she said. "No, I don't know the name."

"But did you see them?" she pressed. "Your enclave saw them in a vision, didn't they? Would you recognise their faces if we were to encounter them?"

Niema shook her head, and Yala wondered if she'd pushed too far in her attempts to convince the other woman to share the details of her mission. Yet her brief flicker of guilt was extinguished by the grim knowledge that if Niema had been able to share more information about their pursuers, Vanat might not have died.

"I'm... I'm sorry." When she spoke, Niema's voice was thick with regret. "I don't know who these people are, and I didn't know they'd kill your friend. I thought—Vanat thought they wanted you both alive."

Yala's hands curled into fists in her lap. "You were both wrong. They slit his throat and tossed him into the dirt as if he was worth nothing."

Why, though? Why did they want us?

Nobody else knew the details of that mission, and even if one of the others had told tales, why would it lead to them being hunted down like animals?

Though Niema knew some of it, didn't she? Whether through this shared vision or on the word of her enclave's leader, she knew Yala's name, and that she'd led the last flight squad to return from the war. Still, these so-called Successors couldn't possibly be related to the Disciples of Life. They'd never have killed Vanat if they'd held his life at any value.

"If you want to continue to the capital," Niema began, "then I'll help you find out the truth, to the best of my ability."

"Starting where?" She couldn't picture Niema venturing into the raucous markets of Ceremonial Square, and she'd be eaten alive in the slums. "Did you have a plan?"

"I'll talk to the Disciples first," Niema replied. "As long as their temple isn't closed to the public, like the Disciples of the Earth's."

"The … Disciples of the Flame." An icy sensation grew in the pit of her stomach. "I wouldn't advise you to go anywhere near them."

"Why?"

Yala didn't answer at first. The mere thought caused her heartbeat to quicken and her skin to crawl as if it was too tight for her bones.

"They care for nobody but their own." She forced out the words. "They're unwilling to help anyone else, even…"

Even the last king, though their neglect to protect him hadn't been intentional. Niema didn't need to know that, but the other truth—that they'd refused to commemorate Dalem's death as he'd left their ranks to join their army—was too personal to share, too. It hadn't mattered a bit that he'd given everything to them and their god. Including his life, in the end.

"Even Disciples?" Niema guessed. "I'll do my best to persuade them to listen to me. We have a shared goal, after all."

Do you? Her words stirred a familiar suspicion. If *they* were somehow involved in the attacks … but again, Yala had trouble imagining Superior Datriem allying with mercenaries. Not that she could imagine him sharing a purpose with Niema either.

When they reached Dalathar, Niema would be forced to

break her silence. Or Yala would break hers, as she had no vow binding her tongue, simply a desire to keep the past where it should be and the knowledge that Niema alone would never be able to answer the questions she'd harboured for years.

Questions, revolving around a single word: *Corruption.*

She would not speak that word with Vanat's grave close at hand, so Yala held her tongue and waited for morning.

———

Following his visit to the Temple of the Flame, Kelan walked to one of the inns designated for visiting Disciples. While he found the bland food and the itchy mattresses tiresome, he could hardly complain about the circumstances he'd landed himself in by losing almost all his coin on the road. At least he had the opportunity to get his clothes laundered and to sleep with a roof over his head that didn't cost him the little he had left.

While the man who'd ambushed their wagon on the road didn't appear to be staying at any of the inns in the city, the following morning brought an unwelcome surprise. As he came down the narrow stairway into the breakfast room, he found the innkeeper in conversation with a female Disciple of the Sky with tightly curled dark hair and a tall, lean frame he knew all too well. Upon seeing his approach, she looked askance at him.

"Laima." Of all the people to run into. "Did Superior Sietra send you here?"

"Kelan," she responded tonelessly. "I thought you left the city."

"I came back." Out of the corner of his eye, he saw the innkeeper make a hasty exit. The inn might be owned by non-Disciples, but that didn't mean they were unaware of the various rivalries and interpersonal conflicts amid their magically gifted guests, nor did they lack the good sense to get out of the way of a potential fight. "Have you spoken to Superior Datriem?"

"If you're looking to steal my mission from under me after you already abandoned your post, you'll be disappointed." She gave him an assessing glance that took in his rumpled clothing and his injured leg. "Run into trouble, did you?"

She sounded as if she was disappointed not to have got there first, which was fair. "You may have heard the local mercenaries are competing over a large bounty."

"Bounty." She rolled her eyes. "What did you do, spend all your coin at the tavern again?"

"No—yes, but that's not the point." Why had he decided talking to someone who'd threatened to throw him out of Skytower the last time they'd spoken was a good idea? "It's not the bounty I want, but the person who set it up. I think they're a possible link to the matter Superior Sietra sent me to look into. Did you hear—?"

"The answer is no, Kelan." Laima reached the front door. "If I can't trust you to keep your attention on me as a lover, I'm not risking my success on this mission on your whims. Try not to get in my way again."

The door swept inward with a gust that would have hit him square in the chest if he hadn't stepped aside. By the time he'd caught his balance again, she'd vanished from the inn.

The innkeeper reappeared, wary, holding a stack of folded Disciple cloaks. "Deserved that, did you?"

"A little." When the innkeeper made to leave, Kelan dragged his gaze from the door. "I don't suppose you've seen that other Disciple? What was his name ... Senik?"

"Nobody here but you two." She ducked into a back

room, saying over her shoulder, "Can you refrain from breaking any furniture if you decide to fight?"

"Ask Laima, not me." She had reason to be angry; it had taken him too long to realise that she'd expected more of a commitment from him than a shared room at the inn between missions, and while there weren't rules against romantic involvement with one's fellow Disciples, Laima had clearly had more in mind than that. Whenever Kelan imagined settling down in a farmhouse with a pack of children, memories intruded of his own early years, running barefoot through grimy streets to pilfer bread from unwary merchants' carts, hoping that a winning smile or a joke would spare him a beating should he get caught. Until they reached the age at which they could be brought before the god of the sky for assessment, children were raised outside of Skytower, and Kelan had fought too hard to escape his poverty-ridden village to want to subject another person to that fate.

In retrospect, he ought to have discussed the subject with Laima instead of backtracking when the truth sank in … straight into the nearest pleasure house. When he'd finally tried to explain, Laima had not been pleased. Harsh words had been spoken, mostly from her, and while it wasn't impossible to avoid her back at Skytower, her presence in the capital was yet another obstacle in his quest to find the source of the rumour that had led to those mercenaries hunting down Yala.

If Senik wasn't here, he might have returned to Skytower for all Kelan knew. Or he might be searching for his mercenary allies. Kelan wouldn't find anyone familiar with the local mercenaries in the upper city, but he hadn't been anywhere near the undercity since before the recent unrest. Still, he could hardly do worse than the past few days' detour, so he left the inn after a hasty breakfast and headed for the gate out of the upper city.

The wall surrounding the centre of Dalathar was far more extensive than the one circling Setemar, but the less prosperous districts outside the walls were practically another city altogether. Close to the upper city wall were the residential areas for workers unable to afford the climbing costs of living in the wealthier centre, along with a thriving pleasure district, but further afield, the conditions grew less salubrious. Slums crowded the banks of the filthy river, and a network of back alleys enclosed the so-called undercity.

The lowest level of the city wasn't literally underground, but it might as well have been for all the light that reached it. Kelan was halfway down the murky stone stairs when a bulky figure barred his path.

"And who might you be?" rasped the figure. "Walk down here dressed like that and you'll be lucky to escape with your fingers still attached."

Kelan squinted at the speaker, but it was too dark to make out much more than a bushy beard. "I appreciate the warning."

He heard the *snick* of a weapon being drawn and summoned a ball of air into his palms, pushing outward. The man stumbled down several steps with an oath. "You have some nerve, Disciple. Think that fancy coat of yours gives you licence to push people around?"

"The atmosphere was rather friendlier the last time I came here." Kelan glided to the foot of the stairs, which emerged into an equally dark street. "You might want to invest in some lanterns."

"You joking?" The man descended the stairs behind him. "You really haven't been here for a while, have you. The lanterns, we took to use as fuel for fires."

Oh. As Kelan's vision adjusted, he made out hand-

EMMA L. ADAMS

constructed shacks lining each side of the winding street. They'd doubled in number since his last visit, he was sure, and so had the beggars sitting outside their door.

Kelan returned his attention to the bearded man, who gripped a short sword in one scarred hand. "Have you seen any other people dressed like me in the undercity recently?"

"Who wants to know?"

"My Superior." He tensed, seeing several other figures emerge from the shadows between the nearby shacks. All were armed, scarred, and glowering at him.

This was not how it was supposed to go.

11

The following morning, they left Vanat's grave.

Mercifully, nothing had disturbed them in the night, and a single night's sleep had restored Niema's energy. Despite this, Yala refused Niema's first offer to ease the pain in her leg and only accepted when the other woman had walked for an hour without any apparent exhaustion.

Despite the pleasant weather, the reminder of yesterday's conversation hovered above them like a storm cloud, and Yala tried in vain to find a way to dissuade Niema from visiting the Disciples of the Flame that didn't involve exposing the details of their last encounter.

If Niema insisted on talking to them, though, it was only a matter of time before the truth came out, whether it was on Yala's own terms or not. She balked at the notion of Superior Datriem learning the details of Niema's mission and not Yala herself, but the other woman remained as close lipped on the details as ever. As much as she hated to admit it, if Kelan had been with them, he might have been able to trick Niema into exposing the truth. He reminded her of Saren, whose shameless habit of charming his way out of tricky situations had so exasperated her as a novice; comparatively, her own blunt approach was utterly ineffective.

The pair of them had a rare stroke of luck that afternoon and managed to find a farmer willing to let them ride in his cart as far as the next town. Yala and Niema seized on the chance to recuperate some energy, and by the time they reached the neighbouring town, the outline of the capital had appeared on the horizon.

They climbed out of the cart and Niema peered ahead, looking to left and right. "We're near the coast, right?"

"You can't see the sea from here," she told her. "Not from the city either, unless you were to stand on the palace complex roof." *Or ask a Disciple of the Sky to lift you up in the air, I suppose.*

"Oh." Mild disappointment flickered across her face before her eyes brightened. "I suppose there's a lot to see in the city."

"Depends what you're interested in." What could she possibly recommend to someone who'd spent their entire life in an enclave in the jungle? Niema would be lucky not to be mugged the instant they set foot in the outer city slums—if she'd had anything to steal, that is. "Whereabouts do you plan to stay? You won't get far without coin, and the best places aren't cheap."

"Aren't there inns for Disciples? I was told there were."

"Might be." Kelan had claimed to be without coin, and he seemed to manage, but he knew the capital, and Niema didn't. "Was that your plan in Setemar, if we'd stayed?"

"My Superior told me that the Disciples of the Earth were willing to take in visiting Disciples."

"Except they didn't answer the door." She'd been too preoccupied with Vanat's capture and the mercenaries' attack to think on the matter at the time, though Yala didn't know the first thing about what the Disciples of the Earth did except run the local mines. "Maybe they were too deep underground to hear you."

"Maybe." A brief pause. "I wondered if Kelan might have driven them into hiding, but that doesn't seem right. Do you think he's in the capital?"

"Without a doubt." They'd likely have reached their destination quicker with his help, but it couldn't be helped. "I'm more interested in the other Disciple he met on the road."

Did that man kill Vanat? The question lingered in her mind, tinged with a cold fury she hadn't tasted in years.

"They must have known one another." Niema's gaze flicked up to the sky. "Though his people aren't like the Disciples of Life. None of my people would turn against each other. We rarely even argue."

"If you can sense one another's feelings, it's no wonder." A handy ability. If her squad had been linked in a similar manner, it might have saved her from having to mediate a few arguments among her squad members … or caused new ones.

"Not all of us can," she said. "Each enclave member is bonded to several others, forming smaller units within the whole. That way we can operate effectively, and if the enclave is attacked, it's possible for us to spread word back to our Superior without needing everyone to be in one place."

"Handy." Yala pondered her choice of words. "Attacked? Does that happen often?"

"No … not in my lifetime." Her halting tone nudged at Yala's mind, and the urge to press further warred with a deeper instinct to avoid the inevitable.

Am I really that much of a coward?

"If you're attacked, would you be allowed to defend yourselves?" she asked. "I gather that the god of life does occasionally make exceptions to the rule."

"If someone were to threaten the enclave's safety, the god of life Herself would be the one to defend us."

Interesting choice of phrasing. "You gave some of your life force to bury Vanat. Could you have borrowed it from another person?"

Niema flinched. "No ... it is utterly forbidden."

Thought so. Yala knew better than to continue that line of questioning, so she sidestepped into another. "I can't imagine the god of life would want you separated from your enclave unless the situation was urgent."

Hadn't Kelan said much the same? He'd hinted at being on a mission of his own, at his Superior's orders—and the strange manner in which the Disciples of the Earth had withdrawn into their home suggested something had them distracted, too.

She stole a glance at Niema, whose mouth pinched at the corners as if she was in pain. Suspicion fluttered in Yala's chest, and a certain word came to her tongue once more. The moment she spoke it, there would be no turning back.

Then again, had that ever been an option? Vanat was dead, Yala had almost joined him, and the rest of her squad might be in the capital, oblivious to the danger they were in.

"Corruption." The word fell between them like a stone dropped from a great height. "That's the threat you were sent to warn the other Disciples about. Right?"

Niema stumbled, her eyes fixed on the dirt road beneath their feet, which was enough of an answer for Yala. *Corruption.* A magic not taught in any temple, whose god had no rites and no worshippers. The power of Mekan, the god of death.

"Your enclave's vision told you that Corruption would threaten you," Yala went on. "Then why would it lead you to me?"

That, she didn't understand. Why would a servant of the

god of life want to protect someone who'd touched Corruption with her own hands? If she had any inkling of Yala's experiences in that last mission … but she'd never seen Yala's scar, nor had she confirmed she knew the details of her escape.

Niema coughed, one hand pressed to her chest. "I … cannot share the details. I'm sorry."

"It's more than a promise to your enclave, isn't it?" Yala took in her clenched hand, the pained lines in her face. "You're magically bound from revealing the truth to anyone."

A jerky nod drew a huff of exasperation from Yala. "I suppose this is the gods' idea of a joke, that *I* have to be the one to speak."

"You don't have to," Niema said. "I-I already know how the last war ended."

"It didn't even start." Her cane beat a sharp rhythm on the sun-hardened earth as they continued down the winding road. "There was no war. The king sent my squad to secure the contested island before Rafragoria did, only to get himself killed while we were absent."

Laria's ongoing skirmishes with Rafragoria over unclaimed offshore territories seemed a petty, inconvenient reason to go to war in retrospect, but at the time, they'd been thirty years and two monarchs into the conflict, and neither side had been willing to give ground. Whether the island held anything of value was immaterial.

She risked another glance at Niema, whose pained expression had given way to careful curiosity. She couldn't possibly know what they'd found on the island, unless her god could see what mortals could not … which was a distinct possibility, now she thought about it.

"You don't want to hear the details." Yala turned back to the road. "I imagine you already know how Corruption works."

The god of life might have been uncompromising in the vows She had forced Niema to swear, but the god of death made the other five deities appear more like harmless idols. Anyone who accessed the magic of death ended up devoured in turn, their flesh rotting from their bones, their bodies becoming fuel for the relentless Void in which Mekan's servants dwelled. For that reason, there was no such thing as a Disciple of Death.

How, then, could Corruption have possibly resurfaced? They'd destroyed the island—or Dalem had—and left no traces of the gruesome inhabitants nor the altars from which they'd sprung. Aside from her spurned attempt to ask for advice from Superior Datriem, Yala had not breathed a word of the mission to anyone outside her squad.

When Niema didn't reply, she said, "I don't know if your warning is right, but if it's true that Corruption is threatening your enclave … there's nothing I can do to help you."

Yala had survived the island by sheer luck, but if anything similar threatened her squad today, she needed to know.

A fierce, disarming certainty gleamed in the other woman's eyes. "It's my belief that you can help us, Yala. You might not believe it yourself, but we all have faith in you."

"You must be short of options." What kind of nonsense had her enclave led her to believe? "No, you need Disciples— or ones who give a shit. Not me. If your god's message told you that I'm the key to helping you, you're mistaken."

Dalem had been the saviour, not her. Yala's only job had been to bring the others home alive, and she'd failed; in fact, she hadn't even managed to hold the squad together in the aftermath.

"No." Niema's hand clenched against her chest again as she fought the invisible bonds of the vow she'd sworn. "The visions Yalet gives us are never wrong. They can be misunderstood or misinterpreted, certainly, but there's no questioning their veracity."

"Are you sure your god isn't stuck in the past?" Yala's cane slapped the ground with each step. "I fought Corruption once, yes. I killed some of Mekan's servants, but you didn't know that when we met, did you? You don't know what that mission cost us."

Stop talking, whispered a voice, but the dam on her half decade of silence had broken, and as Niema didn't interrupt her, the words rushed out in an unbroken current.

"I wasn't sent to that island to destroy Corruption," Yala went on. "None of us knew what we were getting into, and we sure as hells didn't have any special advantage. We still don't. If you want us to help you, we'll all end up like Vanat did. Did your god see *that* coming?"

"No!" Niema's voice was a panicked squeak. "No, and I'm sorry. I don't know who killed him or why. That's the truth."

Yala watched her for an instant, her anger at Niema's misplaced faith warring with the knowledge that it wasn't her *fault* her enclave and her god had sent her on an impossible quest. Yes, her ignorance had almost got Yala killed, but it was unfair of her to pin the entire blame on Niema.

"Let me make one thing clear." Her words were precise, measured. "If you think I'm the key to your success, your mission has already failed. Your enclave is going to have to find another saviour. Sorry to be the bearer of bad news."

Niema made no reply, and they spent the rest of the day in silence.

———

The wind shifted at Kelan's command as he prepared to defend himself. The bearded man sneered, showing no fear, but Kelan had no desire to cause a scene or hurt anyone.

Based on a glimpse of the undercity, they didn't need any further problems to contend with.

"Steady on," said another masculine voice from behind the bearded man. "What're you doing?"

"An intruder," rasped the bearded man. "Another piece of rich scum from the upper city come to laugh at us. I thought we ought to make an example of this one."

"I'm not rich," Kelan protested. "I'm not here to bring trouble either."

That wasn't strictly true, since trouble tended to follow him whether he willed it to or not.

"Then why are you here?" The newcomer stepped up to the bearded man's side, muscular arms folded across his broad chest as he assessed Kelan. Several daggers were sheathed at his waist, while his clothing looked like a discarded military uniform that had seen better days. In fact, the others were dressed similarly. *Former soldiers. I've come to the right place.*

Now he had to avoid getting kicked out.

"I need to find someone," he improvised. "I didn't expect a welcome parade, but this is a little excessive, isn't it?"

"Think you're funny, do you?" The bearded man nudged his companion. "That coat of his will fetch a decent price. So will the sword."

"Not if I run you through first." He didn't intend to use the weapon, but he'd get nowhere by letting himself be intimidated. "I'd prefer not to, mind. You used to be in the military, didn't you?"

"Used to." The bearded man gave a harsh laugh. "Until His Majesty decided we were better off down here in the dirt. What's it to you?"

"I met someone on the way to the capital who you might know." It was a stretch, and the gods knew Yala did not strike him as someone who had many friends, but these people weren't cut from the same cloth as the mercenaries he'd run into, the ones willing to trade one of their own in for a bounty. "She came from the southern Larian jungle. Said she used to be a captain."

"Captain?" The muscular man's arms fell to his sides. "Describe her."

"Curly dark hair, brown skin..." He shook together an inoffensive description in case the other man turned out to be her former lover or something. "She had a thin scar on her face and walked with a limp."

"Not Yala Palathar?" The undercurrent of emotion to the man's voice brought a rush of triumph. *He knows her.*

"That's her," said Kelan.

"Drakeshit," said the bearded man. "Why would she come back to this shithole? He's lying."

"Easy," said his companion. "How many captains are in the southern jungles, really? It's got to be her. She's come back."

"Not yet," Kelan added. "She's on the road. She was looking for someone called Vanat."

"Right." The broad man gave a shake of his head, and then gestured at the others hovering behind him. "Go home. There's nothing to see out here—and no, we're not stealing from him either."

"Good," said Kelan. "I've scarcely a single coin on me."

He didn't know how much his cloak and sword were worth either; both had been gifted to him by his Superior upon taking his vows as a full Disciple, but he had no desire to return to the inn without any clothing. Laima already had enough reason to believe him incapable. At least he'd finally landed on a decent lead, and while the curious bystanders sloped away—with the exception of the bearded man, who glowered at his back as he left—Kelan followed the ex-soldier through the winding street. The smells of human waste and despair were overpowering, while glimpses through the windows of the shack-like buildings showed they contained far more people than were suited for their small size. No wonder the stench was so prevalent, though their proximity to the gushing river didn't help either.

"We can talk in here." The man pushed open a door to one of the shacks. "I'm Machit. Yala kept me alive for nearly a decade, so any friend of hers is a friend of mine."

"I wouldn't *exactly* call her a friend—at least, she wouldn't." With Yala's arrival in the city imminent, there was no sense in setting unrealistic expectations. "We travelled together, though... Is this your house?"

The shack turned out to be occupied by several other soldiers who watched with curiosity as Kelan followed Machit into the cramped room. There was no furniture save for a few sleeping mats stacked against the wall, while a few battered cushions were scattered on the wooden floor.

Machit seized two cushions and carried them into a back corner. "It's not exactly luxury accommodation, I know, but at least we have a roof over our heads during the monsoon season. When the river doesn't flood, that is."

Kelan suppressed a shudder, knowing that the soldiers would attribute his reaction as that of a pampered noble's. His memories of growing up in a similar slum crept in like mould on the walls, and he wished he'd left his robes behind and dressed in ordinary clothing instead. At least then he'd have been able to comfortably sit rather than risk ruining his newly laundered robes. *Maybe part of me is a pampered noble, now, after so many years in Skytower.*

Machit sat on one of the cushions, eyeing him. "What? If you want a chair, we had to burn the last one for firewood."

"No, I was debating the risk of someone running off with my cloak if I removed it," he responded. "Are people selling Disciples' clothes on the black market now?"

"Not often, but your people usually have more sense than to come down here." Machit watched as he reluctantly undid the clasp of his cloak, tucking the garment over one shoulder as he sat down on the other cushion. "Yala ought to have warned you ... but I suppose she wouldn't know."

"She hasn't been here in years." That much he'd worked out, despite her reticence to share the details of her life. "Do her other squad members live down here as well?"

"No, they don't." Machit lowered his voice, glancing at the other soldiers. "Vanat left, and so did Temik. Viam ... she got herself a fancy job in the palace complex, so she has no patience for us lowly scum anymore."

"Really?" Yala hadn't mentioned anyone except Vanat, and that had been under duress due to her desire to track him down. Kelan stifled the impulse to inform Machit of his friend's fate. Better for him to hear it from Yala than a stranger. "Yala left, too."

Machit's mouth twitched into a frown. "I think she felt she had to. It's not as if we're allowed to fly anymore."

"Flying." *Of course. She was in the flight division.* No wonder she'd had no fear of the war drake if she'd spent years of her life airborne.

"Yes. How'd you travel with her without knowing that?" The note of suspicion in Machit's voice grew. "Are you here to interrogate me? Because I don't appreciate that."

"It never came up." Shit. When would he learn to think before he spoke? "She wouldn't talk about her history, and we weren't together for long. I know someone's after her squad, though, and they offered a bounty for her capture. Did you know?"

Machit watched him, his hand creeping towards the daggers sheathed at his waist. "Yes, I did. Is that why you're here? You want the bounty?"

"No." Any thoughts he might have entertained about

turning Yala in had been buried long before they'd found her friend's body on the road. "No, I want to find the person responsible for the bounty, and I know Yala does, too. Who *are* the Successors?"

Machit's eyes bulged. "Don't talk so loudly."

Kelan's attention slipped to the other soldiers, but after he'd removed his cloak and sat down, they'd lost interest in him and Machit and returned to their own conversation. "Do you know who they are? Are they based in the undercity?"

He gave an incredulous snort. "Does anyone down here look as if they can afford to pay out a huge bounty?"

"Who *are* they, though?" he asked. "A gang? A cult?"

"Both fit," Machit said. "Revolutionaries, they call themselves, but I don't know where they get their funding, or what they hope to achieve."

"Why do they want Yala?"

"Shit, I don't know." Machit removed one of his daggers, causing Kelan's shoulders to tense for an instant before he began cleaning the blade with a filthy-looking cloth. "One of them already nabbed and interrogated me, but they let go pretty quickly when they found out I don't know where Yala is. Not that I'd have told them if I did."

"They let you go?" He thought of Vanat's body lying at the roadside, and his chest tightened inexplicably. "I thought they wanted you dead."

"I escaped when their backs were turned." The cloth moved over the blade, a mechanical motion. "If Yala's on her way *here*, they might reveal their faces. How far off is she? When did you leave her?"

Kelan took note of the accusatory hint to his voice. "A day or two away. She wasn't alone—she had an ally from among the Disciples of Life."

Machit dropped the knife. "You're joking, right?"

"No."

"Yala met one of *them?* And didn't drive them away?"

"She tried."

"I bet she did." He gave a short laugh. "A *Disciple of Life?* Aren't they recluses?"

"This one's on a mission." His instincts warned him to tread carefully, though Machit's reaction showed more incredulity than loathing. "I think the Successors might be involved, but I don't know why they're hunting Yala either."

"Involved with what?"

Kelan shook his head. "Disciple business. You don't want to know."

"Probably not." Another humourless laugh. "How'd Yala got herself twisted up in that?"

"I hoped you could tell me that." His shoulders tensed when Machit picked up the knife again. "When the Successors interrogated you, where did they take you?"

Machit resumed cleaning his weapon. "A warehouse somewhere north of the palace. Didn't get the impression it was their permanent base."

"Might be worth a look." When Machit didn't respond, he added, "I expect Yala will want to find them, too, and unlike me, she's at the top of their target list. What're the odds she'll walk straight there?"

Machit groaned. "You know, it'd be just like her to march into their base without any thought for her own safety."

"That's exactly what I thought." He might be a long way from making friends, but if Machit thought Yala's life was at risk, he might be more willing to share information. "It would help if we knew the reason for their interest in her. Was your squad particularly distinguished?"

"For about five minutes." Machit tugged the cloth over his blade. "Before the new king shat on his father's legacy."

Kelan's brows rose at his vehemence. "You wanted to stay in the army? All of you?"

"Me? No." He didn't look up from his blade. "I nearly died a hundred times, but Yala wanted to stay, and hells, we might have been better off if we had."

"You weren't given the option to move to a different unit?" He didn't know the particulars, but when he thought back to the months following the monarch's death, he recalled a series of confused updates on new developments from the capital that nobody had been able to make any sense of. It was bound to have been worse for anyone living in the centre of the storm. "Did Yala meet the king in person?"

"Which king?" Machit returned the blade to its sheath and pulled out a different weapon. "King Tharen flew alongside the flight division, so we all met him, if you use the term loosely. He never spoke directly to us..."

"Except Yala?" As their leader, Yala would have been the liaison between her squad and the upper levels of the army, which might have given her access to information that others didn't have.

"Whatever you're thinking, you're wrong," Machit said. "Yala was never a politician. She was an orphan before she joined the army, same as me, and I can count the number of times she spoke to the king on one hand."

"And the new monarch?"

"Once. When he dismissed us."

Kelan's thoughts circled one another like low-flying drakes. Yala had no magical gift. That much was clear. He'd never managed to convince Niema to share the reasons for her interest in Yala, but he'd put together a few half-formed guesses. If Yala hadn't been in contact with anyone of note since the war, he could only assume that the Successors' interest in her stemmed from her time in the army.

"You aren't going to stop hounding me until I tell you the

details, are you?" Machit sighed. "Look, it's her business. It's also irrelevant. King Tharen is long dead."

"Yes, and a group of criminals wants to capture her." Kelan watched Machit until he lifted his head, meeting his eyes. "This isn't an interrogation. It's a warning. I'm on a mission from my Superior, and so is a Disciple of Life who is under the impression that Yala can help her with some secret quest of a sort. One Yala herself isn't privy to."

Machit sucked in a breath. "You're saying you left her out there with someone who's trying to manipulate her?"

"It's not intentional." Niema was too naïve, almost endearingly so, but the other members of her enclave might have less than honest intentions. "The Disciples of Life rarely leave their enclaves. Not in case of an emergency ... and I'd say Corruption qualifies as such."

He slipped the word in as a test, unsure if it would meet with a reaction. He didn't expect Machit to jump to his feet with an oath, pointing the blade at him in a shaking hand. "What—is this a fucking joke? Get out of here."

"It's not a joke." Kelan rose to his feet all the same. "If you want me to leave, I will, but this Disciple of Life seems to think Yala can help her. Why would she believe that?"

Machit gave a violent shake of his head, then his attention snagged on the other soldiers, who stared openly at the two of them. He slumped back onto his cushion, waving a hand at them. "It's fine. Go on, get back to your conversation."

After a short pause, they did so, though Kelan didn't sit again. He wasn't yet sure the other man wouldn't drive him away.

Machit spoke first. "Listen. If you tell anyone else that, you're dead. Not at my hands either, but Yala's in more danger than you are, and I don't give a shit what happens to me, so..."

"I don't intend to." Kelan watched the other man carefully.

"I know it's none of my business, but wouldn't Yala want to know what the Successors want with her *before* she goes looking for them?"

"Please stop saying that name," he muttered. "Look, I don't know anything about the Disciples of Life, but Yala isn't a Disciple of any sort."

Then where did the rumours come from? "Does she have anything someone would offer money for? Anything from before she left the army?"

"No." Machit drew in a breath. "Well … there was an incident on our last mission. We found … but we were involved by accident, including Yala. There's no reason for anyone to care."

"Are you sure?" Kelan gave him a searching look. "You found something to do with Corruption, didn't you?"

The other man exhaled in a groan. "You'd better sit if you want to hear this. It's a long story."

"I don't have any pressing demands on my time." Wary, he sank slowly onto his cushion again. "Tell me."

Machit drew in a breath. "It started with an island."

12

Yala and Niema spent another day on the road before they had a proper view of the capital's vast outer walls. Farms littered the outskirts, circled by fences to keep out predators, while raptors pulled carts and wagons up and down the dirt roads.

From the outside, Dalathar appeared much the same as her last visit. The exterior wall, fortified against enemy attacks and rampaging war drakes alike, enclosed cobbled streets lined with houses and businesses. A similar wall circled the inmost region known as the upper city, towers positioned at intervals and staffed with guards. Yala's feet knew both regions; the orphanage in which she'd spent her teenage years had been her first introduction to the capital, while the regular military parades she'd taken part in as a soldier had hammered the streets of the upper city into her mind.

With each passing moment, Niema grew more visibly uncomfortable, twisting the hem of her tunic in her hand and glancing up at the sky as if hoping the war drake would descend and whisk her away to somewhere a little less crowded. Yala couldn't say she didn't understand the impulse. At least the barracks were north of the palace complex, so she'd have no reason to risk running into Commander Sranak or any of the upper echelons of the army ... assuming he hadn't been dismissed, too.

Yala drew to a halt on a bridge overlooking the river, wrinkling her nose at the smell of human waste emanating from below. At one time the waters might have been clear, but the dense murkiness was clogged with refuse, and she could have sworn she'd seen a dead body float past at one point. *You'd think the king would have managed to improve sanitation with all the money he's saved from avoiding war.*

"Where do you want to go?" she asked Niema. "If you're committed to talking to the Temple of the Flame, they're in the upper city. You shouldn't have any problems getting in."

A risk all the same but setting foot inside the Temple of the Flame was out of the question. If Niema refrained from mentioning her name, she ought to be fine ... theoretically.

"Where will you go now?" Niema asked.

"To find my allies." Machit and Saren would be in the city, and they deserved to know of Vanat's fate regardless of what they thought of Yala's decision to leave all those years ago. "The Temple of the Flame is on the right-hand side of Ceremonial Square. You can't miss it. When you get there ... please don't mention my name in front of the Superior."

While their discussion the previous day had been the most she'd talked about the mission in years, she hadn't brought up her encounter with the Superior, nor his warning. There was no reason for him to assume she and Niema knew one another, though.

"All right." Niema inclined her head. "If I wanted to find you later, where should I go?"

"Wait for me by the gates," Yala answered. "I don't know

how long it'll take me to find my allies, but I wouldn't wander into the outer city slums alone."

Leaving Niema might be as unwise as releasing a miern into a paddock of hungry war drakes, but at least if she stayed in the central part of the city, she'd be relatively safe. Yala, however, intended to go into the undercity, where she'd last seen Machit. Her leg already ached at the prospect of climbing the stairs.

When Yala reached the other side of the bridge, a breeze tickled the back of her neck, and a voice spoke. "Fancy meeting you here."

"You again?" She spun to Kelan, who'd descended onto the bridge in a flutter of his cloak. "What are you doing here? Slumming?"

"Not exactly," he said. "I met a friend of yours in the undercity…"

Her heart missed a beat. "Who? Machit?"

"Correct."

Machit. "Is he all right? Wait—you didn't cause any trouble for him, did you?"

"No … well, it depends how you define *trouble.*" When she glared at him, he added, "Look, he's fine. The Successors already tried to interrogate him ages ago, and they let him go when he told them he didn't know where you were."

"You'd better be telling the truth." Gods. Did Machit know how close a call he'd had? "Wait—if the Successors interrogated him, do you know where they're based?"

"Not in the undercity," he replied. "They interrogated him in a warehouse north of the upper city, but that might not be their base."

"That would be too simple." Yala's cane rapped on the cobblestones as she made her way into the warren of streets on the other side of the bridge. "I'll talk to him myself—though I suppose he already knows someone's hunting us. I don't know if Saren does. Did Machit mention where he's living?"

"Who, Saren? No, he didn't." Kelan overtook her near an alleyway which she knew to contain a staircase leading down into the undercity. "Where's our pious friend?"

"She's on a mission of her own," Yala said. "I left her to it. Gods, this place smells worse than the last time I was here."

"I thought the same." Kelan lifted a hand, and a breeze fanned her face. "This should help."

"Would your god approve?"

"Like I said, my god is fairly undemanding." He flew behind her as she walked down the alley. "Compared to some."

He hasn't spoken to the Disciples of the Flame, has he? Maybe she ought to have sent him after Niema, though Niema herself wouldn't thank her for that. She couldn't believe Machit had spoken to a Disciple of the Sky, for that matter, but she'd have to question him later. If Kelan had been dropping her name on every corner for the past two days, the Successors might already be on the lookout for her.

Her leg ached before she began descending the narrow stairway to the undercity. Typically, Kelan glided to the bottom in an instant, leaving her to hobble after him. At the bottom, a bearded man she vaguely recognised from her army days barred her path. "What's your business?"

"I'm looking for a friend." Yala mentally skimmed her list of names and paused at Saren. "Do you know where Saren Enthar is living now?"

"I don't keep track of every miserable soul who sets foot down here." He peered at her cane. "You look familiar. Were you in the army?"

"Flight division, yes." She shouldn't have expected everyone in the undercity to recognise her face, given her long absence. "Saren was in my squad. He used to live by the river…"

"Saren what?" A rake-thin woman who was missing her left ear peered up at her. "You. You're Yala—"

"Keep it down," she warned. "I'd prefer for the whole undercity not to know my business."

"*I'd* prefer not to have Disciples wandering in here, disturbing the peace," said the woman, eyeing Kelan with a scowl worthy of a pissed-off war drake.

The bigger man waved them past. "She's no Disciple."

"Definitely not," Yala said. "Do you know where Saren lives?"

"No, but someone in here will."

They continued down the winding street. Shack-like constructions crowded each side, each crammed with anywhere from five to ten people in a single room. Yala asked everyone they passed for Saren's location until someone pointed them straight back the way they came, to a pleasure-house near the river.

"What's he doing there?" Yala's leg shrieked its displeasure at her as she climbed the stairs ahead of Kelan.

"Well." Kelan overtook her in an effortless glide that further enraged her. "According to my extensive experience, pleasure houses are used for a variety of reasons—"

"I know what a fucking pleasure house is, Kelan."

"Fucking is one of them, yes."

Yala jabbed at him with her cane, a motion she immediately regretted when she lost her balance. A gust of air prevented her from falling, and a snarl of frustration slipped between her teeth.

"You know you could have asked me to help you with those stairs," Kelan added when she reached the top. "I wouldn't have minded."

"I would." She followed the sluggish water's path towards

the upper city wall and navigated her way to a cobbled street lined with gambling dens and pleasure houses and ill-kept taverns. The building she'd been directed to sat on a street corner, curtains drawn over the windows and the lanterns by the door that would be lit at dusk.

Yala reached the doorstep and rapped on the door with her cane— the gods only knew what she might walk in on if she didn't, though silence hung over the pleasure distract at this time of day. When nobody answered, she knocked again, louder.

The click of a bolt sliding rang through the empty street, and the door jerked inward. A pair of bleary eyes regarded Yala in dull confusion, set in a thin face she knew as well as her own. "We're closed."

"Saren." Her old friend was draped in what looked like a silk curtain, and the scent of expensive liquor and smoke drifted out of the open door. "What in the hells are you doing here?"

"Yala." His mouth slammed shut, his eyes bulging, and then his jaw unhinged. "Shit."

"Nice to see you too." She jabbed her cane through the crack in the door, preventing him from closing it. "I have to talk to you."

———

Niema followed Yala's directions to the Temple of the Flame, finding that it was nearly impossible to get lost in the city's inmost region. Most streets emerged into Ceremonial Square, a large, paved area dominated by a burnished golden statue that she realised must depict King Larial, the nation's founder. To its north lay the palace complex, a sprawling expanse of land bigger than the grove in which Niema's enclave lived. She glimpsed a towering building within, formed of enormous stone blocks in descending size stacked atop each other up to a large, flat roof. Painted in vibrant shades of red and gold, each layer had been carved with elaborate bas reliefs, while some were adorned with rows of vibrant flowers. They were, she realised, the first plant life she'd seen in the city.

Compared to the capital, Setemar seemed a forested paradise. The underlying stench of human waste that had pursued her and Yala through the outer city might be less pungent here, but almost as unbearable was the presence of other bodies pressing against her from all sides, sweating in the humid air. She tucked in her elbows and made herself as small as possible, but people continued to jostle her on their way past—tourists admiring the palace complex, workers crossing the square to buy lunch, and curious shoppers perusing the markets on the southern side.

Niema might have taken the time to browse the array of goods on offer, but the tide of humanity only made the absence of her enclave members more acute. She could no longer sense their heartbeats alongside hers, nor did she have the sense of being a part of anything amid the chaos around her. She might as well be a smudge in the corner of a vast canvass, at risk of being swept away with a single stroke.

Pull yourself together, she imagined Yala snapping in her ear, giving herself a mental shake. The quicker she got this visitation over with, the faster she'd be able to leave the crowded square behind.

Turning away from the palace complex, she approached the smaller but equally impressive form of the Temple of the Flame. Built along similar lines to the palace but with towering windows occupying each layer instead of flowerbeds, the temple flooded that side of the square with Dalathik's might. Sunlight cut through the windows like sharp eyes watching from the heavens.

Niema climbed the stone stairs in front and knocked, the sound small compared to the thrum of human noise around her. She waited for an answer at the top of the steps as if she were marooned on an island in a sea of loud, vibrant souls. Unlike the Disciples of the Earth, the occupants of the temple wouldn't be hiding underground, but Yala's warning tickled the back of her mind.

As she was on the brink of hopping off the stairs and allowing the crowd to swallow her once again, the door opened. A young woman dressed in a pale orange robe eyed Niema. "May I help you?"

Niema gave a quick bow. "I am Niema from the Temple of Life, here on behalf of my leader, Superior Kralia."

"The Temple of Life?" she echoed. "Ah—did you want to speak to Superior Datriem? He's a busy man, but I can see if he's willing to meet with you."

"I would like to speak with him, if possible." Niema followed the woman—a novice, she assumed—into a room full of dazzling light.

Sunbeams crisscrossed the white marble floor, streaming from above the balconies overlooking the main room and ascending three, four, five storeys up into the sky. A glass ceiling allowed a stream of sunlight to strike the altar in front of a colossal golden statue of Dalathik, god of light. Like all the deities, He was depicted with a reptilian form—a long snakelike body, horns, wings similar to a drake's—but rendered in flame instead of flesh. Real fire licked at the edges of the tail curling around the statue's feet, where candles had been expertly placed to give the illusion that the deity Himself was present in the room. The light made her vision waver and her steps falter as if she trod upon unsteady ground.

Shielding her eyes, Niema jumped in surprise when a man robed in white stepped out of one of the rare shadowy places between sunbeams. His bone-white hair glittered in the daylight, while his clothes were adorned with golden embroidery.

"The Temple of Life?" His gaze swept over her clothing. "I haven't seen one of your people in quite some time. How ... unexpected."

Niema dropped to her knees, as she would to her own Superior, and then straightened upright. "I am Niema, here on behalf of Superior Kralia. It's an honour to meet you."

"And you." His tone didn't quite sound sincere, but after what Yala had told her, she'd expected worse. "Is there a question you wanted to ask me?"

"I am here on an urgent mission from Superior Kralia," she began. "My enclave received a message from the god of life warning of a grave threat to the nation of Laria. I am here to find out if you have received a similar message from your own god."

"A message?" He swept along the floor in a rush of robes, prompting Niema to follow him. Alcoves lay under each balcony, each equipped with a prayer mat and a small altar, all of which faced towards the formidable statue at the front of the room. The sharp tang of burning lingered in the air, growing stronger as they neared the altar, where candles and lanterns glowed despite the surfeit of light and heat flooding the room from above. Up close, faint scorch marks marred the otherwise pristine altar. Superior Datriem halted in front of the towering golden statue.

"Yes." Her voice sounded small, swallowed in the large hall. "A message. Has—?"

"Has Dalathik sent such a message to us?" He reached into his pocket and pulled out a piece of dried sunfruit, tossing it onto the altar. Flames licked at its edges, and as the fire grew, so too did the spark in Superior Datriem's eyes. She watched, heart in her throat, as a similar flame appeared above his

EMMA L. ADAMS

outstretched hand, swaying in a nonexistent breeze, before it vanished in a snap of his fingers.

"This is how we communicate with our god," he said to her. "We make offerings, and He gives us gifts in exchange. That is the extent of His involvement in our lives. Oh, we might pray for favours, we might offer supplication in the hopes of gaining a particular status ... but let us not delude ourselves into believing we are their equals."

"I ... would never believe such a thing." Niema's god might make requests of her Disciples, but She would never ask more of them than they could give.

"Good." He smiled, a twitch of his lips that didn't reach his eyes. "The gods' world is far removed from ours. I believe we are better off keeping our attention on our own concerns, don't you agree?"

But ... this isn't the gods we're talking about. It's humans. Her argument died on her tongue when a second blaze of light ignited in his eyes. Pinned beneath his intent stare, she felt like that piece of fruit, trapped on an altar and doomed to burn.

Niema blinked away the sensation and forced her thoughts back to her purpose. "The warning my enclave received concerns everyone, and all Disciples have a reason to fear the oncoming threat."

"You speak of Corruption."

The word, uttered so casually, jolted her heart. "Have you already received warning from another Disciple?"

Who? The Disciples of Earth and Sea never came to the capital, which left the Disciples of the Sky ... and Kelan had already been on his way here. *Not him. He'd better not have ruined my mission before I got here.*

"Warning? You mistake me." He gave a gentle shake of his head. "Laria has quite the assembly of problems to grapple with, but as of yet, Corruption is not one of them."

"How do you know?" Despite the fear his words had incited, her sense of purpose remained, as solid as the roots of an ancient tree. "My enclave's visions are never false. We believe Corruption is an imminent threat to all of us."

"Tell me, does your enclave study the history of the gods?" His change of subject left her blinking in confusion. "I gather you at least know that when the five gods cast Mekan out of the heavens and into the Void, He was no longer part of their order. His magic is not sanctioned or practised by Disciples in any nation on this earth, and that has not changed in the entirety of recorded history."

"But—it's happened, hasn't it?" Her clumsy words ran up against his smooth confidence, and the limits of her own ignorance. "It's not impossible for someone to become a … a…" A Disciple of Death. Words hard to think, let alone speak.

"Impossible? No … few things are impossible if one is open-minded enough, but I doubt your enclave has anything to fear from Mekan." Another false smile flitted across his face. "If you want to refresh your knowledge of the gods, then I might suggest a visit to the public library. Otherwise, I bid you farewell."

That's it? The dismissal stung, yet her prevailing instincts urged her to leave while she still had breath in her lungs. The instinct had nothing to do with the god of light, however impressive His statue might be, but of the arbiters of His power.

Humans, who could turn her to ash with a touch.

Niema gave a quick bow. "Thank you for speaking with me."

The orange-robed woman reappeared to escort her to the door, and once again, Niema found herself stranded at the top of the stone staircase. Dizziness crept into the corners of her vision, and it wasn't until the clamour of human noise reached her that she realised her ability to sense others had utterly vanished while she'd been inside the temple. In fact, she hadn't been able to access her powers at all.

Careful, Niema. This city had no interest in her kind, and the Disciples of the Flame least of all. Had they treated Yala similarly? Had she warned them...?

The truth hit her like a slap. Yala might not have spelled it out, but the answers had been sitting in front of her eyes from the start. Yala *had* fought Corruption. She might not believe she had achieved any great feat by doing so, but regardless of her and Niema's opposing views on the matter, she'd survived.

If Niema had been in her place, what would she have done? The army was formed entirely of ordinary humans who knew little of magic, and most Disciples were hard for the average soldier to reach. With one exception ... the Temple of the Flame, which stood next to the palace itself.

They were who Yala had confided in. Evidently, they'd dismissed her, the same as Superior Datriem had done to Niema herself, but the glimpse of power she'd seen in his eyes left her raw and shaking. If she hadn't, Niema might not have believed it possible for a servant of the gods to behave in such a manner.

No wonder Yala hadn't wanted to accompany her there ... though if another Disciple had paid a visit earlier, the odds were high that it turned out to have been Kelan.

Niema would look for Yala first, and then she'd hunt down their would-be ally.

13

S aren's mouth hung open, his eyes darting from the cane wedged into the doorway to Yala and then Kelan. "If you're looking to make use of the facilities, the pleasure house opens in a few hours ... though it looks as if you already have company."

Yala shot Kelan a warning glance over her shoulder before advancing into the narrow hall. "That's not why I'm here, Saren. I need to talk to you. Somewhere private. If this place isn't open, why are *you* here?"

"I live in the rooms upstairs." He beckoned her into a room shrouded in darkness; due to the closed curtains, the only source of light came from a small candle someone had left on a windowsill. "We can talk in here."

Due to the darkness, Yala had to use her cane to avoid colliding with the walls on their way to a side door leading into a small office. Yala's leg appreciated the chance to relax, but Saren didn't sit. He paced, made two failed attempts to light a candle in shaking hands before she impatiently offered to do it herself instead, and then vanished from the office and returned with a bottle of dark liquor and two dusty glasses. Kelan, for his part, left them in peace; he seemed more interested in examining the erotic paintings on the walls than in the awkward silence between Yala and her former squad member.

Saren lifted the liquor bottle and poured a sizeable portion into one of the glasses. "Suppose I should offer you a drink…"

"No thanks." Yala had no intention of dulling her senses, though the liquor would at least give her something to do with her hands while she broke the news of Vanat's demise.

"All the more for me." Saren put the bottle down on the desk and perched on the wooden surface, the curtain draping him slipping to reveal he was unclothed underneath. It was nothing Yala hadn't seen before, having shared a dormitory with her squad for years, and she was more concerned with his reluctance to meet her eyes. He contemplated the glass in his hand instead. "It's … it's good to see you again."

I wish I could say the same. The room was too confining, the air thick with unsaid words, and the candle's light revealed the pallor in Saren's sunken cheeks and the dark shadows under his eyes. He coughed and drained half the glass in one gulp.

"Better." He squinted at Yala. "You're really here."

"Yes, I'm here." She rested the cane across her knees and leaned forward. "Who owns this place? Do they mind you stealing their liquor?"

"It's *my* liquor," he said. "Giran, the owner, gave me his entire stash after he stopped drinking. Last year he fell into the river after a drunken binge and nearly drowned in sewage."

"Fascinating," she said. "Did you spend all your retirement money, too? Like Machit?"

She'd made a guess to see his reaction, though she didn't

know for sure how Machit had ended up living in the most deprived part of the city.

Saren flinched a little. "Yes... I tried to talk him into moving here, but he's convinced it's his moral duty to starve in the undercity with the rest of the army."

"What did he spend the money on?" She'd diverged from her plan for this conversation, but there was no good way to summarise a half decade of missed years in the space of a few minutes. "Where's his wife, for that matter?"

"Oh, that didn't last," he said. "No surprise, given that he couldn't walk through a slum without giving up every coin in his pockets."

"Didn't he care that he'd end up out on the streets himself?"

"No." He gave a short laugh. "Some of us are too used to comfort, I suppose."

He drank the rest of the liquor and reached for the bottle to pour another glass, but Yala caught his arm. "I want to talk to you while you're capable of giving a coherent response, Saren. Did *you* know someone put a bounty on our entire squad?"

He shook his arm to loosen her hold. "Did I know what?"

"You heard what I said." Her fingers gripped his wrist. "They killed Vanat, Saren. He's dead."

He twisted out of her grip, knocking the bottle flying. In an instinctive lunge, Yala caught it by her fingertips, alcohol splattering the wall.

"Fuck!" Saren's wide, bloodshot eyes tracked the motions as she placed the bottle back on the desk. "If this is a joke, Yala, it's not funny."

"Would I come all the way back here otherwise?" She stepped close enough that her face was a finger span from his. "I found his body on the road. I'd appreciate some answers."

Saren stumbled to a chair and sank into it with his head in his hands. "So would I."

Scraping together all the patience she could muster, Yala gave a brief explanation of her journey to the capital. It was anyone's guess as to how much of it sank in, but when she reached the part when she'd found Vanat's body, Saren lifted his head, his eyes red rimmed. "You didn't bring him here?"

"I couldn't," she said. "My travelling companion was able to help me perform the last rites, of a sort. The Disciples of Life have some useful abilities."

"Disciples of Life," he repeated. "You travelled with one of *them?*"

"She was on her way to the capital on a mission from her Superior." Yala debated and then said, "It's to do with Corruption."

As she'd expected, Saren jumped to his feet again. "You told her—"

"I didn't tell her anything," Yala interjected. "She knew—her people can receive messages directly from their god in the form of visions. She wasn't allowed to tell me the details, but I guessed. She spoke of a warning of some unknown danger. I'd say Corruption qualifies as such."

Too late, she remembered Kelan. A glance behind her confirmed he wasn't within hearing distance, though he might have left the building altogether, for all she knew.

"Who in the hells killed Vanat, then?" Saren leaned out of his seat. "What the fuck is going on?"

"I gather someone put a bounty on our squad," Yala said. "Whoever they are, they're called the Successors. I thought they wanted us alive—or me, at least—so I don't know why they killed Vanat. Are you sure you don't know anything about this?"

He sank back into the chair with a jerky shake of his

head. "Nobody has mentioned a bounty to me. Not in connection with you."

"They already interrogated Machit, but he got away. Where are Temik and Viam, do you know?"

"I haven't seen Temik in years," he said. "Viam… I haven't seen her either, but I know where she is."

"Where?" When he didn't respond, she pushed on. "Where is she?"

"She works in the palace complex." He gave an unconvincing shrug of his thin shoulder. "Some diplomatic role or other. I don't know too much about it."

"She wouldn't." After the way the king had cut her entire team loose, Viam had gone to work at his side?

"She did," he said. "I guess she wanted to do something worthwhile with that fancy qualification of hers."

"Does she not remember how he treated us?" Yala's voice vibrated with anger. "Does she not remember what his *father* did—?"

"Shit, don't yell at me," he said. "I'm on your side. When I asked, she claimed she wanted to improve the lives of ordinary people, and where better than from beside the monarch himself?"

"She's not helping anyone but herself," Yala said. "Has she even visited the rest of you since the war?"

"No, but neither have you."

I guess I deserved that one. "This is the last place I want to be, trust me. But Vanat died for this bounty, and someone has to answer."

"Wouldn't that be nice." Saren gave a sigh to match her own. "Didn't the old Commander once say justice was for the gods?"

"Fuck the gods."

"I can get behind that." He reached for the bottle and

poured what was left of the liquor into the glass, which he lifted with a wry smile. "To fucking the gods."

"Is that all you have to say?" She watched him drink, incredulity seeping into her tone. "They killed Vanat, and sooner or later, they'll come here, too."

"To find you?"

"Not just me." But he was no longer looking at her, instead contemplating the glass in his hand as if it contained the answers that eluded them. "Do you want me to leave?"

He addressed the glass, not her. "If things were different, I'd gladly let you stay."

I suppose you would. She'd rejected him and the others, and it was unsurprising that they'd reject her in turn. "If I hear you're in danger, I'll come back. I won't lose another of you."

He rubbed the back of his neck with his free hand. "I really am sorry about Vanat. Take care of yourself, all right?"

"That's for me to say, not you." She got to her feet, resting her cane against the wooden floor. "Try not to get killed."

He didn't follow, and neither did she spare him a glance on her way out. So intent on her path was she that she walked straight past Kelan outside the door without noticing him until he cleared his throat.

"What are you still doing here?"

He answered with another question. "Your friend wasn't targeted by the assassins?"

"Yet," she said sourly. "He's lying to himself if he thinks they'll avoid him, but that's not my problem. I'm going to the undercity."

If Machit had been willing to talk to Kelan, he ought to be more open to listening to Yala than Saren had been. Though that he'd talk openly to a stranger was another concern entirely.

Kelan remained an irritating presence as she hobbled across the bridge separating the pleasure district from the rest of the outer city. "Is your other Disciple friend at the Temple of the Flame?"

"Now, why do you want to know that?"

"Just curious."

She gave him a sideways look. "If you think following me around is going to win you my good graces, you're mistaken. Why does any of this matter to you?"

"You forget I was sent here on a mission of my own." He continued to follow her, as persistent as the breeze that tickled her back, and she'd sooner dive off the bridge than admit the cool air was a welcome balm against the humid warmth of the city air. "Did you know that many of your people lived in the undercity?"

"No, but I'm not surprised," she answered. "Our new monarch didn't endear himself to anyone when he down-sized the army. Not just the soldiers, but the farmers and rural folk who have to deal with wild drakes roaming the countryside and eating their livestock."

"Where's the one that came with you, anyway?"

"I have no idea." The last she'd seen of it had been when it had led her and Niema to Vanat's body. "Terrorising some villagers, probably."

"The flight division," he said, inexplicably. "That's why you didn't worry the beast would bite your fingers off."

"Oh, that was always a danger." *Machit told him that.* "But you get used to it. Everyone knows someone who lost a limb. Just in case you're getting any ideas about acquiring one of your own."

"I prefer my limbs to stay attached to my body, personal-ly." His fingers drifted to the bandage wrapped around his thigh. Unlike her, he at least could take the pressure off the wound by hovering above the ground. "How old were you when you signed up?"

"I joined the army at sixteen and the flight division at

eighteen." They crossed another bridge, and she held her breath for a moment to avoid breathing in the stink of the river. "And no, they don't take Disciples, if you're looking for another form of employment."

"I'm not," he said. "You can't blame me for being curious. I've never met anyone from the flight division before. What did you do, dive at Rafragorian troops from the sky?"

"Yes," she said. "The majority of our skirmishes took place over the ocean, and there's not much land troops can do. We don't have a navy either. The chance of being eaten by a sea drake is enough to put anyone off volunteering to fight on the water."

"As opposed to being eaten by a war drake instead?" he said. "That still strikes me as a risky strategy."

"I was a soldier, not a tactician. I didn't make the decisions."

"That was the king."

Shit, what did *Machit tell him?* Yala's mouth shuttered, and she maintained her silence all the way to the undercity entrance. From there, they descended into darkness.

14

Kelan walked behind Yala down the undercity's winding street, undeterred by her attempts to rebuff him. After his exchange with Machit the previous day, he felt he understood her better. To go from a life in flight to being eternally grounded struck him as a tragic outcome, though he freely admitted his own perspective was a little biased. On the other hand, he'd had considerably more trouble reading her actions since she'd returned to the capital. He'd assumed her priority was protecting her squad, but she'd left Saren without a thought. Though if Saren hadn't already been targeted by the people hunting her, there was no sense in her painting a larger target on his head by spending longer in his company.

Kelan had hoped to have gained more of a sense of where the Successors were located by this point, but his conversation with Machit had cleared up several of his questions. And incited new ones—namely, concerning the link between Yala and her squad's final mission and the bounty on their heads. While the story had filled in some gaps in Kelan's knowledge of Yala's history, he remained lost on why the Successors wanted to capture her. If Yala had guessed that Kelan was aware of her narrow escape from an island infected by the magic of Corruption, she gave no sign, but she halted when Machit stepped into their path. "Yala?"

"Machit." Yala embraced him one-handed—which surprised Kelan, as it was the first time he'd seen her voluntarily touch another person—and then let go. "It's good to see you. You look like hell."

"Thanks." Machit's face broke into a grin. "It's hard to get a decent bath down here."

"And to think I expected luxury accommodation." Her mouth pinched at the corners when she took in the dilapidated shacks on either side of them. "How many people are down here?"

"Shit, I don't know. Hundreds." His gaze slid to Kelan. "Haven't found your missing Disciple yet?"

"Who?" Yala spared Kelan a glance. "We're going to be down here a while. If you want to help, go and rescue Niema."

"Rescue?" An odd choice of phrasing—though the capital was bound to be a jarring experience for someone who'd spent her life in the forest. "I take it you didn't leave her in the slums?"

"No, the upper city."

Oh. Of course. She must be at the Temple of the Flame. As for why Yala might think she'd need rescuing—that he didn't know. His own visit to Superior Datriem had proven to be a dead end, but he hadn't exerted a great deal of effort to convince his fellow Disciple that Corruption was in any way a threat.

"Then I will see you later." Neither replied; Yala and Machit's heads were angled towards each other as they walked away from him and towards the shack Kelan had visited the previous day.

Kelan retraced his steps through the undercity, passing beggars sitting in doorways and a few scrawny children playing outside. Not all the undercity's inhabitants were soldiers, though the majority were old enough to have fought in at least one war. He might have asked why none of them had tried to become Disciples instead, but that wasn't an easy path to take, and the Temple of the Flame was rumoured to have particularly gruelling trials. At least according to Machit, who'd told Kelan that one member of their squad had almost sworn his vows to the god of light before he'd defected to join the army instead. Kelan hadn't spent enough time inside the Temple himself to know why fighting a war would be a preferable option to studying under Superior Datriem, though he could make some educated guesses.

Upon reaching the wall to the upper city, he found none other than Niema herself standing outside the gate. "If you're waiting for Yala, she's going to be a while."

"You again?" Her jaw twitched. "What do you want this time?"

"Want?" he echoed. "Nothing. I've already spoken to the Disciples of the Flame, and I assume you were as unsuccessful at winning over Superior Datriem as I was."

Niema took a startled step back, her hands clenching at the hem of her garment. "Yala didn't tell you I was there?"

"I guessed." He offered her a smile that she did not return. "Yala's in the undercity talking to a friend, and it sounds as if they have a lot to catch up on. Were you planning to stay here all day?"

Her gaze darted away from his. "I need to go to the public library, but I wanted to find Yala first. She knows the city better than I do."

"The library?"

"For information relating to my quest."

"Concerning Corruption?" He spoke the word in a

whisper that, nevertheless, gave her a violent flinch. "You surely don't think that information would be left out in public for anyone to get their hands on?"

"No, not that." Niema's shoulders hunched. "It's really none of your business."

"I can show you to the library." He gestured towards the gate to the upper city. "It's not far from the inner wall."

Her eyes narrowed in suspicion. "Why?"

"Why?" he echoed. "For one thing, you don't want to wander around the outer city alone. There are unsavoury people about."

"I can take care of myself." She tugged her garment tighter around her shoulders and lifted her chin.

"Of course," he said. "Though I wouldn't advise you to set a war drake on anyone in the middle of a crowded city. I imagine that kind of activity would get you shot by the king's archers."

Niema levelled a glare at him. "That's not all I can do."

He knew he ought to stop needling her, but it was difficult to resist the temptation when she acted so painfully uptight despite her obvious discomfort in these unfamiliar surroundings. "You can stand here all day and wait for Yala, or you can come with me. It's up to you."

Niema released a faint sigh. "Fine. If you're leading me into a trap ..."

"Then you'll call a plague of rodents to devour me?" Perhaps he oughtn't give her ideas, but despite her wild moment of violence towards him in Setemar, he didn't get the impression she *wanted* to hurt anyone if she could help it. "I'm fairly sure skirrits and giens are the only wild animals you'll find within the city's limits unless you want to steal livestock."

Instead of answering, Niema walked ahead of him towards the gates to the upper city, where a guard of the king's army waved them through. Disciples were free to go wherever they liked, and while Niema wasn't dressed as a typical Disciple would be, nobody would label her as a potential troublemaker. *Assuming she* doesn't *need to unleash that war drake on anyone.*

Kelan had never set foot in the library himself—all Disciples learned to read, but he'd always struggled to make sense out of the various jumbles of letters, and trying to untangle their meaning tended to give him headaches—but the upper city was relatively easy to navigate. He avoided the crowded square, and Niema made no complaint about taking a longer route. Her shoulders were tensed, her arms wrapped tightly around herself.

"Not much like the jungle here, is it?" he said conversationally.

Niema made no reply.

"The undercity is considerably less picturesque," he added. "Smells even worse, if you can believe it."

Niema gave a faint shudder. "I don't know how anyone can live in a place so enclosed."

"They don't have much of a choice," he said. "It's where the work is. It's better than starving in a field."

"Superior Kralia told me of the capital, but she never mentioned it was like this," she murmured. "There's not another living thing in sight, and it smells like rot. If anywhere was likely for—for Corruption to grow, it's here."

"I wouldn't let anyone hear you say that." She had a point, though. Corruption was rooted in death, and they might be walking over several centuries' worth of corpses going back to the founding of the city for all he knew. Yet another reason to be glad he didn't have to put his feet down on the ground. "Do you think it's here in the capital? The source of Corruption?"

"I wouldn't know."

"I would have thought you would have a sense of the general direction." He stole a glance at her as they passed a row of apartments, crossing through the residential area for the more affluent. "Your Superior surely didn't expect you to traverse the entirety of Laria on foot."

"My instructions are between myself and my enclave alone."

"That's rather inconvenient, if you ask me." They rounded a corner, following the path of the wall circling the upper city. "What if you were to run into trouble without your enclave to lend their assistance? I know you have Yala with you, but I assume she remains blissfully ignorant of the true reason you came to her aid in the jungle."

Niema hissed out a breath. "Are you incapable of keeping out of my enclave's business? And Yala's, too? This is nothing to you."

"I already know what Yala experienced in the war." As he'd anticipated, Niema spun towards him, disbelief etched on her face. "I spoke to her friend who clarified the situation, though I admit to being curious as to why you might believe she was uniquely equipped to deal with this threat. It sounds as if her survival was a matter of luck."

Niema's disbelief gave way to anger. "How dare you?"

"It's true, isn't it?" he pressed. "There's no sense in talking around the subject, not when we're both here for the same purpose."

"We are *not* the same." She turned away from him. "I can make my way to the library alone."

"We're already there." He indicated a squat building ahead of them on their right. "Go ahead."

Niema studied the battered wooden door with a frown. "Is it even open?"

"I haven't the faintest idea." He glided up to the dusty

window, which showed a room cloaked in darkness. "I wonder … it's possible that the library closed after the war."

"Why would Superior Datriem send me here?"

"He did?" Her confusion must have momentarily overcome her fury, but her mouth pursed at his words. "Let's see…"

Kelan squinted at the darkened window. Might some books still be inside? It wasn't as if it was against the law to walk into an abandoned building. Granted, they might stumble upon some more soldiers or other beggars who'd decided to shelter in there, but this was the upper city, not the slums.

He tried the door, which didn't open. "It's locked … or something's blocking it from inside."

Niema made a noise of protest, but Kelan extended a hand and sent a flurry of air towards the door. A dull thump sounded, followed by another, and then the door swung open with a creak.

On the other side lay a room wreathed in the musty smell of neglect. Dusty shelves filled most of the space, but there was an obvious absence of…

"Where are the books?" Niema walked in behind him.

"I imagine someone stripped them off the shelves to use for firewood," Kelan guessed. "Or they were moved elsewhere."

"Did you know?"

"Me? Of course not." *It's Superior Datriem she ought to ask.* At a shuffling noise ahead of them, his pace slowed. "We might not be alone in here."

Maybe he'd been right about beggars lodging in here, but he didn't see anyone at first. Light streamed in from the windows onto the centre of the floor, though the areas beneath the balconies that overlooked them from the upper floor were cast in shadow. Kelan trod closer to the nearest wooden staircase leading to the upper level, and a cloaked, hooded figure shuffled into view.

"Excuse me," Kelan said. "We didn't know there was anyone in here."

The person didn't respond or otherwise acknowledge his words, but Niema let out a choked noise and shrank away. "Do you feel that?"

"What?" Kelan peered at the figure's face and recoiled. The man—or it had once been a man—was dead. Strips of decaying skin peeled back from his face, revealing white bones, and blackness filled the holes that had once been its eyes. A horrible stench rippled outward; Kelan had grown so accustomed to the smell of the city in general that he hadn't picked up on it until he stood directly before its source.

Corruption.

Niema let out a choked noise. "No. No, no, no."

She dropped to her knees, and Kelan backed away from the swaying figure. "Niema, I think we ought to leave."

"No," Niema gasped. "No, we can't leave. We have to destroy it."

"Destroy it?" Air swirled around his hands, and at a push, the dead man flew backwards, landing in a heap at the foot of a wooden stairway. "There. Let's move—"

The man rose jerkily to his feet, hardly winded. *He wouldn't be, being dead.*

"Ah." Kelan took another step back. "I don't suppose your powers can bring him down permanently?"

Niema gave a faint moan. "No. Corruption is an affront against nature. I can't…"

"Shit." Kelan hovered, reaching for Niema to pull her out of range if need be—and the dead man pulled a sharp knife out of his cloak. "It's armed. How can it be armed?"

"Because someone—someone doesn't want us in here."

The dead man waved the knife jerkily in their direction. "How can it see us?"

"It can't."

"That's really helpful." Kelan drew his own blade from its sheath.

The dead man moved slowly, no match for Kelan's speed. In one swipe, his foe's head flew off, landing in a grisly heap —but the man's knife kept swinging, slicing at the sleeve of Kelan's coat. With an oath, he sprang back. "It can't die. It's *already* dead."

Somehow, Machit's account of how Yala and her team had found themselves surrounded by the dead hadn't hit quite as hard as seeing one for himself. According to Machit, they'd escaped by setting the whole island ablaze, but the old library didn't appear to contain any lanterns or candles to speak of.

Kelan's next swing took off one of the man's decaying arms. "I suppose this is one way to stop it, but really, there has to be an easier—"

A distinct thud came from somewhere amid behind the shelves. *There's more than one.*

"Niema!" He gave a sharp slash with his sword, sending the dead man's knife spinning out of his hand. "Come to your senses. How do I stop them?"

"Find … find the source of the summoning." She lifted her head, her eyes wide and haunted. "Someone used death magic in here—"

"Really? I never would have guessed." He stabbed the man in his leg, twisting the blade, but the dead figure kept pawing at him with his remaining hand. "Where in hells are the king's guard? Shouldn't they have been watching this place?"

Niema didn't answer. Kelan jerked the knife free and aimed for the other leg, slicing through the decaying tendons. The smell made him gag, but worse was the skin-crawling sensation of facing something *unnatural*. The dead might not affect him as badly as it did Niema, but he felt the stirrings of magic that wasn't his own, that echoed like a voice speaking from an empty tomb, cast like a shadow where there should be none.

While the man dropped to his knees, he continued to paw at Kelan's feet. A blast of air from Kelan's palm sent what was left of the dead body crashing into a nearby bookshelf, shedding pieces of gristle and bone. The body continued to spasm and twitch, but without any limbs remaining, was no longer able to reach him.

"I think I've guessed why the city folk are so adamant about cremating their dead," he remarked. "Would that be proof enough for Superior Datriem, do you think?"

Niema responded by vomiting onto the dingy floor, and he averted his eyes to keep from doing the same.

"I take that as a no." Kelan peered into the darkness ahead, but he had no desire to further investigate and unearth any more dead bodies. "We need to get a lantern, or a candle, and come back."

"Yala," Niema croaked. "We need Yala."

"I sincerely doubt she'd appreciate the invitation."

She'd want them to tell her, though … and despite Machit's insistence to the contrary, perhaps she did have some hidden knowledge as to how to deal with the dead.

———

It was easier for Yala to talk to Machit than to Saren. While breaking the news of Vanat's death was equally difficult, at least Machit wasn't inhibited by drunkenness and denial, and the way he'd embraced her indicated that he'd already forgiven her departure.

"Vanat didn't deserve to go like that." Machit sat upon a

cushion in the corner of the shack Yala had followed him into, having apologised for the lack of chairs. Yala didn't mind; the ache in her leg kept her mind sharp, kept her from drifting away from her purpose. "Why'd they leave his body behind?"

"I don't understand it either," she said. "Evidently, someone wanted to bait me, but they haven't shown their face yet."

"Unless Vanat tried to escape and they wanted to make an example of him," Machit added. "I don't know. You two were always closer than I was ... especially in the last few years."

"It wasn't going to last." She'd already grieved their relationship long before she'd found herself facing the prospect of a life with him no longer in it. The latter, she hadn't faced head-on, not yet. Until her fellow squad members were safe, she didn't have the luxury of mourning. "Speaking of which, whatever happened to your wife?"

He groaned. "We tried, but we were in different places. She was a noble, and I wasn't."

"I'm aware. I came to your wedding, remember?"

Machit rubbed the back of his neck. "You all did, except Temik and Viam. I think that's the last time I'll try settling down."

"I tried," said Yala. "Unfortunately, a wild drake and a Disciple of the Sky destroyed my house."

"Which Disciple of the Sky?" Machit swivelled to her. "The one who came here? He said you were friends ... or as close to friends you get with strangers."

Yala forced a laugh. "He has some nerve ... though we're not enemies, I don't think. I have too many of those already."

"Well, that makes me feel slightly better." Machit dropped his gaze, and Yala's apprehension grew. *What did he tell Kelan?* "He didn't mention—he didn't say Vanat was dead, just that you were looking for him."

"Oh." Somehow, it had slipped her mind that Kelan might have told Machit the circumstances of their separation on the road. Why he hadn't, she didn't know, but it was a small comfort that he'd let her break the news herself. "I can only assume these so-called Successors played a part in his death, but I thought they wanted me alive."

"Sick fuckers," he said. "I *spoke* to one of their people. They questioned me about you, and I was honest because I had nothing to give away. I didn't tell them you were in the jungle, just that you left the city, but I wish I'd said nothing at all."

"It's not your fault they found me," Yala said. "They had people in Setemar, too, and they targeted Vanat to coax me into leaving my home, I think. Whatever bounty they're offering, it's enough to tempt every mercenary with a loose sense of ethics and a looser sense of personal safety."

He grimaced. "I'd help you find them if I knew where they were."

"That's more than Saren offered," she told him. "He wouldn't even acknowledge that he's in danger. At least you're listening to me, though the gods know you have no reason to."

Machit gave a wince. "I-I understand where he's coming from. Saren. He's tired as fuck, same as the rest of us, and seeing everyone as the enemy wears on you after a while. I can't afford to get suspicious of everyone who comes down here. Most people are looking for a way to survive."

"I suppose after so many years of killing, it's easy to go to the other extreme," she commented. "For some of us, anyway."

Machit drew his knees to his chest. "We went through hell back then. This is another kind of hell, but the same rules apply. You find your people and you stick with them. I just have a bigger squad than I used to."

"Saren isn't keen on sticking together." Bitterness coated her tongue. "Neither is Viam, and I haven't a clue where Temik is."

"Nor me," he said. "Viam was always the intellectual sort, though. She never planned to stay in the army."

"Neither did you, given that you tried to run away twice," Yala reminded him. "I thought the notion of living on the streets was the reason you stayed. Did you give away every single coin they gave you?"

He cringed. "Look, I couldn't just watch all these people starve. If there was anything I could do to save one or two of them…"

"I understand." Maybe she ought to feel guilt at not doing the same, but rage and grief and joy at seeing Machit again struggled for dominance inside her and left no room for other emotions. "It's the king who ought to give a shit about his citizens. It's not up to us to keep them from starving. Except Viam, if she has the king's ear, but I'm guessing she doesn't."

"No." Machit lifted a hand to make a sweeping gesture at the room. "We might have felt like kings and queens out there on the battlefield, but here? There's no real need for us. We gave up everything, and what did we get in the end? Glory? Hardly."

Coming from Machit, the words held twice the weight. He'd once been the joker of the group, the one who brought a sense of levity to missions that otherwise would have been mired in darkness. Yala's leg gave a twinge as if to contribute, but she didn't need another reminder. They were a squad no longer, yet Vanat's demise was a stark reminder that someone still hunted them.

"I never cared much for glory," Yala finally said. "I'll settle for finding the Successors and eliminating them."

"Alone?" he asked. "Wait, you were travelling with … a Disciple of Life, that man told me."

"Niema." She'd told the other woman to wait for her by the gates to the upper city when she'd finished her visit to the Temple of the Flame, and while Yala had warned her not to mention her name in front of Superior Datriem, that didn't mean he hadn't already learned of her return to the city. Especially if Kelan had already visited the temple himself. "Yes, she's here on a quest. A ridiculous one, but you know how Disciples are."

"Actually … no," said Machit. "I have no idea how Disciples of Life are. A quest? Really?"

"Of a sort." She drew in a breath, a familiar tension gripping her shoulders. "She believes I can help her fight Corruption."

She'd expected Machit to flinch at the word, but she didn't expect him to groan. "What … no. Where would she get that idea?"

"Supposedly from a vision imparted by her deity." Yala rolled her eyes. "The tricky part is that she's not allowed to talk about the vision without breaking some magically binding agreement, but I don't know what she thinks I can possibly offer her to fight against the dead. The last time didn't end well for some of us."

"She's going to have to learn that the hard way." He glanced at the window. "Whereabouts is she now?"

"At the Temple of the Flame."

He jumped to his feet with a curse. "You *sent* her there?"

"I told her not to mention my name." Perhaps she oughtn't have suggested it at all, but if Kelan had already paid a visit, it didn't matter. "She's a Disciple. She'll be fine. If she's in danger, she can convince any animal nearby to obey her—even a war drake."

"Where would she find one of those?"

"Vanat befriended a wild one before he came looking for me." Her mouth pinched. "He sent it to warn me, and ... it led me to his body."

"Oh." He dragged a hand over his forehead. "You know ... I really thought we'd stick together. Afterwards. Would he have survived if we had?"

"Don't say that." The words snapped out, as sharp as her cane striking against stone. "We couldn't have. Viam and Temik both wanted nothing to do with the rest of us, and Dalem was already dead. And Saren ... if he ends up being the next to die, he doesn't give a shit what it'll do to me."

At least Vanat had been cognisant of the danger, enough that Yala didn't feel quite the same deep-seated sense of responsibility she had for Dalem's death. She might grieve him, might rage at his killers, but she would be able to put them in the ground with her own hands in a way she hadn't with Dalem.

"He'll come around," Machit said. "This is bound to be a shock for him, too ... oh, there's your friend."

Yala turned towards the door, through which Kelan had entered with an ashen-faced Niema at his side. "What happened to you two?"

"We saw something dead," said Kelan. "At the public library."

"You did?" Her heart gave a sickening dive. "By 'dead', you don't mean in the usual sense."

"Exactly." Kelan's tone was unusually grim. "I think we found the source of Corruption."

15

D read coursed through Yala's veins as she listened to Kelan explain what they'd found at the library. A dead man who walked as if he lived, and who'd swung a weapon at them as if directed by an unseen hand.

"I cut off his limbs, and he was still twitching," Kelan said. "Niema wanted to investigate the source and destroy it, but I don't think Disciples of Life are particularly suited to being around the dead."

Niema responded with an indignant croak. "There's a difference between the regular dead and those who have been brought back by M—Mekan's power."

This is going to be a problem. "You should have gone to fetch the city guard, not me."

"Would they have helped?" Machit's hands had clenched into fists that didn't quite hide that he was trembling.

"No, but you'd have more luck with them than the Disciples of the Flame." Yala scowled at Kelan. "You decided to make this my problem, did you?"

"I'd ask my fellow Disciples," he said, "but the only one

I've met in the city so far isn't someone who'd be willing to help me."

"Why am I not surprised?" Despite her best instincts, Yala took up her cane and made for the door.

"You're not going after them, are you?" Machit crossed the room, his stride easily overtaking hers. "Yala ... you know what happened last time."

I know. But if it was one or two dead ... that, she could handle. If she had fire. "Where can I find a lantern?"

"Not down here." Machit resignedly followed her limping path out of the shack. "Yala, this is a bad idea. I thought you weren't going to get involved with ... with *that.* Never again."

"If someone in the city is messing with Corruption, it'll be all our problems sooner or later."

Yala might not be an expert on the subject, but she knew that if someone had raised the dead, there must be a source. If not a temple, then an altar of some kind, and a recent one too. The temple they'd found on the island had been abandoned for centuries; no doubt its original builders had ended up devoured by the magic they'd sought to control, the same as the Rafragorians who'd attempted to seize the island for themselves.

Like all the gods, Mekan demanded a price of His followers to access His power. The god of death's currency was lives, and the wealth He offered in exchange was power over the dead themselves.

Yala's skin crawled as they walked down the undercity's narrow street. "Why were you in the public library to begin with?"

"Niema wanted to acquire research materials for her mission." Kelan gave a laugh. "Superior Datriem was right about that, if not for the reasons he expected."

Yala's heart plunged in her chest "He sent you there?"

"No." Niema's voice was faint. "He was trying to get rid of me when he suggested I go to the library."

"That doesn't mean he didn't know." They'd have to deal with *him* later, though it struck Yala that Niema ought to have stayed behind at the shack. It stood to reason that the god of death's magic would affect her worse than ordinary people, but she was in no state for a fight with anyone, dead or otherwise. "You can't ... dispose of the bodies in any other way than burning them?"

She didn't want to mention Vanat's burial in front of Kelan, though it hardly mattered if he knew. Not when he'd witnessed a piece of the nightmare that had haunted her for over half a decade for himself.

"No." Niema persisted in following Yala and the others to the stairs out of the undercity. "Not here. Not by the source of their power."

"Is fire the only way to destroy them?" Kelan queried.

"Yes." She and Machit shared a glance, grim with the shadow of memory. "Fire ... the god of light's fire is ideal, but unless you want to kidnap a Disciple..."

"No need." Kelan glided ahead of her. "I expect you can buy a lantern from the market, but I find myself woefully short on coin. Unless you want me to steal one instead?"

Yala ground her teeth. "I'll pay, but you'll owe me."

Upon entering the upper city, Yala bought the supplies for setting a fire and distributed lanterns between the four of them. It didn't entirely surprise her that Corruption magic had arisen under Superior Datriem's unobservant eye, but how had someone been able to learn how to use it in the first place? Every trace of the island had been destroyed, and so had the person who'd sent her there. She'd long stopped expecting to ever find out how much King Tharen had known about the island prior to sending them on that mission, though her old suspicions had circled her thoughts like a lost bird with nowhere to go but to roost in the depths of her mind. If someone else had unearthed the truth, though...

Yala's spinning thoughts quietened when they turned into the street that housed the public library, giving way to instinctual dread. The shadows appeared thicker than they should be, and there wasn't a single trace of life, none of the skirrits sniffing at the shadows or giens roosting on the roof that were present in the other streets and alleys. Nature itself avoided this place, and with each step, Niema seemed to diminish further, as if a simple breeze might blow her away.

Yala's cane tapped the ground at the foot of the door. "Please tell me you locked it."

"There wasn't a key." Kelan drew his blade with one hand and reached for the door with the other.

"Wait." Yala turned to Niema. "You should wait here by the door. Machit..."

"I'm coming in." He hefted the lantern she'd given him. "You'd think someone would have noticed the dead wandering around the upper city."

"This place looks abandoned." The whole street did. While the upper city was the domain of the affluent, the capital's struggles weren't confined to the undercity alone.

"I'm not surprised that nobody has time for reading these days," Machit remarked. "Let's go in."

Kelan pushed the door inward, and a familiar dread gripped Yala's chest at the stench of decay emanating from within the library. Her gorge rose when she laid eyes on the dismembered remains of the body Kelan had taken apart, reduced to twitching lumps of flesh.

"Not bad." Yala swung the lantern around, alighting the darkened areas beneath the balconies. "We'd save time if we burned the whole place down."

"And get arrested for arson?" Machit said. "I know, I know, priorities."

"Want me to lure them out?" Kelan lifted a hand, and a gust of wind swirled amid the shelves, stirring clouds of dust. "If they can't see or hear, are they aware we're in here?"

"I'd rather they weren't." Machit lifted his lantern, the light crossing the frightened planes of his face. "Let's go."

Kelan had already sent another gust of air into the library, and this time several thumps sounded. In moments, another dead man came shuffling around a corner, a knife glinting in his hand.

Yala held up her lantern. "There you are."

"He can't speak, can he?" Kelan asked.

"No, but it makes me feel better if I pretend I'm fighting something alive." She hobbled at the man, used her cane to parry the knife, and swung the lantern at him. The dead man stumbled, his trouser leg catching alight, but he continued to advance on their group.

Machit backed up a step. "Shit. I guess the fire of a Disciple of the Flame is more potent than a regular lantern."

"Typical." Yala swung the lantern again, but Kelan got there first. A ball of air flew at the dead man, causing the flames to sweep higher, eating away at the flesh of his leg and groin.

"Ouch," said Machit. "Pity he can't feel any pain."

"He's not alone." The dead man's empty stare brought a familiar bone-deep terror, knowing the force that drove him was beyond the world they knew. The god of death's appetite held no bounds, and unless they destroyed every trace of His magic, they might be devoured, too.

The dead man continued to burn as he staggered forward, his knife swinging jerkily. Yala severed his wrist, and his hand dropped to the floor along with the weapon. Kelan's blade swung in, severing the man's legs at the knees.

"That ought to take care of it." Yala trod on his twitching hand on her way past and swung the torch around to view the hallway from which he'd emerged.

"I wouldn't burn the place down while we're inside," Kelan said. "What are you looking for?"

"Answers." Despite the lantern, the shadows in the corner remained untouched. She trod closer, picking out a dark stain sweeping across the wooden floor. Bile burned the back of her throat. *This is where the men died. Or were sacrificed.*

From the little Yala knew of death magic, accessing Mekan's power required a sacrifice of flesh and blood. That did not mean both men had met the same fate; it was entirely possible that one of the men had sacrificed the other and then died in turn as Mekan's greed drove Him to consume the nearest living being. Whatever the case, that didn't mean Mekan's power had faded with the destruction of their bodies.

Yala held the lantern, aiming it at the patch of unbroken shadow, and alighted on a dark shape.

"Shit!" She held out a hand to stop the others from walking any further as the shadows unfurled into a winged shape, resembling a large bird. A powerful wave of rotten stench hit them, and she heard Machit gag behind her.

"What *is* that?" Kelan coughed.

"Ugly." The monster's wings beat, shedding bits of decaying flesh. *Is it some dead relation of a war drake?*

Yala swung the torch at the winged beast as two more shadowy forms emerged from the darkness behind. The lantern struck its target with a crack that unbalanced her, forcing her to lean on her cane to avoid tipping over.

"Watch out!" A torrent of air whooshed over Yala's head, from Kelan's hands, knocking her attacker into the underside of the balcony.

"Get away!" Machit swung his lantern at the second beast,

while the third descended on Yala like a bloodfly. Her dagger sank into its skull, but these beasts were sturdier than the dead humans, and Kelan's opponent continued to beat its wings even as his blade ripped it open and its rotting guts tumbled out.

Yala's lantern cracked against her attacker, and it recoiled from the heat with an inhuman screeching noise. The sound froze the marrow in Yala's bones, and a hoarse yell from Machit told her that his enemy had gained the upper hand. Blood soaked one of his hands, and Yala ran to help, her leg aching with displeasure. She swung her cane, which struck the rotting creature with a wet smack. Kelan's blade severed its wing, and he brought the lantern down on the remains.

Machit stumbled over to her, his hand slick with blood. "Is that the last of them?"

"I'll check." Yala leaned heavily on her cane as she retraced her path to the shadowy corner, while Kelan glided behind her.

"Where did those things come from?" he asked. "They came *out* of the shadows."

The Void, whispered a voice in her head. Dalem's. *They opened the Void...*

Yala's body thrummed with dread, part of her braced for the floor to give way beneath them, for new horrors to rip their way up from underneath their feet—but the only shadows beneath the balcony were the regular kind, and when Yala swung the lantern, the dark patch on the floor remained immobile. Untouched.

She turned back to the others. "We need to burn the bodies."

"There's not much of them left," said Kelan. "Granted, any city guards who come in here might have questions."

"Good." Yala wanted to burn the entire building, but that would involve destroying the evidence, and the city guard would never believe her claims that they'd been attacked by the dead. "Where's Niema?"

"Here," said a faint voice.

They crossed the library to the door, where Niema had slumped against the wall, the lantern discarded at her feet.

"I told you not to come." Yala reached with her free hand to help her to her feet. "Can you walk?"

"Yes…" She took Yala's offered hand and pushed upright, drawing in a shaky breath. "I-I can't sense Corruption anymore. You destroyed it."

"Oh, good." Machit hurried over and paused with his hand on the door. "What are you doing?"

Niema had released Yala's hand and faced the twitching bodies, whispering words that drove the lingering stench of decay from her nostrils. As she drew in an involuntary breath, Yala inhaled a scent that reminded her of thick-growing forests, of life in abundance. The distant sounds of the twitching dead ceased as Niema's prayer to the god of life came to an end and silence lingered in its place.

"There," she murmured. "That ought to stop them from coming back."

Yala's lantern shone on the decaying remnants of the dead, no longer twitching with unnatural light. "Couldn't you have done that from the start?"

Kelan sheathed his blade. "You've been holding back, haven't you?"

Niema slumped forward; her forehead would have hit the floor if Kelan hadn't caught her arm at the last moment. "Oh. That's why."

Machit peered at her face. "I think she passed out. I'd carry her, but I can't feel my hand."

"Shit." Yala's stomach turned at the sight of the blood coating Machit's left hand and wrist. "We'd better get that looked at. Kelan, can you carry her?"

Kelan scowled, but he was in the best shape of the three of them, and that wasn't saying a lot. "Where do you want me to take her? There's an inn for Disciples…"

"Can they help Machit's injury there?" she asked.

"No … probably not," he said. "They won't have seen that type of magic before. I certainly haven't."

"Saren," said Machit. "He was always the best at treating wounds."

"He also threw me out." Surely even Saren wouldn't turn his back on an injured teammate, though. "Fine."

If one of those beasts had *bitten* Machit, the bite might be venomous for all Yala knew. Her leg burned with fresh pain, but she pushed herself to her limits as they made their way from the library to the outer city gates. She almost hoped the guards would ask why they were in such a state, but the two men on duty barely spared them a glance as they walked past.

"I knew we should have gone to the Temple of the Flame," Yala growled when they reached the other side of the gates.

"Are you sure *you* aren't the one who got bitten by a deadly monster from the Void?" Machit asked. "Do you really think Superior Datriem would have done anything but close the door in our faces?"

"It sounds as if he's the one who told Niema to go there in the first place." Kelan grunted, shifting his grip on the unconscious Disciple. "Why didn't Corruption affect me as much as it did her?"

"I can't imagine the god of life and the god of death being friendly with one another," Yala said. "Other than that, your guess is as good as mine."

"She also stopped those bodies from moving," Machit added. "Please tell me that's the end of it."

"I think so." Niema herself had said so, and she'd know better than any of them if the Void was open in the city.

Whatever had happened in that library hadn't been as potent as on the island, and while someone had undeniably opened the realm to which Mekan belonged, the three creatures they'd encountered had been tiny compared to the beasts that had assaulted them on the island. The library was no temple, and Mekan's insidious magic hadn't crept outside, as far as she knew.

Gods help us all. In the end, the only way to purge Mekan's presence from the island had been to burn the temple in holy fire. Their cheap lanterns would never have been able to deal with a threat on the same scale.

Upon reaching the pleasure district, Machit tucked his injured hand inside his coat to avoid drawing attention. The gambling dens and pleasure houses had yet to open for the evening, but this time when Saren answered their knock on the door, warm candlelight spilled from the hallway behind him. He was dressed in a shirt of crimson silk, his hair damp and curling to his shoulders. "Yala ... shit, what happened to you?"

"What do you think?" Yala spoke in a terser voice than she'd intended. "We need a healer, and he insisted on coming to you."

Machit pushed back his sleeve to reveal his bloody wrist, and Saren recoiled. "Did something *bite* you?"

"You might say that." Yala gestured at her leg. "Remember this? Think *that,* but smaller."

Saren stumbled back into the doorway, the colour draining from his face. "No ... not that."

"It's up to you." Yala's gaze cut into Saren. "I warned you, didn't I?"

The words were cruel, but they worked. Saren sagged against the door frame. "Come in, then."

16

The pleasure house had utterly been transformed in the past few hours. Soft light spilled out through the doors on either side of them, revealing rooms of wood-panelled walls and silken curtains. Several people—the staff, Yala assumed—watched as Saren led them down the hallway to a wooden staircase.

"There's a room you can borrow for a bit." He eyed Niema, draped in Kelan's arms. "What's wrong with her?"

"She had an inconvenient fainting fit." Kelan glided ahead of them up the stairs, while Yala let Machit overtake her. Her leg protested at yet another set of stairs, and on the upper floor, they found a wooden door to a private room containing two narrow beds.

"I'll get the medical supplies." Saren retreated from the room while Machit sat on one of the beds. Kelan laid Niema on the other, where she stirred a little.

"Were you awake the whole time?" Kelan wiped his bloodied hands on his cloak, his mouth turning down at the corners. "I just had this laundered."

"How tragic for you." Yala's lip curled. "Machit, how's the arm?"

"Green." He pushed up the sleeve of his shirt, with difficulty; his entire lower arm was swollen—and yes, it had turned the green of an infected wound. "What *was* that creature?"

Niema lifted her head. "The stories call them demons … or Mekan's creatures."

"Delightful." Yala's gut tightened at the sight of the swelling bite marks on Machit's wrist. "I hope that was the end of it. If those two men acted alone, it's one thing, but if the person who killed them is still out there…"

"Then they'll know we destroyed their monstrous pets." Machit slumped against the bed frame. "I thought we got away from this crap. How'd it end up here?"

"You're asking the wrong person." Yala's skin prickled, and she became conscious of Kelan's questioning stare. "Frankly, I don't understand why anyone would *want* to use magic that's as likely to devour the user as not. Niema, is there likely to be another altar, or temple, elsewhere in the city?"

"I don't know." She spoke quietly. "This has never happened before, at least not in Laria. Superior Kralia said no similar incidents have been recorded in the history of our enclave."

"How long would that be?" Kelan queried. "Your people haven't been around as long as mine, I'm betting."

"It's not a contest." Yala's forehead pinched. "Also, it's not surprising that people who make deals with Mekan don't tend to survive to tell the story."

The god of death did not discriminate between devotee and unlucky bystander when He demanded payment. The scenes they'd witnessed on the island were proof enough.

Saren came back into the room with the medical supplies

in his arms. "I can clean the wound, but ... fuck me, it's green."

"I'm aware." Machit extended his arm. "Might be time to start planning my last rites."

Yala's hands clenched over her cane. Her aching leg urged her to sit, but restlessness kept her upright, her mind ticking over the possibility of Corruption brewing elsewhere in the capital. "Someone ought to talk to Superior Datriem. He might not have known what we'd find at the library, but he'll have a hell of a time denying the existence of Corruption if he sees the proof with his own eyes."

"The *library?*" Saren dabbed at the wound. "Is that where you were attacked?"

"Someone was using the abandoned library to conduct a ritual with the god of death, yes."

"Ow!" Machit yanked his arm away when Saren gave a violent flinch. "Be gentle."

Saren sprang back from the bed, his gaze darting around as if he was contemplating jumping from the nearest window. "The library is in the upper city. How in the gods' names did nobody notice?"

"It's been closed for years, supposedly." Yala eyed Machit. "Did you know?"

"I knew they shut down the library, but not that someone was using it as their lair." He extended his arm as Saren made a second attempt to clean the wound.

"You made a habit of frequenting the library as a soldier, did you?" asked Kelan.

"No," Yala replied. "We had a collection of books in the barracks…"

"Yes, of pornography," Machit said with a snort. "I think Viam stole the few textbooks we had."

Yala grimaced at the mention of their former friend. "You

know what *might* contain texts on Corruption? The palace complex has its own library."

Machit's head snapped up. "You're joking."

"I'm not," said Yala. "Look—someone figured out how to create a scaled-down version of what we saw on the island. They must have had instructions from somewhere."

At one time she might have been careful who overheard, but what did it matter if Kelan and Niema knew? They'd seen the dead with their own eyes, and no threats would still their tongues as they had Yala's. As tempting as it might be to believe the men who'd died in the library had stumbled upon the knowledge of their own accord, they hadn't learned to call on Mekan from nowhere.

Neither had the Rafragorians who'd died on the island, whether or not King Tharen himself had shared in this knowledge.

Nobody said anything. Not even Kelan, whose curiosity might not outweigh the prevailing desire to have nothing to do with Corruption ever again. She knew that feeling well.

Niema sat upright, her hands trembling at her sides. "I didn't know Corruption would have such a strong effect on me, though I should have guessed."

"Dalem said that Corruption repels all living things," Yala recalled. "When we landed on that island, our mounts fled the monsters and left us stranded. There wasn't a single living creature near the library, not so much as a bloodfly."

Saren dropped the cloth. "I've seen that place in my nightmares every night for years. I didn't need it to come here."

"Do you think any of us did?" Yala's leg throbbed as if reminding her that she'd taken that injury while fighting off a similar beast to the ones they'd faced earlier. Based on the state of Machit's arm, she was lucky the wound had been inflicted by a claw and not a tooth.

Nobody contradicted her word. Saren finished wrapping a bandage around Machit's wound and then left the room, muttering something about getting a drink. From the noise downstairs, the pleasure house was nearing opening, and it came as little surprise when Kelan was the next to leave the room. No doubt he already had plans to employ their services later that night, disappearing into some woman's room—or man's, she didn't know which way his preferences lay—but Yala herself preferred an emotional connection with her lovers and derived little enjoyment from fooling around with strangers, even in more pleasurable circumstances than these.

Saren returned with a bottle of liquor and several glasses, which he distributed among them. Yala accepted hers with reluctance; her throat was parched, her hands trembling with the aftermath of their fight and the arduous walk on her sore leg. The strong Parvan rice wine burned its way down her gullet and lit a fire inside her. Niema, too, revived enough to rise from the bed and join Yala near the door.

"I'm sorry," she murmured. "I should have been more help than I was. I failed you."

"You didn't." Yala had no more harsh words for her. "If anyone did, it was the Disciples of the Flame. Or me, since I sent you to talk to Superior Datriem despite knowing he'd lead you astray."

Niema shuddered. "He was ... he was nothing as I expected. My Superior is intimidating, yes, but she is kind, too."

"I thought he'd be respectful of another Disciple. Or as respectful as possible for someone like him, anyway."

"No." Niema consumed the rest of the liquor in a gulp, coughing. "He threatened you, didn't he? When you told him of the island?"

"Yes." Yala lowered her eyes. "I can see why he wouldn't have wanted to risk anyone learning that we found a temple dedicated to the god of death. Granted, it was abandoned centuries ago for all we know."

"Prior to the founding of Laria, I imagine." Niema's forehead scrunched. "It's surprising that the island wasn't discovered sooner, though."

"The place was mired in fog." Yala took another sip of her drink, savouring the sharp burn down her throat. "We could barely see where we were going. I don't know if Rafragoria found it first or if Laria did, but now do you see why I'm not in any position to make decisions on how to handle this? None of us knows what we're doing."

"There's one thing I don't quite understand," Niema said. "You escaped the island—destroyed it. Was one of your squad a Disciple of the Flame?"

"No, he never took the vows." The words tightened her throat. "He knew all the prayers and rituals, though, and he knew that Dalathik's power was the only thing that could destroy the island. He called the god of light and paid his life in tribute."

"Oh," Niema said softly. "Oh, I see."

"Exactly. All I did was kill one of Mekan's beasts, and at a cost." Yala gestured to her injured leg. "Dalem is the one who destroyed that island, not me, and I thoroughly obliterated any chances of joining the Temple of the Flame myself."

"Superior Datriem isn't representative of every Disciple of the Flame, is he?" Niema queried.

"He might as well be." Yala's tone soured. "I only know as much as Dalem told me, and he wasn't allowed to share the details of the prayers or rituals he learned, but he did say that their hierarchical structure is absolute. Superior Datriem makes all the decisions, his council enacts them, and the rest of the Disciples toe the line and obey the rules."

"They allowed your friend to leave, though?"

Yala's hand clenched around her glass. "Allowed? They

told him he'd never hear the voice of the god of light again, and that Mekan would take his soul upon death. You know, I never did think to tell Superior Datriem he was wrong. Dalem did hear the god of light in his dying moments. He chose death on his own terms."

If they'd never been on the island, he need not have died at all, but the god of death's magic had infested the place, and if he hadn't destroyed it, there was no telling how much more damage it would have done.

Niema's gaze travelled to Machit, who'd lain on his bed with his eyes closed. "I'd offer to heal him, but my abilities don't work on wounds inflicted by the dead."

"What?" Yala's thoughts wrenched back from the island. "Will it heal by itself? Or…" Or would they have to cut off his arm? She'd seen several similar cases in her years in the army, and she had no doubt that Machit would rather lose his arm than his life.

"I wish I could help." Niema spoke in a whisper. "If Corruption has already infected him…"

"He'll die." Her throat closed like a cauterised wound. *No. Not again.*

Niema's silence was an answer in itself and Yala found herself looking to her squad-mates. Machit hadn't shown any signs of having heard them, but when Saren met her eyes, she saw a familiar pain staring back at her.

"He's going to die, isn't he?" he whispered when Yala limped to his side.

Yala inclined her head. "According to Niema, there's no cure."

Saren made a choked noise. "This is my fault."

"It isn't," Yala said, and found herself surprised she meant it. "You didn't tell him to come with us. If the fault's with anyone, it's with—"

"Not you." He cut through her words.

"I was going to say with the people who decided to use the public library to conduct a ritual to the god of death to begin with."

"That. Yes." Saren cleared his throat. "I... I lied to you. Before. The name you mentioned—ah, the Successors? I've heard it mentioned downstairs a few times, in connection to a new political movement."

"Movement?" she echoed. "I thought they were a gang of criminals."

"No ... well, they might be, but they also have political ambitions. They want the king to address the needs of the people of Dalathar—*all* the people, not just the nobles."

"What part of that has anything to do with me? With us?" Frustration crawled up her spine like an itch that was out of her reach. "They offered a huge sum of money for my life and might have conducted a ritual with the god of death. What has that to do with the king?"

He lifted his mostly empty glass and drank. "I don't know, raising the dead is one way of starting a revolution."

"This is serious." She fought to keep her temper under control. "Machit is dying. We might be next. If the Successors are the reason we're being hunted, I'd appreciate it if you found out which clients of yours might be working with our enemies. Preferably *before* you throw us out on the street again."

He winced. "I'm sorry about earlier. You can stay here for as long as you like ... and your companions, too. I'm sure Giran won't mind."

Too late. "The Successors, Saren. Who knows their location?"

"I'll ask around." He veered towards the door. "You can ask, too, but—ah, please don't scare away the clients. Giran won't thank you for that."

Yala's objection died on her tongue when Machit

groaned. Her instincts told her it was unwise to get into another confrontation when she was already exhausted, and the state of her clothes alone would be enough to scare off the pleasure house's patrons. This was the first time she'd had access to a proper bed in days, though she needed to return to the undercity to fetch her pack where she'd left it in Machit's house, assuming the contents hadn't already been stolen … but she could hardly bring herself to care. None of that mattered when Machit was dying.

Not when it was her fault.

Yala followed Saren's path downstairs and found Kelan in the hallway, talking to a woman draped in silk and sipping from a glass of liquor. The pleasure house hadn't opened its doors to the public yet, but the soft scent of incense wafted from the nearby rooms.

Yala's cane tapped the ground at Kelan's feet. "Excuse me."

Kalen dragged his attention away from the woman's plunging neckline. "What is it?"

"If you're going to hassle the staff, you might at least try asking relevant questions." Yala did not bother lowering her voice. "Like the location of the Successors."

The woman choked on her drink. "Don't *talk* so loudly."

"You know the name."

Kelan stepped in. "What my, ah, *acquaintance* means to say is that she would appreciate it if you were to point us to someone who knows the location of a certain group of…"

"Revolutionaries." Yala used Saren's term, which sounded mildly more respectable than 'criminals', though that didn't mean they weren't both. "I'm interested in meeting their leader."

The woman laughed. "You and half the city's underworld, sweetheart. Their message hit a nerve."

"I want to know where they're hiding." Yala glared at her. "Can you point me towards someone who'll talk?"

She pursed her lips. "If our clients want to talk, that's one thing, but I can't go ruining the atmosphere by asking them to an interrogation, can I?"

"It's urgent."

"Urgent?" She sipped her drink. "Nobody here is in a hurry, sweetheart."

"I expect not," Kelan said, "but I find myself in need of coin, and I'm told they're offering jobs to mercenaries. I would like to make use of your services, but I have no intention of taking advantage of your hospitality."

Yala rolled her eyes, but the woman smiled. She leaned over to him, flashing an expanse of breast and thigh in the process. "I can think of some less hazardous means of earning a little coin than chasing bounties."

The word 'bounty' made Yala's spine stiffen. "What kind of people are they offering money for, exactly?"

"Haven't a clue." The woman gave Kelan a last appreciative glance before making her languorous way into the nearest room and placing her glass down on a table. "Turns out lots of people aren't fans of the powers that be, though."

"You mean the king?"

"Who else?" She flashed Kelan a quick smile. "If you want to engage in my services later, let me know. We can arrange something."

"I'd be delighted," Kelan said, which earned him a jab in the shin from Yala's cane. "Ouch. What was that for?"

"I want to find the Successors. Tonight." She lowered her voice. "I thought that was your goal, too."

"It is, but I can't say I'm keen for another brush with death today."

"Too bad." She drew in a sharp breath. "Machit is dying. I'm not in a negotiating mood."

"Oh." Guilt flittered across his expression. "Was that creature's bite venomous?"

"Worse." Venom could be drawn out. Corruption could only be erased by holy fire, unless the Successors or whoever had called those beasts into this realm knew another way. "The Successors don't seem to be easy to find, but there's one thing guaranteed to get their attention."

"Offering yourself as bait?"

"It's not ideal, but yes." They wanted her alive. Not necessarily intact, judging by the behaviour of those mercenaries they'd run into, but how else would she be able to meet them directly? "Granted, I'm no closer to finding out their favourite haunts, except the library. Assuming that was them."

"I can look for my fellow Disciples," Kelan offered. "I've wondered where the man we ran into on the road disappeared to, but he might show his face if he learns you're in the city."

"Tell him you have me." She knew the risks, but the notion of waiting much longer was unthinkable. "And if you find the Successors, let them know I'm willing to surrender."

His brows shot up. "You *want* me to tell everyone your location?"

"No, I want to meet them at their hideout," she said. "I'm not going to make the others targets if I can help it."

"So you want to walk into the enemy's home, without any backup?"

"That was implied. Yes." Was he concerned about her? It hadn't been that long since he'd betrayed her location to the mercenaries himself ... though he'd since proven more help than hindrance. Perhaps he did see her as an ally and not an adversary, but Yala had had enough of not knowing who she was fighting.

"If they don't know it was us who ruined their schemes in the library, they will soon," she added. "I'd sooner walk into their trap than let them find me first."

Kelan had to admit that Yala's method was probably the easiest way to get the Successors' location, but there was a hitch. Namely, her allies, who refused to let her surrender herself into their hands—and Niema, who insisted on going with her.

"You shouldn't even be walking," Yala told Niema. She'd called the others back upstairs to discuss their plans in private, since the pleasure house had begun to stir with the arrival of the first clients and they'd already attracted a few confused stares. "Going out after dark is risky already, considering you don't know the way around."

"I'm not letting you surrender yourself alone." Niema was steadier on her feet than she'd been earlier, and when she spoke to Kelan, some of her former disdain had returned. "You can't come with us, though. They'd take your presence as a threat."

"Now, I thought I was the one tasked with finding their location," Kelan said. "Or finding my fellow Disciples, at any rate."

"Go on." Yala watched him, scarcely blinking. He pitied whoever found themselves on the end of that stare next. "Find them."

"No need to rush." He didn't quite manage to meet her cutting eyes. "If I were to run into the elusive Successors themselves, where should I tell them to come looking for you? You'd better pick somewhere far away from the pleasure district."

"The library," Yala decided. "Just in case there was any doubt that we were responsible for ruining their fun."

"Good enough." He caught Niema's eye, but she didn't acknowledge him.

If she wanted to sacrifice herself, it shouldn't be his problem. *Why do I care what happens to these people?* Yes, he'd played his part in keeping them alive for the past few days, but he'd never intended to get this deeply entangled with them. His mission had entwined itself with theirs, and somehow, hearing Machit's recount of their escape from the island hadn't hit quite as hard as experiencing the visceral terror of confronting something that was so far removed from what was natural that every living thing fled from its presence.

Like all Disciples, he knew the name of the god of death, Mekan. The stories said that the other five gods had shunned the sixth and cast Him out into the Void, where His magic festered, searching for living things to feast upon. To access His power required a sacrifice in exchange, and incredibly, someone had managed to access that power here in the capital. A city packed with living souls would be a veritable buffet for the god of death.

That unpleasant thought remained lodged in his mind as Kelan left the pleasure house and conjured a breeze that carried him up onto a level with the rooftops. He easily glided over the wall into the upper city and came down near the library. No movement stirred, but now the sun had gone down, any shadow might hide more of Mekan's creatures.

As Kelan approached Ceremonial Square, he glimpsed another figure flitting across the rooftops. *Laima?* No—the figure was male. Swiftly he rose into the air and moved in pursuit, confirming that the man did appear to be the individual who'd attacked their wagon on the road to the capital. Senik, a newly qualified Disciple and not one whom Kelan knew well.

Upon registering Kelan's presence, Senik spun around in midair and drew his sword. "You again."

Kelan reached for his blade. "Looking for someone?"

"What does it matter to you?" The man pointed his blade directly at Kelan, his cloak rippling behind him. "You attacked me on the road, too. Do you ally with Corruption now?"

"Corruption?" he echoed. "Certainly not. I recall that it was you who attacked the wagon in which I was travelling from Setemar."

"You travelled with a Disciple of Death?"

He doesn't mean Yala? What rumour had the Successors started now? "No, I did not. Were you perchance hoping to gain the bounty offered for Captain Yala Palathar's life?"

"Captain Yala *is* a Disciple of Death."

"Trust me, someone in the city is, and it's not her." Shit. How many others might have heard the same rumour?

Senik gave Kelan an incredulous look. "You don't know? Why did you think the Successors wanted her? They can't have a rival running around."

"A rival." Kelan felt his body sway as if the air itself might give way beneath his feet. "They're Disciples of Death … but what did you plan to do with Yala if you managed to capture her?"

"Kill her, of course." His blade skimmed the air, a finger span from Kelan's neck. "You know where she is, don't you? Tell me."

"I don't think so." Kelan's blade slid out of its sheath, and he glided across the air, the other man in pursuit. "Ah—Senik. That's your name, isn't it? You're newly qualified. This must be your first mission."

"Stop talking." Senik's blade crashed into Kelan's, jarring both their hands. "Does Superior Sietra know you're working with the threat she sent you to eradicate, Kelan?"

He knows about my mission. Yet he was under the impression that Yala was the enemy, and worse, based on the strength of his swings, he was aiming to kill.

Kelan parried, his blade sweeping Senik's aside. The air buffeted them, neither able to gain the upper hand with their

EMMA L. ADAMS

magic alone. "Calm down. I'm not working with Corruption. Listen—"

The man's eyes gleamed with fierce anger as he dove at Kelan, whose blade swung up, aided by the force of the wind. He'd expected to parry the blow, but his blade sank into the other man's chest. A crimson stain bloomed against Senik's blue cloak, and his eyes widened for an instant before the air ceased to hold him, and he plummeted.

Kelan watched him fall, his mind half-numb, half-panicked. *I didn't mean to kill him.*

Then another thought slammed into him: *Yala isn't an agent of Corruption.* But if Superior Sietra believed the rumours, if she'd sent Senik to finish the job Kelan had started…

If that were the case, then if he wanted to fulfil his mission, he'd have to end her life with his own hands.

17

Niema followed Yala's steps out of the pleasure house and towards the gates to the upper city. She'd hoped the night air would help the dizziness that had persisted since she'd called upon the god of life to quell the last traces of Mekan's presence, but the formerly empty street was now awash in brightness and noise. Workers and tourists thronged the pleasure district, and the scent of smoke and incense made the humid air feel even thicker than usual, like breathing soup. While the sun had slipped outside behind the rooftops, lanterns hung from walls and adorned the gate to the upper city.

Upon reaching the gates, Yala paused. "I don't think you should come with me, Niema. This is likely to be dangerous."

Niema tried to steady her breathing. "I'm fine. Besides, Kelan is out there somewhere as well."

"Assuming he hasn't got distracted." Yala turned back to the gate. Since Niema had revealed the fatal nature of Machit's wound, the other woman's manner had changed. Every word she spoke was laced with tension, and every crack of her cane on the cobblestones promised violence to anyone unfortunate enough to stand in her path.

Niema understood why; Yala had already lost one friend in the past few days, and the idea of losing another was unthinkable to her. Yet their encounter with the dead had driven home Yala's fierce insistence that her survival on that island had been due to luck and her friend's sacrifice and not through some ability Niema had yet to witness.

If she spoke true—and Niema had no reason to doubt otherwise—then where did that leave her enclave's vision, and the mission with which Superior Kralia had entrusted her?

When they reached the other side of the gates, Niema scanned the sky for any signs of Kelan. She thought she glimpsed figures up on the rooftops, but the dark sky made it impossible to identify them.

Music drifted from Ceremonial Square, interspersed with waves of talk and laughter, but the back streets in which they'd found the public library remained quiet, deserted. Not in the same manner as before—a skirrit's tail disappearing around a corner indicated that the god of death's presence had departed long enough for life to begin to return—but not only in the form of rodents. Several shady-looking figures lurked outside the library, dressed in nondescript clothing with hoods pulled up to hide their faces. *Mercenaries.* They were a mixture of men and women, the best that Niema could tell, and were heavily armed.

A broad-shouldered man with notable gaps in his front teeth caught sight of them first. "Looking for someone?"

"You might say that." Yala squared her shoulders. "I don't suppose you're allied with the Successors?"

"Who wants to know?"

"I'm Yala Palathar," she said. "I'd like to talk to your leader."

"How about that?" He bared his remaining teeth in a grin. "The elusive Yala Palathar has delivered herself into our hands. Melian was right."

"About what?" Yala took a step toward him. "No more dancing around the subject. What do you want me for?"

"Better take her to Melian," one of his companions called out. "And her friend, too. What're you supposed to be?"

Niema lifted her chin. "I'm Niema, a Disciple of Life."

"Are you now?" The toothless man gave an unpleasant laugh. "Melian *will* be pleased."

All Niema's instincts urged her to run, especially when one of the cloaked figures nudged the door to the library open. *Their leader is in there.* No doubt the Successors had come to see who'd disturbed their attempts to call upon the god of death.

"Why here?" Yala asked. "What did the public library ever do to you? I suppose you've never read a book, but still."

"What's that mean?" The toothless man scowled at her. "Think you can insult my intelligence, *Captain?*"

"Which squad did *you* fight in?" Each beat of Yala's cane brought them closer to the door. Niema's blood ran with dread, and when she faltered, a meaty hand gripped her shoulder.

"No running." Yala hissed out a breath when the toothless man reached for the dagger at her waist. "And no weapons in here."

"Don't touch me." She yanked the dagger out of its sheath with her free hand, the other gripping her cane. When the man tried to take that, too, she shook her head. "That's not a weapon."

"It can be."

"So can a book, if you're creative enough."

"Thinks she's funny, that one does." The man holding

Niema's arm gave her a shake. "As for you, where are you hiding your weapons?"

"I don't carry any." Her voice wavered. "Disciples of Life are forbidden to inflict violence on anyone."

That drew a laugh from the group and a quiet groan from Yala. *At least it makes our surrender convincing.* Though she had to wonder what Yala planned to *do* when they were back inside the room in which the dead had risen from the Void. Did she have a plan? She'd wanted to get here, but it didn't mean they'd get *out* again.

Niema twisted her arm, trying to break free of the man's hold, but he steered her into the library and closed the door at her back.

———

Yala knew that they were walking into a trap. She also knew that they ought to have waited for Kelan to come back, and that Niema should have stayed behind. That Niema had now revealed her status as a Disciple of Life *and* her vow against inflicting violence would only worsen the situation, but if they both ended up dead, she'd have nobody to blame but herself.

Like the pleasure house, the library had undergone a transformation in the past few hours, albeit in the opposite direction. If not for the lanterns the cloaked occupants held, the shelves would have been cast into total darkness. The faint smell of decay lingered, but stronger were the human smells of sweat, dirt, and blood. Somewhere between ten and twenty other people—mercenaries or Disciples of Death— were gathered below the balconies.

"Melian," the toothless man called. "I have an unexpected visitor."

All eyes turned to Yala, taking in her dirty clothes, her

uneven gait, and the cane in her hand. Then a woman stepped into view, short and dressed in a similar hooded cloak to her followers. Her curly hair had been pulled into a bun, while her bronze skin gleamed in the light of the lantern she held. She was also very much *alive.*

"You're the one in charge of all this, are you?" Yala studied her opponent, struck by how ordinary she appeared. She might have passed the woman at the market without a second glance.

"In charge?" Melian pursed her lips. "We're more egalitarian than you would be used to, but I suppose you can call me the Superior. And *you* ... you must be Yala Palathar."

"Out of interest, how much did you offer for my capture?" Yala assessed the room while she spoke. The only route of escape was the door through which she'd entered, though at least five mercenaries were in her way, one of whom held Niema's shoulder in a firm grip. "If I'd known I was worth that much, I might have hired some impersonators to keep you on your toes."

"You have no understanding of your situation." Melian sounded faintly incredulous. "Is this a game to you?"

Yes. A war game. The blood rushed in Yala's veins in a manner she hadn't experienced since she'd left the army. "I thought you turned this into a game when you killed Vanat to lure me here. Was that the intention?"

"No," Melian said. "I'm told he tried to escape his captors, wounding them in the process, so he earned his fate."

Yala's heart thumped louder, echoing in the empty space. "That's not for you to decide, but I suppose dealing with the god of death requires a flexible concept of justice."

The hint of a smile touched at Melian's lips. "You *are* an interesting conversationalist. I expected a dull-witted soldier, but it's almost a pity that you have to die tonight."

"What?" She cast a brief glance behind her, but the other

members of Melian's group formed a solid wall blocking her way to the exit and Niema had disappeared behind them. *Shit.* "You changed your mind about keeping me alive? What was the point in dragging me all the way here?"

If the Successors had been working with the god of death from the start, what did they want with her? If they'd been concerned that she'd destroy their efforts like she had on the island, they'd all but ensured that outcome by bringing her into the city. They'd have been better off leaving her to remain ignorant, ensconced in her jungle cabin.

"The point?" Melian's mouth curved into a smile. "You may have observed that we've made some progress in learning to harness the god of death's power, but Mekan is a rather demanding entity. To gain His loyalty requires sacrifice."

Yala's heartbeat, so loud until now, seemed oddly quiet. "You think my experience on the island makes me a worthier sacrifice? Is that why you need me?"

"Almost right," said Melian. "There's nothing Mekan values more than a fighter, and you slew one of his creatures with your own hand."

Yala's leg throbbed, as if to remind her of the price she'd paid for that victory. "You're out of your mind."

How had she even learned how to use death magic? There weren't temples and ancient texts and scores of other Disciples keen to pass on their knowledge as there were with the other Disciplines. Yet Melian had proclaimed herself a *Superior.*

"Not at all," said Melian. "My mind is clear. The people of this city want change, and I am willing to provide it. What would you prefer to do, die in isolation, or be part of a movement that will change the course of Laria's history? Future generations will remember our names."

"Making a deal with the god of death isn't something I'd

want to be known for." Yala's attention flickered to the library's distant corner. "You already killed two of your own followers. How many more will you sacrifice?"

"So it *was* you who was in here earlier." Melian lowered her lantern, causing the shadows on the floor to shift and Yala's skin to tighten with dread. "As to your question, the only way to defeat one's fear of death is to embrace the inevitability. They were willing to give their lives for the cause and had nothing to lose, and the same is true of myself."

"You always have more to lose." She might not understand Melian's weakness yet—except for a dangerous overconfidence—but she had no doubt one existed.

"I suppose you'd know," said Melian. "Surely you of all people would agree that our current monarch is inept in every possible way and that the country is suffering under his rule. With the aid of the god of death, we will remove him from power and forge a new age."

"Ambitious, but you could have done all this without me."

"I disagree," said Melian. "You touched the Void yourself, and if we give you back, there is nothing Mekan will not grant us in return."

A laugh caught in Yala's throat. "I wouldn't count on it."

She took a step back and collided with a solid, heavy body. Melian gestured with her lantern. "Restrain her."

Yala lifted her cane and swung it at the shins of the nearest target. A satisfying crack rang out, but more bodies pushed against hers, a mass of living flesh. *Where in hells is Niema?*

As Yala fought, hands grabbed hers and then released her equally quickly. Someone screamed, and Yala twisted on the spot, trying to see her surroundings. Lantern lights bounced from empty shelves to the solid figures of the mercenaries, and towards a strange-looking mass creeping across the floor from the direction of the door. Her eyesight picked out beady eyes, long tails, fur. *What—?*

Rodents. Hundreds of skirrits, sweeping into the library like a wave breaking on the shore. Her captors staggered, tripped, or just goggled in disbelief—both at the skirrits and the person behind them. Under the shuffle of countless tiny footsteps and the pants and curses of the mercenaries, Yala heard a distinct high-pitched whistle. *Thanks, Niema.*

Yala's cane struck left and right as she ran for the door as fast as her leg would allow. Skirrits parted around her like the tide, and as she emerged into the street, Niema joined her, still whistling.

One hand on her injured leg, Yala exhaled a sigh of relief. "How'd you do that?"

Niema paused in her whistling. "I called every living creature within range. Skirrits are small enough that it doesn't cost me too much effort, but they won't keep her distracted for long."

"We have to warn the others—warn the guards—shit, even warn the Temple of the Flame if it'll get one of those Disciples to lift a finger for once." Pain blazed in Yala's shin, but she couldn't afford to slow. "Melian's people might be delusional, but they're dangerous enough to be a legitimate threat."

As they rounded a corner, they passed the bloodstained body of a fallen Disciple of the Sky. For a heart-stopping instant, Yala thought it was Kelan, but when she looked closer, she recognised him as the Disciple who'd attacked their wagon on the road.

"Kelan's attempt at negotiation didn't go as planned, then," she said breathlessly. "I wonder where he is."

"Yala." Niema skidded to a halt as a dead man blocked their path. He'd once been a city guard, judging by his uniform, but his face was a shrivelled husk, his eyes empty and sightless. As she made to sidestep him, hurried footsteps came from behind them.

The mercenaries. They'd escaped the tide of skirrits, and now she and Niema were trapped behind the dead and the living.

"Nice try," Melian called. "Now ... I believe one of your friends is currently living above a pleasure house outside of the upper city. I wonder if he'd appreciate a visit?"

18

A meaty hand clamped over Yala's mouth, and a burly man lifted her off the ground. She struggled and kicked, but her size had never been an advantage even before her injury, and they'd taken away her weapons already. Hands ripped her cane from her, stripping away her last defence. More of Melain's allies herded Niema through the gates to the outer city.

They killed the guards at the gate, Yala thought numbly. The continuous music and laughter from Ceremonial Square might as well have existed in another world, and while there should have been guards patrolling on top of the wall, either they were shirking their duty or Melian's people had already removed anyone who might have stopped her.

As they reached the pleasure district, screams ripped through the air, and Yala glimpsed people fleeing left and right as Melian's allies marched down the street towards the pleasure house doors.

"Saren." Yala tried to speak around the hand over her mouth, and when it pressed harder, she sank her teeth in. The man holding her yelped and cursed, trying to shake her off, but she bit deeper until coppery blood flowed into her mouth. While he was unbalanced, she thrust her head back into the soft cartilage of his nose.

He dropped her with a bellow of pain. Yala tried to land in a crouch, but her treacherous leg gave way beneath her, and her knees hit the stone. She swallowed a gasp when a booted foot slammed into her ribs. Clutching his bleeding hand, the man who'd held her gave another vicious kick. "You'll pay for that."

Yala bared bloody teeth at him. "Think I've never taken a beating before?"

She scarcely had time to catch her breath before one of Melian's allies seized Yala's arm and yanked her to her feet. Ahead, Melian had already entered the pleasure house, and clients and staff fled or cowered in the nearby rooms. Dizzy with pain, Yala stumbled over the threshold. In the room on her left, Saren stood with a shattered glass at his feet, and when he saw her, the colour drained from his face.

"I thought we'd vary the entertainment tonight." Melian's voice rang through the room. "What do you think?"

The front doors slammed, and someone let out a scream from behind a silk curtain.

"No need to panic," said Melian. "You fine people won't come to any harm … that is, if my captive behaves herself. Which of you is Saren Enthar?"

"Me." Saren's voice trembled, but he kept his attention on Yala, not Melian, as her captor dragged her into the room. "What do you want?"

"Your friend refused to cooperate with me," said Melian, "so I thought I'd give her an incentive. It's nothing personal."

Yala spat blood at her. Crimson splattered Melian's face, and her eyes narrowed dangerously. "Now, I thought we'd come to the understanding that your friends' safety depends on your cooperation, Yala."

"*Your* safety depends on the cooperation of the god of death." She spoke mostly for Saren's benefit—if she gave him some idea of what was going on, he might be able to scrape together a plan—though the gods only knew how. "I wouldn't bet on those odds."

"Bring him here." Melian drew a wickedly sharp knife and indicated to two of her companions to seize Saren.

Yala wouldn't have blamed him if he'd run, not a bit, and it was a shock when he dropped to a crouch and seized the largest piece of shattered glass at his feet, thrusting it towards one of his attackers.

Behind her, the door slammed again, and a gust of air ripped through the room. Several people ran for the door, seizing the chance to escape, and Yala flew forward out of the mercenary's grip. This time she managed to land on her feet, but the impact jarred her leg yet again. Pain pulsed up her right shin, and she grabbed the back of a chair to keep her balance. Chaos filled the room as mercenaries grabbed anyone who ran past, and Yala twisted around to see Machit standing in the doorway. What was he doing on his feet? She shouted a warning that was lost in the general clamour as she attempted to cross the room to him.

"Run!" she shouted hoarsely. "Machit, get out of here!"

"I'm already dead." He held his injured arm to his chest, his eyes glittering with defiance. "I don't mind taking a few more hits if I can bring these fuckers down with me."

She opened her mouth to protest, and his eyes bulged. An instant later, an arm wrapped around her neck from behind, choking her.

"That's enough from you," growled the mercenary whose hand she'd bitten.

Yala twisted her head sideways into the crook of his elbow to ease the pressure on her throat, but his hands released her almost at once. She hit the wooden floor with a thud, and white-hot pain blanked out her vision. Her leg screamed, and through blurred vision, she saw the mercenaries drag the struggling Machit and Saren across the room.

"Instead of one survivor of the island, we have three," Melian said. "I should thank you, Yala Palathar. Three will more than satisfy Mekan's appetite."

Yala could only manage a groan. Her leg felt as if it had been split anew, and her face was damp with blood or a spilled drink, or both.

"Who the hell *are* you people?" Saren croaked. "Do you really think you can meddle with the god of death and not get eviscerated?"

"They know," Yala managed to spit out. "They don't care."

"Stop talking," said Melian. "I think I'll let you watch me kill your friends first, Yala. You'll be last to die."

"No, that's you." Machit clutched his bandaged arm to his chest. "My only regret is that I won't get to see it."

"How kind of you to offer to go first." Melian approached his kneeling form, her knife sharp and glinting. "To the god of death, I offer this sacrifice."

The knife flashed, and Saren let out a scream when Machit's throat split open. Blood sprayed the wooden floor, and Yala's pain-drunk state broke in a surge of white-hot rage. She wrenched herself forward, attempting to break her captor's hold. A strangled cry ripped from her throat, though if she'd been able to speak, she'd have said, *it wasn't a sacrifice. He was already dying, and he offered himself willingly.*

Cold pressed upon Yala's body, sapping the brief burst of energy from her limbs. Chills rippled over her flesh, caressed her skin. Not the roaring torrent of a Disciple of the Sky, but something else. Something that cast a shadow across the blood-drenched floor, a shadow that belonged to no living creature.

Melian lifted her head with a satisfied smile and spoke.

"It's an honour to conduct business with you, god of death. As you can see, I have two sacrifices from among the squad who slew one of your followers. Will you accept their lives in exchange for loaning me your strength?"

"*Yes.*"

The word tickled Yala's ear, not spoken by any mortal's tongue. Not another sound disturbed the air, save for the faint thud of Saren's head against the floor, and Melian's rapid, excited breathing.

"Our next sacrifice appears to have fainted," she remarked. "Pity, but that doesn't matter to you, does it?"

"Fuck ... you." Yala forced the words between her teeth. Cold air whistled in. The shadows on the floor flickered like dying candles, weaving around Machit's corpse, mingling with his spilled blood. "Get ... away from him."

Yala's pain-dulled sight tracked the movement of the shadows shifting over Machit's body, indicating the god of death taking His sacrifice—and then departing, coalescing into a nebulous form that fixed its eyes upon her.

Cold such as she'd never experienced before cut her to the core. She felt like a body flayed open on a table, except it was as if her *mind* had cracked open, and the eyes had pierced into her inmost depths. Her leg gave a throb of pain, dispelling any notion that this might be a horrific conjuring of her pain-drunk imagination.

"*I know you,*" the presence whispered.

That was when she heard the call of a war drake.

————

Holding Niema around her waist as he hovered above the rooftops, Kelan had to admit that while he'd had worse ideas, he'd also had better ones. The war drake's reptilian form came into sight as Niema's legs continued to flail beneath him.

"Stop wriggling or I'll drop you," he told her. "You'll have to be clear with your directions when it gets closer. We don't want it landing in the wrong place."

"No," Niema said faintly. "We don't. If it does, people will die."

"I'd say the odds are already against us in that regard." Though they were as likely to fall to their deaths as they were to be eaten by the oncoming war drake if Niema passed out again and lost control over its will.

Niema began whistling again, a strident noise that formed a jarring contrast to the chaos on the ground below. Kelan had managed to use the sky god's power to knock the mercenaries inside the pleasure house around, but it hadn't been enough to drive them away. When Niema had whispered her idea to him, he'd been sceptical at best, but he'd agreed to fly her to the city's boundary so that the war drake would hear her cry.

And the beast had answered.

Now, its vast shadow flew over the pleasure district, and Kelan watched as Niema's sharp whistle drove the beast into descent. One of the mercenaries let out a scream as the war drake's claws ripped his head clean off. Blood spurted onto the cobbles, and Kelan stopped short of landing in case he unwittingly got himself decapitated as well. How had Yala ridden one of these beasts into battle, let alone tamed it? That was a question he'd ask later—assuming she was still alive.

Niema's whistling halted. "Put me down. I have to find Yala."

He acquiesced, landing outside the pleasure house, and placing Niema's feet on the ground. Someone had torn down the curtains in the downstairs room, and through the window, he saw a hard-faced woman with a curved knife in her hand standing over the body of Yala's friend, Machit. Yala herself was on her knees, a sight he'd never have imagined he'd see, but his attention slipped when another mercenary came running at him.

"Might want to look behind you." He lifted a hand and blasted air at the mercenary, knocking her into the path of the oncoming war drake. Claws bit into the woman's chest and yanked out her innards, and as she crumpled, the beast's claws swiped at Kelan's neck. He skated back, barely avoiding losing his head. "Niema!"

"Leave him," Niema called to the war drake. "Stop. Don't attack us."

Her words became a whistle, but from the pleasure house, he heard a voice, as deep and cold as a bottomless pit.

"I know you."

19

The war drake's cry echoed in Yala's ears, cutting through the pain and confusion, and the person holding her let go as if burned. Pain continued to ripple through her leg, but while she was vaguely aware of shouts and panic around her, she had eyes only for her squad. Saren, unconscious, and Machit, sprawled in a pool of his own blood.

Dragging her injured leg behind her, she crawled to his body and held her hands over his neck as if to stem the bleeding through sheer will, though intellectually she knew that this was a wound even Niema's powers wouldn't be able to heal. His eyes were empty, soulless, and would never again crinkle in laughter as he joked with their fellow squad members.

Cold air whispered over the back of her neck. The blood spilling from Machit's throat appeared to shimmer, blurring before her eyes like a shadow cast over water … and the fingers of his limp hand twitched. Shadows oozed between the joints, urging the dead flesh to move.

"No." The word tore from Yala's throat, guttural and

desperate. "No. You can't have him."

"I already do."

If Yala hadn't been too dizzy and numb to feel an appropriate level of fear, she might not have replied to the voice, but as it was, she gasped out, "Then leave his body alone."

Whether his spirit had truly been devoured by the god of death was unclear, but she would not allow Mekan to manipulate Machit's corpse like those monstrosities in the library.

"Brave words, from a human. Would you like me to bring him back?"

Yala recoiled as the implication sank in. The god of death was offering her a bargain ... and it was anyone's guess as to what He might demand in return.

"You!" The shriek came from Melian, who stalked towards Yala with a manic glint in her eyes. "Don't you *dare* take what is mine."

"Yours?" It took every bit of Yala's remaining strength to keep her head upright and meet Melian's fury head-on. "Do you claim ownership over the god of death?"

She half-expected another response from the disembodied voice, but a deafening screech from somewhere outside made even Melian look over her shoulder for the source. Nearby, screams mingled with the growls of a wild animal. Yala hadn't imagined the sound of a war drake, but how had one flown into the middle of the city?

Melian whipped around. "We will finish this later, Mekan."

The chilling presence withdrew in a flurry of shadow that left Machit's body limp once more, and Yala's strength gave out. The last thing she saw before her consciousness faded was the final remnant of shadow departing like a curtain closing on the world.

———

As the inhuman voice spoke, the war drake let out a screech that forced Kelan to cover his ears. Niema swayed on the spot, her whistling faltered, and the beast's claws swiped perilously close to her face.

"Niema." He reached for her arm to pull her out of the way, but she shook her head.

"It's afraid. It's not listening to me anymore."

The beast's wings spread wide, and it launched into flight —above the rooftops, and towards the wall to the upper city.

"Niema!" Ignoring her noise of protest, Kelan seized her around the middle and lifted her into the air again. "The guards aren't at the gates. If it gets into the upper city—"

"I know!" Niema squirmed. "I don't know if it can hear me."

"Gods." Kelan moved in behind the war drake and willed the god of the sky to send a gust of power towards the beast's wings. His aim wasn't as strong as when he used his hands, but both arms were occupied trying to keep Niema from slipping. To his relief, a ball of air slammed into the war drake's beating wings, knocking its path off course.

Kelan's second attack reached its mark but had the unfortunate effect of turning the war drake's attention towards him instead. The beast turned midflight, claws swiping at Kelan, and he dodged, breathing a plea to the sky god to loan him all the strength necessary to avoid a gruesome death.

Though given that awful voice he'd heard inside the pleasure house, he wasn't sure that being torn to shreds by an angry war drake was the worst possible outcome of the night.

Niema whistled again, high and shrill, and this time the war drake's head turned to her. At another whistle, its flight path turned away from the upper city. Kelan's shoulders slumped in relief, and in several beats of its huge wings, the beast departed the way it had come, a winged shape merging into the dark sky.

As they descended, they found the crowd around the pleasure house had dissipated, leaving a grisly trail of blood and body parts in their wake. The war drake had certainly done an effective job ripping into the mercenaries, but where was their leader?

Niema took a shaky step towards the doorway. "Is Yala alive in there?"

"Let's find out."

———

When Yala's consciousness returned, she found Saren peering down at her, his eyes clouded with confusion. *Good. He's alive.*

"Yala?" he rasped. "Was … was that a war drake?"

"More than a war drake." That voice she'd heard … she might have believed it to be a product of her imagination if not for the agonising throb in her leg that had permeated the experience.

Yala could scarcely lift her head without her body reminding her of every blow she'd taken, but she didn't see any sign of Niema, nor did she expect her to heal all the damage. Especially if Niema knew the god of death had offered her a bargain. She'd be horrified.

Saren let out a sound halfway between a howl and a sob as he crouched over Machit's body. Yala forced her head upright, wanting to confirm that the shadows that had temporarily infested Machit's corpse had fled … and they had, but so had the one who'd slaughtered him.

Melian was gone. Nobody remained in the room, the staff and clients having fled, until Niema and Kelan entered, taking in the carnage. Their clothes and faces were splattered with gore, and Kelan looked more shaken than Yala had ever seen him.

"So it *was* you." Yala made another attempt to rise and grabbed the nearest chair for balance. "The war drake."

"I was too late." Niema's desolate stare was stark in her blood-splattered face. "Where—where is their leader?"

"Melian?" Yala's mouth twisted. "She must have sneaked out in the confusion."

"Where the hells are the city guards?" Saren lifted his head from Machit's body, his eyes bloodshot. "Someone should have stopped this."

"Melian killed them," Yala answered. "The ones who were guarding the gates to the upper city, and presumably the ones patrolling the wall, too."

Were their rotting corpses roaming around, too? If so, at least the Disciples of the Flame would no longer be able to deny there was Corruption rampant in the capital, though if Superior Datriem knew that she'd interacted with the god of death, he'd probably douse her in holy fire on the spot.

"I'll tell them." Saren approached the hallway on unsteady feet. "Someone … someone has to, and I don't know where Giran is."

"What are you going to tell them?" Yala challenged. "That the god of death was walking around the pleasure district? They'll laugh in your face."

Saren flinched. Hot shame flooded her, and an apology rose to her tongue, inadequate, unvoiced.

Kelan cleared his throat. "And the war drake? If we admit we're the ones who lured it to the city, we'd get arrested for endangering the public."

"Make something up if you must." Yala clambered around the chair and managed to sink into it. "Whatever you do, don't let the blame slide away from Melian. She's the leader of the Successors."

"That's her name?" Saren swore. "What kind of revolutionary causes a massacre?"

"Someone who serves the god of death." Yala closed her eyes, rested her head against the back of the chair. "And who wants to punish me for defying her. This—it's all on me."

"The hell it is." Saren's voice cracked. "I'm the one who—shit, I've heard the Successors' name before, and I never made the connection. Someone mentioned they're building an army of vigilantes."

"An army of the dead?" Yala guessed. "There weren't enough of them to form an army, but if they kill enough people…"

"Fucking hell." Saren veered towards the door. "I'm going to find someone to report this to. They can't have killed every guard."

"I'll go with you," Kelan offered. "I can come up with a plausible story to explain the war drake's presence in the city."

He might cause more trouble in the process, but Yala was in too much pain and too exhausted to go with them. As the pair departed, Niema came to her chair, her face a mask of concern. "You're hurt."

"I'll live." Machit wouldn't be so lucky, and the image of his fingers twitching was all too vivid in her mind. "We … we have to burn the bodies. If Melian and the others come back…"

"They won't," Niema said. "Not tonight. They caused too much of a disturbance to go unnoticed."

"More because of the war drake than the death magic." She coughed, her body aching with each spasm.

"Let me help." Niema extended her hands over Yala's injured leg, whispering a prayer under her breath. Yala's rasped protest went unheard, and she stifled a moan of relief when the fiery pain faded to a dull ache.

Removing her hands, Niema slumped against the chair.

"You shouldn't have done that." Yala's aches remained, but at least she could put weight on her right foot without collapsing in agony. "How much life force did you give up today alone?"

She must have paid the price somehow, and there were no other living things inside the pleasure house except for the few survivors.

"Only a little," Niema said. "The god of life understands that some circumstances make it difficult for me to access Her power, and I have demonstrated my devotion enough times for Her to grant me some ... allowances."

"You saved my life." Before the war drake had arrived, Yala had been at Melian's mercy, and the knowledge awakened a rage she hadn't felt in a long time. *How* dare that deluded would-be revolutionary move into the city and terrorise everyone? How dare she kill Machit?

"I'm sorry I was too late for him." Niema's gaze followed hers to Machit's body. "I-I don't understand why Melian wanted to sacrifice you. You'd never met her before, had you?"

"You heard her, right?" Yala thought of the shadows that had crept over Machit's corpse, and the chilling voice that had tried to bargain with her. "She thinks that because I fought against Mekan's monsters on the island, I'm a more worthy sacrifice to her god than anyone else."

But is she right? The god of death had certainly responded to Melian's request, but how much of that had been Mekan's desire to claim her own life? That was the problem with bargaining with death. It always ended the same.

"She felt threatened by you." Niema sounded far more certain than Yala herself felt. "Since you already fought the dead and won."

Yala snorted. "Threatened? Hardly. Though now she's

given me a reason to be a threat to her."

The trouble was, they'd never located the Successors' base, and Melian might have fled anywhere in the city. Yala knew better than to believe she'd returned to somewhere as obvious as the library, though Yala herself had played a part in covering up the evidence of her collusion with the god of death when she and the others had destroyed those corpses.

The front door clicked open, and Kelan entered the room a moment later. He'd tried to clean the blood from his face but had only succeeded in smearing it into his hairline, and his cloak would likely never be its former colour again. Saren slunk in behind him, equally subdued.

"That was fast," said Yala. "What did the city guard have to say?"

Saren's shoulders slumped. "I don't think they believed us. We told them a group of cultists broke into the pleasure house and started a massacre, which is technically true, but the war drake raised some questions. I'm pretty sure they think the war drake was responsible for killing some guards on the wall, too."

"That was Melian," said Yala. "Though one of the guards she slaughtered was still walking, last I saw."

"What—?" Saren cut off with a noise of disgust as he realised what she'd implied. "What the fuck is wrong with her?"

"If you ask me, the only thing wrong with her is that she's not dead yet."

"She escaped," Kelan said unnecessarily. "Do you know where she went?"

"Unless she's even more unhinged than I thought, she won't have gone back to the library," Yala answered. "It's more likely that she has another hiding place, and I'm guessing the guards won't make finding her a priority if they think there's a wild drake attacking the city."

"I'm sorry," Niema said. "The beast was harder to control than I expected. The presence of death magic broke my spell over it."

"If you hadn't brought it here, Saren and I would be dead," said Yala. "And possibly the king, too."

"The *king?*" Saren gaped at her. "Melian planned to depose him?"

"You knew they claimed to be revolutionaries, didn't you?" Yala said. "They never mentioned that they planned to overthrow the ruling government by raising the dead."

Saren sank into a chair. "Gods. I shouldn't have stayed here while those people were hunting you, Yala."

"I'm the one who led them here," she said. "I thought they wanted me alive, but Melian…"

"She wanted to kill you." Saren spoke in a low, tortured voice. "And me, just because I was here. And Machit…"

"I told the guards that someone needs to clear away the bodies," Kelan said. "If they don't show up to collect the dead by morning, we can ask at the Temple of Flame—"

"Absolutely not." But who else had the ability to ensure nobody would be able to tamper with Machit's body?

Kelan's mouth pinched. "I'm sorry about your friend, but Saren is right. I'll talk to them myself and see if they'll listen."

He sounded sincere, for a wonder. Yala supposed anyone would have had a shakeup in their perspective after witnessing a sacrifice to the god of death.

Saren rose to his feet and heaved a sigh. "I need to find Giran, but if he figures out that I'm the one who brought a war drake to the doorstep, I'll be out on the street."

"I can help clean up the blood." Yala's own culpability wouldn't allow her to sit idle. "Then we'll find somewhere else to lie low until we can figure out where those Successors are hiding."

20

The streets were slick with blood. Kelan's feet didn't touch the ground, but it made no difference; crimson already soaked his ruined cloak, and his rising nausea didn't make it any easier for him to think clearly.

Saren had offered Kelan a room to stay in, but he'd declined. He needed to go back to the inn and see if any of his fellow Disciples were around—but he'd also *killed* one of them. If they'd discovered Senik's body yet, he'd find himself in a bind that even he couldn't explain his way out of. Worse, Senik wasn't the only Disciple who Superior Sietra had sent into the capital. If Laima was following the same orders and had heard the same rumour, he had to explain the truth before *she* went after Yala, too.

The war drake had left a trail of gore in its wake, and the mercenaries' bodies lay in a sea of severed limbs and split skulls. He kept his eyes on the sky, but the scenes were already etched deeply enough into his mind that he knew they'd be the first thing he'd see when he closed his eyes.

Along with Senik's lifeless corpse. *Hells. Why didn't he listen to me?*

Twice, he had to stop to retch in an alleyway before he flew over the wall to the upper city. There, he was somewhat relieved to see guards converging on the gate. No doubt they'd found the bodies of their fellow guards, slain at Melian's hand.

If her plan had succeeded, she might well have tried the same at the palace next. It was in no way *his* responsibility to stop a violent revolutionary from overthrowing the monarch—in fact, if not for the involvement of Corruption, he had little doubt that Superior Sietra would have ordered him to leave the city altogether and let the king deal with the political upheaval himself.

As it was, who other than a Disciple could possibly bring about an end to Melian's scheme? For that reason, he needed to pay the Disciples of the Flame another visit, but they wouldn't appreciate being disturbed at this hour, and Melian herself had long disappeared into the night.

Instead, he entered the Disciples' Inn, where the innkeeper who greeted him at the door took in his bloody clothes and face in shock. "Disciple ... what happened to you?"

"Trouble in the lower city," he muttered, unable to think of a story possibly for the first time in his life. "I don't suppose you could draw me a bath?"

At least the inn kept spare clothes for Disciples, because his cloak was ruined, and his shirt and trousers weren't much better. Viscera and blood splattered him from head to toe, and with shaking hands, he peeled off his cloak, wishing he could as easily strip away the memory of Senik's death—and of the chilling voice he'd heard inside the pleasure house.

Mekan. He had no doubt to whom the voice belonged, but the gods didn't *speak*, not even to their worshippers.

Divine tongues were not for mortal ears to hear, but they had, and whatever Yala had experienced inside that room would make the war drake's rampage seem inconsequential.

Someone knocked on his door. He tensed, hand reaching for his weapon, but it was only the innkeeper asking if he wanted anything to eat. He declined and asked for the strongest liquor she had to offer, which might be the only thing that would help him get any sleep that night.

"Ah—let me know if any of the other guests come back," he added, thinking of Laima. He had to start somewhere, and with the state he was in, it'd be difficult for her to accuse him of lying.

I think. If she'd been given the same false information on Yala, she might act as Senik had and proclaim him a traitor and Yala a Disciple of Death. *Where* he'd got that idea … well, the rumours he'd heard from the mercenaries on the road had been as outrageous, but Corruption was a real and present threat in the capital.

Superior Sietra was the person to talk to, but she was out of reach, back at Skytower. She'd also sent him here to complete a mission, and while she was positively undemanding compared to the likes of Superior Datriem, he was also fairly sure she'd never had to deal with one of her Disciples *murdering* another one.

Until his visit to the Temple of the Flame, Kelan had forgotten how it had felt before he'd experienced the surety of the sky god's presence in his life. He'd been far below the qualifying age when he'd first figured out that the Disciples of the Sky paid annual visits to the towns and villages of southwest Laria in search of new recruits, and he'd known Skytower was his only way out of poverty. He'd waited for them every year until they finally took notice, giving him a test to see if Terethik answered his will. When He did, Kelan had gladly thrown himself on the sky god's mercy, but luckily for him, all Terethik required of His Disciples was for them to participate in a weekly prayer and a handful of annual ceremonies. There were no overly complicated rules or contradictory requirements to contend with, and even before they took their vows, Kelan and his fellow novices had spent hours hurling themselves off the highest floor of Skytower, trusting that the god of the sky would catch them on the way down. He'd never had reason to doubt his deity *or* his fellow Disciples.

Now, though, he found himself holding his breath every time he heard footsteps on the stairs, convinced that someone had come to take him to account for his crimes. After he'd scrubbed every trace of blood off his skin until the bathwater turned red, he positioned himself in the upper corridor to wait for his fellow Disciples' return.

At some point he must have given in to exhaustion, because he woke with a blade a mere finger span from his throat. His eyes jerked open, and he flung a handful of air in the direction of his attacker. A yell and a thump sounded, and he lifted his head to see a bemused Laima staggering down the corridor.

"Ouch!" Laima pressed a hand to the back of her head. "What—were you sleeping in my doorway?"

"Oh." The sour taste of liquor at the back of his throat told him it had been several hours since his return, and he'd fallen asleep outside her room. "Sorry."

"Honestly." She scowled down at him. "You're drunk, aren't you?"

"No ... yes, but that's not the point." He pushed to his feet, grimacing at the renewed ache in his leg. The injury hadn't healed, which was unsurprising, given that he'd had little opportunity to rest in the last three days. "Did you hear what happened last night?"

"It's still night, Kelan." She breezed past him and elbowed

him out of the way of the door—none too gently. "If you were hoping I'd be in the mood to invite you into my bed, you're mistaken."

"That's not..." Given her tone, she hadn't found Senik's body. Yet. "Where have you been all night?"

Laima laughed. "That, Kelan, is none of your business whatsoever."

"Wait." His hoarse objection, combined with his hand on the door frame, prompted her to turn around. "There's something you should know. Someone in the city is dabbling in Corruption, but it isn't who you might think it is."

She stared at him for an instant. "Really, Kelan? This is ridiculous even for you."

"It's true," he said, somewhat put out, though the fuzziness of his thoughts told him the liquor had worked a little too well at taking the edge off the night's events. "Superior Sietra sent me to investigate Corruption. That's the truth."

"That doesn't explain why you're drunkenly sleeping in my doorway."

"You really didn't see any of it?" Incredulity crept into his voice. Yes, the capital was a large city, but how had she possibly missed the chaos on the other side of the upper city gates? "Even the wild drake?"

"Oh, that?" she said. "Yes, I heard some of the guards talking about a wild drake attacking the inner wall. I suppose it was hungry enough to risk getting shot at."

He swallowed. Hard. "The war drake didn't kill the guards. The Disciples of Death did."

"Right, Kelan," she said flatly. "I think you should go back to your own room."

"I will, but if you hear the name 'Yala'—"

She shut the door on him. *That went well.* She hadn't heard of Senik's death, so he'd been spared—for now—but he'd made a mistake in coming back here at all, even if he'd got a hot bath and free liquor out of it. He ought to have been searching for Melian's hiding place … but was a regular Disciple a match for a servant of the god of death?

Superior Sietra might know, but to find out the truth about what *she* believed, he'd have to go back to Skytower.

———

Yala's resolution to help clean up the aftermath of the massacre lasted until she was so exhausted that Niema had all but ordered her to go to bed. It said a lot for her level of exhaustion that she hadn't argued back, and when she'd collapsed onto her sleeping mat, she'd fallen into a mercifully dreamless sleep.

When she came downstairs around dawn, she found Saren half-lying in the hallway, a bucket of bloody water at his side. The last she'd seen, he'd claimed he was going to clean up the mess in the hopes of avoiding retaliation from Giran for the damages, but that'd been hours ago. He was trembling, his hands rubbed raw from scrubbing the blood out of the floors.

"That's enough," she said. "You don't need to punish yourself."

"Look who's talking," he muttered to the ceiling. "You've spent the past few years punishing yourself for what happened to Dalem."

Yala grabbed the damp cloth next to his hand and swatted him on the back of the head. "That doesn't make me an example to follow."

"Old habits are hard to break." He grabbed the cloth from her. "Why are you awake at this hour?"

"Old habits are hard to break," she mimicked him—they'd always risen early as soldiers, dragged out of bed for physical training drills. "I couldn't sleep."

Niema didn't seem to have the same problem; she hadn't stirred as Yala had clattered around their shared room sorting through the contents of her pack in search of clean clothes, but she'd thoroughly exhausted herself yesterday by healing Yala right after the battle.

"I still don't know where Giran ran off to." Saren straightened upright and peered into the room in which Melian had attempted her sacrifice. "He's not among the dead. Neither are the other staff. They have better survival instincts than we do."

Yala's gut tightened. "Where are the bodies?"

"Back there." He gestured to an alcove, where the bodies of Machit and the other unfortunates had been wrapped in the ruined, bloodstained curtains, presumably by Saren himself. The rest of the room looked rather bare, with the furniture moved aside to make it easier to scrub the floors, but it was a marked improvement to the mess Melian had left it in.

The front door opened, prompting Yala to lift her cane in warning, but it was only Kelan. He'd washed the blood off himself at some point during the night, but he didn't look as if he'd slept more than she had.

"Haven't you heard of knocking?" asked Saren.

"I rather thought you'd be reluctant to answer the door, considering the circumstances." He ran a hand through his damp hair, which straggled loose to his shoulders. "This place looks much cleaner than it did last night."

"If you overlook the body bags." Yala paced over to the window and peered outside into the street. Someone had washed away the blood, presumably the city guards, but nobody had come back for the bodies. "Might need to remind the guards to take them away."

Or the Disciples of the Flame, but that would be a last resort.

"Wise idea," said Saren. "If we leave it too long, will the bodies end up like…?"

"Like those people we found in the library?" Unbidden, she glanced at the curtain-wrapped corpses, her imagination conjuring up images of twitching limbs. "I don't have the slightest idea how the god of death's magic works, contrary to what some people seem to assume."

Dragging her gaze away, she watched as Saren lifted the bucket of water and carried it through the hallway to an open door at the back which led into an alleyway. On the left was a set of living quarters that she assumed must be reserved for the staff, though Kelan wasted no time in walking into the carpeted room and planting himself in an armchair. *He's going to make himself at home in here, is he?*

Yala cleared her throat. "Did you speak to any of your fellow Disciples?"

"Yes." He tilted his head back and addressed the ceiling. "Briefly."

"And?" she prompted. "Remember the other Disciple of the Sky we ran into on the road? We found his body in the upper city."

"Ah." Kelan lowered his head but didn't quite meet her eyes. "He confronted me last night, and … and I killed him. I can only assume the guards blamed his death on the war drake or our runaway cultists, because so far nobody has come after me."

"Oh." Considering the upheaval of the night before, she'd forgotten all about the Disciple whose body they'd found in the upper city. "Did he explain why he attacked us?"

He drew in a breath. "He seemed to be under the impression that *you* were the one dabbling in Corruption, not Melian."

Yala stared at him and then gave a humourless laugh. "That explains a lot."

"You're joking?" Saren entered the room, dripping water all over the carpet. "Who in their right mind would believe that crap?"

"You'd be surprised," Kelan murmured, addressing the ceiling once more. "I heard some equally implausible rumours on the road from superstitious mercenaries who were convinced you made a habit of devouring men's hearts."

"Fucking *Melian*." The Successors' leader must have started the rumours, intending to divert the other Disciples' attention. She was too clever by half, and worse, she'd never wanted Yala alive.

"I tried to warn the other Disciple staying at the inn that she might run into similar rumours," Kelan added. "Unfortunately, she didn't seem inclined to listen to me."

"Is there a reason she didn't believe you?" Yala asked. "Do you make a habit of telling outrageous stories?"

He ran a hand over his face. "Hardly outrageous. Maybe one or two were, a little."

Yala rolled her eyes and left the room, mostly so she wouldn't give in to the temptation to vent her frustration upon him. It wasn't Kelan's fault his fellow Disciples had believed Melian's rumours, but it would have been nice if at least some of the city's Disciples were on their side. Though Kelan had also killed one of his fellow Disciples defending her, and accident or not, there'd be consequences to pay.

She entered the room that contained the bodies and counted three, four, mercenaries in addition to Machit himself. Melian had lost a few followers the previous night, at least, but Machit hadn't deserved to die at her hand. While a quick death was preferable to a slow death of a festering wound, he shouldn't have been there at all.

Saren walked to her side, drawing his arms across his chest. "I wonder … where did Melian and her followers get the idea that *you* were dabbling in Corruption?"

The accusatory note to his tone had no business being there. "I have no fucking clue, Saren. You were there on the island. You saw the same as I did."

"I—" He faltered. "I wasn't trying to imply you'd ever... I know you wouldn't. Not after Dalem."

It was the first time he'd uttered their mutual friend's name in years, and Yala's heart contracted. She looked down at the newly scrubbed floor to avoid meeting his eyes. "We burned every trace of that temple to the ground. Nothing was left."

How, then, had Melian learned to call upon the god of death? Without any ill effects, even? Every Rafragorian soldier who'd set foot on the island had died. The god of death had devoured them.

Yala looked up and found the same question in Saren's eyes. Drawing in a breath, she held his gaze. "I can think of one place that might have contained the information. It's right here in the city."

Saren shook his head, uncomprehending. "I don't follow."

"We know King Tharen was researching Corruption." As she'd expected, Saren flinched at the word. "Maybe someone else found his notes, like a disgruntled employee. Remember the Successors' goal is to dethrone the king, and if he's that unpopular with the public, he must have enemies inside the palace as well."

"Then..." Saren trailed off. "Shouldn't we, I don't know, warn him? I don't care for King Delial much, but being murdered by the dead isn't a fate I'd wish on anyone."

"Precisely," said Yala. "Which is why I'm going to the palace myself."

21

W hen Niema awoke, she started her day with an extensive prayer to the goddess of life as a thanks for the power She had given Niema yesterday. She might not be able to hear her enclave members' heartbeats alongside hers, but she prayed to them, too, knowing that they had played a part in loaning her their strength.

When Niema went downstairs, she found that the blood had been scrubbed off the floors and the bodies moved elsewhere. Another door lay ajar on the left of the stairs, revealing several armchairs clustered on a carpeted floor.

Yala's cane beat steadily on the carpeted floor as she paced inside the room, and she acknowledged Niema's presence with a grunt. "I bought you new clothes from the market."

"You bought—what?" Niema glanced down at her garment, which was admittedly a little worse for wear by this point.

"In here." Kelan lifted his head from where he half lay in an armchair, his feet propped on a low table. Despite his relaxed pose, his eyes were as grim and tired as Yala's. "She was on the brink of getting herself into trouble again, so I persuaded her to run some errands instead."

"Have some gratitude," Yala said. "I bought breakfast, too."

Several plates lay upon a table, containing a selection of food that Niema had never encountered before. Most people in the capital likely did not have the time or resources to prepare their own food, so markets had sprung up on every corner selling hot soup in containers, fried meat on skewers of dubious quality, and balls of soft fried dough flavoured with an unfamiliar spice that made Niema cough when she bit into one.

"Where's Saren?" She reached for one of the wooden cups that lay among the plates. At first, Niema assumed they contained liquor, but a closer sniff revealed a fragrance of herbs boiled in water.

"I think he's looking for the owner of this place," Kelan said. "Assuming he ever comes back. Mass murder is bad for business."

Niema had no argument, so she finished her breakfast and then picked up the clothing Yala had acquired for her, which consisted of a pair of trousers and a thin shirt with flowing sleeves that would be handy for keeping the midday sun off her shoulders. The city might be enclosed in some areas, but parts were still more exposed than the thick canopies of the jungle.

"Unexpectedly thoughtful of her, if you ask me," Kelan remarked, seeing Niema examine the clothes. "I notice she didn't buy *me* anything."

"You get your clothes for free," Yala responded. Despite the tired lines underneath her eyes, she looked much better than she had when she'd lain beaten and bleeding on the floor the previous evening. "Try them on. Then we'll go to the upper city."

Niema tucked the clothing over her arm. "Why the upper city?"

"Yala wants to remind the city guard to come and pick up the bodies," Kelan said. "Or the Disciples of the Flame, depending on who's most likely to listen."

"You aren't going there yourself, are you?" she asked Yala. "After yesterday, you should keep a low profile."

"Oh, she doesn't know the meaning of the words." Kelan removed his feet from the table. "She's got it into her head that she has to warn the *king*."

"Someone has to." Yala's jaw set. "He might not want a war, but that's exactly what he'll get if he lets the Successors continue to recruit people to their schemes."

Niema frowned. "Would you get to talk directly to the king yourself?"

"I doubt he's taking visitors," said Yala. "However, someone ought to send warning that he had a narrow escape last night. I expect that if Melian had successfully killed me, he'd have been her next target."

"How did she plan on getting into the palace?" Saren came into view. "I suppose her army of the dead could have taken out the guards, but what then? For that matter, what does she plan to do when she's in power?"

"I don't know that she's thought that far ahead," Yala said. "Whatever the case, one of us needs to warn the king."

"I hope they believe us." Niema thought back to her earlier visit to the Temple of the Flame and supressed a shudder. "I can talk to Superior Datriem myself. I know he's unlikely to be of much help, but he should at least send someone to remove the bodies."

"Or he'll send you back to the library." Kelan rose from his seat. "I'll go with you. He won't be able to dupe two of us at once."

"He might try," said Yala. "Though I'd like to know if he'll try to wriggle out of responsibility again."

Niema's mouth parted. Strangely, she didn't mind the idea of Kelan being there. If nothing else, he wouldn't be as easily intimidated by the Superior's display of his powers. *Or maybe he will. We're both without access to our own abilities inside that temple.*

Yala going to the temple was out of the question, both due to Superior Datriem's prior threats and due to Melian and her allies being elsewhere in the city. After Niema had gone upstairs to change into her new clothes, she returned to the hallway to find Saren loudly objecting to Yala leaving at all, but he caved in when Yala pointed out that Melian was as likely to show up at the pleasure house again as anywhere else.

"If you see any signs of trouble, go and hide in the under-city," she told Saren as they were leaving. "Machit's friends are down there, they'll help you."

"All right." He stood back to watch them leave, one hand resting on the doorframe.

Someone had cleaned up the street outside, washing away the blood and removing the bodies, but Niema's stomach turned whenever she caught the faint stench of decay, mingling with the smell of the river.

The streets leading to the upper city entrance were unusually quiet, while the guards initially refused to let them through the gate until Kelan and Niema revealed their Disciple status.

"The cheek of it," Yala muttered when they reached the other side. "I'm the reason they aren't corpses like the guards Melian killed."

"Be glad they aren't blaming you instead," Kelan said, earning a glare from both her and from Niema. "What? It's true."

Despite the relative quiet of the outer city, the central region was its usual chaotic entity, with crowds of workers and merchants filling the streets. The crowd bothered Niema less than it had the previous day, but all she could think of when they passed the bustling market stands was how narrow an escape these people had had.

So had they, for that matter. Nothing Superior Kralia had told Niema had prepared her for the reality of encountering the god of death face to face, while Yala's narrow escape made her claims that her survival on the island had been a matter of chance seem less unlikely to Niema than they had previously.

When they emerged into Ceremonial Square, Kelan nodded to Niema. "Ready?"

She did her best to squash down the panic squeezing her chest. "I hope Superior Datriem is willing to listen to us this time."

Kelan's doubtful countenance mirrored her own, though navigating the crowd was much easier for Kelan than for her, as most people took one glance at his cloak and stepped out of the way of his gliding path. They reached the steps to the temple before Niema had mentally prepared herself for the prospect of facing the Superior again.

Kelan knocked, and as before, an orange-robed novice answered the door. "May I help you?"

"I hope you can," Kelan answered. "We need to talk to Superior Datriem. We also need to arrange funerary rites for several individuals. You may have heard from the city guard already that there was a massacre in the pleasure district."

"A *massacre?*" echoed the novice.

"Isn't that the term used to describe a large number of violent deaths?"

Niema shot him an exasperated look, wishing she'd come alone instead of leaving him to handle a delicate situation with all the finesse of a rampaging war drake. She cleared her throat. "It's true, and we need help."

The novice withdrew, but while Niema stayed on the doorstep rather than crossing the threshold, Kelan didn't appear concerned that entering the temple would cut off access to his own magic. Holding the door open with one hand, he peered into the hall, from the towering windows to the balconies and the large altar at the back.

"What are you doing?" Niema whispered.

"Looking around," Kelan said out of the corner of his mouth. "I didn't get to see much of the temple before."

"This isn't an idle jaunt, Kelan. These people are dangerous."

"I'm aware." His fingers curled around the door frame, while his feet were firmly planted on the ground. Otherwise, he showed no signs of discomfort at being deprived of his magic. "This might be our last chance to look, considering…"

His words trailed off when Superior Datriem himself approached them. While the Superior was dressed as impeccably as ever, half-moons underlaid his eyes that made her wonder if he'd had a night as restless as their own.

"Back again?" He looked between the two of them. "I'm told you require our assistance with funerary rites?"

Niema dipped her head. "Yes, at—"

"At the pleasure district in the outer city," Kelan finished, pointing behind him. "It might also interest you to know that some of them were attempting to make a sacrifice to the god of death."

"Did they?" To Niema's consternation, Superior Datriem scarcely blinked. "They were unsuccessful, I take it."

"Actually, no." Kelan's tone was casual, but a spark appeared in the depths of Superior Datriem's eyes that sent a quiver of dread through Niema's nerves.

Kelan surely saw too, but he pressed on regardless. "The

conspirators succeeded in gaining the attention of the god of death. If not for the quick intervention of our Disciple of Life, we wouldn't have survived. However, some escaped, and I believe it's your Temple's responsibility to help us hunt them down."

The Superior's lips compressed. "*My* responsibility? I thought the two of you were sent by your respective Superiors to investigate this issue."

Niema gaped at him. No longer was he denying the threat existed, but his casual unconcern was somehow worse than outright denial. He and the other Disciples of the Flame might be safe from the dead behind their secure doors, but the same was not true of the rest of the city.

"I thought you said there was no evidence of Corruption," said Kelan. "Which turned out to be untrue. In fact, we found an attempted ritual to the god of death inside the public library—which if memory serves, is the place you told Niema to go in order to research the subject. Strange coincidence, don't you think?"

The spark in Superior Datriem's eyes darkened to a flame, and Niema's throat went dry.

"I'd consider your position carefully before you make accusations," he said. "Perhaps you should look more closely at your own allies instead."

"What does that mean?" Kelan hissed out a breath when the door closed in his face. "He knows. He *must* know."

"What are we supposed to do if he does?" Niema backed away from the temple's doors, her heart swooping downward. "Did you have to challenge him to his face?"

"Yes." There wasn't a hint of humour in his voice. "He's unfit for his position, if not an outright conspirator himself. We don't have the authority to remove his status, but he can't be left where he is."

Niema threw her hands up in exasperation. "Is now really

a good time to remove the leader of the one branch of Disciples who can stop Melian?"

"Probably not," Kelan said, "but I think it's time I went back to Skytower to ask my own Superior for aid with the next step."

————

Yala approached the gates slowly, using her cane to navigate the crowd thronging Ceremonial Square. The palace itself loomed over its north side, an impressive structure of towering stone adorned with murals and decorated with layers of flowers that certainly hadn't been there when King Tharen had been in charge. The statues of past monarchs remained on either side of the stone stairs leading to the doors, as did the two armoured guards standing outside the towering gates, sweating in their thick drakeskin clothes. One, a female guard with the bronze skin tone of a northern Larian, accosted Yala. "You look familiar."

"I'm Yala Palathar," she said. "I'm here to talk to the king, or to a representative, about a possible threat to His Majesty's safety."

"Yala Palathar?" Her gaze dropped to Yala's cane, then lingered on the scar on her face. "I've heard your name several times recently, and never in a pleasant context."

People in the palace complex had been talking about her? *Please tell me they didn't pick up on Melian's ridiculous rumour about me dabbling in Corruption.*

"First I've heard," she said. "If I can't talk directly to His Majesty myself, I'd appreciate it if someone passed on my warning. I don't know if you heard about the incident last night, in the pleasure district…"

"If you're concerned that His Majesty might be in danger

from rampaging war drakes, let me reassure you that the palace is well protected."

Against the dead, though? "It's not the war drake that concerns me. You might have heard of the group calling themselves the Successors. I ran into them last night—"

The second guard, an ebony-skinned man with a shaved head, turned sharply towards her. "Ran into them, did you? Or do you mean to say you attended a meeting?"

"They tried to kill me." She didn't have to tell them everything, but she'd infuse enough truth into her words to sound convincing. "The woman in charge—Melian—she claimed she wanted to overthrow the monarch, and based on what I saw of her, she's certainly mad enough to try."

The male guard grunted. "They'll have to get in behind the other thousands of people with the same complaints."

Right. Nobody is satisfied with the current state of things, so why would Melian's people be any different? "They claim to have the allegiance of the god of death, and I have reason to believe they were telling the truth."

The two guards exchanged sceptical looks, and the woman grunted. "These revolutionaries will say anything to get people to follow their lead."

Yala stifled a sigh. "Whether you believe me or not, I need you to pass on a message. If not to the king, then … I don't know if either of you know Viam Tiathar, but she was part of my squad in the army. She works at the palace."

"I know her," said the male guard. "Quiet, scholarly type. Can't you speak to her yourself?"

"I don't know where she lives," said Yala. "If either of you see her, can you tell her I'm staying in the pleasure district in the outer city?"

For now, anyway. It was anyone's guess as to how long it would be before Melian returned for a second attempt to sacrifice Yala to her god, but Viam might not have any interest in talking to her regardless. No more than Yala desired to speak to Viam herself, but if Melian's source of knowledge on death magic had come from inside the palace, Viam was bound to end up involved sooner or later.

Viam had been on the island as well. She might have left the rest of the squad behind, but like the rest of them, she knew what Corruption was capable of.

22

After making her way back from the palace gates, Yala found Kelan and Niema outside the Temple of the Flame, staring at its closed doors as if hoping the place would catch alight. A sentiment Yala could get behind. "Your visit went well, then?"

Niema turned to her. "Superior Datriem shut the door in our faces."

"He also implied our own allies are more of a concern than the Successors," added Kelan. "I can't say I know if he was referring to you or to the other Disciples."

"How inconvenient," she commented. "Please tell me he at least offered to send someone to remove the bodies."

"No," said Niema. "Instead, he foisted the responsibility of rooting Corruption out of the city onto us. Did you manage to talk to anyone at the palace?"

"Yes, but it sounds as if His Majesty already has a substantial number of enemies, so I can't guarantee they'll make this one a priority." She glanced over at the towering expanse of the palace complex, wondering how well defended it truly was.

"That's not a surprise, given the general state of affairs," Kelan remarked. "I expect they're used to fending off dissidents."

"Fending off the dead, though?" Yala shook her head. "I don't know what more proof I can give them if Melian herself remains in hiding. They think she's a revolutionary spreading tall tales—which is a little better than believing *me* a Disciple of Death, I grant."

Niema's gaze roved over the tall windows of the temple. "I confess, I thought the word of Superior Kralia would have had more impact on Superior Datriem than it did. Would the other Disciples be more inclined to listen if he wasn't there, do you think?"

"I doubt he ever leaves the temple," Kelan said. "No, I think the quickest way to find more Disciples is for me to fly home to Skytower and speak to Superior Sietra."

"You're leaving?" Niema sounded surprised, but Yala wasn't. He'd already offered more help than she expected, and while their list of allies was dwindling, it was nice to imagine this Superior Sietra would be willing to send backup. *Or not, given that Kelan* killed *one of them.*

"I can fly, remember?" he said. "You won't be deprived of me for too long."

Yala gave him an eyeroll, though despite his light tone, the grimness from the previous night hadn't faded from his eyes. "If you're sure, then go. I have a possible ally to speak to, too, an old friend who works in the palace. I asked the guards to let me know if they see her."

"You have a friend who works for the king?" Niema asked.

"I don't know how close she is to him, but yes, she took a job inside the palace complex after leaving the army," said Yala. "The guards didn't believe my warning, but Viam ought to be willing to listen."

If I'm lucky. While part of her itched to hunt down Melian, wherever she was hiding, she didn't know where to start. Besides, with Kelan gone and Saren in no fit state to fight off any more attackers, she didn't want to get herself and Niema killed for no reason.

What else was there to do? Yala racked her thoughts and then landed on the undercity. Did Nahen and the others know Machit was dead? If not, she'd have to pass on the bad news herself.

That will hit them hard. They worship him down there.

A familiar churning grief arose within her at the thought, and she gripped her cane tightly. The others deserved to hear the truth from her, and at least talking to the undercity folk would distract her from the frustration of Melian's escape.

Niema shifted. "Are there any other Disciples in the city I can talk to? Outside of the Temple of the Flame?"

"Well…" Kelan paused. "There's at least one staying at the inn, but she's not the cooperative sort. Not with me, at any rate."

"Does *she* know you killed one of your fellow Disciples?" Yala asked.

Niema flinched. "He did *what?*"

"The man who attacked our wagon tried to ambush him yesterday," Yala clarified, having forgotten that Niema hadn't been present when he'd arrived at the pleasure house that morning. "He believed Melian's lies."

Niema's mouth parted, her gaze darting towards Kelan, whose lips twisted in a scowl. "Nobody else knows but us, and I'd prefer to keep it that way until I can explain myself to Superior Sietra."

I hope he knows what he's doing. Yala hadn't the faintest clue how the Disciples of the Sky punished transgressors, since they dealt with matters within their own ranks without deferring to an outside force, but he must be willing to take the risk of punishment.

Niema's mouth tightened with disapproval. "I'll talk to your companion."

"That doesn't strike me as a good idea," Kelan said. "She might not be alone—though my people would never attack a Disciple of Life."

The man Kelan had killed had attacked their wagon, but Yala decided against reminding him. After all, the Disciples of the Flame certainly wouldn't help, and the other Disciples were too distant for them to reach. "If you want to find me, I'll be with Saren."

Yala left Kelan and Niema in the upper city and made her way back to the gates, skirting market stalls and flocks of well-dressed upper-class folk who seemed a world away from the filth and desperation in the undercity. She did see more guards than the previous day, patrolling atop the wall and around the square. *It would have been nice if they'd been that attentive last night.*

Once she passed through the gate to the outer city, the signs of discontent began to make themselves seen. The number of boarded-up buildings had grown notably in the past few years, while the crowds of workers were somewhat shabbier-looking than the merchants and nobles in the upper city, their clothes stained with the grime that seemed to linger everywhere in the city. Even the sweat Yala wiped from the hand that held her cane had a greyish tint.

At the entrance to the undercity, the bearded man from the last time came to accost her. "Back again, Captain Yala? What did you do with Machit?"

He doesn't know. "You didn't hear?"

"Hear what?" Nahen asked.

She swallowed against her dry throat. "I thought you

would have heard. There was an attack in the pleasure district last night, and he was killed."

"Who was killed?" Another former soldier limped into view, lean and scarred. "Not Machit?"

"I'm sorry," said Yala. "I know a lot of you must have been close to him—wait, where's his ex-wife?"

"Back with her noble family, I expect." The scarred man scowled. "You'd better have a good explanation for this, *Captain* Yala. I thought you came to find your old friends, not get them killed."

What to say? It *was* her fault he was dead, at least partly. "The Successors killed him. Not me."

"What?" Nahen's expression darkened. "I thought they took him once already and gave him back."

"No, he escaped," she corrected. "This time he wasn't so lucky. Listen—did anyone new come down here last night?"

Might Melian be hiding out in the undercity? No guards patrolled this part of Dalathar, and hiding among the desperate was one way to avoid attention.

"New?" echoed the scarred man. "Like who?"

"The Successors' leader, Melian, escaped before I could take off her head for killing Machit." Explaining the rest would take too long, and there were a few hundred others down here who deserved to know what had happened to him as well. "I have no idea where she ran off to, but nobody's caught her yet. She killed some of the city guards, too."

"What's she look like?" asked Nahen.

"She's..." The trouble was that Melian didn't *look* particularly remarkable. Her manner of speaking and her attitude were what set her apart. "Clean. Larian, like us, with long brown hair and brown skin. Not an ex-soldier. She didn't have any obvious scars or injuries, and her way of speaking is more like a noble. She was dressed in a plain black cloak, nothing too fancy, though I think she's used to masquerading among the upper class."

"Isn't she more likely to be in the upper city, then?" queried Nahen.

"Yes, but I'm not taking any chances," said Yala. "She's plotting to overthrow the monarch, and after what her people did last night, I can believe she'll give it a fair shot."

"Overthrow the *king?*" The scarred man sounded intrigued. "With what army?"

An army of the dead. "She's smooth talking enough that she convinced a bunch of mercenaries to follow her. She killed Machit for getting in her way, and for all her talk of revolution, I don't think she gives a fuck about the undercity either."

"How'd he end up in her way?" asked the scarred man. "Your doing, I assume."

Yala's jaw tensed. "It's a long story, but it ended in a massacre at the pleasure district, and I have no reason to believe she won't try it again. This time it might be you who's in her way."

"Shit," said Nahen. "Well, if you want to look for her down here, I won't stop you."

"Thanks." She descended the stairs, glad that Niema had healed her leg enough that the climb wasn't as painful as the last time. "Is there anyone here Machit was particularly close to?"

She knew he didn't have family; like her, he'd been an orphan who'd joined the army under duress and had tried to run away a few times before Yala had convinced him he'd be better off sticking with her squad if he wanted to survive. Even she'd been surprised that he'd stayed after reaching the end of his compulsory service, but also like her, he'd had few prospects elsewhere.

Curious faces watched her from windows of the shacks as

she passed, many of whom she'd seen standing in line with her fellow soldiers at one time. Perhaps she was imagining the judgment in their stares, reprimanded her for abandoning them to their fates, but what could she have done? Handed over every coin she owned like Machit had? *That'd have been better than what I did do, I suppose.*

Guilt had driven her from the city. She'd failed to protect her squad, failed Dalem, and every moment she spent in Dalathar was a reminder that nothing she'd achieved had mattered a bit. Yet guilt had brought her back, too, and now it urged her to talk to these people. To hear their stories.

One person couldn't make up for the mistakes of so many others, she knew, but it was a start.

———

Kelan walked Niema to the Disciples' Inn and then departed, presumably to return home. A wild impulse urged Niema to ask him to take her with him—not to Skytower, but to a place outside of the city, somewhere quiet with clean air where she could sit and pray to Yalet in peace. The city made it hard to breathe, and part of her feared that if she stayed long enough, she'd lose her connection to both her enclave *and* her god.

That notion scared her more than any potential threat from Corruption, but she forced herself to focus on her mission, on her purpose.

Niema knocked on the door to the inn, and a matronly woman answered. She wasn't dressed as a Disciple, so she must be one of the inn's staff members. Niema hadn't known they employed non-Disciples, but she imagined the job must be well paid if they had to deal with Disciples like Kelan making constant demands on their attention.

"Excuse me," she began. "I'm Niema, a representative of the Disciples of Life."

"Looking for a place to stay?" The woman's brows rose. "I can't say we've ever hosted a Disciple of Life before."

"No—not yet." She hadn't given a thought as to whether she might want to find alternative accommodation to the room Saren had offered her; last night, she'd been lucky to have a bed to sleep in at all. *Or to be alive to see the dawn.* "I hoped that I might talk to some of your guests, if they're willing. I understand that Disciples of all kinds stay here, and I'm looking to consult with them on a mission from my Superior."

She blinked. "Well, you have good timing. Two guests just showed up. They're upstairs."

"Thank you." Niema accepted the invitation to enter and climbed the narrow stairway to the upper floor.

A door lay slightly ajar, affording her a view of a modest but pleasantly furnished guest room. Two blue-cloaked Disciples of the Sky, one male and the other female, turned towards her, and Niema gave a hasty bow.

"Greetings," she said. "I am Niema, of the Disciples of Life, and I am here on behalf of my enclave."

"A Disciple of Life?" The woman looked down at her, her dark hair curling to the nape of her neck. "Interesting. I'm Laima, and this is Tremin."

The man—broad and square jawed—gave a tight nod. Suspicion was etched into his features.

"It's a pleasure to meet you," said Niema. "I travelled here from my enclave in the southern jungle on the orders of Superior Kralia. Are you here on a similar mission?"

The man's brow twitched. "Mission?"

"Yes." Caution urged her to tread carefully, but she'd gain nothing by skirting around the subject. "I was sent here after my enclave received a warning from our god that there was a threat in the capital ... a threat from Corruption."

The word prompted a subtle change in atmosphere, as the Disciples' shoulders tensed and their hands shifted their cloaks aside, revealing identical curved blades at their waists.

"Corruption," said Laima. "Did you talk to Kelan about this?"

Kelan. Had they seen him from the window when he'd walked her to the inn's doors, or had she made a guess? Sweat gathered on the back of her neck; Niema was not a natural liar. "Kelan is on a similar mission, yes, but I'd like to talk to you. Have you seen any signs that someone in the capital is dabbling in death magic?"

"Death magic?" Tremin echoed. "You were with the agent of Corruption yourself: Yala Palathar."

A breeze lifted Niema's hair as if from an open window, but she knew better. One or both of the Disciples had called upon their god. "You're mistaken."

"I think not." Laima's lip curled. "Tremin has enlightened me on the company you keep. Kelan tried to spin me a tale of his own last night, but I was disinclined to believe him, and my instincts proved right."

"He..." *Gods. They think Yala is working with Corruption ... and Kelan, too.* "We met on the road, yes, but Yala isn't dabbling in Corruption, and Kelan is—"

"A murderer," Laima cut in. "Tremik tells me that the body of one of our Disciples was found earlier this morning in the upper city, with injuries that suggested he was dropped from a great height. Since the only other Disciple in the city at the time was Kelan, it's clearly his work."

Niema's skin went clammy, as if she was trapped within the crowd at Ceremonial Square, scarcely able to breathe. "I don't know anything about Kelan. I'm here to investigate

Corruption, and I would never have spent any time in Yala's company if I believed she was involved."

"Then you don't mind leading us to her?" said Tremin.

"She's innocent." Niema lifted her head, trying to ignore the glint of their weapons and the cold breeze stirring the air. "I'm a representative of the god of life herself, and She would never suffer to be in the company of Corruption. The god of life is incorruptible."

"But are you?" The woman drew her blade and pointed it at Niema. "I don't think so. Get into that room, and if you try to escape, I'll cut your throat."

23

A fter he'd left Niema at the inn, Kelan made his way
to the western edge of the city, reasoning that he'd
draw less attention that way. He would have taken
a shortcut over the wall, but the number of guards milling
around suggested the army was on the move after the attack
from the war drake last night, and he didn't want to be taken
as a threat.

He'd almost reached the gate to the outer city when he
heard footsteps behind him. An instant later, a sharp blade
kissed his throat.

"Going somewhere?" asked a feminine voice.

He tilted his head, an unpleasant sinking sensation in his
chest when he recognised the female mercenary whose
wagon he'd helped Yala steal on the road out of Setemar.
"What are you doing here?"

"In Dalathar? Or in the upper city?" Her blade shifted
against his neck, drawing a faint trickle of blood. "I imagine
you're surprised I managed to get here after you stole my
transport, you pathetic excuse for a Disciple."

"This is unnecessary," he said. "If you wanted to talk to me, you didn't have to put a knife to my throat."

"Ah, but we're getting paid for this, you see." She pressed harder until he jerked back, straight into the burly arms of one of her companions. The man's hands gripped Kelan's shoulders from behind, while the blade hovered a finger span from his neck.

"Paid for what?" He gritted his teeth as the man swivelled him around, the blade nicking the skin of his neck in the process.

"The Disciples of the Sky don't look kindly on taking the life of one of their own." The mercenary woman walked beside him while her companion manhandled him down the street. The tight grip on his shoulders and the blood trickling down his neck combined to quash all notions of escape.

"One of *my* people put you up to this?" he asked.

"You never know who you might meet on the road." Laughter entered her voice. "I can thank you for that, Kelan, since if you hadn't stolen my transport, I'd never have been able to take this job."

"You don't know what you're doing." *Shit.* His fellow Disciples wanted to enact punishment on him, no doubt, and not on Superior Sietra's orders either. She couldn't possibly know of Senik's death if his body hadn't been discovered by dawn, but if some others had already been on their way to the city, and had found him... "Who told you my name? Laima?"

"You did." Her breath hissed against his ear, close to the edge of the knife blade. "You never asked mine. It's Rianem."

"Pleasure to make your acquaintance," he said through gritted teeth, as a bead of blood trickled down his neck. "We could have come to an arrangement, you know. One that didn't involve you running off and leaving me to pay for your room."

She laughed softly. "Don't tell me you haven't tried that one before."

Their steps took them back to the inn, where he'd left Niema. Another unpleasant jolt hit him. *Niema.* If she'd said anything that had unwittingly given away the company she kept, she'd be in as much trouble as he was.

He had no chance of explaining himself to these mercenaries, though. They guided him to the door, at which point the man let go of his shoulders. "Go in."

No doubt he'd receive a knife in his back if he attempted to tell any of the staff he was here by duress, so he pushed the door inward and entered the inn. Nobody was in the entryway, but he heard voices upstairs, and recognised Niema's among them. *Gods.*

When Kelan began to climb the stairs, the voices ceased. At the top, Laima greeted him from an open door on his left. "Tried to sneak out of the city, did you?"

"To explain the events of last night to Superior Sietra," he said. "I didn't know you made a habit of hiring mercenaries."

"I didn't know you were the sort of scum who'd kill one of our own." She lifted a hand, conjuring a blast of air. Instinct drove him to defend himself and he caught her attack in his palm, causing both of them to stagger. He glimpsed another Disciple of the Sky behind Laima—Tremin, a brutish man who he'd always found unpleasant—and Niema, who sat with her back against the wooden bed, her arms bound behind her.

"Kelan," she gasped. "I tried to tell them you were innocent, but—"

"Quiet," growled Tremin. "You, get in here."

Kelan reached for his blade, with reluctance—he didn't want to worsen the situation more than he already had—but the other two had no such qualms. Twin blasts of air struck him in the chest one after another, and when his back hit the wall, Tremin's fist slammed into his gut so hard that the breath fled his lungs. Grasping the front of Kelan's coat, the other Disciple seized his blade at the hilt—Kelan tried to grab it, his fingers sliding over the sharp edge and drawing blood—but Tremin released his cloak and dealt an open-palm blow to his jaw.

Pain rang through Kelan's skull, and he heard Niema shouting his name from inside the room. Tossing Kelan's blade to Laima, Tremin seized his cloak again and hurled him over the threshold. When he tried to rise, two pairs of booted feet kicked his ribs repeatedly.

"Stop!" Niema shouted. "Stop hurting him. He's not—we're not what you think we are."

"Nobody else could have killed Senik." Laima stepped away from Kelan, leaving him struggling to catch his breath.

"I didn't—" he wheezed. "I *did* kill Senik, but he didn't give me much choice in the matter."

"What did he do, badmouth that Disciple of Death you're spending all your time with these days?" Laima queried. "I didn't believe you earlier, but you only told half the truth even then, didn't you? You saw Corruption with your own eyes because your ally is the one who used it."

"No." He coughed, spitting blood onto the floor. "The Successors—they're the ones dabbling in Corruption, and they wanted Yala to take the fall for them. Senik believed their rumours, and he would have killed her if I hadn't stopped him."

"It's true," Niema said from her position against the bed. "I think the Successors are putting out the rumour that Yala is a Disciple of Death to divert the blame from their own activities."

"I have to admit I didn't expect this kind of behaviour from a Disciple of Life," said Laima. "Granted, you've travelled with Kelan, which doesn't indicate good judgement."

"We're not friends," said Niema.

"Thanks." He pushed to his knees with one arm wrapped around his bruised ribs. "I told you the truth, Laima. Niema and I met on the road. We were both sent by our respective Superiors to find out if it was true that someone was dabbling in Corruption."

"It sounds more like you got into bed with it," said Laima.

"No!" She couldn't possibly have misinterpreted the situation more wrongly if she'd tried. "Absolutely not. Yala would throttle me before she let me bed her."

"She would, too," Niema put in.

"At least one person has good judgment," Tremin remarked. "Even if she's a Disciple of Death."

Kelan was beginning to wonder if anyone in this gods-forsaken city was on his side at all, or if he was doomed to drown in a sea of his own bad decisions. "She isn't a Disciple of Death, but that's not the point. You can't possibly believe Superior Sietra would want you to hold an ambassador of the Temple of Life hostage. Punish me for my mistakes if you must, but Niema did nothing wrong. She ... she's not very experienced with the world outside of her enclave."

"Thanks for that, Kelan," Niema muttered.

"Just returning the favour."

Laima regarded the pair of them with an expression of faint incredulity on her face and then turned to her companion. "This is unbelievable. Tremin, he's right on one part. We can't keep Niema here, but I don't trust her not to go running straight back to her Disciple of Death friend if we let her go."

"Then she can lead us directly to her," Tremin said. "How about that?"

"In what universe did you think a Disciple of Life would befriend a Disciple of Death?" Kelan asked his captors, silently begging one of them to see sense. "Is it not more plausible that the rumours are false?"

"Quiet," said Laima. "*You* aren't going anywhere."

"So I'm a hostage now? Or are you planning to enact justice upon me yourselves without consulting Superior Sietra?"

"Does he always talk this much?" Tremin asked.

"Unfortunately, yes." Laima considered him. "Superior Sietra is the one who typically decides the punishments for traitors, true, but that doesn't mean we have to deliver him to her in one piece."

Shit. She might be bluffing … or not. "If you're going to torture me, I'd appreciate it if you were quick about it. I urgently need to talk Superior Sietra myself."

"And spin one of your tales, I'm sure." Laima moved over to Niema and began to undo the ropes binding her hands. "Don't try attacking either of us. It won't end well for you."

"My people are pacifists," Niema protested. "But he's telling the truth, and so am I. The dead attacked the city last night, and it wasn't Yala who sent them."

"Stop talking before I change my mind about letting you go." Laima pulled the ropes loose and gave Niema a push in the direction of the door. "Go on."

Niema briefly caught Kelan's eye, displaying a flicker of guilt, and then hastened out of the room. In her place stood Tremin, who bared his teeth in a grin. "Now let's see if I can shut that trap of yours."

———

When Yala left the undercity, she felt as drained as if she'd walked from the barracks to the upper city in the midday heat. Drained, yet somehow satisfied, as if part of the weight of guilt had lifted from her shoulders despite the grim news she'd brought.

Her thoughts came jolting back to the present when she reached the pleasure district and saw a well-dressed woman standing on the corner. The puffed sleeves of her white shirt stood out starkly against the grey backdrop, and the silken skirt was equally impractical for the uneven cobblestones.

"Viam." Yala approached her former friend, unsure why she was stunned by her transformation from soldier to scholar. Viam wore her hair longer than she'd been allowed to as a soldier, and her elegantly pleated hairstyle and expensive clothes were a marked contrast to the desperation Yala had seen in the undercity.

"Yala." Viam looked equally startled at the sight of her former squad leader, though Yala's cane and scars hadn't changed in the half decade since the war. "You wanted to talk to me ... is this where Saren's living now?"

"Yes." Yala indicated the closed door. "Come on in."

They entered the dark hallway with its freshly scrubbed floors. The first thing Yala noticed was that the bodies were no longer inside the room on the left, and the second was that Saren lay sleeping in an armchair in the living area, a bottle of liquor on the table next to him.

Yala rapped her cane on the floor. "Saren."

He woke with a start, catching his balance against the edge of the armchair. "What—oh, it's you, Yala."

"Where are the bodies?" she asked. "Did they already take them away?"

"Yes, the Disciples came and..." he trailed off, seeing Viam behind her. "You."

"Me," said Viam, a touch of defensiveness in her voice. "What bodies? What are you talking about?"

Instead of answering, Saren addressed Yala. "An hour ago,

a group of novices from the Temple of the Flame came in to take the bodies. They said they'll cremate them tonight."

So Superior Datriem had kept his word despite his dismissal of Kelan and Niema's warnings. "Including Machit?"

"Machit is dead?" Viam blanched. "No."

"Yes, and so is Vanat." Yala found her sympathy for Viam's discomfort evaporating at the reminder of her twin failures, and the knowledge that Viam had been in the lap of luxury while her fellow soldiers had suffered in the undercity. To Saren, she added, "Please say that they at least separated Machit's body from the scum that murdered him."

"I tried," said Saren. "They came in, took the bodies, and left. Wouldn't listen to a word I said, and since Giran wasn't here to back me up, they didn't want to know."

"Murdered him?" Viam said in a hushed voice. "Why?"

"Sacrificed is the more accurate term." Yala watched the colour drain from her former friend's face. "I don't know what the palace guards told you…"

Viam backed towards the nearest chair. "Did you say *sacrificed?*"

"Yes, by a group of would-be Disciples of Death."

"No." Viam sank into the seat. "Not … not them. It's not possible."

Yala had wondered if Viam had played a role in the information getting outside of the palace after all, but her reaction of abject horror would have been difficult to fake.

"Yes," she said. "A group of would-be followers of the god death have been learning how to use the power of Corruption. They took Vanat hostage to lure me to the capital and then killed him when he tried to escape, and then they tried to slaughter Saren, Machit *and* me last night. Turns out she thinks anyone who survived the island is a worthy sacrifice in Mekan's eyes."

Viam let out a soft noise, her beseeching eyes seeking out Saren. "Is it true?"

"Would Yala lie to us?" he said. "She tried to warn me. I didn't listen, and now Machit is dead. Worse, the woman who tried to kill us escaped. Oh, and her followers are planning to usurp the throne, too."

"Is that all?" Viam placed her head in her hands, a strand of hair escaping from her pleat. "I can see why you want to warn the king, Yala, but I … I can't imagine anyone would believe me."

"I'm not unfamiliar with that issue," said Yala. "The priests at the Temple of the Flame are content to bury their heads in the mud, too, which isn't new for them."

Colour flooded Viam's face. "They shouldn't have. And I know how you feel about the king, but I took the job because…"

"Because you wanted to help," Yala guessed, ignoring Saren's derisive snort. "I know this sounds like an outrageous tale, but you're the only person I know of who might be able to get word back to the king before they try again."

"It would help if I took some kind of proof with me."

"Proof?" Yala scoffed. "I might have directed you to the public library where we interrupted one of their rituals, but I had to destroy the evidence to stop it walking outside and attacking people. You've seen for yourself how persistent the dead can be."

Viam shuddered. "I believe you, but I can't imagine anyone in the palace has ever seen … ever seen that before."

"Is King Daliel aware of his father's brief interest in Corruption before his death?" Saren lounged in his chair, his head propped on one elbow. "Or did King Tharen bury the evidence?"

Viam winced. "Don't—*please* don't say anything like that near the palace. It's as good as treason."

"Really." Saren sat upright, a challenging glint in his eye. "I almost want to try it to see how they react."

"Saren!" Yala snapped, wondering what in the world had got into him. "I have my share of grievances with the king, too, but really—we need His Majesty's cooperation."

"I don't much care for gaining the cooperation of the prick who cost us our jobs—sorry, *almost* all of us."

Viam's face turned mauve, while Yala held up a hand. Saren had been holding as much pent-up rage as the rest of them, and no doubt Machit's death and Viam's reappearance had served to break the dam—but his anger would help nobody. As usual it fell to Yala to calm them down.

"You don't want the Successors to kill the king, do you?" she asked of him. "If they do, we'll both die, and probably a lot of other innocent people will, too."

"Wouldn't be the first riot in the capital," he said. "Though usually the bodies don't get up again."

"Saren!" She threw up both hands in exasperation. "Enough."

When they'd been soldiers, she'd have told him to go and spar with one of the others to work off his frustration, except both he and Viam hadn't picked up a weapon in years, and with Saren's current mood, he'd either injure himself or someone else.

"I should go," Viam said. "I'll tell my supervisors as much as I can."

"Tell them the Successors are behind this," Yala said. "They'll have heard the name. They might even know that the Successors want the King dethroned, but not that they intend to ally with Mekan to achieve their goals."

"You might also remind them that there's an awful lot of dead in this city," Saren added. "They have no shortage of recruits for their army."

"That's also true." Before Viam left, though, Yala had one

more question. "That reminds me—are there any texts in the palace library concerning death magic?"

"No, of course not," Viam answered a little too quickly. "I've spent enough time in there, so I should know."

Hmm. Maybe King Tharen had hidden his research, not least from his heir, but Melian must have found out somehow.

"Are you sure about that?" Saren's lip curled. "It's strange that these Successors seem to know the details of our squad's own encounter with death magic. Where would they get it into their heads that sacrificing Yala to the god of death would gain them an advantage?"

Viam's jaw dropped. "What?"

"That's what their leader said, in her own words," said Saren. "Oddly enough, the only people who knew the details of our last mission were those of us who were actually there. Oh, and the old king, but he's buried at the bottom of the ocean."

Viam jumped to her feet. "You think *I* told someone?"

"It sure as hells wasn't the rest of us," he said. "It wouldn't be the first time you'd used your friends for your own gain."

Viam backed towards the door. "I don't appreciate that accusation. I took the job because it was the only one I was offered, and I'd *never* betray any of you like that."

She ducked her head—not before Yala saw the wet sheen in her eyes—and retreated down the hallway. When the front door closed behind her, Yala said, "What the hell was that, Saren? You weren't supposed to make her leave."

"I thought you were thinking the same," he said defensively. "What? Someone leaked that information, and she's been *inside* the palace."

"Don't forget even King Delial didn't know what his father was up to," said Yala. "Besides, she's not the only person from our squad who's unaccounted for. There's also Temik."

"Oh, he's never gone near the palace," he grunted. "He lost his best friend that day."

"True." Yala's chest tightened. "That might have been our only chance to get word to the king, though."

"Since when have the higher authorities ever been any help to us?" he said. "King Tharen sent us to our deaths and then died himself. I doubt he cares if we keep his secrets."

"I don't think Viam would have told anyone about the island," Yala said. "Not least because she might have lost her job or worse. You know who else has access to the king."

Superior Datriem might not meet with His Majesty on a regular basis, but several of His Disciples had once been among King Tharen's personal guard, and it would have cost him little effort to track down anyone else who spread information that might endanger the peace. After Yala's own experience, Viam wouldn't have dared utter a word.

Saren reached for the bottle on the table beside him. "The new king has no more interest in magic than he does in war. Though I thought the same of King Tharen, too, and look where that ended."

"He might not have been dabbling himself," Yala said. "I'm more inclined to think he sent us to the island so Rafragoria wouldn't get there first, without knowing he was endangering us in the process."

Generous of her, perhaps, but if the king had so much as whispered in the ear of the god of death, someone else would have known. Wouldn't they?

Saren fumbled on the table for a glass. "Rafragoria didn't know what they were getting into either. Honestly, the only reason we're both still breathing is that nobody on that island had a fucking clue what they were doing."

They didn't ... but Melian does.

"Anyway." Saren tipped liquor into the glass with shaking hands. "Want to drink to Machit's life? And Vanat's, while we're at it? Might as well make the most of however much time we have before Giran comes back and kicks us out."

Yala knew dulling her senses wouldn't help, but the cremation would take place in a few hours, and she'd need more than righteous fury to get through it. "Why not."

24

Niema waited around a corner, out of sight of the inn, thinking hard. She was rather short on ideas as to how to remove Kelan from that guest room without breaking her commitment to nonviolence, and the other two Disciples of the Sky were more misguided than malicious. They believed they were acting in accordance with their deity when they'd captured Kelan ... but they wouldn't actually kill him, would they? The Disciples of the Sky were nothing like her own people; she could no sooner have inflicted damage on one of her enclave members than she could cut off her own limb, but Kelan had taken one of their lives with his own hand.

For that reason, if her fellow enclave members had been here, they'd have told her to leave the other Disciples to resolve their issues among themselves. But Kelan had also saved her life, and if he hadn't helped her bring the war drake into the city the previous night, Yala might have died.

A skittering noise at the street's end showed a skirrit disappearing into an alley, perhaps a remnant of her trickery the previous night. While her diversion hadn't slowed Melian and her allies down much, she needed a short-term solution that wouldn't inflict any lasting damage. *All right.*

Niema whistled softly, and a flurry of footsteps answered. The rodent reappeared, followed by another, and Niema directed them to scurry ahead of her. Then she made her careful way back towards the inn, wishing she shared Kelan's ability to levitate above the ground so that she'd be able to ensure the others weren't looking out the window at that precise moment.

Instead, she pressed herself flat against the wall of the adjacent building and shuffled along, listening for any sounds from upstairs. As she whistled, more skirrits came out of the alleys and converged on the inn, one of them nudging open the front door. She half expected to hear immediate screams from the staff, but Kelan's captors might have ordered them to leave, to prevent anyone from realising they held someone captive in one of the upstairs rooms.

In any case, nobody challenged Niema at the front door. She entered, beady-eyed skirrits gathering around her feet, and her ears pricked, hearing Kelan's captors talking in the upstairs hallway.

"I'm not comfortable with this," Laima said in a low voice. "I know it's *Kelan*, but there's a limit, and frankly, his complaining is driving me out of my mind."

"I can knock him out," Tremin offered.

"And what if he's telling the truth?" Footsteps sounded at the top of the stairs, causing Niema's shoulders to tense. "You know Senik was a reckless piece of crap as well. It wouldn't surprise me if he was hiring mercenaries to help him capture people to exchange for bounties."

"We hired mercs ourselves, didn't we?"

"They said they knew Kelan," Laima said. "And they've

worked with the Temple of the Flame before, too. Never mind them. I think we should take him back to Skytower and let Superior Sietra handle the punishment herself."

Niema whistled, urging the rodents she'd bewitched to scurry upstairs. She held her breath and waited for the inevitable exclamations of shock.

"What the fuck?" Tremin bellowed, as Laima shrieked in the background.

Niema climbed the stairs as swiftly as she was able without tripping over a rodent and found Laima and Tremin backing away from the oncoming tide of rodents. Both shouted at the sight of her, but a piercing whistle from Niema caused the skirrits to leap at the unfortunate Disciples' ankles.

While they were distracted, Niema entered the room in which they'd shut Kelan. He watched in bewilderment when she shoved the door closed behind her, his face bruised and one eye swollen shut. His hands had been bound, and blood trickled from a thin cut on his neck.

"Niema." He blinked—or his unswollen eye did—and tried to rise to his feet. "What's going on?"

Thumps sounded, which sounded rather like a number of large rodents being flung against the walls. "Never mind that. We'll have to escape out the window."

"Can't you untie me first?" On his third attempt to stand, he managed to stagger upright, leaning on the bedframe for balance.

"No time." She ran to the window, but it was closed with some mechanism she wasn't familiar with. They didn't have glass windows in the enclave.

The door swept inward and Laima and Tremin stalked in. Niema gave a sharp whistle, directing the skirrits to launch at the two Disciples from behind, while Kelan swore, his brow furrowed in concentration. A gust of air blew the window open while their pursuers let out cries of anger as the skirrits' sharp teeth and claws dug into the skin of their ankles. While they attempted to dislodge the rodents, Kelan climbed onto the window ledge in front of Niema.

"You'll have to hold onto me if you don't want to break an ankle," he told her. "Ready?"

I can't believe I'm doing this. Niema grabbed his arm as he stepped out of the window, a current of air lifting them skyward. As they wheeled above the city, a strangled scream caught in her throat, and she tightened her grip until her nails dug into his arm. With a grunt, he descended equally rapidly. Her stomach rose into her throat, and when they landed near Ceremonial Square, she gladly released his arm.

Kelan hissed a painful breath between his teeth. "I take it clawing someone's arm off doesn't violate your vows of nonviolence?"

"Better that than falling to my death." Niema reached for his bound hands. "I'll remove these…"

"It'd be easier with a knife."

Niema knew ropes markedly better than she knew windows, however, and he exhaled with relief when she undid the bonds and let the ropes fall to the ground. "You owe me now."

"I'll add it to my list of debts." He touched a hand to his bruised face. "I doubt you'll get any mercy from them if they find us again."

"If they were fool enough to spill the blood of a Disciple of Life, they'd deserve any misfortune that might befall them."

Kelan scooped up the ropes and then slipped them into one of the pockets of his coat. "Out of curiosity, what would happen if they did?"

"A painful death."

"Really?" He tugged his collar up to hide the blood on his neck. "That seems rather brutal for a god of life."

"Some would call it merciful." Now the rush of their escape had worn off, she became conscious of the crowded markets, and their proximity to the Temple of the Flame. *Hang on ... didn't Laima claim they worked with mercenaries? What did she mean by that?*

"That's one way of putting it." He touched a hand to the bruise on his cheek. "Where's Yala?"

"How should I know?" she asked. "I was too busy planning a rescue to look for her."

A bewildered smile flickered across his mouth. "I didn't think you were the type to hold that over my head. Though I'm surprised you saved me at all."

So was she, for that matter, but there'd be time enough to wonder if she'd made the right choice later. "Where do you want to go now? We can't stay in the upper city."

"I'd like to go after those mercenaries who brought me in," he said, "but I'm more interested in what Laima said about them working for the Temple of the Flame."

"You heard that, too?" Her brow wrinkled. "Which mercenaries brought you in?"

"The ones whose wagon we borrowed." Kelan rotated on his heel, shielding his eyes with one hand from the sun blazing through the back of the Temple of the Flame. "Strange. I didn't know the Disciples made a habit of hiring mercenaries. I wonder…"

"We already got thrown out once today, in case you've forgotten," she said. "Superior Datriem won't be any more welcoming if you show up looking like you've been trampled by a raptor."

"I expect not, but I have to wonder what else they might

say behind closed doors that they prefer not to show on the outside."

"You want to spy on them?" Was one imprisonment and beating not enough for him? "Won't your people be watching the sky for you?"

"Yes—the sky, not the ground." He stepped out of the way of a group of passing workers, who eyed his bruises curiously but didn't otherwise pay them any attention. "Also, they're not going to capture me in full view of the public."

"I wouldn't count on that." While they were in equal danger anywhere in the capital, that didn't make her any keener to stay in the upper city, especially as Kelan's injuries would draw attention. She waged an internal war with herself over the benefits of healing him that ceased when he caught her staring at his face.

"What?" he asked. "I've looked better, I'll allow."

Oh, fine. "If you want me to heal your bruises, I can."

"You—what?" His unswollen eye blinked at her. "You can heal injuries?"

"You don't know much about my people, do you?"

He touched the bruise on his jaw with a fingertip. "That tends to be the case when they make a habit of hiding deep in the jungle."

"That it does." She cast a brief glance around in case anyone was watching, but the market crowds were too occupied with their own affairs to notice the pair of them. "Well?"

"All right." He reached for the bandage on his leg. "This is bothering me the most. Yala certainly knows how to make an impression."

Niema extended a hand and whispered a prayer to the god of life. Healing energy flowed from her palm, and Kelan stiffened, his leg straightening as the wound sealed. She raised her hand to his face and watched the bruises fade into smooth skin.

"That's better." He gingerly felt his ribs. "The rest I can live with. I don't think that brute Tremin broke anything."

"You'd better hope he doesn't come back." She didn't think it was a wise idea for them to walk into full view of the Temple of the Flame either, but Kelan seemingly had no such misgivings.

The thick press of bodies in Ceremonial Square would at least make it easy to tell if there were any other Disciples around, and she stayed close behind Kelan as the breeze he conjured parted the crowd on each side.

When they neared the Temple of the Flame, he led Niema to an alcove between two market stalls. "You should wait here while I have a closer look."

"You do realise they'll be able to see you coming, don't you?" Niema said. "What do you expect to find there?"

Kelan didn't answer. Niema hadn't the faintest idea what he was thinking, except that if the Disciples of the Flame were hiring mercenaries, Superior Datriem wasn't as oblivious to the outside world as he pretended to be. What else *was* he hiding?

Kelan rose into the air on a breeze that carried him up to the rooftops. Given the size of the tower's windows, it seemed improbable that nobody would have spotted him. When he'd been up there for a full minute, Niema waved a hand to get his attention.

"Do you *want* them to see you spying on them?" she hissed when he descended slowly, without looking at her. "Well?"

His arms lowered to his sides. "Melian is in there."

"What?" That couldn't be right. *"Melian?"*

"That's where she's hiding." He murmured. "I think we have our explanation as to why the Disciples of the Flame are so reluctant to act against the Successors."

"That's impossible." Melian had tried to summon the god

of death. Why would the Disciples of the Flame invite *her* into their temple? Granted, they didn't necessarily *know* that she was the one responsible for the previous day's massacre, but their behaviour towards herself and Kelan indicated that they usually shunned outsiders. Then another horrifying possibility struck her. "Are the bodies—the bodies from yesterday in *there*? Inside the temple?"

Kelan's eyes widened. "That is a good question. I wouldn't be surprised if the Disciples kept the bodies destined for cremation somewhere in their temple, or nearby, at any rate."

Nausea rose in Niema's throat. "We can't let her stay in there. Someone has to tell them they have a Disciple—a Disciple of Death inside their own temple."

"I'll enlighten them." Kelan moved towards the doors, and Niema's hand reached out, snagging his sleeve. "Kelan, think. Why would they take our word over hers? She got there first."

Kelan tugged his sleeve free. "She'll find it harder to hide her handiwork than she thinks, if the bodies of her followers are indeed in the temple."

Niema wasn't so sure. Like the other Disciples of the Sky, they might well be convinced *Yala* was the Disciple of Death, and the only reason Niema hadn't been turned away from their doors at first was because they hadn't known she and Kelan had been travelling with Yala.

The door opened almost as soon as Kelan reached the foot of the temple's stairs, and a novice greeted them. "Superior Datriem said you were outside. He wants to invite you in."

"We'll come in when he tells us why he has a Disciple of Death inside your temple," Kelan said. "Otherwise, no thanks."

Niema stifled a groan, though the novice simply looked

bewildered. "Tell him…" She faltered. "Ah, tell him we're here for the cremation."

"That isn't until sunset." The novice backed into the doorway, beckoning to Kelan. "He insisted on you coming in, though."

"You again." Superior Datriem himself appeared, gesturing to the novice to move aside. "Did your Superiors send you to spy on me and my fellow Disciples?"

"That woman you have up in the library isn't a Disciple," Kelan told him. "Not one of yours, anyway. She's Melian, the leader of the Successors and would-be Disciple of Death."

Superior Datriem gave no reaction to his words, though she heard the novice gasp behind him. "Melian is an ally of ours who's been helping in our search for the perpetrator dabbling in Corruption in the capital. If you'd like to discuss the subject further, you're welcome to come inside."

Kelan didn't budge. "I wonder how many of your acolytes know you're colluding with Corruption yourself?"

"Kelan," Niema hissed, tugging at his sleeve. "Get back—"

Superior Datriem's eyes flared white, the colour of holy fire, and several other robed figures appeared on either side of him. "Bring him in."

In moments, they had Kelan surrounded. Before they could catch her, too, Niema ran.

———

Yala woke with the taste of rice wine on her tongue and a chair cushioning her back. Somehow, she'd slept better in an armchair than she had in a bed the previous night, though as a soldier, she'd learned to sleep anywhere she could—which had included a drake's saddle on more than one occasion. Her gaze travelled to the window, whose curtains were closed, rendering the room in darkness aside from the light streaming in from the hallway.

Saren looked up from where he lay sprawled in his own armchair. "It's not dusk yet, don't worry."

Yala rose to her feet and stretched, releasing a series of popping noises in her shoulders and neck. "Speaking of dusk, the cremation will take place at the temple, won't it?"

"I guess," said Saren. "Won't be at the palace, at any rate. They don't hold fancy funerals for reprobates like us."

"He shouldn't be burned together with those criminals either." Though if the ceremony took place in the Temple of the Flame itself, how in the hells was she supposed to avoid drawing Superior Datriem's attention? They were lucky not to be on that pyre themselves as it was.

"I don't disagree." Saren climbed to his feet and reached for the near-empty wine bottle. "Your friends aren't back yet."

"Kelan and Niema, you mean?" The former wasn't a surprise, but the latter was concerning. Niema had mentioned her intention to talk to the Disciples of the Sky who were staying in the city, but it shouldn't have taken this long.

Saren tipped the dregs of the wine into his glass. "Strange company you keep these days. Did I mention that?"

"Is that anything new?"

"Ha." He tipped back the glass and drank, his eyes closed. "Guess you've got to replace us somehow, since we keep dropping dead."

"None of that talk," she said. "Look, going to a public event is a risk even if it isn't at the temple. Any ideas as to how to avoid attention? Short of disguising ourselves?"

"I think there are costumes in one of the back rooms."

"Absolutely not," she said. "I can't hide my limp, can I? Whether I carry a cane or not, they'll know it's me."

"Machit would find it fucking hilarious if we showed up dressed in military regalia." He chuckled to himself. "Vanat, too. Might as well give those costumes a try. I don't think Giran's coming back to reopen this place for a while."

"Unless he's waiting for me to leave first." The more time she spent under this roof, the higher the chances of Melian returning to finish what she'd started the previous night. Yes, Saren had been a convenient target, too, but it was Yala that Melian wanted dead above all else. "Moving somewhere else isn't the worst idea."

"What are you saying?" Saren asked. "You aren't going back to the jungle?"

"No," she said. "I can't. Kelan destroyed my house."

"He didn't, did he? I thought he was an ally."

"We had a somewhat difficult start." And his loyalties weren't the most dependable. Niema, on the other hand... Where was she? "I'd have to fly to another nation to escape, and the closest is Rafragoria."

"I think you could pass as Rafragorian," said Saren. "Just tell everyone you got that leg injury from fighting a war drake."

Yala gave a snort. "The only phrases I know in that language are the insults their soldiers have yelled at me on the battlefield. I think that would give me away, don't you?"

Saren picked up the wine bottle, realised it was empty, and pulled a face. "Do you ever think about it?"

"Huh?"

"Those people we killed." He crossed the room to a cupboard at the back. "They weren't there for their own enjoyment. No more than we were."

"They might have been." Rafragoria didn't have a compulsory military service period for all able citizens the way Laria had once had, though Yala and her squad had stayed in the army years past their allotted time.

"I doubt it." Saren emerged from the cupboard carrying another bottle. "Even if they were, it wasn't their choice to go to war with us. Someone else gave the order."

"Their empress," she recalled. "I wonder if Rafragoria is in as much of a financial hole as we are."

"No clue." He reached the armchair and sank into it. "We didn't even know what it was like in the rest of the country, did we? Not until we left the barracks."

That was true. The army had been a different world, a simpler one based on survival and trust. Maybe that had been the point; they'd had no choice but to focus on lasting each day and protecting those within their power. Those simple rules had got her squad through years of training and more years of campaigns, and none of them had ever thought of what might come after.

Yala watched Saren pour out another glass and declined one of her own. "I'd like to be able to remember Machit's cremation. Wouldn't you?"

He gave a shudder. "Not if Superior Datriem is there."

"Don't remind me," said Yala. "I hope Viam did manage to get word back to the king, at least. I don't know if she'll be there…"

Saren's head bowed. "I know I was a shit to her. I needed someone to hurt, and she…"

The front door slammed open. Yala peered out into the hallway as Niema came rushing in, her face panicked. "What's going on?"

"The Temple of the Flame," said Niema. "Melian is in the Temple of the Flame. And—they have Kelan."

"They *what?*" All other concerns slid from Yala's mind. "Melian is in there?"

"She's pretending to be helping them, and Superior Datriem believes her." Niema's breath came in sharp gasps.

"When Kelan tried to argue otherwise, the Disciples had him surrounded. I had to run."

"Damn." Part of Yala had suspected that the Temple of the Flame had played a part in spreading the rumours concerning Yala's involvement with Corruption, given that Superior Datriem had known of her experiences on the island where few others had—but why would he work *with* Melian? He couldn't possibly *want* a Disciple of Death in the city, let alone inside his own temple. "What did they do to Kelan?"

"I didn't see," Niema said. "I had to hide from their novices among the market stalls, and I barely got out of the upper city without being caught."

"Why were you back at the Temple of the Flame to begin with?"

"Kelan, of course," she said. "He wanted to spy on them after he heard they'd been working with mercenaries..."

"Mercenaries?" *Is that where they heard the rumours?* It was typical of Kelan to challenge Superior Datriem to his face instead of telling her first, but she couldn't leave him to his fate. Not when the Disciple of Death was inside the tower itself, along with...

Yala's blood chilled. Machit's body was in there. If Melian intended to do more meddling with the dead... *No. I won't allow it.*

Saren stared at her. "You're not going to rescue him?"

"It's not just him who needs rescuing," said Yala. "They have Machit's body, remember?"

"Gods." His mouth twisted. "Machit wouldn't want you to get yourself killed, though."

"It's only a matter of time before they come here to find me," she said. "The only reason we've lasted this long is because the Disciples of the Flame never leave the upper city, and because we forced Melian to change her plans after we confronted her yesterday. No doubt she's working on convincing Superior Datriem that I'm the problem, not her."

"Then you want to tell him otherwise?" Niema guessed. "Expose her?"

"I'm unlikely to be believed," Yala acknowledged, "but we can't let her near those bodies. I'll drag her out of that temple with my own hands if I have to."

25

K elan had never considered what it might be like to face a Disciple of the Flame in open combat, let alone their leader. The already humid air thickened with heat as the Disciples flanked him, and while part of him irrationally hoped someone in Ceremonial Square would notice he was not entering the temple of his own free will, they didn't.

Even if they had, nobody without magic of their own would be able to challenge them. The breeze he conjured to his fingertips vanished the instant the Disciples steered him over the threshold into their temple, and thanks to Laima and Tremin taking his blade, he was without any other means of defending himself.

The door thudded closed at his back, the sound echoing off the high ceiling above the glittering altar. Superior Datriem swivelled to Kelan, the former greyish brown of his eyes almost entirely smothered by the embers of Dalathik's flames. "I have to admit that I would rather not create unnecessary conflict with Superior Sietra by maiming one of her

Disciples, but I'm sure she'd be horrified if she heard of your actions today."

"What about inviting a Disciple of Death into your midst?" He glanced at the balcony near where he'd seen Melian through the window, but all he saw were curious novices and Disciples peering down at him. "I have no desire to incite unnecessary conflict, but that woman caused a public massacre the other night. It's her who's responsible for those bodies in the crematorium—"

"Absurd," said Superior Datriem. "You claim to wish to avoid conflict, but you've caused needless distress to my people during your short stay in the capital. I think it'll be better for all of us if I were to put you somewhere you are unable to cause any more strife until someone from your own temple comes to collect you."

Meaning Laima and Tremin, no doubt. His stomach lurched when he finally spotted Melian, who gave him the barest smiles from the balcony above. When he jabbed a finger in her direction, someone seized his arm from behind. Scorching pain seared his skin, as if he'd plunged his arm into a firepit, and he bit back a gasp as the Disciples manhandled him across the lower floor. His feet halted at the top of a wooden ladder leading downward into darkness.

Kelan hadn't known the temple had any areas that weren't blazing with light, but it made sense that their prison would be underground. The Disciples pushed his feet onto the upper rung of the ladder, giving him little choice but to climb, and when his feet hit the ground, they pulled the ladder up, out of his reach.

"Wait—"

A trapdoor slammed on him, leaving him in darkness. It was suffocatingly hot, and his brief glimpse of the room from above had shown him it was barely bigger than a cupboard. On the whole, he'd much preferred being locked up at the inn. He might have been restrained, but at least he'd been able to see his surroundings.

Kelan walked backwards until he hit a stone wall, his hand clutching his burned arm. An accident—or a warning of the god whose power inhabited these walls. If he tried to reach *his* god, he doubted his prayers would reach Terethik's ears. The air here was thick and musty, and several minutes passed in the darkness while he tried to formulate a way to convince Superior Datriem of Melian's guilt. Unless he *knew* she was a Disciple of Death and had kept her here to prevent her from unleashing his power against his own temple… Kelan had little doubt that the Superior was capable of that level of duplicity, but why would he willingly support the rise of Corruption? The Disciples of the Flame were supposed to be incorruptible, like the Disciples of Life.

Or so he'd thought.

Some indeterminate length of time later, the trapdoor lifted and Superior Datriem's face peered down at him. "Uncomfortable, isn't it?"

Kelan shielded his eyes in answer; the sunlight cutting through the open trapdoor was twice as dazzling after an hour or more in total darkness. "Do you normally treat your guests with such disrespect? Given that Melian is walking around upstairs, I suppose not."

"Still, you stand by your lies."

"They aren't lies." He tilted his head back to see if Melian was watching him, but Superior Datriem's towering form prevented him from seeing any more of the room above. "I'm curious, though … when did Melian start working for you? What did she do to convince you that she's trustworthy?"

"Her work has helped us uncover a number of individuals in the capital who foolishly tried to bargain with the god of death," he responded. "In addition to pointing us in the direction of others outside of the city who also have ties to Corruption."

Meaning Yala. "Because she's *with* them and as disloyal to her helpers as everyone else."

"Enough." Superior Datriem's eyes blazed like the surface of the sun. "I have never needed to imprison another Disciple before, and it gives me no pleasure, but I cannot allow you and the company you keep to continue to endanger the people of this city."

Yes, he's definitely referring to Yala. Kelan might have pointed out that the Disciples who'd founded this temple would have thought twice before risking the wrath of another deity, but the trouble with Terethik was that He was a little *too* lenient. The sky god's general casualness towards prayer and worship meant that He was unlikely to notice a Disciple making desperate pleas to get His attention, especially when they were imprisoned in another temple.

"What do you plan to do with Niema if you catch her?" he asked. "She's a Disciple of Life, so any harm you do to her will rebound upon you."

I think. Niema hadn't specified if *her* god would be able to harm anyone inside the temple, but he guessed not.

"Short of trusting the wrong people, she has done nothing wrong," said Superior Datriem. "I hope that she'll return to her home without further putting herself in danger."

"She wants to eradicate Corruption in the city, same as you," Kelan said. "Is there any reason you turned her away when she first visited? You're welcome to dislike my approach, but Niema is as pious as yourself."

Presumably, it had been Melian who'd convinced him to accept no other outside help, but Kelan wanted to hear the justification from his own mouth.

"Eradicate Corruption?" he echoed. "I'm afraid that is impossible, Disciple, but we *can* prevent Corruption from gaining a foothold by removing anyone who accepts Mekan's help."

"You gave one of them a job," he pointed out. "You think Yala's the Disciple of Death, don't you? You had a hand in spreading the rumours that lured her to the capital, but you don't realise that Melian wants to offer Yala as a sacrifice to the god of death herself."

"Rumours?" Superior Datrim shook his head. "Not rumours ... truth, of a sort. I assume Yala never told you of her last mission as part of King Tharen's army, when she slew a creature of the Void herself?"

"Actually, she did." Hadn't the Superior disbelieved Yala when she'd told him of that mission? Threatened her, even, from what he'd gleaned from talking to Machit and then to Yala herself. "She left their temple burning in holy fire, so I don't know how you can rationalise that she somehow decided to start studying Corruption magic from an isolated shack in the middle of the jungle." He threw in enough true details to make his claims as convincing as possible, though the gods only know what story Melian had conjured up to convince the Disciples of her innocence and Yala's guilt.

"She didn't return from that island alone," he said. "She brought something back with her."

"What are you talking about?"

Hurried footsteps sounded nearby, and a novice ran into view. "Superior Datriem, Captain Yala is here."

"She's *here?*" Shit. What was she thinking?

"So it would seem." Superior Datriem lifted the end of the trapdoor again. "I'll be back later to finish our conversation, Kelan."

"Wait—" His words were swallowed by darkness when the trapdoor came down once more.

———

Yala's heart jangled in her chest like a sack of coins as she made her way across Ceremonial Square, Saren's arguments ringing in her ears. To say he didn't approve of her plan was an understatement. Niema neither, though she'd acknowledged that they had little choice but to comply if they wanted to bring a halt to Melian's supposed alliance with the Disciples of the Flame. It was little comfort that Melian would be unable to use death magic inside the temple itself when Kelan was equally powerless, and according to Niema, he had already been captured by his fellow Disciples of the Sky earlier that day.

The sun had progressed across the sky so that its light bathed the western side of the temple more than the east, though its bright windows were as dazzling as ever. While Niema insisted on coming with Yala, she'd ordered the other woman to wait at a far enough distance that she'd be able to escape if necessary. It would do no good for them both to be captured at once, and while Niema claimed to have bewitched the city's skirrits to help her rescue Kelan, the Disciples of the Flame would not be so easily cowed. No doubt they could burn any rodent infestation to ashes if necessary.

Yala strode up the stone stairs to the temple door, knocked, and held her breath.

When an orange-robed novice answered, she fixed on a smile. "Greetings. I believe Superior Datriem would like to speak to me?"

The novice gawped at her. "You're Yala—"

"Yala Palathar," another voice said, and echoes of her own name swept across the temple's lower floor.

Several moments later, Superior Datriem came into view, his robes billowing around him and a mixture of triumph and curiosity on his face. "Yala Palathar. To what do I owe the pleasure?"

"I'm here to surrender, of course." She raised her voice a fraction as she stepped into the temple's entryway. "I already saw one friend die at the hands of your deity. I'd like to avoid seeing another suffer the same fate."

A chorus of gasps rose from the acolytes behind him, bringing a perverse sense of satisfaction at briefly breaking the iron control Superior Datriem held over them. He'd already designated her as the enemy and a Disciple of Death, and there was nothing she could do to sink any further in his estimation.

His sole response was a mere tightening of his brows. "I have no intention of harming your ally, though I would have thought you of all people would know the difference between a murder and an intentional sacrifice."

"I nearly became the latter last night, so yes, I do."

More murmurs rose from among the novices. Superior Datriem's jaw twitched. "I'm sure you've concocted a story to justify your decisions, but I would ask you to come with me to speak in a more suitable location."

Didn't he think my account of what we found on the island was a lie, too? He'd been in denial, at any rate, and had been willing to risk threatening her with bodily harm if she didn't hold her tongue. Then again, years had passed, and there was no telling how long Melian had been whispering in his ears. She was far cleverer than Yala would have believed after her behaviour the previous night.

Superior Datriem led her up a curving staircase to the upper level, affording her a view of the wide hall with its alcoves and prayer mats, and the large golden statue of the god of light above His slab-sized altar. Part of her had expected to be sacrificed upon that altar, but instead, Superior Datriem beckoned her through an avenue of shelves to what appeared to be an office. *Is he inviting me into his private room?*

297

The notion of being alone with him made the sweat on the back of her neck turn cold, and her feet stopped in their tracks.

He beckoned to her again. "Come on, Yala. I might have imprisoned you with your ally, but I thought it was only fair to let you talk to the one who turned you in before I send you to join him. You might know one another."

Melian? Despite the dread gripping her body like the claw of a war drake, Yala's feet moved, carrying her to the open door. A man stood inside the office, dressed in the orange robes of a novice Disciple of the Flame. His hair was longer than it had been as a soldier, but the righteous glint in his eye was the same as when Yala had last seen him.

"Temik."

"Yala." He spoke without emotion. "So you're back."

"I thought you left." Meaningless words, but all her thoughts were smothered by blank shock—and below lay the sickening certainty that she ought to have known. Temik was the only member of her squad who'd been unaccounted for since her return to the city, and of everyone, he'd made no secret that he blamed her for Dalem's death. But this... "You ... you told everyone I was a Disciple of Death?"

"It's true," he said. "You slew a beast of Corruption and in the process forged a bond with the god of death. None of us knew at the time, of course, but it makes sense."

"I'll tell you what *doesn't* make sense," she said. "You being in the same room as Dalem's killers. Yes, he gave his life to save ours, but that doesn't change the hand that wielded the knife, does it?"

If Superior Datriem had any reaction to her words, she didn't see; Temik commanded her attention, fully and completely.

"You're mistaken," said Temik. "Dalem gave his life in

order to destroy that temple. The god of light honoured his sacrifice."

"So that's your goal, is it?" she queried. "To kill me with your own hand and claim you're serving the god of light?" She'd known his anger burned deep, but he couldn't have come up with this scheme on his own, could he? Melian must have worked her spell upon him, but the room was empty aside from the three of them.

"No." He shook his head. "You have it wrong, Yala, though Corruption is so little understood that it's unsurprising that even you have no idea of your potential."

"Potential?" she spat. "Listen to yourself. Vanat and Machit are *dead* because of you, and the latter was sacrificed to the god of death himself. If you think for a minute that I'd condone that, you couldn't be more wrong."

His mouth pinched at the corners. "I had nothing to do with their deaths."

"Melian did," Yala went on. "She slit Machit's throat, and almost did the same to Saren and me."

"That's enough," Superior Datriem said. "Novice Temik, I brought Yala to you so that you could talk face to face, but I little thought she'd be so cruel in her lies."

"Lies?" Yala scoffed. "Melian is the one who has been deceiving you. She's intending to sacrifice my life to gain the service of the god of death."

"You do not deny that you have Mekan's touch upon you, then?" he said. "I see it myself, as clear as day, and I am afraid that I have no choice but to put an end to you myself."

As he always wanted to. Strange, how hearing the truth from his lips removed a weight from her shoulders that had been there for years. "I was under the impression that sacrificing people who aren't members of your temple was against the law."

Yes, she knew that the god of light and flame was unforgiving, and those who crossed Him died for their mistakes, but there were some lines even the Disciples weren't allowed to cross.

"In circumstances like these, we must follow the guidance of our deity," said Superior Datriem. "Recent events have made it clear that the law alone will not stop the eradication of Corruption. You'll die at the pyre tonight, Yala Palathar."

"Did you ask Melian what she plans to do with the bodies?" She kept her attention on Temik, despite his clenched jaw and refusal to meet her eyes. "They have Machit's body here, waiting to be cremated. Right next to a Disciple of Death—"

A gasp of pain escaped when Superior Datriem seized her shoulder and steered her out of the office. His touch scorched her skin, and the smell of burning reached her nostrils. *He's not holding back this time. He truly means to see me die.*

She would burn, and the Disciples of the Temple of the Flame would be there to watch.

26

Niema watched Yala disappear into the temple with a familiar sense of creeping dread. It was like watching her enter the library to face Melian all over again—only worse, because this time Melian was aided not by mercenaries but the might of the Disciples of the Flame themselves. Kelan was a captive, too, unable to access his power. That left Niema the sole person who might be able to get them both out alive, but a swarm of skirrits wouldn't be enough to cause every Disciple of the Flame to abandon their prisoners.

No … she needed to call on the war drake again. While she hadn't *needed* Kelan to hold her aboveground in order to draw the beast into the city, she'd found it much easier to give directions from the air. On the ground, there was far more potential for her plan to go awry and for the war drake to attack innocent civilians.

When the temple door opened and several novices exited, Niema hastened to duck behind the nearest market stall to avoid being spotted. They must be on the lookout for any of Yala's allies, and while Niema had expected Superior

Datriem not to be fooled by her easy surrender, that didn't make Niema's own plan any easier to accomplish while under pressure.

She whistled, intending to reach any skirrits that might remain in the upper city after her rescue mission at the inn. They might not help her get into the Temple of the Flame, but they could at least distract the novices while she directed the god of life's message further afield.

Niema continued to whistle as she made her way through the market stalls, many of which were packing up for the evening. Live animals weren't sold at Ceremonial Square markets, no doubt due to the mess they would inevitably cause, but she'd seen mierns, hogs and other animals at the smaller markets throughout the city, and even a few wagon-pulling raptors. Her whistle might not reach them all, but she cast her influence wide, and was rewarded when a gien flew to land on the roof above her, then a second bird joined the first.

Go to the temple. Distract them. Niema scarcely paused for breath, so intent was she on infusing her whistle with her will, and with her devotion to the god of life.

Yala is the only one who can stop the Disciples of Death. If she dies in there, nobody can stop them.

Niema might have had some doubts as to Yala's ability to stop Melian earlier, but she couldn't afford to let any wayward thoughts get in the way of her plea. With a singular focus, she directed the god of life's power to reach outward and cast a wide net throughout the city. More birds changed their flight paths, converging on the temple.

People in the square began to stare at the sky, pointing and exclaiming. She was drawing attention—too much, perhaps—but every moment Yala spent inside that temple increased the odds that she and Kelan wouldn't walk out again.

Distract them! Niema's mental cry split the sky like a bolt of lightning, and every bird circling the square flew at the Temple of the Flame. The robed novices ran to the steps with shouts of alarm, and as the door opened, a Disciple lifted a hand and directed a handful of flame at the oncoming birds.

No. Niema's stomach twisted at their cries, their pain, and her whistling ceased as she dropped to her knees. The order had already been given, though and she heard the birds echoing her whistle…

And, once again, the cry of an oncoming war drake.

C***

As Superior Datriem directed Yala towards the stairs, a commotion echoed from below. The door slammed once, twice, and gasps and shouts arose from amid the Disciples and novices. Through the large window above the balcony opposite hers, Yala glimpsed the confusing sight of what appeared to be feathers showering upon the temple. When she followed Superior Datriem's confused stare to the vast window in place of a ceiling, she saw the source: birds, a hundred or more, diving at the temple with shrieks and cries.

Niema. Yala had to admire her ingenuity, given the comparative lack of wildlife in the city. It looked as if the giens and freks that liked to roost on the palace complex roofs had brought their entire flocks in, and Yala seized the chance to slip out of Superior Datriem's grip and descend the stairs as fast as her leg would allow.

Instinct told her to run for the door, but she'd come here to find Kelan as well as answers. Superior Datriem had spoken of sending her 'down' to be imprisoned with her ally, so he must be on the lowest floor, but she didn't see any locked doors. She *did* see a wooden ladder lying on the floor underneath the balcony, and nearby was a closed trapdoor.

When she ran towards it, she heard an unmistakable hoarse shout from below her feet.

As Yala gripped the edges of the trapdoor—at least it wasn't locked—a screeching cry could be heard outside. *The war drake.* Niema had taken a major risk bringing it to the most crowded part of the city, but she must have felt she had little choice.

Yala ignored her leg's pained twinge as she wrenched the trapdoor open. Below was a small, dark room without any windows; upon seeing her, Kelan broke into a coughing fit, shielding his eyes from the blazing light above. "Thank you. I can hardly breathe in here."

"The trapdoor wasn't locked. Couldn't you have flown out?"

"I can't use my powers in the temple." He reached upward, but he wasn't tall enough to grasp the edges of the trapdoor. "Can you get the ladder?"

Someone shouted her name, and Yala cursed. "No time. Grab my arms and try not to pull me in there with you."

"I'll do my best." He reached upward and grasped her forearms, and she braced herself for pain as she gave a firm tug. While Yala tried to keep her weight on her good leg, she hadn't lifted another person since she'd left the army, and the awkward angle made it impossible for her to keep her balance. She fell sideways with an oath, and when she came upright, she saw that Kelan had managed to half climb out.

"Come on." She beckoned, impatient, as he pulled himself the rest of the way out. His blue cloak was specked with dirt and grime.

"Thanks." He scrambled upright, eyeing the commotion by the front door. "What's going on out there?"

"Niema." Yala retrieved her cane, which she'd dropped. Outside came a loud thud, like a heavy body landing on stone, followed by several screams. "We'd better get out of here before every guard in the city tries to arrest her."

Kelan didn't need any encouragement to cross the hall, where novices cowered behind pulpits and in alcoves and hardly seemed to see him and Yala running past. The door itself was blocked by a row of full-fledged Disciples, flames dancing in their palms as they faced the oncoming beast.

"You can't burn a war drake," Yala called from behind. "Get out of range before it eats you."

Burned feathers littered the stone steps in front of the temple entrance, and when Yala and Kelan elbowed their way through the Disciples to the door, the war drake landed in Ceremonial Square, its tail striking the golden statue of Laria's founder.

"Yala!" A wide-eyed Niema waved at her from near a cluster of abandoned market stalls, the sole person outside the temple who remained on this side of the square. Yala struck a Disciple in the kneecaps with her cane and emerged from the temple's doors beside Kelan—but as she did, the war drake's stare turned upon them.

"Shit." Kelan lifted a hand, causing a gust of air to rush towards the war drake and slam into its open mouth. The beast lashed its tail in anger, knocking down several more market stalls and causing Niema to drop to the ground to avoid being knocked flying.

"Kelan, don't make it angrier than it already is." Yala descended the steps in a pained hobble, not daring to take her eyes off the reptilian beast.

When Kelan glided ahead of her, the war drake turned towards him, raising a clawed foot to strike.

"Stop!" Niema waved her hands at the beast, whistling between her teeth, and the war drake's claw crashed through a window instead of through Kelan. "Yala, *how* did you fly on this beast?"

"I didn't bring it into the most crowded part of the city, for a start." Yala ducked another Disciple who attempted to grab her arm from behind. "Kelan, get out of the way!"

She ducked, pulling him down along with her, as one of the Disciples flung a ball of fire at the war drake. The beast's attention returned to the temple, but Kelan was prepared. Before Yala could utter a protest, he'd locked his hands around her arms and leapt down the steps, an air current carrying them to the square.

"What the—?" She broke off when he let go, depositing her beside Niema. "Tell me next time you intend to pick me up without warning."

"You're welcome." He backed up a few steps as another fireball came from the temple; evidently, the Disciples of the Flame had yet to recognise a losing battle. "I'm guessing this is where your plan ran out?" he added to Niema.

She scowled in response and began whistling again. The war drake's head turned towards her, growling when another fireball hit its chest and fizzled out like a firework dropped into the ocean. Fire had no effect on the war drake, but she and the others were entirely too flammable.

Yala prodded Kelan in the shin with her cane. "Help me think of somewhere to run that isn't the pleasure house and isn't likely to have Disciples in it."

"Skytower," Kelan said instantly. "Yes, it's my people's home, but they won't do either of you any harm."

"How do *you* know that?" Admittedly, the Disciples of the Flame had no interest in targeting Saren, and while Melian did, Temik seemingly hadn't known about her role in Machit and Vanat's deaths until Yala had told him. Putting her faith in someone who'd betrayed her was not much of a plan, but Saren would be in even more danger if she stayed in the city much longer.

Niema's whistling reached a higher pitch, and the beast's

huge wings beat, carrying it into the air. Sweat dripped down her forehead from the effort of keeping her attention on the war drake when the Disciples continued to hurl fireballs at it. Ceremonial Square might be considerably emptier than it had been earlier, but onlookers gawked from nearby windows and street entrances. There were far too many human targets.

"I'd say it's a safer bet than staying here," Kelan remarked. "Can you ride on the war drake?"

"What?" Yala cursed when the war drake swung its huge tail, knocking more of the market stalls flying. "They're meant to carry a single passenger, and they'd prefer to carry none most of the time." Yet she'd flown on a war drake with two passengers more than once, and if it was the only way to escape without dooming her allies…

Niema's whistling paused. "Kelan, didn't you say wild drakes often *attack* Skytower?"

"I'll go ahead of you and tell them you're no threat," said Kelan. "This is not the time to be picky."

He had a point there, but mounting a war drake without a stirrup or saddle would be tricky even if she hadn't had an injured leg to contend with. "Niema, if you can get the war drake to lower its head to the ground, it'd be appreciated."

"This isn't as easy as it looks, you know." Niema took the lead as they ran across the square, skirting the golden statue of King Larial, and gave another sharp whistle.

The war drake landed on the flat stones with a thud, and at Niema's whistling command, it lowered its head so that its flat chin rested against the ground. Yala approached, all other noise fading into the background as the war drake's pit-like eyes studied her with a faded version of its former intelligence. Niema had the beast entirely under her power … but would that hold when they were up in the air?

A burst of fire flew across the square, striking the stone

and leaving cracks in its wake. *Fuck it. I'd rather die in the air than on the ground.*

"Hurry up!" Kelan shouted, hovering several handspans in the air—he must have tried to distract the Disciples while they mounted the war drake. "Both of you."

Yala climbed over the war drake's neck, her legs settling into a rider's position without conscious thought. "Niema, you'll have to lean on me. Those scales are rough, and you don't have drakeskin clothes." Though Yala herself hadn't thought to wear them. She hadn't expected to fly again.

"I'll survive." Niema climbed in front of Yala. "Come on!"

Yala squeezed her legs—and the ground fell away beneath them in a lurching motion that caused her to drop her cane. Stunned faces watched their rise, from regular spectators on the streets to the Disciples of the Flame outside of their temple. Yala could have sworn she heard someone shouting the words to an old military song through an open window, but all sound faded into the background as the upper city dropped out of sight, becoming nothing more than a mass of stone and beating hearts. Yala's pulse surged, and a sense of rightness flowed in her blood as it hadn't in years.

In front of her, Niema whimpered. "I'm not sure I like this."

"We can't all be like Kelan." She looked for him, seeing his lone cloaked figure ascending above the city walls. "We'd better hope his fellow Disciples don't follow us, too."

The war drake's vast wings beat, carrying them over the outer walls of the city. Niema straightened in her seat with a startled gasp when the blue curve of the ocean appeared on the horizon.

"Look at that." Yala nodded to the glittering mass at the city's northern edge. "There's your ocean."

"I didn't expect it to be like this." Niema's voice trembled. Yala kept a close watch on her, like she might have done to a novice rider new to the saddle, to make sure she didn't tumble out of her seat. The absence of any riding gear increased the risk, but Yala had flown in more adverse conditions before, and anything was better than being a prisoner.

"Just be glad it isn't raining." She shifted in her seat, knowing that without her drakeskin trousers protecting the insides of her legs from the sharp scales, she'd be in considerable discomfort soon. "Take it from me, flying through a storm isn't fun."

Yala kept an eye on Kelan, the only one who knew the way over the terraces and fields that sprawled west of the city. Yala had grown up on a farm somewhere down there, though little remained after the fire that had caused the deaths of her parents. She knew from Dalem's stories that the mountains in which the Disciples of the Sky made their home lay southward, but her flights with the army had been confined to the coasts, and while she could have guided a war drake along the curve of Laria's north coastline with her eyes closed, the rest of the country remained unmapped in her mind.

Most military maps only covered the north coast and the capital, since the rest of Laria shared no borders with their enemies, and its jungles were of little interest to anyone except when they needed to burn down a stretch of trees to make way for more farmland. From above, Yala was reminded of how small Laria's cities were when compared to the rest of the landmass, despite five hundred or more years of human intrusion. Laria's history was one of constant struggles—if not against their neighbours, then against the wildlife that had lived here long before King Larial had flown here from the northernmost continent and founded a nation of his own. If not for the Disciples, nature would have won, a fact that was easy to forget in a time when Disciples lurked at the edges of the world and not at its centre.

In those stories, the Disciples had moved oceans and carved cities out of stone. They'd burned or moved swathes of forest to make space to keep the vast winged creatures that had become a defining feature of Laria's armies—but they hadn't fought in wars. Much less started them. What would happen if Melian did exactly that? If the Disciples of the Flame had already chosen a side, the others would have to do the same, including Kelan's people.

Not a pleasant thought, though at least it took her mind off the grim knowledge that Temik was Melian's ally. Temik ... she'd known he'd been furious after Dalem's death, but did Dalem's enmity with the Disciples of the Flame no longer matter to him? Why would he willingly ally with the people who'd treated his closest friend so cruelly, let alone look the other way when his new allies murdered two more of his fellow squad members?

Unanswered questions flocked around Yala's mind like the birds Niema had unleashed on the temple, and she dragged her attention back to the present when she realised that she'd lost sight of Kelan. The sun had set as they flew, with the result that the patchwork of fields and forests below were cast in shadow.

Niema lifted her head to the horizon. "Yala ... is that Skytower?"

Yala squinted ahead of them, picking out a low rise of hills or cliffs cutting through the landscape. In their midst, a towering stone structure rose into the sky.

"Skytower," Yala murmured. "We're here."

As they flew, the cliffs grew more visible, rocky promontories from which Skytower arose like a flag planted upon a deserted battlefield.

"These are the mountains?" Niema asked. "I thought mountains were taller ... and covered in snow."

"Snow?" Yala let out a bark of laughter. "Where'd you see

that, in a storybook? In the Parvan Empire, maybe, but not here."

"Don't laugh at me," Niema said. "I've never been this far west before, have I?"

"No offence intended." Yala, who'd thought the sea was solid when she'd first seen it, could hardly fault her for ignorance. She had to admit that even without snow, the idea of someone building a *tower* up in those rocky cliffs struck her as highly risky. It must have originally been built by the Disciples of the Sky themselves, surely, its stone expanse rising to at least five stories and merging with the darkening sky.

She spied Kelan hovering nearby, surveying the tower as if trying to figure out how to land a war drake without being taken as a threat. If they disembarked down in the valley, it'd be a long climb—*oh, shit*. Two more human figures arose from the cliffs near the tower, approaching at speed. Kelan veered closer, but it was too late to change their flight path.

A gust of wind knocked them sideways, causing the war drake to growl. Yala gripped its sides tightly with her knees, but she felt Niema slide out of her seat an instant before her sore legs gave out, sending her tumbling into the darkness.

———

Kelan crossed the air in a blur, hands outstretched, as Niema and Yala fell off the war drake's back. Yala slammed into him, knocking the breath from his lungs, and when he glimpsed Niema tumbling past, he shouted at the nearest Disciple, "Catch her! She's a Disciple of Life!"

His heart sank when Niema continued to fall, but a whistle reached his ears, and the war drake dove towards Niema. Had she directed the beast to catch her while falling to her death? Impressive—but one of the Disciples reached her first, grabbing her arms and halting her fall.

As the Disciple carried Niema higher, Kelan flew in behind them, Yala gripping his shoulders with both hands. "Don't you dare drop me."

"I thought you didn't want me to carry you." When she called him a foul name, he added, "You're handling this better than Niema did."

Kelan kept an eye on the Disciple who held their companion as they flew towards Skytower. Kelan's feet touched solid ground, and he released Yala. She broke away from him, swearing under her breath when she saw the number of Disciples crowding the platform. The man who'd caught Niema landed first, but he did not release her.

Kelan raised his voice. "Let go of her, Lakiel. We're here to talk to Superior Sietra."

"Kelan." Lakiel jerked his head towards him. "You're wanted for questioning in connection to Senik's death."

Of course I am. "I'll gladly submit to questioning, but the others—"

"Is one of them the Disciple of Death?"

"Who, me?" Yala tensed when the Disciples broke into whispers, shouts, jostling her on the platform.

Kelan instantly regretted bringing her with him. He hadn't exactly expected a warm welcome, but it seemed that the false rumours of Yala's involvement in Corruption had reached the tower despite Laima and Tremin still being in the capital.

"Take them to the roof." Lakiel handed a dazed-looking Niema to another Disciple, while a burly man seized Yala around the middle. She twisted out of his grip, her elbow colliding with his chin, but she was outnumbered and had no way out of the tower except a swift fall to her death.

As his fellow Disciples hauled Niema and Yala away, Lakiel approached Kelan. "You, too."

He raised a brow. "This is unnecessary. I did say I wanted to talk to Superior Sietra, didn't I?"

"The Superior is busy, and you're in the company of two unknown Disciples." Lakiel pointed upward. "Go on."

Resigned, he drifted up from the platform on which they'd landed, rising parallel to Skytower itself. He flew past the lower levels, which contained the common areas for Disciples such as the cafeteria and sparring rooms and the dormitories in which novices slept, and ascended past the upper floors, which were reserved for the fully qualified Disciples and some which were for the Superior alone. They halted at an open terrace on the roof, the starkest and coldest part of Skytower. Unlike the Temple of the Flame, the tower didn't have a dungeon, but the roof served the same purpose.

Kelan touched down behind the other Disciples, who'd placed Yala and Niema upon the terrace, inside the flimsy fence that existed as the only barrier between them and the steep drop.

"Don't try to escape," said one of the Disciples. "It's a long way down."

Kelan strode towards them. "You know I can easily get down from here, right?"

"I assume you have more sense than to jeopardise the chance to explain yourself to Superior Sietra," he said. "That's what you wanted, didn't you?"

Yes, he had, but not like this. As the other Disciples descended out of sight, a cool breeze rising in their wake, Niema sank onto the roof. Yala remained standing, her body swaying a little; she'd lost her cane at some point and her clothes were designed for the heat and humidity of the city or jungle, not this freezing rooftop. Kelan tucked his arms into his cloak, glad of the thick layers that were so much of an inconvenience in the city.

Niema spoke through chattering teeth. "I can't sense the war drake anymore. I'm not sure my powers even work."

"They don't?" Yala eyed Kelan. "Is that normal? Don't other Disciples' powers work inside their rivals' temples?"

"It's why I couldn't use my abilities to get out of the Temple of the Flame." They hadn't tortured him, but the heat and lack of air had been punishment enough, and his throat was parched. "I forgot that would happen to you here, Niema."

Yala gave a short laugh. "I'll give the Disciples points for ingenuity in their prisons."

"They didn't throw us from the tower, at least," Kelan ventured. "Superior Sietra will be willing to listen."

Yala scoffed. "To you, perhaps. Me, though? Everyone's heard the rumours."

"I killed one of my fellow Disciples, remember?" Kelan's plan seemed more unwise by the instant, but he refrained from saying so aloud. "I'll speak to Superior Sietra first and vouch for you."

"You can't deny I'm a Disciple of Death when Superior Datriem confirmed it, can you?" Yala sat down, slowly, her injured leg stretched in front of her. "I'm so notorious that even I don't have an inventory of all my crimes."

"Superior Sietra wouldn't unthinkingly accept the word of a stranger she's never met," he said, referencing Melian. "Superior Datriem claimed you brought something back from the island, which I assume was another of her lies."

"Or Temik's." Yala drew her arms tight around her chest, her face grim. "I think he's feeding the Disciples enough information about that mission that they're willing to go along with the rest."

"Temik?" he echoed, the name unfamiliar.

Yala heaved a sigh. "My former squad member."

Niema gasped. "One of your squad members is with Melian?"

"Apparently so." Yala's voice was laced with emotion. Despite her current vulnerable state, she was as tense as a drawn bowstring, and he didn't want to be the one standing in her way when she snapped.

Rather than risk saying something unwise, Kelan removed his cloak and tossed it to Yala and Niema.

"What are you doing?" Yala eyed the cloak as if it might contain a hidden weapon.

"You're both freezing, and I'm likely to be questioned before the two of you," he replied. "I don't have two, but you can trade."

The wind cut right through his thin shirt and further aggravated his dry throat, but the others needed the cloak more than he did. Despite his encroaching exhaustion and the shakiness in his limbs reminding him he hadn't eaten in hours, he paced the terrace to keep warm until two robed novices rose to land on the platform.

"Kelan," one of them said. "Superior Sietra will see you now."

"Good." He strode to the edge of the roof and descended to the upper floor which contained Superior Sietra's office.

Superior Sietra occupied the entire topmost floor of the tower, and her command to enter reverberated in the air as he pushed open the office door. He entered the wide room and knelt upon the mat in the centre, a formality she didn't normally insist upon—which was a good thing for him, because he always forgot.

Superior Sietra watched him from beside the large window that overlooked the mountains. Tall and regal, she towered over him even from the high-backed chair in which she spent most of her time, due to a childhood illness that had cost her the use of her legs. She wore robes of a deep ocean blue and a headdress braided in gold topped her curled nut-brown hair. Despite her fondness for imposing fashion choices, the intimidating factor mostly came from the knowledge that she could have flung Kelan across the room with little more than a flick of her fingers. The god of the sky always served His most ardent worshipper first, so nothing he did would have been able to stop her.

"Kelan," said Superior Sietra. "Do you think grovelling will lessen the punishment?"

"No." He straightened upright and walked to the wide desk behind which her chair sat. "However, I need to explain myself."

"Yes, you do." She gave him a piercing stare, her eyes as sharp as lit coals. "I'd very much like to know why Senik is dead, reportedly at your own hands, as well as why you brought two potential allies of the god of death here to Skytower. Did you not go to the city to root out the cause of the Corruption, not to befriend it?"

For once, words failed him. He'd never noticed how cold it was in the temple without his cloak on, and the chill did nothing to help him think clearly. In addition to Superior Sietra, he also stood beneath the eyes of the god of the sky Himself, whose reptilian form graced a mural on the wall. Terethik, rendered in a vibrant blue and gold mosaic, regarded the room with a satisfied smile upon His face, the tiny figures of humans sitting in front of His clawed feet and coiled tail.

"Kelan?" Superior Sietra said, an impatient bite to her voice.

He cleared his throat. "There has been a miscommunication. One of the individuals currently imprisoned here is a Disciple of Life. The other has no magical skill but was wrongly accused due to a rumour spread by the true Disciples of Death."

"Explain."

It was difficult to know where to start, so he began with his initial arrival in Dalathar. He didn't steer away from his own mistakes along the way as he once might have, including his attempt to capture Yala and his dealings with the mercenaries in Setemar. He left out some details on Yala's squad and their own tangled histories, but otherwise held nothing back.

When he'd finished, Superior Sietra regarded him with a frown. "If you're telling the truth—and this is *quite* the tale, Kelan—then you leave me in a difficult position. You undoubtedly killed one of our own."

"I know." He bowed his head. "I acted rashly, but so did he. If I'm to be punished, I'd ask you to spare my companions. Niema is a member of the Temple of Life, and she came to the capital on the orders of her Superior."

"Then she will be welcome as a guest, if she speaks true," said Superior Sietra. "However, I cannot offer hospitality to a Disciple of Death."

"If destroying one of Mekan's creatures makes one a Disciple of Death, I might say the same for myself, since I killed one, too."

"You were already a Disciple," she said. "And Corruption is little understood, it's true."

"Superior Datriem has a Disciple of Death inside his temple, and it isn't Yala," said Kelan. "Melian has won his trust by betraying her allies, and if Corruption rises, it'll be under his eye."

"It's outside of our scope to intervene within the ranks of another temple," she said. "I intend to send more Disciples to the capital to speak to him, but I cannot ask them to challenge another Superior."

"Then we might be too late," said Kelan. "Melian's goal is to overthrow the king. Her followers call themselves revolutionaries, and with Corruption in their hands, they have a fair chance of achieving their aims."

"They wouldn't be the first to try," she said. "You forget we Disciples have watched many dynasties rise and fall over the years, yet we have always endured."

"Corruption will affect us all," he said. "I thought that was why you sent me there."

"Yes," she said. "I did, and if even the Temple of the Flame is unable to deny its rise, it's too late for us to prevent the inevitable."

His heart sank. "What are you saying?"

"I am saying that we all have difficult choices ahead." She lifted a hand, and a breeze nudged the door open behind him. "I'll decide on your punishment after I talk to your allies."

27

Yala watched the remnants of the day seep out of the sky, the cold air biting at her exposed skin. Kelan had yet to return to the roof, but he was more likely to be given allowances than the two of them were. He'd also left his cloak, but Yala let Niema claim it; she was less used to discomfort than Yala was.

"What did Kelan mean?" Niema asked after a long stretch of silence. "When he said—Superior Datriem thought you brought something back from the island?"

"I don't know." She twitched her wounded leg, wishing she hadn't dropped her cane. "Except…"

"Except what?"

Yala thought back to the possessions she'd left behind in the upstairs room of the pleasure house. "I did keep the claw that stabbed me, but it's hardly proof that I'm a Disciple of Death. No, that was another one of Melian's lies … or Temik's."

"He—" Niema fumbled the words. "He was part of your squad? On the island?"

"Yes." She knew Niema had more questions, but so did

Yala herself, including what had driven Temik to join forces with the people who'd treated Dalem so cruelly. "I'd say he's been smoking lakeweed, but I don't think they allow that in the Temple of the Flame."

"I should have believed your warning to stay away from them." Niema shivered, pulling Kelan's cloak tighter around her shoulders. "I know my people are seen as excessive in our devotion, but I cannot imagine any other Temple willingly taking in a Disciple of Death, let alone someone who presents a threat to the nation. Didn't the Disciples of the Flame used to help protect the monarch?"

"At one time," said Yala. "I guess His Majesty did away with that tradition as well."

King Daliel had no need of Disciples to defend him when he hid away in his palace instead of flying out to war as King Tharen had done, but she didn't know if he still discussed diplomatic matters with Superior Datriem as his predecessor had done. She hoped not, given Melian's proximity to the temple. *Does it matter? None of them will listen to me either way.*

"The Disciples of the Sky are supposed to be fairer," Niema added after a short pause. "According to Kelan, anyway. They won't keep us here indefinitely."

"You, certainly not," said Yala. "If they have any sense, they'll let you go back to the capital."

"I won't leave without you." Niema lifted her chin. "It would defeat the purpose of my mission."

She still thinks I'm the person who can help defeat Corruption? "Did you forget the Disciples of the Flame *and* Melian's people will be searching the streets of Dalathar for me? Twice I've surrendered, and twice I've escaped, but I can't keep running forever. You have obligations to your enclave, too, not just me."

"I don't know how to explain what I've done to my other enclave members." Niema's hands clenched in her lap. "Not only have I made enemies of two branches of Disciples, but I violated my vow of non-violence against living beings when I set innocent creatures upon the Temple of the Flame and let them burn."

Yala looked at her blankly and then remembered the burning feathers that had surrounded the temple when she'd escaped. "If there'd been another way to get me out of there, I don't know of one. You saved my life. Kelan's, too."

Before Niema could reply, a gust of wind arose, bringing a robed Disciple to the edge of the roof. "Our leader would speak to you."

Niema stood, discarding Kelan's cloak, and they vanished in another swirl of cold air. Yala reached for Kelan's cloak. Why he'd given it to them ... well, she'd found him slowly cooking in a dungeon earlier, so maybe he was glad of the cooler temperature. As it was, she would have paced to keep warm if her leg didn't object, so she wrapped the cloak around her shoulders and tried not to think of the inevitable interrogation ahead of her. If Superior Sietra decided she was guilty the way Superior Datriem had, she might as well have thrown herself over the edge and save them the bother.

No. After she'd gone through so much effort to survive, she refused to die in captivity, and she owed it to the rest of her team to make it back to the capital. Except for Temik, but if anything, her desire to know what had driven him to make the choice he had surpassed her anger at his claims that she had some affinity with the god of death. *Mekan's touch.*

This wouldn't be the first time Temik had hurled accusations at her; he'd never let her forget that it was she who'd decided to land on the island and drawn the attention of the force that had claimed it. Never mind that she'd barely put one foot inside the temple. She certainly hadn't interacted with the god of death.

Not then.

I am not dabbling in Corruption. Mekan might have spoken to me, but I didn't listen to him. I didn't do anything.

The thought of Machit's body stirring brought a shudder to her skin. She hadn't asked Dalem for the details on exactly how Corruption magic functioned—hadn't had time, given that they'd been running for their lives—but she knew the death god's power could linger for long after the humans who'd called upon Him were dead. Mekan had been taunting her, nothing more.

I didn't make a bargain with him. He has no hold over me.

Convincing Superior Sietra of that would be harder, however.

After perhaps an hour, the Disciple who'd taken Niema downstairs came for Yala. "Don't try to fight. You'll only fall to your doom."

"I'm aware." She held her breath, tense, as the Disciple seized her arms and lifted her into the air. If she'd closed her eyes, she might have been able to pretend she was flying on the back of a wild drake, but their flight was much more elegant, much smoother, and much showier. The Disciple's cloak streamed behind them as they carried her downward and glided through an opening between two pillars one storey below the rooftop.

Skytower's design was peculiar. Based on her admittedly limited view, it looked as if each storey was slightly smaller than the one below and ringed by an exterior balcony. The result was that when she leaned over the edge, she could see all the way down to the foot of Skytower and the platform on which they'd initially landed. There were no stairs either, that she'd seen, but why would Disciples of the Sky need them when they could take flight from the instant that they took their vows?

"This way." The Disciple who held her arms steered her away from the view and alongside the stone wall until they came to a wooden door. A rap upon the door announced her presence, and it swung inward.

Yala entered the Superior's office, feet echoing on stone, her leg protesting the lack of a cane. On left and right, murals adorned the wall—on the right, a battlefield, and on the left, a depiction of the god of the sky. Talathik was depicted as a figure clothed in gold and blue, towering over a prayer mat upon which human figures knelt.

His human ambassador was equally impressive. Superior Sietra was seated in front of a large window that displayed the impressive landscape beyond the mountains. She wore a headdress of gold plating and robes of a deeper blue than the other Disciples of the Sky.

"Superior Sietra." Yala inclined her head—a Disciple would kneel, but despite everyone's beliefs, she wasn't one, and with the fragile state of her legs after her flight, she'd be lucky not to keel over. "I'd say it's an honour to meet you, but I wish the circumstances were more ideal."

"You must be Yala Palathar." Superior Sietra's sharp eyes took her in, from her injured leg to the scar on her face. "You were a soldier, correct?"

"I was, yes," Yala said. "Captain in the flight division."

"I imagine you must appreciate the view." She gestured behind her, where the dark landscape of Laria's south spread outward below the tower. "I expect the roof is more picturesque, but also rather colder."

Yala wasn't sure if she was intending to make a joke or relieve the tension, but she didn't let her guard down. "Yes. I spent, ah, eight years in the sky. Ten if you count my apprentice years."

"Impressive," Superior Sietra said. "Kelan gave me a thorough account of how you met, but I'd like to hear it from you, too."

So far, she'd made no direct reference to Yala's supposed

status as a Disciple of Death. While Yala didn't believe it would be far from Superior Sietra's thoughts, she was glad of the chance to explain herself. That was more than Superior Datriem had offered her.

Yala drew in a breath and gave an account of the events that had led to her arrival in Skytower, leaving out little except Temik's involvement. That was private, and she didn't know the details of how he'd joined the Disciples of the Flame nor how Melian had gained knowledge of Corruption to begin with.

Superior Sietra studied her for a moment when she was finished. "That's quite a story, but it matches Kelan's, and you don't strike me as much of a fanciful storyteller as he is. If it's true that the Disciples of the Flame are compromised, there is little we can do from here, and they are the Disciples whose power is uniquely equipped to deal with Corruption."

Yala's hands clenched. "So ... you're staying here? No matter what happens in the capital?"

Had she truly expected more? The Disciples had never involved themselves in the affairs of kings in the past. Even when they'd fought as soldiers prior to the peace treaties in the past century, they were always set against their fellow Disciples from enemy nations, not against Corruption.

"I will stay here, yes," said Superior Sietra, gesturing at the chair in which she sat. "While the god of the sky cares little for mortal limitations when He chooses His followers, entering the Temple of the Flame would see me stripped of any access to His power and thus render me grounded. Superiors are no exception to the rule."

"Oh." Yala's face burned as the implication sank in. "I didn't know that until Kelan lost his abilities in the Temple of the Flame. Is it because one god's power supersedes the others?"

"In a temple, where faith is strongest—yes," she said.

"Otherwise, each has their own strengths and weaknesses. Yes, even Corruption."

Yala licked her dry lips. "Ah—I suppose the fact that most people who use Corruption tend to drop dead is a disadvantage of sorts."

"That is true," she said. "It's not against our rules to host another Disciple in our temple, but a Disciple of Death…"

"I'm not a Disciple of anything." She ought to have guessed that Superior Sietra was waiting for the opportune moment to bring up the subject. "Melian started the rumour because she needed to give the Disciples of the Flame an obvious target."

"Undoubtedly," said Superior Sietra, "but she drew the rumour from somewhere, and if you truly glimpsed the Void itself…"

"The rest of my squad looked into the Void, too," Yala said. "I don't claim to be an expert on the subject, but who is?"

"I've studied the matter," said Superior Sietra. "I have also visited other nations, ones that have different roles for their Disciples. The Parvan Empire entrusts them in positions of power, did you know?"

"Not Disciples of Death." Yala's knowledge of other countries was as limited as one would expect from her patchy education, but she knew that no nation condoned or practised Corruption magic. "Isn't it illegal in the Parvan Empire?"

"In most nations, yes," she said. "Especially the ones in which Disciples of the Flame hold the highest status. Our own deity is more open-minded, so we do not disallow our scholars from studying the theory."

A chill swept through the room, making Yala aware that she'd dropped Kelan's cloak at some point on her flight down from the roof. "I didn't know there were any texts on the subject."

"Mostly in translation, but there are," she said. "It's not so unusual for us to want to understand the workings of other Disciplines, and Mekan's history is entangled with the other deities', whether we acknowledge it or not."

Yala's attention went to the mural again, but no other gods accompanied Terethik. "The stories say the other deities kicked Him out of the heavens…"

"And He created the Void in defiance, yes," Superior Sietra finished. "The specifics vary depending on the tale, but I think we can agree that Mekan's demands are ill suited for founding a nation upon."

"You mean sacrificing lives?" Yala's thoughts went to Dalem, unwillingly. "I've seen other deities take the lives of their followers if they ask for too much."

It was a risky statement to say in front of a representative of one of those deities, but the question had been gnawing at her for years. Corruption was evil, undoubtedly, but how could the Disciples of the Flame claim superiority after everything they'd done in their own god's name?

Superior Sietra smiled, inexplicably. "Yes. It's a point few other Disciplines would wish to acknowledge, that we all have the potential to use the deities' power to inflict harm. What sets Corruption apart is that the law of most nations generally eschews taking innocent lives or views the practise as a moral wrong."

Was she implying that there was a way to use Corruption *without* making such compromises? Surely not. Though Niema's revulsion at the deaths of the birds she'd unleashed upon the Temple of the Flame were a reminder that the strict laws her enclave had put upon their members might be for their own protection as much as anything else.

"In any case," said Superior Sietra, "Corruption was not

outlawed officially in Laria, mostly because it was believed to be extinct, and none of our past monarchs has had much interest in magic."

"Until…" *Until King Tharen.* Yala couldn't finish the sentence, so ingrained within her was the fear of retribution. The floor, however solid beneath her feet, seemed as if it might slide away and leave her to fall. "Until Rafragoria found that island."

She'd always assumed Rafragoria had been the first to spot the island off their shore, though she'd never had it confirmed.

"You want to know if any of us were aware of what was on the island," Superior Sietra said. Yala hadn't, but now curiosity prickled at her skin. "No, the affairs of monarchs and militaries are not ours, and while I made sure to stay updated on each new development in the wars, I did not know until afterwards that the island had contained a temple devoted to the god of death."

"Who told you, Superior Datriem?" Anger churned in her gut. "He threatened me into keeping quiet, but he went around telling the other Superiors?"

"Only Superior Dovial of the Temple of the Earth and me," she replied. "The others were too far afield, and he was frightened of repercussions."

"Frightened." A bitter laugh escaped. "Did he mention my name? He can't have met Melian by then, so she didn't have time to poison his mind with lies about me."

"No, but he requested that my Disciples keep an eye out, should you return to the capital."

"Why? In case I might teach myself to contact the god of death?"

"Yes," she said, without as much as a twitch in her expression. "If you engaged in an active pursuit of Corruption, you would become a Disciple."

"With what texts? What leaders?" Yala fought to reel in her temper like a fisherman taming a large catch. "I don't want anything to do with the other Disciples at all, especially Superior Datriem. Though if joining another Temple would erase any potential influence Mekan might have on me—"

"Unlikely," said Superior Sietra. "None would allow a Disciple of Death to enter their ranks."

Temik had the same potential as I did, but he lied. Her nails bit into her palms. "Then what? Do you plan to have me killed? If so, you'll be helping the enemy ... though Melian won't be pleased, I suppose, because she got it into her head that she ought to be the one to kill me herself if she wants to win over the god of death."

"She was right."

"I—excuse me?" Despite the cold air biting at her skin, the room abruptly felt as confined and as suffocating as the Temple of the Flame.

"Given the choice between a regular person and a Disciple, Mekan would always take the latter. Yes, I know you're untrained." She held up a hand as Yala began to object. "However, nobody but a Disciple can hear the voice of a god."

The breath punched from Yala's lungs. *I ... told her I heard Mekan.* She'd thought nothing of it at the time, assuming everyone had heard. Though Saren hadn't been conscious at the time, and Melian...

Fuck.

Superior Sietra's attention returned to the window, as if to give Yala time to process the truth of her words. *I am a Disciple of Death.* No wonder Melian wanted her gone. The knowledge also somewhat justified Temik's decision to join another Temple if he'd wanted to avoid Mekan's influence, too, though she didn't know how he could have known beforehand. Yala still had far too many questions, but Superior Sietra had not dismissed her yet.

"And what part does my own will play in this?" Yala said. "I have no intention of using death magic. None. I want Melian brought to heel before she overruns the city with the dead and assassinates the king."

"Understandable," said Superior Sietra. "I might be unable to travel to the capital myself, but I will send in a team to watch the situation. I have no personal quarrel with Corruption, and as the god of death is unlikely to be a threat to us, I will allow you to stay in my temple."

"Stay?" *For how long?* Yala knew she ought to thank Superior Sietra for her generosity, but her words carried the underlying hint of steel that made her suspect she was being given an order.

"Yes." She lifted a hand, and the door blew open behind Yala. "Kelan, enter. You too, Niema."

Yala stiffened as her companions walked into the room. She hadn't known they were outside the office, but it made sense that Superior Sietra would want to talk to the three of them together.

"Now I have heard an account of recent events from all of you, I would ask what you intend to do."

Kelan answered first. "With your permission, I intend to return to the city and finish my mission... that is, if Laima and Tremin can be convinced that I am not an ally of Corruption out to undermine them."

"If they do not come back to Skytower by morning, I will request that any Disciples I send to the capital will speak with them," she said. "I will let you know by then whether I think you capable of resuming your mission or not."

Kelan dipped his head, a restrained gesture of respect that nevertheless looked odd on someone normally so self-possessed. Superior Sietra's approval meant a great deal to him, and why wouldn't it? Yala had been the same towards her superiors ... right up until the moment the king had knocked the foundations of her world from underneath her.

Niema cleared her throat. "And me? I would like to return to the city, too. I also need to warn my people of the impending threat."

When Yala tried to catch her eye, a sharp glint of anger and resentment struck her like a spear. *Oh. She knows I'm a Disciple of Death ... and I can no longer deny it.*

"Do as you like," Superior Sietra said. "You may leave whenever you desire, but I'd advise you to spend the night here and begin the journey when it's light. Kelan, I can trust you to find a room for our guest, can't I?"

Kelan glanced at Yala, and she detected a flicker of guilt in his expression. "Yes. What about Yala?"

"As I said, I see no issue with her staying here," said Superior Sietra. "It seems to me that allowing you to travel back to the capital would give the enemy a considerable advantage."

"What?" Yala stared at her. "Look—my allies are in the city, and Melian is looking for them as well as for me. If they come here next—"

"They won't," said Superior Sietra. "The tower is quite safe."

Safe. Yala would almost have preferred death to imprisonment, whichever form it took. Niema said no words in her defence, though Kelan wore a frown of discontent. "Yala does have allies, including inside the palace itself. She can help us."

Viam. Did she *know Temik joined the Disciples of the Flame?* They'd never discussed the subject.

"Enough." Superior Sietra's tone rang with steel. "You forget you're awaiting punishment for murder, Kelan, and if not for the urgency of the situation, you'd be joining Yala in confinement."

"You're sending me back to the roof?" Disbelief bled into her tone.

"As a precaution," said Superior Sietra. "Mostly for your own safety. There are some who are less accepting than I, or who would believe letting you survive is too great a risk. I will ensure you're kept as comfortable as possible, given the circumstances."

Yala's mouth opened, but no argument came out. Numbness gripped her body, infiltrated her mind, and she was scarcely aware of being escorted out of the office.

Two Disciples seized her arms and carried her back up to her prison on the rooftop. It was full dark by now, and colder than ever, though someone had put out a sleeping mat and a blanket for her. She had to admit the view of the night sky was spectacular, and when her captors departed in a sweep of their cloaks, she found herself arrested by the sheer majesty of the blots of whiteness shining out of the gloom.

Staying here might not be such a tragedy. It might not be quite as comfortable as the home she'd built in the jungle, but her cabin was gone, and that was all she'd really wanted, wasn't it? A place to retire, to live out her remaining days without being beholden to anyone. Human or god.

Mekan couldn't reach her here. If she'd been tied to Him ever since she'd flown to that island, it was no wonder death dogged her every step.

Yet the old morose thoughts didn't carry the same weight as before. She and the rest of her squad had walked away from that mission changed, undoubtedly. In their own ways, they'd all given up on the future they'd once thought they had, though not by choice.

Who was to say if they had any sway over their own destinies? In the end, no level of denial had prevented the god of death from seeking her out. Not the threat to her life, nor her mishandled isolation from her squad. Even the message the god of life had imparted to Niema's enclave had proven false, though not for the reasons Yala had initially believed.

Niema will probably never speak to me again. The truth lay heavy on her soul, but she found it hard to regret a choice she'd never made to begin with. The god of death had marked her, but that didn't make her a Disciple. Dalem, for one, had proven that nothing was foretold, and nobody's fate was written in stone.

The choice would be Yala's. The gods knew she'd made some bad ones lately—even leaving the capital had been a mistake—yet her conversation with Superior Sietra had brought a level of clarity that Yala hadn't felt in a long time. Damned or not, she was willing to risk anything to bring Melian down.

Even becoming a Disciple of Death.

28

Kelan had thought that being back at home in Skytower would make him feel more at ease, but it did not. Part of it was that word of his role in Senik's death had spread throughout the entire tower, and whispers trailed him wherever he went. Meanwhile, Niema was in a taciturn mood after Superior Sietra's revelation concerning Yala's connection to the god of death, refusing to speak to him as they walked down the draughty corridor where the guest rooms were located.

"I can show you around Skytower while they're preparing your room," he offered, but she merely grunted in response. "We don't have guests often."

Each Disciple had their own private room, though the novices slept in dormitories on the lowest floor until they took their vows and gained access to the benefits of being a full Disciple. He'd hoped Niema might take an interest in the ways in which Skytower differed from her own experience as a Disciple, but she didn't even react to his explanation of how the wastewater was carried out of the privies through the open holes in the floor, nor his offer to show her the bathing rooms, which were positioned for easy access to the freshwater from the fast-flowing rivers on the mountainside. He'd thought she might at least want to clean off some of the city's grime, but she remained stubbornly silent until they reached her guest room.

"Dinner will be served soon," he told her. "I'll have to carry you to the lower level, though … we don't usually need stairs."

"No." It was the first word she'd spoken to him since they'd been on the rooftop dungeon.

"You can ask a novice to bring a meal to your room, but—"

"Good, I'll do that." Without looking back, she disappeared into the guest room and closed the door.

Kelan sighed. Did she think he'd intentionally kept Yala's secret? She might have, or she might see them as conspirators—or else the revelation had reverted her back to her former dislike of him. In any case, he was wasting his time arguing with her, so he went down to the cafeteria on the lower floor with the intention of taking a meal to Yala in case they forgot to feed her.

Lakiel had other ideas. The other Disciple snatched the second bowl from Kelan's hand when he walked past. "You're not to visit the prisoner, Superior Sietra said."

"Fine, as long as you aren't starving her," he responded. "Did the Superior send for me?"

"No, she said that she'll contact you tomorrow."

Evidently, she had yet to decide on his punishment. Kelan carried his own meal up to his quarters to escape the stares from his fellow Disciples, resigning himself to waiting until Superior Sietra had concocted a plan to deal with the situation in the capital before he faced the consequences for killing Senik. No doubt those consequences would worsen if he acted on one of his half-formed schemes to rescue Yala from the rooftop, as tempting as they might be.

As the evening wore on, Kelan found himself kneeling on his little-used prayer mat and asking for guidance from Terethik for possibly the first time since he'd been a novice. He rarely thought of those days, but with the renewed uncertainty over his fate came memories of a time when he'd feared that Terethik might take away Kelan's gift and leave him with nothing. He'd never been a high achiever as a novice, but his confidence had mounted with each passing month until he all but forgot he'd ever doubted himself at all.

Now? Certainly, Superior Sietra must have had some level of trust in him if she'd sent him to investigate Corruption before anyone else, but he'd undoubtedly fucked up, and the least of what he might expect as a consequence was confinement to the tower for the foreseeable future. It was better than death or exile, certainly, but if he and Yala were both unable to leave Skytower, would anyone be able to stop Melian from making a second bid for power?

Terethik provided no answers, and Niema refused to answer when he'd knocked on the door to her guest room, no doubt stewing in fury over Yala's supposed change in loyalties. She at least would be allowed to return to the capital the following day, but it was anyone's guess as to whether she'd be able to stop Melian single-handedly. Short of unleashing an army of war drakes upon her—and no doubt the Disciple of Life would have prepared a list of reasons that wouldn't be possible.

After a sleepless night in which he was unable to get comfortable no matter how he lay on his mat, the morning brought another unwelcome surprise. As Kelan watched the sun rise from one of the balconies overlooking the lower terrace, he spied two figures land on the platform below. Laima and Tremin. He'd forgotten their impending return, and while he'd hoped they wouldn't spot him standing above —not least because he was without any weapons to defend himself against another beating—Laima's eyes locked on him right away.

"Kelan?" she called to him.

"You're back." His body tensed at the memory of their last encounter when she flew up to meet him. "Did you already cross paths with Superior Sietra's envoy?"

Tremin joined her, wearing a scowl that didn't ease Kelan's apprehension, but Laima's expression held none of the hostility it had the last time he'd seen her. "There's no need to look at me as if I'm going to throw you to your death, Kelan."

Kelan made sure he wasn't standing too close to the edge all the same. "Then you did speak to Superior Sietra?"

"Yes," growled Tremin. "I don't know how you convinced her to ignore the evidence of your wrongdoing."

"What evidence?"

"Senik's dead body."

"She knows I killed him." His gaze flicked up to the tower's topmost floor. "I told her the reasons, and you're free to believe me or otherwise, though I'd rather you refrained from any more violent interrogations."

"Tremin," Laima said. "You were supposed to apologise for that."

"What?" Kelan turned to her, startled. "You believe me?"

"I believe we might have been a little hasty, yes," she said. "Though you didn't help the situation when you decided to fall asleep in front of my room."

"If you had a night like I did, you'd have been drinking, too," Kelan told her. "I was waiting for your return, and I thought you'd hear of Senik's death sooner than you did. I wanted to explain myself before you handed me in…"

"Enough." She held up a hand. "I've heard the full story

now, and while I can't grasp how the Disciples of the Flame are involved in this, I'm not going to question that you had anything but a good reason for turning on Senik."

"And Yala?" he asked. "Do you believe she's not the villain everyone seems to think she is?"

"I assume Superior Sietra has a good reason for sparing her life," said Laima, "but that's not our main concern. We need to deal with the problems brewing in the capital before anything else."

"Yes, and Yala can help with that."

"Is your mind stuck on nothing but this woman?" she said, exasperated. "This is about more than your prick, Kelan."

"That's not what I—" He broke off, unsure how much of Laima's anger at him was misplaced jealousy, and how much was her overlooking the advantage of having a potential Disciple of Death on their side. What Yala thought of the matter was another issue, but it was plain to see that Superior Sietra did not believe she presented a threat to his fellow Disciples.

"Regardless of the prisoner's situation, Superior Sietra has asked me to lead a group of Disciples to the capital to speak with the Disciples of the Flame," said Laima. "You'll come with me, to prevent any misunderstandings. Tell our guest, too."

"Right. Niema." She *wanted* him to go back to Dalathar? *I suppose there aren't many other witnesses to the recent events.* "I'll tell her. When—?"

"Two hours from now," Laima answered. "I expect you to be presentable by then."

Presentable? Weren't they going to join—if not stop—a war? Admittedly, he wouldn't get far without any weapons, and he'd need to get his cloak back, too. He'd left it on the roof with Yala.

337

Reasoning that Niema would have no choice but to answer the door this time, he made for her guest room. To his disconcertion, Laima and Tremin followed him, waiting expectantly for him to knock on the door.

Kelan rapped his knuckles on the wooden surface. "Niema? We're leaving for the capital in two hours."

She answered the door a moment later, her head held high and a haughty tilt to her chin. "Good. Wait, did you say 'we'?"

Tremin stepped in. "Niema, I apologise for how we treated you at our last meeting."

"As do I." Laima lowered her head in a gesture of respect. "Do let us know if there is anything we can do to assist you."

"Superior Sietra said that I would be permitted to leave the tower today." Niema's tone was flat, almost contemptuous, but she addressed Laima instead of him. "I will require an escort back to the capital."

Not me, I assume. Though he had to question what Niema planned to do upon their arrival. Without Yala, the odds of surviving their next encounter with Melian were lower than ever.

"Kelan, where are you going?" Laima called after him as he moved away from Niema's door.

"To talk to Superior Sietra." He reached the platform edge and glided upward to the top level, hoping they didn't follow him this time.

"Come in," Superior Sietra called after he knocked on the door, and she showed no surprise when she saw him enter. "Kelan. You already spoke to Laima and Tremin?"

"Yes. They said I was to go with them to the capital. Is that true?"

"Correct," she said. "After the situation in Dalathar is dealt with, you'll come straight back here to serve out your punishment."

His spine prickled. "Which is…?"

"You'll be confined to the tower for a period of time—a month should do it," she said. "And stripped of your rank as a full Disciple for that long. I think it's only fair."

Some of his apprehension eased. "Thank you. Ah—and Yala? Is she to remain imprisoned?"

"Yes," she said. "You may take your other guest with you when you depart for Dalathar."

He shouldn't have expected any more, and yet… "I understand why you want to keep her confined, but I truly believe that she can only be an asset in the coming fight, not a hindrance."

"My hope is that you'll find a way to avoid a fight, Kelan, if at all possible."

"I doubt Melian will make that a viable option."

"Her plan hinges on sacrificing Yala, doesn't it?" she queried. "Essentially, she's forced to keep the god of death at a distance, no doubt relying upon the protection of the Temple of the Flame until she is able to amass enough power —enough sacrifices, if you will—to gain strength enough to break into the palace and displace the monarch."

Kelan's mouth parted. Superior Sietra was an accomplished enough strategist that he shouldn't be surprised that she'd figured out Melian's plan, but it didn't seem complete to him. Couldn't she do the same without Yala? "There are others like Yala … other Disciples of Death. I'm sure Melian isn't the only person with a bond with the god of death in the capital."

"No, but we don't need to make her job any easier, do we?" she said. "Let us assume I've anticipated and countered all your arguments, Kelan. You have a long day ahead of you, and you don't want me to change my mind and start your confinement early, do you?"

"No." That would do even less to help the situation,

though his own abilities to stop Melian were debatable at best. "You do have time to change your mind, though."

"I do, but it is unlikely."

Kelan sighed inwardly. "Can I at least fetch my cloak? I left it on the roof."

"Ask someone else. You're not the only person in this tower who can fly, Kelan." She lifted a hand, and the door swung open behind him, a clear dismissal.

No, but I might be the only person willing to get Yala off that roof.

Unfortunately, there were few angles from which he could approach the roof without being spotted, and the other Disciples were stirring by now. Blue-cloaked figures thronged every platform and terrace, and while his fellow Disciples weren't *quite* as cold towards him as the previous evening, he doubted they'd assist him in any more transgressions.

He found Niema inside the cafeteria on the lowest floor, sitting stiff-backed on a bench next to Laima and Tremin and picking at a plate of fruit. He grabbed a plate of his own from the selection on the back table and joined them.

"I take it your attempts to talk Superior Sietra into freeing your companion were unsuccessful?" said Laima.

"Yes, though I need someone to go to the prison and fetch my cloak. For some reason, she doesn't trust me to go get it myself."

Laima arched a brow at her companion. "Tremin?"

"No," Tremin growled. "I'm not running errands for him. Can't he get a new cloak?"

"All my money is in the pockets of that one." Not that there was much of it. "I also find myself without any weapons. Did you leave mine at the inn?"

Laima's face flushed. "Ah, yes, but you're allowed to visit

the weapons room, you know. You aren't under confinement yet."

"Good to know." He tried to catch Niema's eye, failed, and returned his attention to his plate while he contemplated ways to get Yala out of prison without ending up joining her.

An hour later, Kelan waited on the terrace with the other Disciples selected for the mission, equipped with both his cloak and a replacement for the sword he'd left in the capital. While he'd asked a novice to fetch his cloak from the roof without setting foot up there himself, Laima kept glancing in his direction as if she suspected him of trickery, which wouldn't be inaccurate.

"We're leaving now," she told the gathered Disciples. "Tremin will lead the way, and I'll bring up the rear."

Typical. Laima watched the others leave one at a time without moving herself. If he wanted to avoid being found out, Kelan would have to join them, and then let himself be overtaken and double back towards the tower without Laima noticing.

As he took a step forward, she held out a hand to stop him. "Kelan, wait a moment."

"What is it?" he queried. "Changed your mind?"

She pointed upward. "You want to get your friend out of there."

Words of denial rose to his tongue, but he discarded them all, knowing none would fool her. "If we don't get her out, there's a fair chance she'll try to climb down and die in the process."

Next to him, Niema's mouth twitched into a scowl, but she didn't say a word.

"You mentioned Yala knows the person who's threatening the city," said Laima. "Does Yala have a plan to stop her?"

"Not … not exactly, but I think she's more likely to be able to than any of us." There was no point in underplaying the issue. "Her past experience with death magic has given her insight into how we might get the upper hand on Melian. She's no typical Disciple."

Laima exhaled. "Fine. Go on, and I'll make sure nobody follows you up there."

"Really?"

She inclined her head. "Yes, but you'd better move quickly."

Kelan needed no encouragement, though he saw Niema's face twist in disgust or perhaps anger when he rose into the air. He glided upward, taking a route that avoided putting himself within view of Superior Sietra's office window, and then touched down on the roof.

Yala startled, half rising from the sleeping mat on which she sat. "Are you supposed to be up here?"

"Absolutely not."

She groaned. "Don't tell me you're defying your Superior again."

"With any luck, she won't realise until we're gone," he said. "You want to go back to the capital, right?"

Yala pushed to her feet. "Is Niema...?"

"She's with Laima," he said. "Laima is on our side, don't worry."

Yala huffed out a sigh and limped over to him. "Then I'll surrender my dignity for a while."

"It's not all bad." There was no way to carry her that she wouldn't object to, so he settled for gripping her shoulders from behind so she could at least see where they were going. Then Kelan stepped off the roof, calling a breeze that carried them both downward to the platform on which Laima and Niema waited.

Upon seeing him, Laima took to the sky with her passenger, who didn't give either of them a second glance.

"I assume she's going home," Yala murmured. "Niema,

that is. I can't fault her for wanting to warn her enclave. About Melian … and me."

"She'll realise she was wrong." Kelan didn't know if that would reassure her but felt compelled to try. "I expect she's struggling to reconcile your, ah, connection with the god of death with the rather stringent requirements of her own deity."

Yala made a sceptical noise. "I'm not sure that's a struggle I'm likely to win."

He sought a change of subject that didn't involve their potential imminent deaths. "Your leg doesn't hurt, does it?"

"No. Less than flying on a war drake, if you can believe it." She gave a quiet laugh. "Though if we're attacked by one of those in the air, I can't say I like our survival odds."

"I expect yours returned to the wild." He didn't see any winged creatures above the forests and fields, and a war drake would be hard to miss from up here. "Or it'll be waiting for you near the capital."

"Hardly," she said. "They aren't loyal to anyone. Niema's ability is the only reason that one didn't take off my head."

"You seem to have survived years in the flight division in one piece."

"Not everyone did," she said. "If Disciples had been part of the military, we might not have had to use war drakes, but that would have brought problems of its own."

"You aren't wrong." He thought back to Superior Sietra's sharp assessment of the situation. "I never would have guessed that I'd see the Disciples involving themselves in politics."

"Not enough of them," Yala muttered. "It'll take more than a small envoy like this to counter Melian's allies."

"I hoped for a bigger team, too," Kelan agreed, "but I think the other Disciples of the Flame can be swayed. We can all agree that the murder of our monarch and handing our capital over to the god of death would not result in anything other than terrible consequences for everyone, except perhaps for Melian."

"Or me." Yala was silent for a moment, watching the fields below. "It depends if you view being a Disciple of Death as an advantage."

"Don't you have to choose to be a Disciple?" A rhetorical question, it was undoubtedly true, at least in his experience. The deity might choose their followers, but the followers had the right to choose, too.

"Theoretically." Another short pause. "What if you have two choices, both shitty ones?"

That, he didn't have the answer to. "Then you make the choice you can live with, I suppose."

"Temik's choice isn't one I could have lived with." Her voice was quiet enough that he wouldn't have caught the words if the back of her head hadn't been pressed against his chest.

"Your squad member?" Curiosity reared its head, but he knew that he couldn't push her to confide in him, and that she was likely only talking to him out of the lack of any other available options. Niema was no longer a possible confidant, after all. "He joined the Disciples of the Flame?"

"Yes, and he's the one who told everyone I was a Disciple of Death."

"Why?" He knew from the irritated noise she made that she found the question annoying, but she answered regardless.

"Because he blamed me for Dalem's death, I suppose," she said. "I can't figure it out either. The Temple of the Flame treated Dalem like shit. He had to join the army to get away from them, and they refused to acknowledge him as one of theirs even when he died in their service."

"Strange." Kelan had his own suspicions, but he didn't

know Temik, not like Yala did. "Stranger is that Superior Datriem accepted the rise of Corruption as inevitable."

"So did Superior Sietra." Yala heaved a sigh. "And you wonder why I don't have a high opinion of Disciples."

"I might remind you that a Disciple is the reason you aren't falling to your death."

She twisted one arm out of his grip and gave him a rude gesture. He winked in return, though he didn't want to push his luck now that she'd finally accepted him as an ally. There was no telling what would happen when they reached the capital.

As Dalathar's walls came within view, Laima and Niema separated from the rest of the group, heading eastward.

"She's leaving," Yala murmured. "I thought … well, she hasn't completed her mission, but I suppose there's not much else for her to do. The existence of Corruption is a direct threat to her people, so I expect she'll want to warn them to prepare in case it eventually spreads out of the capital and reaches their home."

"Denial doesn't work as a strategy either."

"I know," said Yala. "I already tried that one."

Neither spoke again until they angled towards the outer wall of the city. "Where do you want to land?"

"Near the pleasure district," she replied. "Assuming the Disciples of the Flame didn't pay a visit and force Saren into hiding."

"All right." He angled south of his fellow Disciples to avoid them accosting him and carried Yala over the wall to the outer city. While he knew he'd face questions when he joined them, he had no regrets concerning his decision to rescue her.

When they landed on a bridge near the pleasure district, he released Yala. "You can walk from here, right?"

"I can." She turned to him, her windswept hair tangling around her face. "Thank you. I guess I owe you one."

"If you still had that war drake, I'd ask you to return the favour when Superior Sietra confines me in the tower for the next year."

Yala gave a short laugh. "Unlikely. I'll meet you in … how long will your meeting with the Disciples of the Flame take?"

"I think we'll discuss strategies first," he said. "We won't go there right away. You have time to talk to your friends."

"Give it an hour, then," she said. "Then come and find me. If I'm not here, I'll be in the undercity… assuming we're both alive."

"I enjoy how optimistic you are." He grinned. "I'll come back as soon as I have news."

29

Niema asked Laima to leave her near the outskirts of the city. While she'd have a long journey home from there, it would give her time to think over how she was going to break the news to Superior Kralia, both concerning the return of Corruption and Yala's true nature.

Delivering her unwelcome message in person was essential; the enclave had no other way of knowing what was going on in the capital, and it would be worth the risk of cutting herself off from any updates herself for a short while. *Or a long while, if Superior Kralia insists that I stay in the enclave after my return.*

Perhaps that was why the notion of leaving the city gnawed at her, aside from the bitter knowledge that she'd failed in her mission. Realistically, there was little for her to do in the capital other than get in the others' way, and even if she *was* confined to the enclave upon her return, she owed it to her people to warn them. Honestly, she ought to be grateful that she'd been afforded the chance to see so much of the world outside of her home in the first place.

Yet her doubts multiplied as she walked away from the city. Superior Kralia and the rest of the enclave would be scandalised to know Niema had spent so much time around a Disciple of Death. *Let's face it, I'll be lucky if she ever lets me leave the jungle again.* To top it off, they might send people to challenge Yala themselves … assuming she survived the upcoming conflict.

That was the more pertinent issue. If Melian's plan succeeded, she wouldn't stop with the capital. She'd want to ensure the other Disciples wouldn't stand in her way, including Niema's enclave.

Niema's steps halted when she reached a fork in the path and met with the inexplicable sight of the war drake sitting near an abandoned shack that might have once been a farm. As if it were waiting for someone. Not her, surely … yet when Niema approached, the beast lifted its head. It must recognise her as the person who'd worked magic upon its will, because Yala had made it clear that the beasts had little loyalty to individual humans. Without Niema, the others would never be able to call upon its help again.

"What is it?" she asked of the creature.

The beast growled, its claw raking furrows in the soil. Maybe it didn't know either, but the influence of her powers must have left an impression, rather like the time she'd spent with the others had left one on her. A bad impression, Superior Kralia would say, though Yala herself wouldn't disagree.

Her heart contracted. Whatever her personal thoughts on Yala, the other inhabitants of the capital would suffer if they lost this battle. And if the war drake, or Niema herself, ended up being the defining factor in their fight, could she truly walk away?

Niema met the war drake's eyes, gave a short whistle. Then she turned around and began to make her way back towards the outer gate again.

———

Yala tried the door to the pleasure house and found it locked. Worry fluttered in her chest, but she told herself that Saren was more likely to have taken her advice and gone into hiding in the one place the Disciples of the Flame wouldn't deign to set foot in. Namely, the undercity.

Provided nobody had seen her return, she had enough time to find her allies without fearing her presence would endanger their lives. The rough and uneven cobblestones made her miss her cane but retrieving it from Ceremonial Square was out of the question. Upon reaching the undercity entrance, she halted when Nalen, the bearded man who seemed to have appointed himself the guardian of the undercity following Machit's death, barred her path.

"Is Saren in there?" she asked him.

"He is," Nalen confirmed. "Thought you left the city."

"I'm back. Provisionally," she said. "The Successors haven't been in the undercity, have they? Or the Disciples of the Flame?"

"No," he said. "You'd better not have anyone on your tail."

"I don't." When he moved aside, she descended the stairs, her leg protesting at every step. Yet another disadvantage to Niema's departure was that she'd no longer be able to heal any wounds she or the others might suffer.

Yala followed the narrow street until she reached the shack in which Machit had once lived. Through the window, she saw Saren slumped on a cushion in a far corner. Despite the hood he'd pulled up to hide his face, she'd recognise him even in a crowded room. Everyone seemed to come and go as they pleased, but she knocked on the door, then waved at Saren through the window to get his attention.

Saren leapt to his feet and ran over to meet her. "Yala?"

"Who else?" She wrapped an arm around him, her other

349

hand gripping the door frame for balance. "I took a brief detour to Skytower."

"You went *where?*" He released her. "Where's Kelan?"

"He's with the other Disciples of the Sky," she replied. "The rest is a long story, but the good news is that the Disciples of the Sky no longer see me as the enemy."

"And the bad news?" He beckoned her into the shack, where he'd filled the far corner with a jumble of possessions, including what looked like the entirety of his liquor cupboard and half his wardrobe. "Aside from the Temple of the Flame being allied with Melian?"

"There's ... worse." The words caught in her throat, but one escaped. "Temik."

"What about him?"

"He's a Disciple of the Flame."

"What?" Saren's eyes rounded. "No."

"He started this." She couldn't look directly at him, couldn't face the impact of her words upon him. It seemed too cruel, so soon after Machit's death. "He told them everything. He's the reason Vanat and Machit are dead."

Saren slumped to the grimy floor. "No. He wouldn't do that to us."

"It makes no sense to me either, but I spoke to him myself." She half crouched beside him, stretching out her injured leg in front of her. "I don't know how long he's been working for them, but it explains how Melian found out the details of our squad's last mission."

Saren made a choked noise. "I believe you, but I don't understand why he'd overlook what they did to Dalem."

"Maybe he's using them for his own ends, but that doesn't matter, does it?" Bitterness laced her words. "Superior Datriem has resigned himself to the inevitable, which means he won't lift a finger if Corruption infests the entire city. Intentional or not, he's on their side now."

"And the Disciples of the Sky." He lifted his head. "You escaped the Temple of the Flame and went straight to another group of untrustworthy Disciples? Do I have that right?"

"Believe me, we had limited options," Yala said. "The Disciples of the Sky are at least acknowledging Melian as a threat, but they don't have the forces to challenge another Superior. Don't forget they can't use their abilities inside the Temple of the Flame, and there'd be repercussions if they started a public fight with Superior Datriem. Look at how much damage a single war drake caused to Ceremonial Square."

"I don't give a shit, to be honest." Saren reached into his cloak and pulled out a bottle of liquor. "They can fight it out and leave the rest of us alone."

Yala grabbed his hand to stop him from opening the bottle. "Saren."

"What? I'm too sober for this conversation." He yanked his hand away from her. "And the odds are high that I'm going to fucking die today."

"You won't be the first to die. I will."

That got his attention. "What's that mean? You *want* Melian to sacrifice you to her god?"

"No." She drew in a breath. "It turns out that she was right, at least concerning my potential as a Disciple of Death."

Saren's mouth hung open, the bottle of liquor forgotten, as she spilled out the details of her meeting with Superior Sietra. She spoke without pausing and without checking to see how he reacted; she didn't think she could bear the notion of him turning away from her like Niema had.

When she'd finished, she risked a glance up at him. While a frown marred his face, he hadn't recoiled from her in

351

disgust. "You … you've never actually *used* Corruption magic, have you?"

"No," she said, "but when Melian had us restrained and was ready to sacrifice us, the god of death spoke to me. According to Superior Sietra, only Disciples can hear His voice."

He gaped at her for another moment. "I suppose the voice of the god of death isn't something you can mistake."

"Definitely not," she said. "He recognised me from the island, I think. He wanted to bargain. I said no."

"I should damn well hope so," he said. "You know what happened to the Rafragorians who tried to make a deal with the god of death."

"I know," she said. "But that's why Melian wants to be the one to kill me, and why she won't let anyone else get there first. Not even Superior Datriem. Maybe I can use that against her somehow."

"How?" He blinked. "What, set her allies against one another? That's way too risky."

"We're running out of time, Saren," she said. "Niema's gone. She left the city rather than fight on the same side as a Disciple of Death, and I doubt she'll be the only one with that opinion."

"Not here." He gave a sweeping gesture around the room. "You think anyone down here gives a fuck? After everything else we've been through, I'd be a hypocrite if I turned my back on you because you have a slight affinity with dead people."

"Ha." She almost managed a smile. "Melian is out of her mind, but it would seriously piss her off if the Disciples of the Flame tried to kill me before she gets her chance. That's why I wondered … perhaps I should have let Superior Datriem stick me on a sacrificial pyre last night after all."

"He wanted to do *what* to you?" Saren's mouth twisted,

sickened. "What makes the Disciples of the Sky think they can negotiate with these people?"

"Kelan doesn't," she said. "Unfortunately, he's outvoted."

There was no telling what else the Disciples of the Flame might have been up to in the past half day since she'd left the city—not to mention Melian herself. Had she left the temple or stayed hidden among their number, secure that they wouldn't turn against her?

What did *she* think of Superior Datriem's intention to have Yala condemned to death? Granted, Melian might have another target in reserve, like Viam, or Saren or even Temik himself, though the latter had spurned the god of death when he'd sworn himself to another temple.

Yala didn't know if Viam or Saren shared the same potential as she did. Saren had been unconscious when the god of death had spoken, and she couldn't see him willingly taking up that mantle. Though he understood her position, it took a weight off her shoulders to have at least one friend on her side. Unless you counted Kelan, and she didn't know if she *did* count him as a friend, even if he'd helped her escape Skytower.

She'd been a fool to confront Melian alone, but she wouldn't make the same error again. Whether others offered to fight for her or if she had to strike a deal with the god of death, she'd ensure Melian didn't succeed in her plan.

No other outcome was acceptable.

———

Kelan caught up to his fellow Disciples at the inn, where they'd taken over the downstairs room. Laima came in soon after Kelan's arrival, with Niema no longer at her side, confirming his guess that she'd requested to be left at a convenient place for her to start her journey home.

The inn's staff were somewhat startled to have a sudden influx of guests. Laima spoke to the owner while the others settled themselves in every available chair on the downstairs floor. Once the innkeeper departed, she walked to the front of the room to address everyone.

"Disciples," Laima called out. "You all know I've been put in charge of leading the negotiations with the Disciples of the Flame. I've already spoken to each of you individually, but before we leave, I wanted to ensure nobody else has any unanswered questions or concerns."

"I have plenty of questions," said Tremin, who'd presumably only been chosen for the mission in case they needed to apply brute force. "Such as why we're not challenging them directly. They're sheltering an enemy inside their temple, aren't they?"

"Strictly speaking, the Disciples of Death—if they exist—are not considered to be our enemies," said Laima. "Those are the words of Superior Sietra herself, so if anyone has an issue with the claim, feel free to ask her when we return to Skytower."

"Then why're we here?" Tremin growled. "Is it worth endangering our lives over someone who isn't an enemy of ours?"

"Melian *is* a threat to us," Kelan said, before he could think better of the decision. "She has no limits to her ambitions. She secured the Disciples of the Flame as allies to ensure nobody would stand in the way of her intention to oust the king, and I doubt she'll let the other Disciples remain neutral. She'll want their allegiance, too."

A murmur of discontent travelled among the other Disciples. Laima must have hand selected the team, and she hadn't picked anyone Kelan would have considered a friend, but if he didn't try to warn them of the danger Melian posed, none of them would leave the city alive.

"Then what are we to do?" queried one of the other Disciples. "Stand and watch as this Disciple of Death takes over the Temple of the Flame from inside? Is that her intention?"

"It's not possible for one branch of Disciple to displace another," said Laima. "I also believe she's stripped of her connection to the god of death while she's within their temple. Is that correct, Kelan?"

He blinked in surprise at being directly addressed. While he didn't believe for a moment that she'd forgiven him, she must have accepted that the best way to succeed in their goals was to ask the only one of their group who'd personally faced both Melian *and* the Disciples of the Flame.

"That's correct," he responded. "Her abilities don't work inside the temple, but neither do ours, so if the Disciples of the Flame take our presence as a challenge to their own authority, we're likely to find ourselves at a severe disadvantage."

"Then we wait for her to leave?" someone asked.

"If we wait for her to leave the temple, we're running the risk of being too late to stop her," Kelan said. "Yes, I know we aren't supposed to interfere directly in the affairs of another branch of Disciples, but the Disciples of the Flame all deserve to know who they brought into their midst."

"Didn't you befriend a Disciple of Death yourself?" Tremin called across the room.

He ignored the murmur that travelled among the others. "I don't condemn Melian because she's a Disciple of Death. I condemn her because she's a mass murderer planning to infest the city with the dead, and quite possibly slaughter half the Temple of the Flame in the process. Once they've stopped being useful to her, that is."

"There's no proof of that." Laima raised her voice over another chorus of mutters. "I don't disagree that she has to

355

be stopped, but I can guarantee that Superior Datriem won't turn her over to us because we asked him to."

True ... unfortunately. "What else did you have in mind? Did Superior Sietra give you an alternative?" *Aside from asking nicely, which didn't work for Niema.*

"We talk to him first," she said. "A small group of us will discuss the possibility of cooperation, should Corruption prove a threat to both of us."

Kelan assumed he wouldn't be part of that group, given his history with Superior Datriem, but he had no illusions that negotiation would work. Superior Datriem's mind was already made up. Whether he would ultimately take Melian's side or simply look the other way while she stormed into the palace didn't matter.

Kelan sat back and watched as Laima selected the team that would go to the Temple of the Flame. He knew better than to offer to go himself, though it was gratifying when she turned down Tremin as well.

While the six chosen Disciples gathered near the door, Laima beckoned him to talk alone. "Kelan, I'd appreciate it if you didn't try to undermine me in front of an audience."

"That wasn't my intention," he said. "I respect Superior Sietra's orders, but I also think a cautious approach is more likely to backfire on us than not. The Temple of the Flame has already declined to work with us directly, and if Melian realises that we've brought enough people to the city to pose a potential threat, she'll change strategies. Fast."

"She would come to that realisation whether we went to the Temple of the Flame ourselves or otherwise."

"True, but we have to be prepared for the possibility that she already has people waiting to ambush any negotiators," he said. "If she saw us approaching the city, she'd be prepared."

"Mercenaries are hardly a threat."

"Dead ones are." He glanced around the room at the robed Disciples, none of whom had the slightest idea what it felt like to face the nerve-shredding presence of Mekan's power. "On that note, I think that it's worth telling everyone here the best way to deal with Mekan's creatures. They can't be killed, not by conventional means."

She gave an uncertain laugh. "Well, they're *dead*, so I expect not Kelan. They have no will of their own, Superior Sietra told me. Isn't that all there is to it?"

"They have no will of their own, but they'd driven to kill and under the control of the person who brought them back from death," Kelan told her. "If she orders them to attack anyone who steps into their path, they'll do so. They also feel no pain, and no injury will slow them down."

Unease flickered across her face. "Melian can't use her abilities inside the Temple of the Flame, which includes raising the dead, doesn't it?"

"Yes, but it wouldn't surprise me if she already accounted for that," he said. "We found some of her past victims in the abandoned library, and there might be more hidden around the city. Don't forget she has access to the crematoriums, too."

Her eyes widened as she took in his meaning. "Did that woman—Yala—really want to take her on alone?"

"She still does," he replied. "I can't say I envy her position, but it's personal. Melian has killed several of Yala's friends."

"She's a Disciple of Death," Laima said. "Yala is. That's why Melian wants her so badly."

"Wants her death," Kelan corrected. "Or sacrifice, I should say. Badly enough to hide among the Disciples who have the ability to stop her in her tracks, if they knew what she was. She's playing a dangerous game."

"Yes," gasped a voice from the doorway. "She is."

Kelan stared as a breathless Niema sprinted into the inn,

the door slamming behind her. Had she run all the way here from the city gates? "Niema? I thought you were going back to your enclave."

"No ... that can wait." She straightened upright. "I'm here to ally with your people against Melian, on behalf of the Temple of Life."

Kelan turned to an equally bewildered Laima. "Does that work for you?"

"You already spoke to the Disciples of the Flame yourself?" Laima asked Niema.

"Yes, but Melian seems to have already convinced them not to ally with any other Disciples outside of their own ranks," said Niema. "What did you plan to do, surround the temple so she's too afraid to leave?"

"That's not a bad idea," Kelan said. "Not a permanent solution, but if she's backed into a corner, she might feel pressured into showing her real motives."

"There's no guarantees," said Laima. "If our people were to surround the temple, the Disciples of the Flame would see us as a threat, and they'd be right to."

So would Melian, though. Maybe Yala had a better idea, but she'd have even less patience than Kelan did for the Disciples of the Sky's reluctance to avoid a direct confrontation. There was also the fact that he'd brought her back into the city against Superior Sietra's direct orders. Laima might have helped him do so, but the others would be less supportive.

"If your team can verify if Melian is currently inside the temple, it'll be a starting point," he said. "She might have left."

"She's the only person in there who isn't dressed like a Disciple," Niema added. "I can point her out to you..."

Laima raised a brow at Kelan. "Did Niema cause as much trouble for them as you did?"

"Not unless they realise she's the one who dropped a war

drake on their roof." Which was a fair possibility. Their departure from the city hadn't exactly been inconspicuous.

Niema winced. "Yes, there is that, but I can at least watch out for trouble while you talk to Yala."

"Meaning me?" Kelan guessed that Niema herself had no desire to talk to Yala. "All right, but try not to get caught."

30

While Yala waited for Kelan's return, she changed out of her filthy clothes. Saren had brought her pack with him into the undercity, for which she was grateful, and putting on her drakeskin trousers felt like slipping on a second skin, one she'd forgotten she'd shed. They were a little stiff and uncomfortable, but they'd be an asset if she took another unplanned flight.

Assuming the war drake comes back. Niema isn't here, after all.

Still, wearing her old military gear brought a sense of clarity she hadn't expected. Melian was another problem for her squad to solve, another foe to overcome.

As she was adjusting her weapons belt, Kelan came into the shack and did a double take. "You kept your uniform?"

"Yes, why?" She finished sheathing the dagger at her belt and let it fall against her thigh. "How'd negotiations go?"

"There's a team on their way to talk to Superior Datriem at the temple," he replied. "Laima dismissed my idea of surrounding the place to stop Melian from escaping, unfortunately, though I understand why."

"Pity, considering Melian can't use her powers in there,"

360

Yala commented. "You won't get far trying to negotiate with Superior Datriem."

"*I* know, but none of my fellow Disciples have met him—or Melian," he said. "I don't think they understand how quickly this situation might slide out of our grasp."

"That's the problem," she said. "The ideal scenario is that Melian exposes her treachery and the Disciples of the Flame turn on her." Though there was Temik to consider, too, and whether he'd pick up the pieces of Melian's plan in the event that she failed.

"I can guarantee it won't be that easy," Saren said from the corner. "What if they knew she was a Disciple of Death all along?"

"Temik did, certainly." She watched him blanch at the mention of their old friend. "As for Superior Datriem... I don't know."

"If the other Disciples of the Flame don't share his opinion, I can't think of a time when the other Disciples have challenged their Superior and won," Kelan said. "They'd be gambling their faith against his."

"I wouldn't take that gamble either." No—if Superior Datriem retained his position, Yala could only assume that the god of the flames didn't care if Corruption sank its teeth into the ranks of His followers. Though He had answered Dalem's request for help on the island ... *wait.* Yala's heart gave an unpleasant jolt. "The bodies ... did they go ahead with the cremation yesterday?"

Saren winced. "I don't think so, but I didn't dare leave the undercity."

"You made the right choice there," Yala told him. "Machit would have understood. I spent last night trapped on top of a tower, besides."

Kelan opened his mouth as if to respond, then his eyes widened as Niema came bursting into the shack. *Wait. She stayed in the capital after all?*

"You might have to change your strategy," she said, addressing Kelan. "The Disciples of the Flame…"

"They already shot down our negotiation?" he guessed.

"They sent their team to the inn first."

Kelan swore. "They must have been watching the skies for our return."

"Apparently so." Yala rose upright. "If Melian is inside the temple, we need to make sure she doesn't leave. Is Superior Datriem in there?"

"I didn't see otherwise," Niema answered without meeting her eyes. "Does the temple have any exits aside from the front door?"

"One," Kelan said. "At the back. Oh, and there's the rooftop, too, but they won't make an escape that way. I should go back to the inn…"

Right. Kelan understandably didn't want to abandon his fellow Disciples to their fate, but where did that leave Yala? She had little to offer in a fight between the gods. "Maybe I should parade outside the Temple of the Flame until Melian herself walks out to confront me. Even if Superior Datriem turns both of us to ashes, it'd be worth it."

"No." Saren stepped in. "You aren't sacrificing yourself. Besides, what about Temik? If Melian dies, he might take over from her. None of us knows what he's capable of anymore."

True. Damn. I wish I could talk to him alone, without Superior Datriem hovering over my shoulder.

Niema cleared her throat. "There's another way. We already know war drakes are immune to their fire…"

"You want to bring the war drake back in?" Yala suppressed her growing annoyance that Niema refused to look at her. What did it matter when she'd come back to help them, regardless of her personal feelings on the issue? "I thought last time made it clear that setting a wild animal loose in a public square is not a strategy we want to repeat. The beast has gone, anyway."

"I ran into it outside the city," Niema mumbled. "I wasn't thinking of setting it loose in the square this time, though. I think... I think you should fly on it."

Yala's heart missed a beat. "You think what?"

Niema shrugged one shoulder. "Melian might think twice about trying to sacrifice you if you're sitting on the back of a giant war drake."

"You aren't wrong, but it's a hell of a risk." Sitting on the war drake's back would put Yala in control, though she didn't have Niema's ability to bend the beast's will to match her own. Her training hadn't been for nothing, though, and Yala knew that there was no better way to evacuate the square than to descend from the sky upon the back of an enormous, winged reptile.

"Last time, people had the sense to run away," Kelan said, as if he'd sensed her thoughts. "They might have vacated the upper city if two different groups of Disciples are about to go to war with one another."

War. Yala's jaw tensed. "Niema, how close is the war drake to the city?"

"As close as I could bring it without drawing attention."

Not close enough, then. "Kelan?"

"You want me to carry you there?" he guessed. "All right, but I'll have to move fast."

"It won't take long," Yala said, feeling a pang of guilt for dragging him away from his allies—though they'd no doubt be grateful for any extra aid he'd be able to bring them. "Let's get this done."

Stepping outside the shack, Yala waved goodbye to Saren and then allowed Kelan to lift her off the ground. When she leaned forwards, it felt almost like flying on a war drake, if one ignored the fact that she had no control whatsoever over their direction and that her life was in the hands of another person.

As opposed to a deadly wild animal. Let's face it, this is a fucking reckless plan that's as likely to get innocent people killed as not.

In moments, they flew over the outer city's wall, where she caught sight of the war drake roaming around an abandoned-looking neighbourhood. "Put me down on its back. It's easier."

Kelan complied, circling the beast from behind. He moved swiftly enough that the beast scarcely had time to raise its head before he placed Yala upon its back. The war drake growled when it felt her settle into place with her knees on either side of its wide neck. Her legs wouldn't thank her for this, even with her drakeskin trousers giving her some protection this time, but a little pain was nothing compared to what Melian might unleash upon the city.

"Good luck," she told Kelan as the war drake growled and raked a claw on the ground. "You should fly ahead of me. I might be out of its reach, but I can't stop the beast from taking a bite out of you."

"Fair point." Kelan glided across the air, away from the war drake's mouth and claws. "Good luck to you, too."

As he flew back over the city's outer wall, Yala coaxed the war drake into flight. As if it had been waiting for her signal, the beast's wings bunched and then extended, carrying them into the air. Gusts of wind swept in their wake, and a familiar rush filled Yala's blood as they glided over the outer wall and towards the boundary circling the central part of the city.

Atop the inner wall, guards stopped their patrolling, instead pointing at her and shouting.

"Yes, I know," she muttered as the war drake's body

rippled with a displeased growl. "Ignore them. Let's get in there before they start throwing spears at us."

At least she didn't see any signs of a magical battle on the ground; the clash between the Disciples of Flame and Sky had yet to escalate into a war.

"This way." With a nudge, she urged the war drake to angle across the section of wall near the Temple of the Flame, which would take them too close to Ceremonial Square for the guards to risk trying to shoot arrows at them. It would also expose them to the Disciples of the Flame, but she'd lost the element of surprise a long time ago.

Her last option was to make a big enough spectacle to distract them.

"Slow down." Yala urged the beast to slow as they passed the towering windows on the temple's west side, ensuring that everyone inside had a clear view of her. Cloaked figures gathered behind the windows, mouths agape, faces pressed to the glass.

Come out and face me, Melian.

Yala circled the temple once, twice, before the front door opened. She hoped to see Melian on the steps below, but instead, Temik walked out. Alone.

"Come down, Yala," he called to her. "I know you want to talk to me."

She brought down the war drake to hover above the area in front of the staps—high enough that the beast's claws weren't able to reach out and skewer him, though he deserved no less. "I want to talk to your deranged cult leader, not you. Is she around?"

Temik eyed the war drake. "You always did have a flair for the dramatic, Yala."

"It wasn't so long ago that you rode one of these, too," she said. "Is Superior Datriem hiding? Is that why he sent you?"

365

"Datriem is dead," he said. "I'm the new leader of the Disciples of the Flame."

The bottom dropped out of her stomach, and the war drake growled when her hands dug into its scaly neck. "What? You killed him?"

"You can't pretend you didn't want to do the same."

"*This* is what you wanted." The truth hit her like a flurry of falling rocks. "You always planned to stab him in the back."

"Of course." Disgust permeated his words. "How could you have thought otherwise, after how he treated Dalem?"

"You helped Machit's killer, too, in case you've forgotten." Through the temple's front window, she glimpsed a blur of faces gawping at them both, but nobody came out to join Temik. "There's nobody who regrets Dalem's death more than I do, but this isn't what he would have wanted of you. Of any of us. There's still time to turn back."

"Back to what?" Temik's mouth flattened into a thin line. "To being a soldier? That life is over, Yala, and I'm not content to run away and hide like you did. Dalem would have wanted us to make his death meaningful, and what better way to do so than to enact change in the country that sent him to die?"

"By killing the monarch and replacing him with a Disciple of Death?" Incredulity crept into her tone. *He's as mad as Melian is.*

"No. Melian's goals aren't mine." He lifted his chin. "She already planned to kill Superior Datriem, though, and I was in place to take advantage of that."

"Are you even a full Disciple yet?" Not that it necessarily mattered, if the god of the flames had let His most ardent supporter meet a gruesome end at Melian's hands—and inside His own temple, no less. "Never mind. Can you tell Melian I want to talk to her?"

He gave a harsh laugh. "I always liked how direct you

were, Yala. You know, I did have faith in you, once. You were our leader. I was willing to follow you into the mouth of the Void."

"I'm honoured," she said flatly. "Does your god know you used Him as a means to an end?"

"He doesn't care," said Temik. "The gods are like us. They're flawed, prone to distraction, and indifferent. Whether we worship someone living or dead, it doesn't make a difference, does it?"

"You can't possibly think Melian would be an improvement on the current king?" she said. "No Disciple should rule this country."

"Disciples rule other countries," he said. "It can be done."

Not like this. She'd wanted someone to pay for Dalem's fate for so long that she'd thought Superior Datriem's death would bring her more relief, but this … this was worse. Temik might be justified in the revenge he'd taken, but did he have the right to control the fates of innocent people?

"You can't think *Melian* would be a good ruler."

"Is she the worst the capital has to offer?" he asked. "At least she has the desire for change. She didn't run away like you did."

If he'd hoped the words would sting, he was only half successful. "I'm not running now, am I? If you'd told me your intentions a few years ago, I might have given you a chance, but you hated me too much to consider that I might have been able to help you."

"I hated you for a while, yes," he said. "You refused to acknowledge that you made mistakes."

"I took full responsibility for Dalem's death," she said. "As you know full well. Yes, he made the choice to sacrifice his life, but he wouldn't have been on that island if not for—"

"King Tharen," he interjected. "Yes, I'm capable of

changing my mind, too, Yala. I accepted that it was his fault more than yours a long time ago."

"Do you expect me to thank you for that? You allied with someone who wants to slit my throat on an altar." The war drake's impatient growl thrummed beneath her, a reminder that if she didn't figure out how to handle Temik, the beast would make the decision for her.

"It doesn't have to end that way," he said. "There's room enough for more than one Disciple of Death in this city."

He thinks I'd fight on the same side as Melian? Even if the woman hadn't wanted her dead, she was depraved.

"Sorry, Temik," she said. "The answer's no. But you never expected me to agree, did you? You wanted to say your piece, to ease your conscience before you offer me up to Melian."

"Right you are." The voice spoke from behind him, within the shadow of the door, and Melian herself stepped into view. "I thought you'd have enough nerve to face me on the ground, but I guess I was wrong."

"Oh, I know you're not interested in playing fair, so it seemed a waste of time to pretend otherwise." The war drake growled as if eager for her blood. *Soon. You can feed soon.*

"Temik was right—it does suit you, sitting on that beast's back," said Melian. "It's a pity you couldn't have been an ally. You could do a better job of governing the city than the useless pricks in power."

"Hardly." She had to be joking. "I earned the title of squad leader, but it worked because my team members weren't scared shitless of me. If I'd threatened to burn people alive or sacrifice them if they didn't cooperate, do you think we'd have survived a single battle?" She addressed the last part to Temik, whose jaw twitched.

"Sometimes sacrifices are necessary," he answered.

"Are *you* scared shitless of me?" Melian asked with barely suppressed glee.

"No, I'm not. I feel sorry for you." She did, too—or at least Temik, whose fate might easily have been hers. If Superior Datriem had welcomed her rather than slamming the door in her face.

"Then you're a fool." Melian gestured to someone out of Yala's line of sight, and the sound of shuffling footsteps drifted from the alley that ran alongside the temple.

She tensed as a number of figures staggered into the open. Some were mercenaries, but others were dressed in regular clothing, and only the bloodstains and their dead-eyed expressions gave away their true nature.

Including Machit, whose dead eyes brought a chill to Yala's bones.

Why? they seemed to ask. *Why did you let her take me?*

"As you can see," Melian said, "people can still be useful as hostages even when they're dead."

———

Hoping Yala managed to keep the war drake firmly under her control, Kelan skirted the outer wall and made his way towards the central part of the capital. He'd never asked Niema how many Disciples of the Flame had come to the inn, but he doubted they would have left the temple at all if they didn't expect trouble. Superior Datriem kept them on a tight leash; Kelan had heard they weren't even allowed to leave their temple to visit taverns and gambling dens and pleasure houses, as the god of the flames allegedly looked down upon such activities.

Really, it was no wonder the Disciples of the Flame were so uptight. They had no idea how to have fun.

Kelan caught up to Niema, landing beside her on the inside of the upper city's gate. Her jaw twitched, but she didn't tell him to leave.

"Yala's on her way," he told her. "On the—"

The war drake came soaring over the wall near the Temple of the Flame, and he cut off midsentence. *If she wants to draw their attention, that'll certainly achieve her aim.*

Niema paced ahead of him. "I saw at least five Disciples of the Flame approaching the inn. Maybe more."

"Good to know." That meant the Disciples of the Sky had them outnumbered, assuming there weren't more mercenaries lurking nearby, which there might be. He wouldn't have put it past Melian to have filled the upper city with her allies.

When they rounded the corner into the street where the inn stood, he glimpsed several robed figures outside. All were dressed in the pure white of high-ranked Disciples of the Flame, and upon hearing their approach, one of them turned on his heel.

"You." The Disciple's robes gleamed with the kind of elaborate golden embroidery gifted only to the upper ranks. "You're the one who escaped our temple yesterday, aren't you?"

"I didn't know you made a habit of taking prisoners," he replied. "I wasn't aware it was within your rules to lock up other Disciples for disagreeing with your Superior's choice to harbour a criminal either."

"You've convinced your fellow Disciples to believe your lies, too." The man's brow tightened with disapproval. "Superior Datriem is right … your people are degenerate and a disgrace to the gods."

"Not lies," Kelan answered. "In fact, I've been more truthful in the past few days than possibly my entire life up to this point."

He saw Niema roll her eyes at him, but he'd successfully drawn their attention away from his allies—for a moment at least.

"Regardless," said the man, "we're offering you a reasonable choice. Either you are to leave the city and return to your Superior, or we will take your presence here as a declaration of war against our temple."

War. He's serious. No doubt Melian had pushed them towards this decision, but hadn't anyone considered the damage a fight between Disciples might cause to the city?"

"This is excessive," Laima said from inside the inn's doorway. "We came to talk. The reason we brought a larger team than usual is because there's evidence that Corruption has been present in the city recently, and we didn't want to take any chances."

"That sounds like a convenient excuse, if you ask me." The Disciple eyed Niema. "You've drawn a Disciple of Life into your lies, too. Did you drive the Disciples of the Earth into hiding as well?"

"No, of course not," Niema said. "I don't know why they closed the doors, except that they feared Corruption—and who wouldn't?"

A reptilian growl from the direction of Ceremonial Square prompted the Disciples of the Flame to lift their heads.

"You brought a Disciple of Death here with you." The Disciple's eyes lit up with piercing whiteness. "You made your choice."

"Not all of us," said Tremin, elbowing his way to the front of the group thronging the inn's door. "Some of us aren't here to fight you. Kelan—"

Kelan raised a hand and sent a gust of air buffeting into the larger man's chest, sending him sprawling to the ground. He'd intentionally avoided aiming near the Disciples of the Flame, but the man in the embroidered robe lifted a threatening hand towards him. "That's enough. Come with me. Superior Datriem wants to see you."

"Superior Datriem is dead!" The cry rang out from around the inn's corner, and a breathless, orange-robed novice came running into view. "He's dead!"

Flames ignited in the Disciple's hand, which he raised at Kelan. "This is *your* doing."

"Stop!" Niema's shout rang out, sharp enough that even the Disciples of the Flame turned towards her. "The dead are here!"

An instant later, Kelan caught the unmistakeable scent of rot in the air. His blood chilled, and the quarrelling Disciples ceased to argue, undeniably struck by the same otherworldly sensation of all-consuming dread.

Someone had called on the god of death, and Mekan had answered them.

31

Yala watched Machit's staggering approach, blood sluggishly oozing out of his gaping throat. More dead emerged from the alley, too, some missing limbs and others trailing blood from gaping wounds. Some must be other victims of the war drake's massacre and Melian's attack on the pleasure house, but there were other, older bodies among them, too, skeletal and bloated and rotting. The scent of death caught in her throat, making her gag.

Then the war drake gave a chilling cry and beat its wings upward, nearly tipping her off its back. *Shit.* The god of death's power repelled every living creature, and the war drake was no exception. Yala squeezed her knees tight and urged the beast to remain still.

"You're sick," she said to Melian, trying hard not to look at Machit's blank, lifeless eyes.

I should have buried him myself. I should have asked Niema to take care of his body the way she did Vanat. Anything other than this violation.

Temik had backed up against the temple's front doors, the

colour draining from his face, and Yala glared at him. "You're as bad as she is. Dalem would be ashamed of you."

Her words made him flinch, but he straightened his spine. "Machit's spirit is gone. He can't have any way of knowing or caring what anyone does to his body."

"I thought the Disciples of the Flame believed the dead must be burned with divine fire to set their spirits free." One would have thought Temik would at least pretend to follow their beliefs, especially if he'd made himself their leader now.

Temik's jaw twitched, but he otherwise ignored her comment. "Melian, did you want to start with her, or deal with the Disciples of the Sky first?"

"Your people will keep the other Disciples from getting in my way, won't they?" Melian smiled. "I can handle the rest."

As she spoke, Yala saw several *living* people crossing the square to join her. Mercenaries. "You know it won't be long before the Disciples of the Flame realise you killed their leader, don't you?"

"I rather think they'll have more pressing concerns," said Melian. "Come down, Yala, and face me on the ground."

"What makes you think my death will get you what you want?" Yala raised her voice, so that each word echoed across the square, to everyone who might be within hearing distance. "For that matter, what makes you think this is likely to end in anything other than your own destruction? Didn't Melian tell you that you're more use to her dead than alive?"

She directed the last part at the living mercenaries gathering near the temple, but Melian herself appeared unconcerned. "They know what they signed up for. As you did when you joined the army."

"She's right, Yala," Temik said. "We knew what we signed up for, didn't we?"

"We didn't have a fucking choice," Yala spat. "Not at first. You have a short memory, don't you? Besides, what makes you think fighting for someone like her is any better than fighting for a king?"

"We aren't fighting for anyone," Temik responded. "We're fighting for change, and we answer to no monarch nor anyone else."

Why was she attempting to reason with these people? If they were willing to die, it didn't matter what she said to them.

"You had your chance to surrender," Melian added. "If you must bring this to open conflict, remember that innocents will die because of you."

"The city won't bend to your will either," Yala said. "You might not have taken the time to get to know us, but most of us don't like being told what to do by someone who hasn't earned our respect."

"We'll see," said Melian. "Friends, I think Yala might have trouble climbing down from that war drake. Can you assist her?"

Mercenaries both living and dead turned towards Yala, weapons in hand. The war drake might be impervious to fire, but swords and spears would bring it down eventually, and the dead had already spooked the beast.

"Strike them down," she hissed in its ear. "The dead are harmless."

Melian certainly wasn't, but if the war drake lost its nerve and fled, Yala would lose all chance of survival. She gave the command to strike once more, and the war drake swivelled, claws cleaving through the nearest dead man. The others gave no reaction to their comrade's fall, but she hadn't expected them to.

"Destroy them!" she shouted. "Kill her!"

Yala urged her steed to veer towards the temple, but a jet of flames brushed past the war drake's side, forcing her to change her path to avoid being singed. The dead fell upon the beast, its claws and teeth rending flesh and bone. They might be frail, but they had her outnumbered, and when an axe sank into the war drake's foot, it gave a chilling shriek. One of the mercenaries staggered, letting go of the axe, which remained wedged in the war drake's foot. As the beast roared in pain and kicked out in an attempt to dislodge the weapon, someone threw a spear straight through one of its wings.

Blood sprayed, and the beast tipped sideways, breaking Yala's hold. She hit the ground with a thud that jarred her injured leg, and rolled over to avoid being grabbed by dead, clammy hands. There was nowhere to run, and the war drake's piercing cries filled her ears as the dead swarmed her.

———

Niema's gorge rose at the sight of the dead lumbering out of every street and alley within sight, trailing gore and viscera in their wake. How could Melian have raised this many undead followers? *Did she sacrifice someone?* Not Yala—Niema had seen her war drake descending above the temple not long beforehand—but the god of death did not grant His power freely. For Melian to have gained control over so many of His creatures, she must have pleased Mekan greatly.

It was her. She killed Superior Datriem.

Kelan reached for his blade, but most of the other Disciples remained transfixed, staring in shock at the oncoming dead. They wouldn't have experienced the eerie chill of Mekan's presence, and Disciples of the Flame had already been reeling from the revelation that their leader was dead. The man who'd spoken to Kelan recovered first, wrenching his gaze from the oncoming dead, and lifting a shaking hand.

"Your friend's work, I assume." He gestured towards the oncoming dead. "This is what you ally yourselves with?"

"The dead aren't on our side," Kelan told him. "They have no will of their own. If Melian tells them to attack anyone who gets in their way, they won't distinguish between our people and yours."

"Enough talk." A flame kindled between his fingertips. "Our leader is dead. There will be blood for this."

A screeching cry echoed from the square. *The war drake.* Niema lifted her head but was unable to see over the rooftops, though the sickening sound of claws slicing through flesh was unmistakable.

The Disciples of the Flame moved away from the inn's entrance, drawn towards the fighting, but the dead moved, too. They blocked every street, blank faced and relentless.

"Melian must have given the orders to attack." Kelan lifted his blade, glancing behind him at the other Disciples. "You remember what I said about how to stop the dead, don't you?"

A dead man drew a sharp cleaver-like weapon and advanced on Laima, who stood frozen in shock. Kelan blasted air from his palm, sending the dead man flying, but a second lumbered in to take his place. The dead might move slowly, but there might be hundreds standing between them and Yala, and the mere scent of Mekan's magic made Niema's head swim with dizziness.

"Get into the inn," Kelan told her. "I can't guarantee the dead won't follow you in there, but you aren't their priority."

"How do you know she didn't tell them to kill every Disciple in the city?" Niema backed up against the wall, while Kelan hovered above the ground, summoning another ball of air to his palms. "I can't leave her."

Meaning Yala. Disciple of Death or not, if she died, who else might be able to stop Melian's rampage?

At her words, Kelan groaned. "Fine. I'll clear a path to the square, but I'd appreciate some help."

Laima took a hesitant step forward, her eyes on the line of dead blocking their way. One took a swipe at Kelan, who was nearest, and he countered by slicing the man's head clean off. The dismembered head flew several handspans to the right, yet the dead man kept advancing, sword swinging jerkily. Niema's stomach turned over, and she heard someone gagging behind her.

Laima lifted a hand, sending a gust of wind towards the dead, and addressed the Disciples hiding in the inn's doorway. "Come on. You all volunteered for this, didn't you?"

"Some of us didn't," Kelan said over his shoulder. "The person responsible for this is—*was*—in the Temple of the Flame. If she goes down, so will her army."

"She can't be inside the temple anymore." Niema's hands clenched at her sides, her mind and body roiling at the violation of nature at work around her. *God of life, help me survive this.* "She can't use her powers in there—"

The wind rushed over her head as the Disciples of the Sky finally launched their attack, and Niema ducked to avoid being caught in the whirlwind. The dead staggered, some of them dropping their weapons, and more Disciples of the Sky moved out of the inn to join Laima and Kelan.

"This way." Kelan pointed over the rooftops towards the square. "Niema—if you must come with me, stay close behind me. Unless you can conjure up a few skirrits again?"

"Do you think skirrits would make any difference here?" She kept an eye on the towering form of the Temple of the Flames as he led the way down the street, certain that was where the commotion came from. "Yala needs our help."

The war drake's cries filled the background, guiding their way through to the square. While Kelan and his fellow Disciples of the Sky easily took down the dead, they found the entrance to Ceremonial Square blocked by the white-cloaked Disciples of the Flame who'd come to the inn. They stood with their backs to the new arrivals, hands aglow with holy fire.

"Can you move?" Kelan said with his typical level of politeness, hovering off the ground to see over their heads. "Shit—the dead are all over the square."

"Where's Yala?" Niema lifted her head, trying to see, but she didn't have the handy ability to fly.

A sharp knife split the skin of her shoulder, causing her to stumble. The source was a dead man lurking in a doorway, who Kelan stabbed through the neck. "We have to find another way around. Niema—do you want me to take you to the undercity instead? It's safer."

"Safer?" Her thoughts landed on the filthy river and the neglected streets, and a sudden rush of panic hit her. "What're the odds that Melian's spell has affected the dead elsewhere in the city, too?"

Kelan took off the dead man's arms with a swipe of his blade. "Higher than I'd like."

Niema whispered a prayer to the god of life, and the stinging pain in her shoulder eased. "Yala can't win this fight alone. Even if she ... even if she does have a connection to the god of death, she doesn't know how to use it."

Kelan grinned over his shoulder at her. "So you're willing to accept her newfound talents now?"

"Fuck you, Kelan."

That drew a surprised laugh from him. "Might want to save that until after the battle."

"You—" Her words were cut off by a deafening screech, followed by the unmistakeable thud of a large creature falling out of the sky.

The war drake was down.

32

Yala fought off the grasping hands of the dead and managed to stagger to her feet, her leg cramping in protest. She'd lost sight of Melian amid the melee, but on the other side of the square were several white-cloaked individuals. Disciples of the Flame. It would be difficult for any of them to deny that someone had used Corruption magic to flood the upper city with the dead, but the person responsible was notably absent.

"I thought you wanted to face me in person, Melian," Yala called out, her dagger slicing through the wrists and hands that grabbed at her. The war drake snapped and flailed nearby, but countless spear wounds had brought it to the ground, and thick blood dripped onto the paving stones.

As Yala felled another dead person, a spear struck the beast in the throat, spraying crimson. Its huge body convulsed, and the dead scattered, some crushed beneath the war drake's fall, others knocked aside by its lashing tail. Gut tightening, Yala kept her distance from its death throes as she made her way to the temple steps.

Melian might be nowhere to be seen, but Temik stood

outside the front doors, watching the carnage with indifference.

"Where's your ally?" Yala shouted to him. "Hiding inside?"

"No." He beckoned to her. "If you don't want to find yourself turned to ashes or taken to pieces by that war drake, come with me."

"Now you're offering me help?" She backed away as the war drake's tail swung around and knocked over a mercenary who'd been crouching outside the temple, one of the few living people left in the square. *Cowardly pricks probably ran when the dead started walking.*

When Yala stumbled over the temple's lower step, Temik reached out and grabbed her arm. "Don't struggle. I don't want to hurt you any more than I have to."

"A likely story." She yanked her arm free and struck him across the face in a vicious backhand. The briefly stunned expression on his face brought her up short—she'd never hit any member of her squad before, no matter how they annoyed her. The act went against her instincts.

"Don't touch me again," she told him. "Keep your fucking hands to yourself."

His mouth gaped open, as if being hit by his former squad leader had shocked him as much as it had her. A high-pitched cry drew their eyes back to the war drake, which lay on its side, its breath rattling in its ruined throat. The dead continued to stab and swipe, unseeing and unfeeling. *Poor creature.*

Yala's heart spasmed when she glimpsed Machit among the other lumbering corpses, too far away to reach.

Temik wiped his bleeding nose on his sleeve. "What is it? Are you sad about that war drake?"

Yala motioned towards the dead. "No, I'm sad that Machit isn't close enough to hit you, too."

"I didn't ask Melian to raise him from the dead as well as

the others." His mouth pinched at the corners. "We can negotiate. I'll ask her to give his body back if your allies
surrender."

"What allies?" She glimpsed the Disciples of the Flame on
the other side of the square, but she saw no signs of the
Disciples of the Sky, including Kelan. "Those are supposed to
be *your* allies, though if they've figured out that you're
helping the person who summoned the dead, they won't be
for long."

His mouth flattened. "If they don't like my leadership,
they can leave."

"Like Dalem did?" His flinch brought her a bitter rush of
satisfaction.

"Don't say his name," he rasped. "Superior Datriem
treated him terribly, but I won't be the same."

"Since when did you want to lead anyone?" Light flashed
as the Disciples of the Flame cut down the dead, but once
they reached the temple, Yala would be their next target.
They saw no distinction between her and Melian.

"Since you," he said. "You inspired me, Yala. You might
have been unquestioningly devoted to the king, but you gave
us the choice to follow you or not. It seems only fair to offer
you the same choice."

"What choice?" she queried. "Melian wants to sacrifice me
to the god of death. There's not much room for compromise
there."

"You'd be surprised." A thoughtful look flitted across his
face. "You *are* a Disciple of Death. Imagine what we can
achieve together."

"Together?" she echoed. "We haven't been together since
you turned your back on our squad after the war."

"Speak for yourself," he said. "You can't be that fond of the
king, surely, not after what he did to us."

"As opposed to King Tharen?" Despite herself, her long-buried curiosity over how much King Tharen had known flickered back to life. "Did you ever find out if he intended to claim the magic inside that temple for his own use? Or did you stop caring when you decided your own ambitions mattered more than anything else?"

"He didn't," said Temik. "He wanted the island solely to keep Rafragoria from seizing the temple themselves. Honestly, he needn't have died, but I understand why some people would have felt threatened by the temple's existence and would have sacrificed anything to keep it a secret." His mouth tightened on the word *sacrificed.*

"Who told you that?" Not King Tharen himself, nor his son either. She was reasonably certain that Temik had never spoken to either of them. "Are you incapable of any thoughts that aren't lifted directly from Melian's mouth?"

"I didn't do this because of her." He gestured at the temple behind him. "I don't *want* this to escalate into a war. There's no reason we can't rule together—the Disciples of Death and the rest of us."

"Rule together?" A laugh caught in her throat. "You want Melian to be my tutor? To instruct me in the fine art of Corruption? I thought she was making it up as she went along, not following a textbook."

"She did have instruction ... of a sort," he replied. "Don't forget we have a friend with access to the palace library."

Viam. Yala's heart contracted. He'd confirmed her worst suspicion about Melian's source of information, and she fought to keep the turmoil from showing on her face. "I take it the new king was unaware?"

"Obviously," he said. "I almost feel sorry for the fool. His guards will no doubt have warned him to hide underground by now, but there's nowhere to hide from the dead."

Yala couldn't see the palace gates from here, but now she looked in that direction, the Disciples of the Flame were no longer at the other side of the square. The war drake's corpse blocked some of the view, but the dead had also veered away from the temple, converging on a spot out of Yala's line of sight.

Melian. Yala's gaze picked her out on the other side of the golden statue—and a white-cloaked Disciple lying dead at her feet. White flames flickered elsewhere in the square, and while the dead were weaker than the living, even a Disciple could be overcome by strength of numbers.

"Does anyone else want to challenge me?" she asked, her voice ringing across the square. "Choose wisely."

Temik leaned closer. "Come inside the temple, Yala. You'll be protected from her."

"What makes you think I want protection?" Yala forced a laugh. "I doubt your fellow Disciples will be as keen to welcome me among their order."

"They won't challenge you." His breathing quickened. "Yala, I meant it when I said I didn't want to harm you. The other Disciples... I had them drink to their new Superior, and I laced the barrel of wine with enough bitterleaf to knock them out for an hour or so."

Yala's next laugh was less forced. "Do you want me to thank you for knocking out your own supporters?"

"No, but it's easier this way, isn't it?" His gaze drifted towards Melian. "I can't stop her from hurting you."

"I'd prefer to die with what's left of my dignity intact."

His jaw twitched. "So be it."

He stepped towards the temple door and vanished inside, leaving Yala alone at the top of the stone stairs. As the door closed, Melian smiled at her.

"I think that's enough fooling around," she called across the square. "Come here, Yala. Bring her to me."

Mercenaries emerged from either side of the temple, climbing the steps. Grasping her dagger, Yala lunged at the nearest attacker, but her blade scarcely drew blood before another pair of hands seized it from her. Two more mercenaries grabbed her by the upper arms and hauled her across the square towards Melian.

"That's better." Melian brandished her blood-soaked knife, beckoning to Yala with her free hand. "Did your friend offer to protect you? He must care for you despite your poor treatment of him."

"Hardly." Yala struggled to free herself from the hands gripping her arms, to no avail. "Though I assume that's an unfamiliar concept to you."

"I'm not averse to sharing power, if you're concerned that I might take his life the way I did Datriem's," she said. "Datriem's goals and mine weren't the same. He never would have accepted my true nature."

"Neither will this city, Melian," Yala said. "You're overestimating people's tolerance for murderous nobles dictating their lives. You *were* a noble, weren't you? You certainly didn't fight in the war, and nobody else was exempt from military service." Technically, nobles hadn't been either, but they were more likely to have parents willing to spend large sums of money to convince the army to look the other way when their children hit the age of conscription.

Yala didn't much care for the particulars of Melian's life, but if she had any weaknesses to exploit, any gaps in her armour, this would be her last chance to extract the information from her.

Melian gave a shrug. "Noble? Hardly. My parents were modestly well off. The war had already ended by the time I reached conscription age."

Yala mentally added the dates and bit back a laugh. "You're practically a child."

She couldn't be much older than Niema. Foolishly, Yala had been envisioning Melian as someone who'd known of

EMMA L. ADAMS

King Tharen's interest in Corruption from the start, but that wasn't the case at all.

At her comment, Melian's eyes glittered with what might have been anger. "I wouldn't mock me, Yala. Your life is in my hands, remember?"

Yala gave another lunge for freedom, which failed, as the mercenaries pushed her to her knees at Melian's feet.

"I think it's fitting to spill your blood at the feet of the man who started the military order to which you devoted so much of your life." Melian indicated the towering golden statue of King Larial in his military gear, imposing and grand despite being worn by age and splattered with fresh blood from her recent massacre. "In answer to your concerns about whether the people of Dalathar will offer me their support, I've found that people will be swayed to act against their own interests if they believe there's a greater reward awaiting them... and there will be. The city will be in good hands after you die."

Her knife extended, aiming for Yala's throat.

———

When the war drake fell, the Disciples of the Flame broke apart enough for Kelan and Niema to reach the square, only to find themselves forced to back away to avoid being hit by a stray fireball.

"Nice to see them attacking the right targets for once," Kelan remarked to Niema, who didn't quite agree. The Disciples would find it easy to aim at Yala now she was no longer upon the war drake's back; its flailing limbs thrashed and writhed in a sea of the dead, and Yala had vanished somewhere among them.

I have to get her out. Niema scanned the square for a clear path across and found none. The Disciples of the Flame might have fire at their fingertips, but the writhing, dying war drake forced them to remain at a distance, hurling fire at the dead.

"Are the others hiding?" Kelan sliced the arm off another dead mercenary and then skewered him with his blade. "Or did someone lock the temple door?"

"Can you blame them for keeping their distance?" Niema gagged at the stench as the dead man fell, his rotting guts spilling at Kelan's feet. "Can you see Yala?"

"Not from here." Kelan hovered far enough above the ground to avoid treading in the viscera, but any higher would run the risk of him being hit by a stray weapon. The dead weren't only using ground weapons, but arrows and spears flew left and right, and they'd even felled the war drake.

A sudden suspicion gripped Niema, and she craned her neck to see figures moving atop the upper city wall. "Kelan, does Melian have people on the wall, too?"

"It wouldn't surprise me if she did." He descended, dodging an ill-judged fireball that struck a nearby building and left a smoking hole in its wake. "Someone will have to pay for this damage."

"Kelan!" She jabbed a finger across the square as she glimpsed Yala on the stone steps outside the temple, talking to someone—a man dressed in the robe of a Disciple of the Flame.

"That must be Temik." Kelan twisted his blade out of a dead man's gut. "He's not attacking her, at least."

"That doesn't mean she's safe." Her hands fisted, and she wished she could do something useful. The Disciples of the Flame might have scattered, but the dead remained … and so did Melian.

Niema's heart leapt into her throat when she saw Melian fighting alongside the dead, her curved knife cleaving through the body of a Disciple of the Sky. Kelan let out a low noise of outrage, ducking another flying spear as he glided towards them.

"Does anyone else want to challenge me?" she called. "Choose wisely."

Niema's eyes found Yala, who exchanged more words with the cloaked figure before he vanished into the temple. Her heart dropped when Melian called out. "I think that's enough fooling around, don't you? Come here, Yala."

A dead man wandered into Niema's path, blocking her line of sight. She hit out blindly and was struck by the thought that the vows she'd sworn were against causing harm to *living* creatures, not dead ones.

Pushing down her rising revulsion, Niema crouched and grabbed a sword someone had dropped. Kelan stared in confusion when she stabbed wildly at the oncoming attackers, managing to sever a dead man's arm. "I thought you weren't allowed to harm people."

"Living people—and that hardly matters now, does it?" she gasped in response. "Help me get to Yala."

The mercenaries had reached her first, and two of them hauled Yala down the temple's steps, while Melian waited near the golden statue of Laria's founding monarch, her knife held aloft.

Kelan sent a gust of air buffeting into the dead, driving them back, but they kept coming. No matter how many Niema stabbed, she drew no closer to her target. Worse, a *living* man was next to block her path, a bulky mercenary wielding an axe.

"Shit." Kelan's blade caught against the axe, causing him to stagger and lose his footing. Blood seeped from his wrist, and as Kelan struggled against his opponent, Niema stabbed the nearest dead soldier and then gave him a frantic shove into the axe-wielding man's path.

Another glance at the statue showed her Yala was on her knees, Melian's knife at her throat. *No.* A scream ripped from Niema's lungs, and she lunged forwards, hitting at dead and living alike, trying to get closer—

The knife swiped, blood sprayed out, and Yala's body crumpled to the ground.

———

Kelan saw Yala fall, saw Niema lunge forward with a shriek— he shouted a warning to her that went unheard—but the dead abruptly ceased their attack. Instead, they turned away, blank-faced, towards Melian. As if waiting for her instructions.

Melian held her blade—awash in Yala's blood—and a chill blanketed the square, as if the sun had set early. Shadows crept around Melian, as if she were circled by an unseen figure, and Kelan could have sworn he heard an unearthly voice whisper, *"I accept your sacrifice."*

"No." Niema was on her knees, her hands outstretched as if to bring Yala back by sheer force of will. "No, *no.*"

"Stop." He spoke through numb lips, half out of his mind with terror. That *voice*—even Melian's mercenary allies were backing away, none of them paying him the slightest bit of attention. Kelan's stomach gave a jolt when he recognised the ones whose wagon they'd stolen. *They joined forces with Melian. I wonder if they regret that now.*

Niema convulsed, spraying the ground with vomit. Screams and howls rose and fell, distorted by the general confusion, and he was scarcely aware of Melian walking out of his line of sight until the terror gripping his nerves loosened enough for him to see her disappear into a side street, followed by the dead soldiers she'd recruited.

Around the square lay the grisly remains of the battle—

body parts twitching, fallen dead doing their best to rise again, and the less fortunate among the Disciples who'd fallen under Melian's blade. Kelan lifted a shaking hand and found blood soaking into his sleeve. *Right ... I should deal with that. Get Niema out of here first.*

Niema—

Kelan swore. Niema had crawled around the statue to Yala's body, grabbed her shoulders, and begun to drag her across the stones. While Melian had vanished from sight, Niema was in plain view of the remaining Disciples of the Flame and anyone else who might remain from her army. Yet Niema didn't seem to notice or care.

When Kelan reached her, Niema had released Yala's shoulders and placed her hands upon her neck. Her powers didn't work on the dead, as far as he knew, but Niema remained stock-still, hands splayed over Yala's open throat.

"Niema." He reached her side, crouched beside Yala's body. "I'll carry her to the undercity. Let me help."

"No." Niema shook her head fiercely. "No. I can heal her."

"You can't. She's dead." Not that the word meant much, given the pieces of dead flesh littering the square, stirred to a mockery of life by the god of death's power. "Niema..."

"God of life," she whispered, "give me your strength."

A prayer slipped from her tongue, by turns poetic and pleading, as Niema held out her hands over the gaping wound in Yala's neck. Despite his lingering sickness and horror, Kelan found himself arrested by the sheer power of her faith. The outside world had simply ceased to exist for her. Didn't the god of life require something in exchange, though? Something *living?*

"Niema." He reached out a hand, and she slapped him away. Shocked, he let his arm fall to his side. "Don't give up your own life. You'll die."

You don't say, a mocking voice in the back of his head said.

Niema had made up her mind, that much was clear, but there was no telling if her plea would work.

His breath caught. A shimmering glow ignited in Niema's palms, brightening, spreading over Yala's throat. Kelan had to screw up his eyes against the glare, and when his vision cleared, the wound in Yala's neck had...

Gone.

"Niema." He stared at Yala's now perfectly intact throat. "How...?"

Niema lifted her head, her eyes shimmering with the same eerie green light, and then passed out at his feet.

———

Yala had expected her death to be bloody. She'd expected discomfort and pain. Yet her imaginings, and the years of idleness that had elapsed in between, didn't do it justice. Her neck was a torrent of pain and slick with blood, but the flashes of pain were an anchor she gripped onto despite the encroaching darkness.

A familiar voice whispered in her ear. *"Your flesh is mine now."*

"No," she wanted to say. "I'm not. I'm..." But the words wouldn't come, stoppered by the ruin of her throat.

As a Disciple of Death, one would think she'd have been given an opportunity to negotiate with Mekan, but the god of death was more interested in flesh than spirit. No doubt her body would continue to function long after she was gone...

"How inconvenient," whispered the voice. *"It seems we have a little more time to wait."*

"What does that mean?" Again, her reply remained unspoken, but some sense of awareness returned when a familiar pain jolted her shin. *Ouch.* Had her injury followed her into the afterlife? If so, that was hardly fair.

Did Disciples of Death go to the same afterlife as regular people? Or did they remain in Mekan's hands, like in the stories Dalem had shared from his time in the temple, doomed to eternal imprisonment in the realm of their god?

Her leg throbbed again. A tilting sensation told her someone was carrying her, someone who wasn't being nearly careful enough with her injuries.

Except ... wait. Her leg might be throbbing, but her neck no longer hurt. How was that possible?

Her eyes flickered open to see Saren's aghast face peering down at her. "No ... no. She's dead."

"She isn't," said Kelan. "I *hope* she isn't, because I left Niema unconscious in an alley. I couldn't carry both of them at once."

"Right—shit, I'll take her." Saren held out his hands, and she gave another groan when his unsteady grip shook her leg. "She *is* alive."

Niema had healed her? Her voice still wouldn't work, and her thoughts were too fuzzy to grasp.

This time when her vision darkened, no voice greeted her on the other side. Only silence.

33

K elan carried Niema to the undercity entrance after he'd left Yala in her friend's admittedly unsteady grip. When he glided past, the bearded man stared at him, taking in the bloody state of Kelan's clothes and the scent of rot that lingered from the dead. A relative calmness filled the outer city compared to the area on the other side of the wall, and when Kelan reached the shack where Saren had brought her, he saw Yala lying on a sleeping mat that Saren must have brought with him from the pleasure house. Upon seeing Kelan enter, he dragged a second sleeping mat over for Niema.

"She's exhausted, I think," Kelan told Saren as he laid her down on the sleeping mat. "Niema probably burned through all her favours with the god of life when she healed Yala."

"But they'll be all right?" Saren leaned over Yala and dabbed at the blood on her neck with a cloth. No traces of the knife wound remained, as if her throat had never been cut.

"There's an army of the dead loose in the city, and the

head of the Disciples of the Flame has been murdered," said Kelan. "I can't say anyone's long-term survival is certain."

Yala groaned. "I'd fucking better survive after that. Gods, it hurts."

"You're awake." Saren dropped the cloth and leaned over to peer into Yala's eyes. "How do you feel?"

"I don't recommend getting your throat cut."

"Not on my plan, believe me." A relieved smile broke over Saren's face. "Niema healed you."

"Guess she no longer thinks I'm an abomination." Yala coughed a laugh, sitting halfway up and then flopping onto her back again. "Where did Melian go?"

"I don't know, but she took the dead with her," Kelan replied. "She left ... she left several of my people dead in the square, and the Disciples of the Flame, too."

"And ... Temik?" Saren spoke in a hushed voice, his smile fading.

"Alive," Yala said. "He claims that he's the leader of the Disciples of the Flame, since Melian killed Superior Datriem, which was apparently part of his plan all along."

"Oh." Saren slumped on the filthy floor at her side, resting his elbows on his knees. "I should have guessed he planned to slay the old bastard when his back was turned."

"For Dalem." Yala gave another cough. "Gods, my throat hurts."

Saren reached for a bottle of liquor and handed it to Yala. "Drink this. It'll make you feel better."

She gave a hollow laugh. "It can hardly make me feel worse."

As she drank from the bottle, Kelan's attention turned to Niema, who hadn't stirred yet. She wouldn't be able to perform a similar miracle for anyone else, but it was a wonder it hadn't cost her own life. *Fool.* She seemed to have no concern for her own safety, but he had trouble believing that she'd saved Yala purely out of her belief in the vision her deity had shown her. Not if she'd accepted Yala's status as a Disciple of Death.

No: she'd saved Yala to give the rest of them a fighting chance against Melian.

Where is Melian now? On her way to the palace? While Kelan wrapped a bandage around his wrist—a shallow wound, luckily—he wondered how many of his fellow Disciples had managed to get away. Laima had been in charge of giving orders, so if she was wounded or worse…

"Where are you going?" Yala asked as he turned towards the door.

"I'm going to the upper city to look for my fellow Disciples," he said. "Melian might have left, but I don't trust her."

"Neither do I." Yala's gaze shadowed. "Try not to get killed, will you?"

"I've been luckier than you have so far." Though maybe he shouldn't tempt fate, given that he'd heard the god of death speak, and he was lucky to have escaped notice. Likely, he and Niema were of no interest to Melian, unlike Yala.

Securing the bandage around his wrist, Kelan left the shack, passing Niema's unconscious body on the way out. *Fool*, he thought, again. *Selfless fool.* If Melian figured out that Niema had helped Yala escape Mekan's claws, she might come to the undercity to look for her next. Someone had to stop her first.

Kelan reached the stairway to the surface and found his path barred by several of the undercity's former soldiers, including Nalen.

"What's going on?" Kelan asked.

"Trouble."

"What—" He lifted his head and saw two men blocking the way upstairs. They were dead, and based on the state of them, they'd come out of the river—ragged clothes dripping with filthy water, eyes blank, bloated bodies waterlogged.

"Oh," he said. "That kind of trouble."

———

As Yala revived enough to give Saren the gist of how she'd ended up bleeding out in Ceremonial Square, Kelan ducked back into the room.

"The dead are blocking the way out of the undercity," he told them.

"Shit." Had Melian already figured out that Yala had survived, or was she simply trying to ensure that anyone who might challenge her remained trapped underground? "How many?"

"Enough to cover all the exits," he said. "I think they came from the river."

"Typical." She imagined the bloated corpses she'd seen floating in the shallows rising from the river at Melian's command. "She must have pleased the god of death, if He's helping her even without my sacrifice."

"I doubt it," Niema muttered, startling Yala, who hadn't known she was awake. "I bet the god of death thrives on this sort of chaos, regardless of who's giving the orders."

"I can fly out of the undercity," said Kelan, "but I don't know if Melian gave the dead orders to attack anyone trying to get past."

"She might have." Worse, the people of the undercity had nowhere to run if the dead flooded the streets.

"Why does she want us trapped down here?" Saren asked. "Does she think we're a threat to her plans?"

"I doubt it," said Yala. "Most of her attention will be on the upper city, but I guess she's not taking any chances."

A commotion came from outside, drawing her eyes

towards the window. She glimpsed a pair of armed former soldiers wrestling someone outside the shack—a smartly dressed woman who looked somewhat out of place among the grubby and worn undercity folk.

"Viam." Yala pushed upward, but pain and blood loss made her head swim, and she gripped the sleeping mat with one hand to keep from passing out. "Saren—stop them."

Saren didn't move, but Kelan leaned out of the window and called to the ex-soldiers, "What are you doing?"

"We found this one trying to sneak in," said a scarred female soldier who was missing an ear.

"Let go of her." Yala knelt, her arms trembling and her leg aching. "What do you mean, 'sneak in'? I thought anyone was allowed into the undercity."

The ex-soldiers released Viam, who staggered towards the shack. Kelan opened the door, allowing her to enter.

"Thanks." Viam's gaze found Yala, and she stifled a gasp when she saw the blood. "Yala, you're hurt."

"I'm fine." Yala grabbed Saren's cloth and rubbed irritably at the blood on her neck. "What are you doing down here? How *did* you get past the dead?"

"I'm sorry I dropped in like this, but I've been looking for you since yesterday, when I heard you left the city," Viam said quickly. "Nobody would tell me where you'd gone."

"I'm not surprised." Saren's lip curled. "If you'd worn your old uniform, you might have had more luck."

"I... I don't have that anymore." Her cheeks flushed. "Look, you can judge me if you like, but I came here to help."

"You gave Temik access to the palace's library, didn't you?" After his revelation earlier, Yala had half expected the next time she saw Viam would involve her waiting at the palace gates to welcome Melian with open arms. "You gave Melian the tools to learn Corruption."

"I'm sorry." Her voice broke. "I brought Temik the texts

because I thought … I thought he was going to expose the truth about what the former king did."

"You thought *what?*" Saren burst into humourless laughter. "*You're* the reason Melian learned how to use Corruption? I should have known."

Viam ducked her head, hands clenching at her sides. "I didn't know. The king never figured out how to do it, and I thought it wasn't possible without access to a place like the temple on the island."

Niema lifted her head from where she lay on the sleeping mat. "King Tharen was learning about Corruption? The books Melian used were *his?*"

Everyone ignored her except for Viam, who said, "He got the books from the Parvan Empire, I think. They were translations and were more theoretical than practical. It's not as if I gave Melian an actual guidebook on how to contact the god of death."

"You might as well have," Saren said, but there was less heat in his voice. "He knew what we'd find on that island."

"Yes, but Rafragoria never figured out how to use Corruption. They had no more idea than we did."

"They knew enough to have our king assassinated." Yala surveyed Viam. "Did you ever find out why?"

Viam shook her head. "No. Everyone at the palace says they've been keeping to themselves since the war."

"They never expected retaliation?" Temik's words came back to her, unbidden—*he needn't have died.* A sudden suspicion gripped Yala. "What if it was never Rafragoria who killed him?"

"Then who?" Saren's questioning stare told her he'd never considered the matter before.

Kelan hissed out a breath. "Not the Disciples of the Flame?"

Everyone swivelled towards him, and Yala inclined her head. "Temik implied that King Tharen was killed because some people would have taken the mere existence of the temple on that island as a threat. Superior Datriem had access to the palace through the king's private guard, didn't he? Even if King Tharen didn't tell him, it wouldn't have been impossible for him to find out and order his fellow Disciples to put a stop to him."

There was nothing the Disciples of the Flame had despised more than Corruption … at least they hadn't before they'd unwittingly let Melian into their ranks.

Saren gave a hollow laugh. "Another reason to be glad Superior Datriem is dead. Pity it had to be Melian who killed him."

Viam made a choked noise. She'd backed against the wall, her arms wrapping around her chest. "It's unthought of for the guard to turn against the monarch they're supposed to protect. If you said that in the palace, you'd be arrested on the spot."

"I rather think the king and his retinue have more important matters they have to deal with," Saren said. "Such as the dead wandering the streets and Melian's scheming to take His Majesty's place."

"Also, King Tharen deserved what he got," Yala said, unable to help herself. When Viam's expression turned scandalised, she added, "What? That doesn't mean I supported the people who killed him—nor do I agree with the rest of the drakeshit Temik and Melian came out with, for that matter. But look at how much trouble a single Disciple of Death has managed to cause."

Viam shook her head. "I don't believe the king would ever have let the information fall into the hands of someone like Melian. He'd have kept it quiet."

"Would he have let us walk away, if he'd lived?" Saren

gave her a challenging stare. "Or did his death save our lives?"

"Don't be absurd, Saren," Yala said. "King Tharen wouldn't have known that we might return from the island as Disciples of Death ... but I'm willing to bet Superior Datriem did."

He'd wanted to keep an eye on her for a reason, and not only because he thought she'd tell tales. She hadn't been paranoid all those years. If he'd believed her a threat, he'd have sent his people to burn down her cabin without hesitation.

"That might be true," Viam said. "From what I read, it sounds as if all of us have an equal chance of being able to learn to control the dead. We all looked into the Void and fought Mekan's creatures."

"Oh, no." Saren raised his hands. "I am *not* sacrificing people to gain control over dead bodies. Why would I *want* to?"

"Because they're currently blocking every entrance and exit to the undercity?"

"Hold on." Yala swivelled to Viam. "You did that to get in here, didn't you? You didn't sneak in at all."

Viam's cheeks coloured, and Saren gave a wild laugh. "Seriously?"

Kelan raised a brow at Yala. "She has a point."

"You can fly." Yala shot him a glare and then Viam. "You didn't sacrifice anyone to get in here ... did you?"

"No, of course not." Viam lifted her chin. "Sacrifice is only required for something big, like opening the Void itself. Otherwise, controlling the dead is no different than another Disciple conjuring a small flame, or flying, or—"

"The Void." Yala's blood iced over. "That's what Melian plans to do?"

Of course it is. There was a reason she'd wanted to sacrifice Yala that went beyond calling upon an army of the dead. She wanted to gain power over the realm to which the god of death belonged, and to bring that nightmare into the waking world.

Viam inclined her head. "Yes. It'll be like on the island, only worse, because there are far more people in the capital than there were in the temple. And the more people who are killed in the aftermath, the stronger Mekan will grow."

Kelan eyed her. "If she does open the Void, what then?"

Yala's mind filled with images of the ground splitting open, of monstrous beasts emerging to feed on the living. "Imagine what we saw in the library, extended over the entire capital. Melian will be protected—at least until the god of death decides she's no longer useful to Him—but the rest of us will be torn to shreds."

"No thanks." Saren gave a shudder. "Wait, doesn't that include Temik, too?"

"I bet the Disciples of the Flame have some level of protection—or at least the ability to fight off the dead." Yala thought back to their confrontation in the square. "Melian must have accounted for that. She'll want to ensure they don't get in her way."

"Shit." Saren sank to the floor. "You're serious. That's what she's planning."

"Of course I'm serious," Viam said. "I'm not supposed to have left the palace, and I'd be safer in there, but I had to tell you. We're the only ones who might be able to stop her."

Yes, but she's had months or years to learn how to use Corruption magic. I haven't even had a week.

Niema pushed into a sitting position. "Don't. Yala, don't. If you turn to the god of death, there's no going back."

"I died once today already." Yala watched Niema, who'd finally met her eyes. "I'm glad you saved me, believe me. I'm grateful, but I can't stay here."

Viam watched as Yala pushed shakily to her feet. "You want me to teach you how to control the dead?"

"That won't be enough." Yala drew in a breath. "Melian has an army of the living as well."

"Then what?" Saren looked up at her, for all the world like a soldier waiting for orders.

Yala flashed him a smile. "I think it's time we rallied an army of our own, don't you?"

34

While Kelan was intrigued to see Viam teach Yala how to use the magic of Corruption to move the dead blocking the way out of the undercity, he'd stayed here long enough. Laima might think he was dead, assuming she'd survived herself.

If he were Melian, he wouldn't have wanted to risk any other Disciples standing in the way of the path to the king.

After leaving the shack, Kelan approached the nearest staircase and rose into the air, careful to angle himself so that he would avoid colliding with any of the dead who blocked the way to the surface. The overhanging buildings from the street above made this trickier, but he navigated his way upward until he broke free of the gloomy darkness. If anyone was watching the skies for him, he ran the risk of being spotted, but that was the domain of his own people, not Melian's. With luck, she was too busy trying to wrangle her new undead army to notice anything that went on in the undercity.

The dead showed no signs of having noticed him either, though they weren't only blocking the undercity entrance.

Groups wandered the streets and bridges of the outer city, blank faced and exuding the stomach-turning stench of rot. More sinister was the fact that nobody seemed to be controlling them. While Melian might have given the order, the dead moved as if at their own will, and it came as no surprise that he found the streets devoid of living people. Terrified faces peered from the windows he passed, while others had the curtains drawn, and nobody dared to step outdoors.

When he reached the gates to the upper city, he found another line of dead blocking his path. A quick glance at the wall showed it was occupied, no doubt by Melian's followers. If he tried to fly over, he'd blow his cover and get himself knocked out of the sky.

Kelan backed into a side street, and someone grabbed his arm from behind. He spun on his heel, reaching for his weapon, but Laima released him and pressed a finger to her lips. *What's she doing out here?*

She beckoned him to follow her, and he did so, too bewildered not to. When they'd left the gate behind them, she hissed, "Where in hells have you been?"

"I was trapped in the undercity by the dead," he said. "Like the ones at the gate. How'd you get out?"

"Melian's people attacked the inn," she replied. "Those of us who managed to escape over the wall are probably the only survivors."

"Shit." She must have secured the entire upper city against interference while she pushed ahead with her plan to infiltrate the palace. "How many got out?"

"Not enough." She beckoned to him again, leading the way down a cobbled street to what appeared to be an inn, albeit not as polished as the one in the upper city. "The gentleman who owns this place was generous enough to offer us somewhere to lie low."

"Better hope he's not secretly working with Melian." He

followed her into a dingy room that had certainly seen better days. The scent of mildew and rot permeated the downstairs room of the inn, where several blood-stained Disciples sat in a state of stunned silence on the grimy bench that served as the only seating area.

"Kelan." Lakiel looked up at him through a rapidly swelling black eye, one arm in a sling. "You're alive."

"I've been periodically going out and looking for survivors," Laima told him. "Melian's people cleared the guards off the wall, but they aren't watching every tower, so it's possible for us to fly over if we're careful."

"Good," Kelan said. "She's going for the palace. We don't have much time to stop her."

"Stop her?" The words came from Tremin, who Kelan was disappointed to see among the survivors. "Not a chance. We'd die."

"If we stay here, Melian will hunt us down before she's killed the king, or else her dead will," Kelan told them. "She's not going to let any other Disciples remain in the city."

"She has the dead guarding every major street, as well as her mercenaries on the wall," Laima said. "It's suicidal to go back to the square."

"That's what Yala's doing."

"*Yala.* Isn't she dead?" Laima asked. "Wasn't her throat cut?"

A murmur of disbelief arose between the other Disciples, while Tremin narrowed his eyes. "Hold on. Is that where you've been—with the Disciple of Death?"

Kelan ignored him. "Niema healed her. Melian doesn't know, which gives us an edge over her, as she never got her sacrifice."

"I don't think…" Laima trailed off. "Kelan, I don't want Melian to kill the king and take control of the city, but this is an impossible fight. We can't win."

"What about the Disciples of the Flame?" he countered. "There must a way to reach them. Don't forget their abilities prove more of a threat to the dead than anyone else. The original island Yala's team found was destroyed by holy fire."

"Really?" Laima watched him through narrowed eyes. "This had better not be one of your stories, Kelan."

"Don't be ridiculous," Kelan said. "There's the city guard, too. She can't have killed all of them."

"I saw some running away," Lakiel ventured. "From the dead. Honestly, I don't blame them."

I suppose not. Hadn't Niema said that the dead repelled all living beings? It probably said a lot for his own ability to assess risk that he hadn't fled the city himself, but there wasn't anywhere to run to that wouldn't eventually lead him straight back here.

No, the only way out was to challenge Melian directly. Yala planned to do so, and she was barely a Disciple. Kelan might not have an affinity with the god of death, but he didn't have the same target on his head that she did. And Melian didn't know anyone had survived.

Kelan faced the battered, bloodied Disciples. "We came here to talk to the Disciples of the Flame, to cooperate with them. I imagine they'll be grateful for our help in ousting Melian from the city."

"How did you plan to do that?" Tremin asked. "You're all talk, you are. Anyone who listens to you is going to get killed."

"Don't you think it's strange that a group of people with the skills to bring down Melian's army are hiding inside their temple?" Kelan asked. "Granted, she might have locked the doors or otherwise taken them out of action, but Superior Datriem can't have fooled all of them, and after his death, they'll want answers."

Laima nodded. "True, but getting over the wall is enough of a risk. We'll be exposed."

Kelan thought back to Yala's dramatic entrance on the back of a war drake. "I think the portion of the wall behind the Temple of the Flame is unguarded, or at least unoccupied. The war drake flew over without being struck down."

Laima gave him a considering look. "I hope you're right."

"You're going with him?" Tremin's voice rang with outrage. "You're all going to die."

"It's your choice." Kelan addressed the others. "I'll lead the way over the wall, and anyone who wants to come with me is welcome to. Let's see if any of the Disciples of the Flame will volunteer to help us stop Melian."

"I doubt it," Laima said. "At least some of them must have been on her side, or else they'd have already come forward."

Hmm. "The man who's put himself forward as their new leader is Melian's ally, but he might have gone to the palace with her."

He didn't know that for certain, but it was entirely possible the Disciples of the Flame would spurn him like their former leader had regardless of whether his replacement was present or not. Even if he revealed that Melian threatened the king … though as he'd learned in the past hour, some of them had likely killed the last monarch with their own hands.

Laima drew in a breath. "I suppose we might as well try. I'll go with you. Anyone else?"

A handful of others stepped forward, including Lakiel. Tremin grumbled under his breath, but when everyone had volunteered except those too injured to fight, he joined them, glowering at Kelan the whole time.

"If we die, it's on you," he said.

"That's fine with me." Given the bruises on his ribs from the impact of Tremin's fists, he wouldn't shed a tear if

Tremin didn't walk away from this alive. The others had volunteered for this.

As they left the inn, Kelan found himself walking alongside Laima. This was the first time they'd managed to talk without arguing in a long while, which was a breakthrough, if not a sign that she'd forgiven him. After all, they might both die today, one way or another.

When their group neared the back of the Temple of the Flame, Kelan found that he'd guessed correctly about that portion of the wall being unguarded. As he led the way, the others flew behind him, careful to keep themselves concealed behind the temple's towering expanse. Hovering above the wall, Kelan peered around the temple's side and saw the giant form of the dead war drake, sprawled across the square where it had fallen. Otherwise, Melian's army had vanished from sight.

"There's a door somewhere down there," he whispered to Laima. "Let's go."

"What if it's locked?"

"We'll get to that part later." Maybe Temik had the key, or another Disciple of the Flame who'd taken Melian's side, or one of her mercenaries. Getting a proper look through the temple's windows would help them figure out what was going on in there.

Kelan and Laima descended over the wall into the narrow passage that ran between the temple and the building behind it. Darkness shrouded the alley; while the sun shone directly through the windows facing the sun, the temple's rear remained shadowed, including the stone steps that led up to the wooden doors at the back.

Kelan climbed the stairs ahead of Laima, who came to an abrupt halt. "Kelan ... there's someone else out here."

He turned around, seeing a number of armed figures stalking down the passageway behind the temple. Mercenaries, without a doubt … wait. Weren't they the ones whose wagon he'd stolen? *Oh, shit.*

The woman with the shaved head gave him a sharp smile. "Hello again, Kelan."

―――――

"The first thing you need to know is that the god of death accepts one form of payment," Viam told Yala. "The flesh and blood of any living creature, including yourself."

Niema suppressed a shudder as she watched Viam instruct Yala in the use of Corruption, part of wondering if she shouldn't have put her foot down in a more vocal manner. Superior Kralia would have wanted her to intervene, but after the amount of life energy she'd expended raising Yala from the dead, Niema could scarcely sit on her sleeping mat without being overcome with exhaustion. She was lucky not to have died, and in the moment that she'd healed Yala, she was certain her enclave would have sensed something was wrong.

There was nothing she could do to explain to them, though … nor could she think of another way to clear the dead from barring the way out of the undercity.

"You mean to say I have to cut off one of my limbs?" Yala asked, in response to Viam's words. "Or a finger? I have to say I'm not keen on that idea either."

"No, a few drops of blood will do." Viam held up her hand, revealing several bandaged fingers stained with fresh blood. "I took more than I needed to when I was first figuring out how to do it, but unless you try to open the Void like Melian did, you won't have to cut anyone's throat."

"Good." Yala drew her own dagger from its sheath. "A few drops of blood are enough to control one dead person? Or two?"

409

"It's not that precise," said Viam. "Honestly, it depends on how generous the god of death is feeling at that particular moment, if you've used Corruption before, and probably other factors I don't know about."

"This is why it's a bad idea," Saren said. "You're gambling with forces that nobody understands. *Nobody.* Even the people who built that temple centuries ago ended up being eaten alive."

"We don't know that for sure," Viam said. "The risk is minimal if you're dealing with small amounts of power. Making a dead person move around is the equivalent to a Disciple of the Flame conjuring up a single spark, or a Disciple of the Sky levitating aboveground."

"Flying is useful," said Saren. "So is conjuring a flame, but making the dead move around is good for nothing but scaring the shit out of people."

"Or dealing with situations like this," Viam said. "It's easier to manipulate the dead if another Disciple of Death has already reanimated their bodies."

"How would I turn them against Melian?" Yala queried.

Viam's forehead scrunched up. "You can try commanding them to attack her, but I don't know how it works when two Disciples of Death attempt to influence the same target."

"I imagine the strongest Disciple would win out," said Saren. "So, unless you're willing to go to the same lengths as she is…"

"No," said Niema, unable to help herself. "How do you transfer the blood you offer to the god of death? You don't have an altar or anything…"

"No, which is why you need something from the Void itself to complete the offering," said Viam. "I was getting to that part."

"Then what's Melian using to make her offerings?" Yala

narrowed her eyes in suspicion. "How would she get something from the Void?"

"Temik must have brought something from the island," said Viam. "I didn't give her anything except the books, Yala. That's the truth."

"What are you using?" asked Saren.

Viam reached into her pocket and pulled out a patch of dried skin covered in obsidian scales. "Temik gave me this. I think he hoped I'd take lessons from Melian."

"And you didn't?" Yala tilted her head. "Are you *sure* you're not on her side?"

"I wouldn't have come here if I was," said Viam. "I'm supposed to be in the palace complex, actually, and if I survive this, I've probably lost my job."

"Better than your head," said Saren. "Look, this is not a solution. Moving the dead out of the way might help you get to the upper city and find Melian, but you'll end up getting your throat cut again."

Yala scowled but had no argument. Neither did Niema, who wouldn't be able to revive her from death again. They might have got one miracle, but they wouldn't get another.

Niema cleared her throat. "You mentioned an army?"

Yala turned towards the window. "I did, but I don't know that I'll have many volunteers from among the people of the undercity. Granted, they won't want to stay trapped down here indefinitely, and most of them used to be soldiers, too."

Saren frowned. "I don't see them rising up to defend the king either."

"Maybe not, but it's not him we're trying to save, is it?" Yala said. "It's us."

"That's true," Viam said. "If you think you can convince them…"

"I'm willing to try." Yala's eyes simmered with determination, and Niema realised she'd finally caught a glimpse of the person who'd led her squad into the Void itself and brought them back alive.

If anyone could overcome Melian, it was her.

———

Yala started with the people who'd been closest to Machit and who'd helped him protect the people of the undercity. Viam and Saren remained inside the shack, though both said they'd accompany her to confront Melian along with anyone she managed to convince to follow her.

"You're alive, then?" said Nalen when she approached him. "You looked dead."

"Luckily for me, it wasn't permanent," Yala answered. "The dead are still up there?"

"Yes," he said. "What in the gods' name is going on in this city?"

"The Successors have decided to make their play for power," she told him, seeing several other former soldiers had come to listen in as well. "Melian, their leader, is a Disciple of Death, and she sent the dead to guard every major entrance to the undercity to ensure none of us come out and challenge her."

"She's the one who tried to kill you?" He eyed the blood streaking her newly healed throat. "And now she's going after the king?"

"Yes, but she won't stop there." Yala took in a quick breath. "Listen. I know I'm asking for a lot, but if someone doesn't stop Melian, she's going to have everyone in the city obeying her every command under threat of getting killed by one of her dead allies. She claims this is a revolution, but she doesn't give a shit about anyone except herself."

"You want us to fight back?" Nalen guessed. "I don't see

how we can. The dead won't budge for anything. When Nekal tried to move one of them, it stabbed him in the hand."

Yala grimaced. "That's because Melian gave them orders to attack anyone who tries to leave. Let's assume I can get the dead to move out of the way without anyone getting hurt. What then?"

"What then?" he echoed. "How did you plan to convince a bunch of dead people to move?"

"I'll explain after you give me your answer," Yala said. "If Melian dies, her army falls apart. She thinks I'm dead, so she isn't going to be looking for me. She won't expect me to sneak up and stab her from behind, but I can't do it alone."

Nalen exchanged glances with the other soldiers, who eyed Yala warily. She hadn't convinced them yet.

"You can try talking to people," he said, "but you're not local here, so there's no guarantee they'll listen. Machit might have been able to convince them…"

But he was dead, and his corpse wandering the upper city at Melian's command. Yala's hands clenched. "Too bad. You get me instead. Oh, and if anyone has a spare cane I can borrow, it'll be much appreciated."

Five minutes later, Yala returned to the street's end with a newly procured cane in hand and rapped on the door to the nearest shack.

"Everyone outside!" she called to the people within. "I'm calling a meeting of everyone in the undercity at the Crossroads."

The Crossroads was the area in which all the streets in the undercity converged and had once been used for gatherings of dissatisfied workers and other fringe political groups who wanted to avoid drawing the attention of the city guards. Yala moved to the next house without waiting to see how many people followed her order; she knew not everyone would listen or care for what she had to say. As she

413

knocked on each door and repeated her message, a few people began to emerge. Saren came to help her out, though he lacked Yala's ability to project her voice so that the whole street could hear.

Before long, a jostling crowd had converged on the Crossroads. Reasoning that she was unlikely to draw a bigger audience than this, Yala hobbled to the front. A crowd of sceptical faces swam in front of her, and various shouts of 'what do you want?' arose amid the clamour of general conversation.

Yala drew in a breath and called on all her years of barking orders at reluctant soldiers, often from the other side of a field and surrounded by growling war drakes. "Listen to me!"

While the crowd didn't fall into total silence, most of them quietened enough for her to make herself heard.

"You might have noticed we're currently being held hostage by the dead," she said. "*Our* dead, to be precise. Someone has decided to make a play for power in the city by defiling the bodies of our friends and families and using them to keep us trapped down here while they take over the upper city. You might know the name they once used. They called themselves the Successors."

Murmurs of recognition stirred amid the audience, some of whom exchanged sceptical glances.

"Their leader, Melian, claims to be a revolutionary," she went on. "Some of you might have gone to her gatherings in the past or met with her. If so, you'll know her goal is to overthrow the king and take his place."

Her words drew a few accusing stares and mutters, as if they thought she was a royalist in disguise, but she pushed on. "I don't care if she assassinates the king, but she's the one who killed Machit."

Shocked exclamations followed her words. Yala gave the

crowd a moment to express their grief and anger before speaking again.

"Melian slaughtered him because he stood in her way," she said. "And she'll do the same to any of us, given the chance. Right now, we're only alive because she doesn't think we're worth her notice. She's got her dead holding us hostage in the undercity, and nobody else is going to help us. The city guard certainly won't."

"The city guard had never done shit to protect us," someone muttered.

"That's true." Yala raised her voice a fraction as several others chimed in agreement. "They have no intention of helping us, and neither does Melian. Imagine she does successfully unseat the king—do you really think she'll remember the rest of us? She's not a soldier and never has been. She's a Disciple."

"You travel with Disciples," someone called to her. "I saw."

"Who are you, anyway?" asked another person.

"Captain Yala Palathar," she said. "Former captain, that is, relieved of duty after the war. I imagine some of you have similar stories. The king cast us aside, and Melian took advantage of our desperation. She's never been one of us, and she's perfectly happy to leave us all to die."

"What's the alternative?" demanded a man with a deep scar running down one side of his face. "It sounds to me as if you're trying to convince us to join *your* army. I don't know about the rest of you, but I've had enough of dying for no cause."

"I'm offering you the choice." Yala did her best to ignore the number of heads nodding and murmurs of agreement with the man's words. "I'm not going to force anyone to fight, but I'd wager some of you have had enough of being ignored. When are you going to have the chance to get into the upper city and in front of the people with the power to enact change?"

"We might still die," said the speaker, unconvinced.

"You might," said Yala, "but it'll be on your own terms. I don't know about you, but I'd prefer that to hiding down here and waiting to be slaughtered."

She tapped her cane on the ground pointedly, and someone cheered. Saren, who stood near the back, and gave her a grin of approval when he saw her looking.

"It's up to you," Yala told the crowd. "I'm going there regardless, and I'll give you half an hour to decide if you want to join me. If you do, we'll get weapons, anything you need. If you have questions or concerns, I'm here to listen."

As she climbed off the stage, a few more cheers followed, but otherwise, it was hard for her to gauge the general level of approval. Perhaps it had been naive of her to expect support from people whom she'd turned her back on years ago, and she was a hypocrite to ask them to die for her.

Yet if Melian did succeed in opening the Void... Last time it had taken the burning divine fire of Dalathik to drench the dead in flames. This time, she had nothing more than a few bedraggled and beaten-down former soldiers spoiling for a fight. She counted five, ten volunteers, which was better than zero, but nothing on Melian's force of the dead.

So be it. Yala returned to the shack, where Viam met her outside the door.

"That was a good speech," she said. "Listen, I know you can't overcome Melian using death magic yourself, but if you want to use it to get to the upper city, you have the claw from the beast that stabbed you, don't you?"

"How in the gods' names do you know that?" Yala asked, disarmed. "Yes. I have it somewhere."

Yala entered the shack and went in search of her belongings, where she riffled through her pack until her hand closed around the curved claw the beast that looked so much like a war drake had plunged into her leg. The claw looked more like a war trophy than a source of Corruption magic, but there seemed no reason for Viam to have lied, and all other Disciplines required tools. Why would Corruption be any different?

She turned to see Viam and Saren watching her and held the claw aloft. "I bet it's as sharp as the day it stabbed me."

"You aren't going to use that, are you?" The feeble whisper came from Niema's direction. She'd curled into a fetal position on her sleeping mat as if the mere presence of Corruption had sapped her remaining strength. Yala felt a twinge of guilt; Niema had saved her life, despite her natural fear and hatred of Corruption, and she must be struggling to accept Yala's choice.

"I hope I don't need to," Yala said. "Saren, are you coming with me?"

"Of course." He approached the corner where he'd left his pack and fished out a dagger identical to Yala's. So he had kept some of his old army-issued weapons after all. "Can't promise I'm much use in a fight these days, but I'll always have your back, Yala."

"So will I." Viam reached for a knife she'd concealed in her pocket, which looked somewhat odd next to her fine clothes. Her wary countenance suggested she expected mockery from Saren, but he gave her a nod and nothing more. Better than hostility.

Yala led the way into the street, cane in hand, and her new followers filed in behind her. Not a lot—she counted maybe thirty or so—but it was better than nothing, and she was willing to bet they could give Melian's followers a great deal of trouble. At least the living ones. The dead were the real problem.

Yala asked Nalen to keep her followers back from the

stairs while she went ahead of them to clear the way. As she climbed, Viam and Saren hurried in behind her. Her leg protested at each step, but the pain became a lesser concern. As they neared the top, three dead people barred their way, blank faced and waterlogged, weeds and grime trailing from their hair.

Yala fought back a retch at the smell and reached for her belt, to which she'd attached the Void beast's severed claw.

"Do you want to deal with them or should I?" Viam asked her.

Yala lifted the claw in answer, running her fingertip over the edge before she could think better of the decision. A droplet of blood beaded on the surface, and a cold sharp breath of air entered her lungs.

The crimson sheen of the blood on her finger brightened, glimmering. Yala drew in another breath of cold, stale air and whispered, "I offer my blood to you, god of death, to gain control over these dead."

Saren swore behind her, and Viam sucked in a breath. A cold breeze caressed Yala's skin as the droplet of vanished through the surface of the claw, and the sound of dead flesh moving filled her ears.

The dead's blank faces turned in her direction. As if waiting for orders.

"Move," she whispered. "Don't attack anyone. Move aside."

The dead stirred, their rotting limbs brushing against one another as they shuffled back. Yala watched, hardly breathing, while the dead retreated, leaving the path out of the undercity clear.

"Fuck," Saren whispered. "Was it always that easy?"

"Don't speak too soon," Yala muttered back. "It was probably only easy for me to control them because Melian isn't paying any attention to the outer city."

"Still." Viam flashed her a pale smile. "It's a start."

Yala called over her shoulder, "Follow me, everyone. Be as quiet as possible, and if the dead attack you, disarm them or cut off their hands. They can't feel pain, but they can't stab you if they don't have any way to hold a weapon."

If anyone was having second thoughts, this would be their last chance to turn back, but nobody did. Yala's makeshift army followed her upstairs and out of the under-city, where she picked out the swiftest route to the upper city gates. They ran into a few dead wandering around, but the streets were otherwise deserted. Nobody spoke much; though the dead couldn't hear them, the eerie silence brought a chill to Yala's skin. It was as if all the living people in the entire city had gone into hiding.

When the gates to the upper city came within sight, Yala held out a hand to stop the others. As she'd predicted, a row of blank-faced dead blocked their way through, but before she could order them to move, her gaze snagged on a horribly familiar shadowy fog sweeping upward into the sky from somewhere behind the gates.

A cry rang out across the square, a resonant echoing call that reverberated in her very bones.

Melian had opened the Void.

35

K elan looked upon the mercenary with whom he'd shared a pleasant evening and wondered if he could ever have imagined they might end up here. No, even his wildest tales could never have conjured up anything as unlikely as he and Laima standing outside the back door to the Temple of the Flame while Rianem pointed a knife at him.

"Is this really what you wanted?" he asked of her. "The dead swarming the capital is going to make it difficult for you to earn a living."

"Opportunities are everywhere," Rianem said. "I don't have to stay in the capital."

"You can't possibly think Melian will stop here in Dalathar?" he said. "She wants to rule the whole of Laria."

"I doubt it'll have any effect on my life," she said. "Sorry, Kelan. No hard feelings?"

"Kelan!" Laima's shout drew his attention to the sky above the temple, in which a cloud of darkness rose into the air like smoke from a fire.

Even the mercenaries stared at the rising darkness, which

420

appeared to come from somewhere on the temple's right-hand side. It wasn't smoke or fog, but shadow, and with it came a chill that crept under his skin and crawled through his nerves. Kelan was vaguely aware that the mercenaries were in a perfect position for him to disarm, but fear held him captive, every muscle locking into place. Yala's words came back to him. *That's the Void*.

A guttural cry arose, and a winged shape followed, detaching itself from the shadowy mass. The mercenaries began to back away from the temple, instinct overcoming the terror that had frozen them as they looked up at the spine-covered, black-scaled beast.

Kelan, too, unfroze. "Imagine that across the whole country," he said to the mercenaries. "Are you sure that's what you want?"

In answer, they fled to left and right, leaving him and Laima alone in the narrow passage behind the temple. Laima cursed and tried the door. "Locked."

"Thought so." His mouth moved faster than his thoughts, which were slow to shake off the numbing terror of the dark shape emerging from the Void. He pressed a hand to the door and pushed air towards it, but no other god's power could touch the Temple of the Flame. "Shit."

The monster's roar echoed across the square as it launched into flight, not unlike a war drake. Perhaps that was what it had once been, when it was alive, but Mekan's realm had twisted it, stripping away the flesh and leaving a mockery in its place.

"What *is* that thing?" asked Laima.

"A beast from the realm of Mekan Himself," said Kelan. "From the Void."

The colour drained form her face. "If it's dead, it can't be killed, right?"

"Yala managed it," he said. "With help."

The beast let out a cry as it rose from the fog on the temple's other side, the female mercenary struggling in its grip. Teeth flashed, and the mercenary released a scream he'd never heard a human utter before. Laima sagged against the back door, her hands clapped to her mouth.

"Fuck." Kelan rapped his knuckles on the door, to no avail, and from the ground, they couldn't see what was going on inside the temple itself. They'd need to cross to the windows... which would also put them within sight of the monster.

Well ... it is a little distracted at the moment. Gods help us.

"Kelan, what are you doing?" Laima hurried behind him as he glided around the temple's side to peer through the windows. The creeping fog obscured the view, however, and he hovered, trying not to listen to the beast's claws ripping open the unfortunate mercenary.

Through the shadowy haze, Kelan saw a cloaked figure kneeling in front of the window. The Disciple was slumped on the floor, head down. Kelan didn't see any blood, so he was reasonably sure he wasn't dead, but when he reached out and tapped on the window with his knuckles, the man didn't stir.

"Stop!" Laima's scream came from behind him, and air rushed past a moment later. His head snapped upward, seeing that the war-drake-like beast had made for its next target—the Disciples of the Sky who'd been descending over the wall.

"Hey!" He flew upward to join Laima, drawing his blade in one hand and making a supplication to the god of the sky with the other. "Laima, the Disciples are unconscious. We won't get any help."

Yala's 'friend' Temik had drugged them or otherwise put them out of action. Laima swore and sent another jet of air at the beast, but it shrugged off her attack with one beat of its massive wings. Curved spikes jutted from its spine, while its flat head was topped with pointed horns and similar spikes marked each wing joint. Its body was skeletal, but its obsidian scales were solid as iron, and even its claws rapping against the glass of the temple window didn't make any of the Disciples stir.

"Let's try again," he told Laima. "Both of us at the same time. One, two…"

Twin bursts of air hit the beast's wings, this time knocking it back and drawing its attention. While the Disciples of the Sky on the wall seized the chance to move out of the way, the monster dove at Kelan and Laima, claws and teeth at the ready.

Laima lifted a hand, and a torrent of air struck the beast, causing it to slam into the side of the temple. Despite its size, the beast made no impact on the solid stone—evidently the Temple of the Flames was built of stronger stuff than Yala's cabin—but Kelan took advantage of its lost balance to duck underneath and drive his sword into its exposed wing. One of its clawed feet came close to catching him in the face, but he dodged, dropping in height so that he hovered on a level with the temple's window. Inside he glimpsed more unconscious Disciples sprawled on the floor, oblivious to the deadly fight outside.

Come on, god of the flames. Do you want your people to stay trapped inside while their city is overrun by the dead?

The beast dove again, its claws swiping at Kelan's head. He swerved, swinging his blade at the beast's wing as he ascended at speed. While his blade drew a gaping hole in the wing, one of its spines nearly caught him in the eye. *That's what got Yala,* he thought, ducking underneath.

Laima descended with her own blade in hand, bleeding from a cut on her face. Two more Disciples flew in to join them.

"We can bring it down," he told the newcomers. "Get the wings first—and watch out for those spikes."

The beast's tail lashed as it swung towards Kelan, knocking another Disciple flying back at the wall. A spear flew upward, hurled by one of the mercenaries below, but he couldn't tell if they were aiming at the monster or at the Disciples trying to take it down. Most had fled, though the foggy darkness flooding the square made it hard for him to see anyone on the ground.

When the monster dove at the newcomers, and Kelan took aim at its wing from behind. His blade sank deeply into the joint, but a sharp spine caught him in the shoulder. *Fuck.*

Kelan gasped in pain, eyes watering. He heard someone shouting his name, but his shoulder burned with agony, and he could scarcely keep his grip on his blade.

The beast's tail whipped around, and this time it caught him in the chest. Kelan flew back, his sword slipping from his hand and into the darkness, and this time the god of the sky didn't catch him when he fell.

———

As she urged the dead to move out of the way into the upper city, Yala saw Kelan and another Disciple of the Sky fighting against the beast from the Void near the Temple of the Flame. Her leg twinged in sympathy as the beast's claws swiped, but with so many targets to occupy its attention, it didn't notice Yala or her new ally.

Yala entered Ceremonial Square and saw the sprawled body of the dead war drake lying in a puddle of blood amid a thick layer of shadowy fog seeping through the square. Melian was nowhere to be seen, but the darkness blotting the sky in front of the palace complex suggested that she was moving closer to the king with each passing instant.

Given its position, walking directly through the Void was the only way to reach Melian. Or flying over it, but the few surviving Disciples of the Sky were preoccupied with their airborne adversary. If the war drake had survived, she might have had a chance, but...

Yala dragged her gaze away from the palace and glanced behind her at the makeshift army she'd brought from the undercity.

"What do you want us to do?" Saren asked from her side, in tones that sent her mind back to the days when he'd been their squad's scout, sent to assess each new situation and to report back to Yala before they landed. From the knowing look in his eye, he'd had the same thought.

"I need to get into the palace," Yala muttered. "But I'm not walking through the Void, and I'd also prefer to avoid the dead taking me."

"Then what?" Viam stepped to her side, anxiously eyeing the fallen war drake. "Is that drake dead?"

"Definitely." Her body tensed when the beast attacking the Temple of the Flame released a chilling cry, and its claw sent one of the Disciples flying in a spray of blood. "But that doesn't mean it can't be useful to us. Viam, Saren, can you make sure nobody ambushes me?"

"What about us?" asked Nalen.

"For now, stand back," she replied. "Also, try not to die."

It sounded an unnecessary order, but the god of death had quite enough reanimated bodies to influence without adding more to His ranks.

Yala approached the dead war drake and reached for the claw belonging to a similar creature that had risen out of the depths of Mekan's realm. A chill raised the hairs on the back of her neck, and she could have sworn a shadow fell over the blood spilling from the war drake's numerous wounds as she neared.

EMMA L. ADAMS

"No," Saren said in a hushed voice. "You can't— You want to raise *that* from death?"

"I don't see why not." Yala ran her blood-encrusted finger over the tip of the claw and whispered to the god of death, "Well? How much do you need?"

More than that, whispered Mekan's voice.

Yala scowled, then touched the claw to the dried blood on her neck where Melian had cut her throat. "Didn't I already give you enough?"

Yes... I always appreciate a willing sacrifice.

"Yala ... what are you doing?" Viam flinched back, hearing the voice.

"I touched death," Yala whispered. "I came close to being yours, didn't I? Take all the blood I spilled as a gift and let me raise this war drake."

A shadow crept over her vision like the wing of some huge bird, carrying a cold breeze that caressed the wound in her neck. Chills pricked her skin, and she could have sworn she heard the god of death give a faint sigh of satisfaction. The shadow lifted, and she tracked its movement towards the thick grey-black fog converging around the pool of blood beside the fallen war drake. Darkness crept over its scales, tendrils curling around its limbs.

Yala raised a hand ... and the war drake's massive leg twitched.

Saren let out a muffled exclamation. A thrill raced through Yala's veins when the beast's huge body gave a tremendous shudder. Its limbs twitched, legs popping and creaking as it began to rise to its feet.

"Watch out," she told the others. "This is bound to draw attention. If not from Melian herself, then her followers."

"You think?" Saren said faintly. "Fuck me. It's ... it's really moving."

426

"Yes, and if either of you wants to come with me to face Melian, now's the time to decide."

"It can't carry three of us," Viam said in shaky tones. "I—I'll come. I should have been inside the palace from the start."

"All right." Yala knew there was a good chance neither of them would walk out again, and the grimness on Saren's face said the same.

"Please try not to die," he said. "I couldn't stand it if the only members of our squad left alive were me and *Temik.*"

"I'll try not to." She handed her cane to Saren and then approached the towering form of the war drake's newly risen body. "Ready?"

"Absolutely not." Viam sounded as if she might pass out, but she stepped up to Yala's side regardless. Good. If two of them went in, at least there'd be someone left with a chance of stopping Melian in the event that one of them died.

Yala swung a leg over the beast's slumped neck, trying to ignore the clammy stickiness of the blood on its scales and the eerie manner in which it gave no sign of recognising the presence of a human passenger. Viam climbed up behind her, her breaths shallow.

"Go." Yala squeezed the war drake's neck with her legs, and its wings gave a jerky beat. "Let's fly."

They rose into the air, slowly, and lopsided with the weight of the spears protruding from the war drake's wings. Holding her breath, Yala looked into the Void smothering the area outside the palace complex entrance. Through gaps in the grey-black haze, she saw bodies lying inside the grounds —guards, perhaps, who'd tried to stop Melian's entry—but two figures stood upon the towering stone stairs leading into the palace itself.

As they flew over the gates, it became clear that Melian and Temik had reached the palace, but they appeared to be arguing. They stood on the steps, between two large statues of previous monarchs, hands gesturing at the towering building before them. If Yala had to guess, someone had locked the doors from the inside. Melian must have had a plan to get around that hitch, surely.

"Put me down near the palace," Viam whispered in her ear. "Before Melian hits the war drake and we both fall."

"If I land, they'll see us." A giant undead war drake was a little difficult to hide, and while they might have landed behind one of the other smaller buildings within the complex—the homes and workplaces of the various ministers and other officials—that would prevent Yala from seeing what Melian herself was doing. Though she had to admit that it was considerably easier to control the beast in its current state, and it responded to the merest nudge of her foot without so much as a growl of annoyance. "I need to take out Melian first."

The trouble was that the god of death now served both of them, and Melian had offered a considerably higher number of sacrifices than Yala had. If that was the sole deciding factor, she hadn't a hope of winning ... if not for the paradox of being a Disciple of Death. The god of death demanded flesh, and He wasn't picky about where it came from. Sooner or later, Melian would ask for too much, and the price would be her own life.

If Yala failed to kill her outright, she'd have to push her to that point of desperation.

As they flew around the swirling darkness of the Void, Melian lifted her head. Fury and disbelief flooded her expression.

"You!" Melian bellowed. "You're dead."

"Not quite," Yala called back. "My steed is, but you taught me that that doesn't have to be an impediment."

She flew directly at Melian, who ducked in a moment of panic that Yala hadn't expected from her, and then steered the war drake sideways to allow Viam to jump free of its back.

Yala briefly considered joining her, but she had more chance of hitting Melian from up in the air. While Temik watched her with equal disbelief, Yala lifted a hand in a wave. "Fancy meeting you here, Temik."

Melian lifted her head, outrage simmering in her eyes. "I gave you these lives, god of death. I command that you give me control over this beast."

The beast's body heaved with a shudder, but Yala held on tight even as its wingbeats slowed.

"You already told me you would obey," she growled, half at the war drake and half at the god of death Himself. "I thought you didn't go back on your word."

The beast's body gave another shudder, and as Yala gripped its neck, she was vaguely aware that her own hands had turned a shadowy grey in colour, as if Mekan's touch lived beneath her own skin. She held on grimly and *willed* the beast to descend, claws outstretched.

Melian's eyes flew wide, and then she twisted her hands as if trying to push the beast away from afar. The war drake's body tilted sideways in the air, but Yala's response was simply to hold tighter and push her own will straight back at the beast until it regained its balance.

Melian let out a scream of frustration, and Yala grinned. Melian might have the power of the god of death at her fingertips, but she'd never flown on a war drake before, dead or living. She didn't know how many hours Yala had practised to avoid being thrown off her steed no matter what kind of manoeuvres she attempted. She'd had to avoid spears in midair, tackle opposing war drakes, and even catch a falling team member in flight. This was nothing.

Such was Melian's frustration that she failed to notice Viam emerge from behind a statue with a dagger in her hand

—but Temik did. He shouted a warning, and Melian spun towards Viam.

The momentary distraction gave Yala the chance to catch her balance on the war drake's back. Diving forward, she directed her steed to reach for the back of Melian's cloak.

Melian screamed as the war drake's claw dragged her off her feet and lifted her into the air. Unlike Yala, she was unused to being airborne, and as she kicked out, panicking, Mekan's whisper returned to Yala's ear.

"If you kill her, you will gain everything she has and more. What would you ask of me first?"

"Close the Void," she whispered. "Leave the city. That's what I ask of you."

"It's too late to ask that, Yala. I'm already here."

Yala recoiled, and Melian twisted in the war drake's grip, her face a mask of hate. As she jabbed a finger at Yala, the beast tipped sideways—

Flames shot outward from Temik's palms, striking the back of Melian's cloak. As the fabric caught ablaze, she lost her grip on the shadows. A startled scream escaped her—and she fell, her body plummeting towards the ground.

Melian landed with a crack that sent blood fanning outward from her shattered skull. As the war drake caught its balance, Yala's eyes landed on the culprit—Temik, whose outstretched hand glowed with flame. His face was ashen, fixated on Melian's fallen body.

She was dead, but the Void remained, a blot of darkness against the gates, a swirl of fog seeping into the city. What would the price be to get rid of it? What did she have left to give, save for her life?

Yala directed the war drake to land in front of Temik. He watched, dazed, his mouth slack. "You can't be here. You're dead."

"Things don't have a habit of staying that way around us, though, do they?"

"I killed her," he mumbled, indicating Melian. "That was for Machit, and for Vanat."

"Do you want us to thank you?" Viam stepped into view, raising her dagger. "I should cut your throat for what you did."

"Don't," Yala warned. "Look! The Void is open, like on the island. Mekan isn't keen to leave the city."

"What?" The remaining colour drained from Temik's face. "Why didn't you tell me that would happen?"

"You're still intent on blaming us for your mistakes?" Yala said incredulously. "Melian is the one who opened the Void, and unless someone figures out an alternative, it'll remain here indefinitely, spewing horrors out across the city."

Unless the god of the flames saw fit to intervene, but when Dalem had called upon Dalathik's aid, the price had been his own life. Nobody here was brave enough to make that bargain, including Temik, who stared helplessly as if he was waiting for someone to tell him what to do.

As if he was waiting for Yala's orders.

The bitter irony struck her; even now, she was the one who had to make the hard decision. She caught Temik's eye, seeing the frightened soldier he'd once been, and the words stuck in her throat.

"It's your choice," she finally said. "I can't say I have much of a hope of winning the support of the god the flames, but I'll give it a fair shot."

Temik lowered his head for a long moment, and when he looked up again, a film of tears covered his eyes. "I'm sorry, Yala."

"Bit late for that now." She heaved a sigh. "Honestly, I'm sorry, too. I fucked up in a lot of ways, and hells, maybe letting the king go back to ruling Laria is another, but…"

She trailed off when Temik walked past her, his eyes fixed on the dark mass of the Void. As he walked, he murmured under his breath. She strained her ears to catch the words, and a jolt of familiarity hit her.

"Wait—!" Yala slid from the war drake's back, landing clumsily on her aching leg, but flames already licked at Temik's fingertips.

Horror washed over her as she watched the fire spread, outlining his body, scorching his skin—and as he burned, he kept walking, deep into the shadow of the Void. Briefly he turned back, flashed her the ghost of a smile. She saw him mouth a word—*Dalem*—before the flames smothered his face, too. Then he was gone, in a flash of fire that swept up the darkness of the Void like a firework catching alight.

She thought she heard the god of death roar with rage, but it was equally possible that she'd imagined it, as well as the shadows whirling around her in a dervish. As the shadows fled, Yala closed her eyes against the blazing fire.

36

Yala's memories of the moments following the battle consisted of a series of sharp, vivid images. The palace grounds, drenched in blood and littered with corpses. The monstrous drake-like beast toppling to the ground, felled by the embattled Disciples of the Sky. Saren and Viam supporting her as she walked across Ceremonial Square. The inhabitants of the undercity surrounding her, bombarding her with questions.

Somewhere along the way, her consciousness faded, and her next clear memory was of waking up in what appeared to be a private room at an inn. To her bewilderment, a concerned Niema peered down at her.

The other woman hastily backed away when she saw Yala was awake. "Are you ... ah. Are you all right?"

"I think so." The words tasted of dust in Yala's mouth. "I'm not ... shadowy or anything? I don't look like I have the god of death hovering on my shoulder?"

Niema blanched. "Was ... was it you who got rid of Mekan?"

"No. Temik did." She sank back on the bed, a familiar

hollowness in her chest. "The god of death refused to listen to me, so Temik gave his life. It was his choice."

"Of course it was." Saren sidled into the room, balancing a tray on one hand. "I brought sustenance."

"Thanks." Yala reached for the tray, which was laden with food from the markets. "How long have I been here?"

"Hmm ... two days?" Saren handed her a wooden mug, which she sniffed to make sure it wasn't liquor before she drank from it. "It took a while for us to find an inn willing to let us rent a room for you. We found this place on recommendation from—"

Viam entered behind Saren. "You've been sleeping like a rock."

"Lucky for some people," Saren said. "The rest of us haven't been able to rest for more than an hour since the battle. Giran has officially kicked me out of his pleasure house. He brought a contingent of city guards, and they're already pissed at having to clean up the dead bodies."

Yala drained the mug—the fresh fruit juice was a balm to her sore throat—and coughed. "Didn't those guards run like the hells from the same dead bodies when they were walking?"

"They did, but we held them to account." An inexplicable smirk appeared on Saren's face. "Nalen hauled a couple of them down to the undercity and showed them those water-logged corpses from the river. I think they're going to find it hard to ignore any other bodies that end up in the water, considering they might get up again."

"Finally, some good news." Yala thought back to the confusion of Ceremonial Square. "Speaking of the dead, where'd that war drake go?"

"Good question," said Saren. "It's not around the palace complex, or we'd have heard. Probably flew off and dropped dead in a field somewhere. The Disciples managed to kill that monster from the Void, too."

"Good … wait, where's Kelan?" She recalled seeing his fellow Disciples being knocked out of the sky by the giant beast, and abruptly lost her appetite.

"He survived," said Niema. "He's at the inn, I think … they have healers there."

"Oh, good." Yala ran through a mental list of their other acquaintances. "The Disciples of the Flame?"

"Mostly alive, though they're confused," said Viam. "I had a look through the windows on my way here, and I think most of them were unconscious during Temik and Melian's coup."

"Temik drugged them." Yala still had little respect for those who'd supported Superior Datriem, especially with her new knowledge of their role in King Tharen's death. "Hope their next leader isn't as much of a prick."

"Depends how they make the choice," asked Saren. "What do they do, put it to a vote?"

"I think their deity is the one who picks the leader," Viam answered. "Dalathik hates Corruption, so I don't see Him choosing any of Melian's allies."

"I wouldn't speak too soon," said Yala. "Superior Datriem despised Corruption enough that he had our last monarch killed for it, and he didn't see Melian for what she really was until it was too late."

Saren grimaced. "About that… Viam, are you going to tell the king?"

"What?" Viam shuddered. "Am I going to tell King Delial that his father was murdered by his own Disciples? Hells, no. Can you imagine?"

"He might not believe you," Yala added. "If he was genuinely ignorant of what his father was up to, and he has no interest in Corruption himself…"

"He doesn't," Viam said. "I know you have grievances with him, and I do, too, but he's trying. King Tharen left us drowning in so much debt it's a wonder we aren't halfway below the ocean."

"The undercity might as well be," Yala said. "There'll be more riots, more unrest, if he continues to ignore them."

"I don't disagree." Viam's wary gaze went to Saren, who seemed to have set his own grudge aside, though that might change once the aftermath of their brush with death wore off. "I... I don't know that they'll listen to me, given that I disappeared without a trace in the middle of a crisis."

"I'm sure His Majesty would understand why you left," Saren said. "Half the palace guard got slaughtered."

"That's true." Viam's mouth tightened. "It's going to be weird going back, knowing everyone will want an explanation from me."

"Better that you get to set the narrative yourself than leave it up to the surviving Disciples of the Flame." Though Yala didn't envy her the fine line she walked. While King Daliel had been utterly oblivious to his father's interest in Corruption magic, if ever he asked the question of how the texts on the subject had ended up in Melian's hands, it would be hard for Viam to explain without giving away her own role in the matter.

Still, at least Viam had a job to return to. Yala did not. She could assist with the clean-up in the city, she supposed, but other than that, she'd made the same mistake she had as a soldier—namely, assuming she wasn't going to survive long enough that she'd have to worry about the aftermath.

No ... she'd eat and rest first. Have a bath. Find clean clothes. And, when she felt a little more human and had enough fortitude to brave the stairs, she intended to pay a visit to the undercity.

———

To her astonishment, when she did enter the undercity, Yala was met with a chorus of cheers.

"What did you tell them?" she asked Nalen in bewilderment, assuming he must be to blame.

"Nothing," he said. "That was all you."

"I didn't do anything." She looked out at smiling faces in the shack windows, at soldiers emerging into the narrow passage to wave at her. Quieter, she whispered to him, "Their lives aren't any better than they were before."

"Trust me, no longer being held hostage by the dead is an improvement," Saren said from behind her. "And the city guards actually listened when we told them how awful conditions are down here."

"I hope they carry on listening and actually do something about it," she replied. "If you ask me, they ought to hire some of the soldiers who came with me to the upper city rather than running away to replace the people they lost."

"Funny you should say that," Nalen said. "I brought up the same point to them. We'll see if it comes to anything."

"I hope so." Yala might have money, but her funds would only stretch so far, and she had her own bills to pay. The innkeeper might have offered her free accommodation in exchange for saving the city, but she could only tolerate charity for so long, and there was Saren to think of, too. When they walked back to the inn, she caught him sidling towards the pleasure house again.

"I'm not letting that fucker Giran steal my liquor," he said, when he saw she'd followed him.

"I thought you said he didn't drink."

Saren gave a soft snort. "He didn't, before the god of death attacked his home. Do you blame him for giving up that resolution?"

437

"That doesn't mean you'll be able to get away with sneaking into his property," she said. "When's he reopening?"

"Before I leave, I hope." Kelan stepped into view, one arm heavily bandaged and his movements considerably less graceful than usual.

Yala raised her cane in greeting. "You look like shit."

"You look considerably less like shit than the last time I saw you." He indicated the door. "I see the owners have returned."

"Yes, and kicked us out," Saren said. "As if we didn't clean up the mess."

"We're staying at an inn someone recommended." Yala beckoned, and both of them followed her the short distance to their new accommodation.

"You're alive, then," Niema emerged from the building, presumably having heard their voices.

"I have to admit I expected a warmer welcome." He nevertheless entered the inn behind Yala. "I'll have to return to Skytower in the next day or so. Laima insists I should stay behind and recover, but Superior Sietra needs to hear the full story, and only I can give some of it."

"How many…?" Niema broke off. "How many were killed?"

Kelan's eyes shadowed. "Four of my people, and most of the Disciples of the Flame who were sent to negotiate with us. The majority of the others were drugged, though they should recover."

"Lucky them." Saren led the way into the main room, which was unoccupied except for one chair in the corner. There, Viam sat reading a book—she hadn't wanted to come with them to the undercity, feeling as if she wouldn't be welcomed there—which she put down when Saren claimed another seat. "The rest of us remember the nightmare, don't we?"

"Yes, we do." Kelan didn't sit, instead hovering above the ground in a manner that didn't quite conceal the thick bandages under his coat. "The Disciples of the Flame destroyed that monster's body, by the way."

"Oh, good." Somehow it'd slipped Yala's mind that the beast from the Void would have potentially provided a new batch of Disciples of Death with the means of contacting Mekan. "Ah … how many people know I raised the war drake from the dead? Specifically, the Disciples?"

"Well…" Kelan paused. "My people, certainly, but the Disciples of the Flame mostly slept through it."

Saren shrugged. "Nobody in the undercity cares."

"I'm a little concerned that the other Disciples will view me as something that ought to be stamped out. Like Superior Datriem did." She looked at Niema, who flinched.

"I won't tell Superior Kralia, if you don't want me to," she said. "I can tell them your friend ended the battle, which is true."

"Temik. Yes." Yala caught Kelan's attention sharpen, curious, as he hadn't seen the battle inside the palace grounds. "Or the god of the flames, to be more accurate. The god of death rejected my request to close the Void when I asked Him. Just in case anyone was wondering if I'm a full-fledged Disciple of Death."

Kelan nodded. "Superior Sietra already knows your capabilities, so there won't be any surprises there. Niema, are you going to tell Superior Kralia that the former monarch might have been researching Corruption?"

Niema grimaced. "I don't *want* to, but she'll get suspicious if I leave out too many details.

She'll also want to know how accurate our vision was."

"What *did* your vision show?" Yala asked. "Are you allowed to tell us now it's over?"

Niema drew in a breath. "You've guessed, haven't you? I saw your squad facing down the Void."

"That's it?" Disbelief bled into Yala's voice. "Then you knew we beat Mekan's creations by sheer accident."

"Not as far as my Superior interpreted it." Niema cut a glare at Kelan, who was hiding a smirk. "What?"

"That's what you based your entire mission on?" Kelan exchanged raised eyebrows with Saren, who looked equally sceptical. "Not your skill, or...?"

"She saved my life," Yala reminded him. "If not for her, Melian would have let me bleed out in the square."

Niema scowled at Kelan. "I don't remember you being much use in the battle either."

"You were asleep for most of it," he retaliated.

"Hey!" Yala threw up her hands. "Honestly. I've barely been awake a few hours and you're already at one another's throats."

"That's why we need a squad leader to keep us in check." Saren shot a mischievous grin at Viam, which she returned. *So they forgave each other. For now, anyway.*

"I don't remember volunteering." Yala eyed Kelan, who'd backed out of the doorway. "Leaving already?"

"Yes," he said. "If I don't, Laima will leave out my role in saving the city when she gives her account to Superior Sietra, which would be a tragedy for everyone involved."

Yala rolled her eyes at him. "Good luck with that."

As he left, Niema watched with her eyes narrowed. "He doesn't know the first thing about me *or* my people."

Yala smothered a sigh, wishing they'd waited until more than a day had passed since the battle before they started bickering again. "Niema ... this isn't going to be an isolated incident. I think you'll have to tell your Superior that there's a strong chance there might be Disciples of Death popping up all over Laria."

"You think someone else will try?"

"I'd like to hope that anyone who might have been getting dangerous ideas would think twice after hearing what I did to the last person who tried raising the dead." She gave a shrug. "Depends on what the rumours end up saying I did, but it worked well enough the last time."

"I suppose." Niema paused. "I'm sorry I reacted the way I did when I found out the truth. If you hadn't been able to step in, we'd have all died. And—I'm sure I can make Superior Kralia understand, too."

Yala doubted it, but she also had no intention of ever meeting Superior Kralia, and it didn't matter what Niema's enclave members thought of her decisions. She had more than enough people to be accountable for, and while she had her share of regrets, allying with Mekan to save her allies wasn't one of them.

———

When Kelan returned to the Disciples' Inn, he found the other Disciples of the Sky waiting in the downstairs room.

Laima met him at the door. "You're supposed to be in bed."

"You didn't specify *whose* bed," he said, in tones that might have been convincing if not for his thickly bandaged shoulder and the fact that he was having so much trouble breathing around his broken ribs that vigorous physical activity would be out of the question for a while.

"Honestly," she said, "I know you went to say goodbye to your friends, but are you sure you want to fly back to Skytower now?"

"Yes." The thought of a long flight did not appeal, but Niema hadn't offered to heal him this time around. He'd hardly endeared himself to her, though spending half a day unconscious and then waking to a great deal of pain had eroded what little patience he had left for her enclave's ridiculous superstitions. She might as well have said she'd seen Yala's victory in a dream.

Still, against all the odds, the city was standing and so was he. The second part seemed more of a miracle, though Kelan suspected the god of the sky had had a hand in how he'd survived when that monster had flung him out of the sky. The healer at the inn had told him he was lucky to still be able to use the arm the creature had stabbed, and that it would take several weeks before he was able to fight with a blade again. He could fly home, though, which was more than he could say from the Disciples who hadn't survived the fight. While he expected his return to Skytower to be greeted with a lecture from Superior Sietra for his role in Yala's escape, he retained the hope that she'd backtrack when she found out how Yala had steered the city out of the jaws of disaster.

Kelan fetched his belongings from upstairs and returned to the lower room, where Laima was addressing the other Disciples.

"The Temple of the Flame haven't appointed a new leader yet," Laima was saying. "I think someone ought to stay and keep an eye on that."

She gave Kelan a pointed look, and he shrugged his uninjured shoulder. "I rather think Superior Sietra would want me to come back to serve out my punishment for helping her prisoner escape."

"I highly doubt she'll be punishing anyone for that," Laima said. "You spoke to Yala again, right?"

"Yes," he said, sensing the others' attention on him. "And she has no interest in becoming a Disciple of Death, despite her actions in the battle."

"No interest?" echoed Lakiel. "Didn't she raise a war drake from the dead?"

"Yes, but there's no branch of Disciples for her to join, is there?" he pointed out. "The Disciples of the Flame won't let anyone set up a rival temple if their new leader is anything like the old one."

"Given the circumstances of their Superior's death, I don't see them intervening in other Disciples' affairs at any time soon," said Laima.

No, but they killed the last king. He hadn't told the others, though it didn't necessarily matter if they all knew. Matters involving the monarch weren't supposed to be any of their business at all, but he intended to tell Superior Sietra at the least.

Their bruised and bedraggled group left the inn and rose to ascend over the city wall. While Kelan had had no intention of taking any detours, for once, he broke apart from the others when he glimpsed a lone figure approaching the gates to the outer city. Niema glanced up, startled, as he swooped down to land at her side.

"What is it?" she asked.

"I'd offer to help you reach the gates faster, but that's not possible at the moment." He twitched his bandaged arm. "No, I came to apologise. I'd prefer for us not to part on bad terms."

"Apologise for what?" An indignant flush darkened her cheeks. "Mocking my people at every turn? Implying I was of no use in the confrontation with Melian?"

"Yes," he answered to both. "You're going all the way back to the southern jungle now? That's a long journey to make alone."

Surprise flickered in her eyes. "Yes. I know the way."

"Are you certain you'll be met with a warm welcome?" he queried. "Given your involvement with a certain Disciple of

Death? I know your people don't look kindly on those who consort with Mekan, and it's not an inaccuracy to believe they might see Yala as an enemy."

Her gaze dropped. "It's not like that. Some interpret our vows more strongly than others."

"While you're more flexible, I know." He shot her a wink, mostly to make her flush more deeply. "If I don't hear from you for too long, then I'll come to see if Superior Kralia has held you hostage."

"No," she said. "Absolutely not. You can't come to the enclave."

"Are you sure?" He laughed under his breath as she broke into splutters of annoyance, feeling more upbeat than he had since before the fight for his life. "If you need my help, send a messenger bird to the Skyhold. Or a war drake, though that would be less popular with my fellow Disciples."

"I will *not* need your help."

Kelan grinned at her and then rose into the sky.

———

Unbelievable. Niema shook her head as Kelan departed, becoming a distant figure gliding upward into the sky. He might be insufferable, but she hoped his last comment hadn't been serious. Niema could only imagine what a stir it would cause if he showed up at the enclave and announced that he'd come to drag her back to the stinking hole of the capital.

Though strangely enough, she'd almost grown used to the stench over the past few days. While she didn't miss the crowds, in comparison to the enclosed streets, the country-side appeared dizzyingly vast and open when she finally sat in the back of a wagon. As the raptors began to pull the wagon down the road leading out of the city, she found herself a touch overwhelmed by the landscape stretching around her. From the sky, it had seemed small, but she had a long journey ahead of her.

To pass the time, she reminded herself of all the things she'd been looking forward to upon her return to the enclave. The quietness, the proximity to nature, more crucially, the closeness of her fellow enclave members, and the sensation of their hearts beating alongside hers.

While part of her remained apprehensive about Superior Kralia's reaction to her report, she was reasonably sure that once she'd explained herself and gave her time to adjust to the idea of the new challenges they'd be facing, everything would return to normal. She might even be chosen for the next mission to the capital. Preferably without Kelan having to intervene, or send a...

Wait.

Niema squinted ahead as they rattled along, her gaze locking on a bizarre landmark. A war drake sat at the roadside—alert, upright, and unmoving. The driver cursed, and the wagon tilted as they swerved to avoid hitting the creature, but its eyes were dull, and Niema knew that if she tried to use her power to control the beast, the touch of the god of life would have no effect upon it.

Nevertheless, she had no worry that the beast would follow her. It might have no desires or thoughts, but it would remain by the city until its master called it again.

The wagon bounced upright, the driver expressing bewilderment at the smile creeping onto Niema's face as they left the war drake behind and continued along the long road home.

Maybe you'll get to fly again after all, Yala.

ACKNOWLEDGMENTS

Thank you to my amazing editor Sarah Chorn, my keen-eyed proofreader Trish Long, and my fantastic cover artists at Deranged Doctor Design.

I also want to thank my dedicated assistant Mary Fields and my Patrons over at my Patreon - and everyone who backed the Kickstarter and helped me bring this dream to life.

ABOUT THE AUTHOR

Emma spent her childhood creating imaginary worlds to compensate for a disappointingly average reality, so it was probably inevitable that she ended up writing fantasy novels. She has a BA in English Literature with Creative Writing from Lancaster University, where she spent three years exploring the Lake District and penning strange fantastical adventures.

Now, Emma lives in the middle of England and is the international bestselling author of over 30 novels including the Changeling Chronicles and the Order of the Elements series. When she's not immersed in her own fictional universes, Emma can be found with her head in a book or wandering around the world in search of adventure.

Find out more about Emma's books at www.emmaladams.com.

Ingram Content Group UK Ltd.
Milton Keynes UK
UKHW011821190423
420451UK00004B/59